HER PLAYBOY'S
PROPOSAL

BY
KATE HARDY

MILLS &
BOON

Published in Great Britain 2016
By Mills & Boon, an imprint of HarperCollins*Publishers*
1 London Bridge Street, London, SE1 9GF

ISBN: 978-0-263-25423-5

Dear Reader,

Her Playboy's Proposal is all about trust—learning to trust again when someone's let you down, and learning to trust yourself when you think you're the one who's let everyone down.

And how do you learn to trust? In Harry and Isla's case, they discover that love is the answer. Except they take a while to realise it—and it takes a life-changing moment to make them both realise that they can trust each other *and* themselves.

The story's set partly in Cornwall (if you're thinking *Poldark*—absolutely!), partly in London, and partly on the coast in Dorset. And there are weddings, best men, best women, and a speech I really, *really* enjoyed writing.

I hope you enjoy Harry and Isla's journey.

I'm always delighted to hear from readers, so do come and visit me at www.katehardy.com.

With love,

Kate Hardy

To my fellow Medical authors—because you're
a really lovely bunch and I'm proud to be one of you. xxx

Books by Kate Hardy

Mills & Boon Medical Romance

Italian Doctor, No Strings Attached
Dr Cinderella's Midnight Fling
Once a Playboy...
The Brooding Doc's Redemption
A Date with the Ice Princess
Her Real Family Christmas
200 Harley Street: The Soldier Prince
It Started with No Strings...
A Baby to Heal Their Hearts
A Promise...to a Proposal?

Mills & Boon Cherish

Behind the Film Star's Smile
Crown Prince, Pregnant Bride
A New Year Marriage Proposal
It Started at a Wedding...
Falling for Mr December

Visit the Author Profile page at
millsandboon.co.uk for more titles.

CHAPTER ONE

Isla took a deep breath outside the staffroom door. Today was her second day at the emergency department of the London Victoria Hospital, and she was still finding her place in the team. She'd liked the colleagues she'd met yesterday, and hopefully today would go just as well— with new people who didn't know her past and wouldn't judge her. She pushed the door open, then smiled at the nurse who was checking the roster on the pinboard. 'Morning, Lorraine.'

'Morning, Isla. You're on cubicles with Josie and Harry the Heartbreaker this morning,' Lorraine said.

'Harry the Heartbreaker?' Isla asked.

Lorraine wrinkled her nose. 'I guess that's a bit of a mean nickname—Harry's a good doctor and he's great with patients. He listens to them and gives them a chance to talk.'

'So he's very charming, but he's a bit careless with women?' Isla knew the type. Only too well.

'Harry dates a lot,' Lorraine said. 'He doesn't lead his girlfriends on, exactly, but hardly anyone makes it past a third date with him.'

And lots of women saw him as a challenge and tried to be the exception to his rule, Isla guessed. 'Uh-huh,' she said. She certainly wouldn't be one of them. After what had happened with Stewart, she had no intention of dating anyone ever again. She was better off on her own.

'OK, so he'd be a nightmare to date,' Lorraine said with a wry smile, 'but he's a good colleague. I'm sure you'll get on well with him.'

So professionally their relationship would be just fine; but it would be safer to keep Harry the Heartbreaker at a distance on a personal level. Isla appreciated the heads-up. 'Everyone else in the department has been lovely so far,' she said, smiling back. 'I'm sure it will be fine.'

Though she hadn't been prepared for quite how gorgeous Harry the Heartbreaker was when she actually saw him. The expression 'tall, dark and handsome' didn't even begin to do him justice. He would've been perfectly cast as one of the brooding heroes of a television costume drama, with dark curly hair that was a little too long and flopped over his forehead, dark eyes, a strong jaw and the most sensual mouth she'd ever seen. On horseback, wearing a white shirt, breeches and tailcoat, he'd be irresistible.

Harry the Heart-throb.

Harry the *Heartbreaker*, she reminded herself.

Luckily Josie had already triaged the first patient and was ready to assist Harry, which meant that Isla had enough time to compose herself and see the next patient on the list.

Harry was a colleague and that was all. Isla had no intention of getting involved with anyone again, no matter how gorgeous the man looked. Stewart had destroyed her trust completely, and that wasn't something she'd be able to put behind her easily.

* * *

Harry finished writing up his notes and walked into the corridor to call the next patient through. He knew that Josie had gone to triage her next patient, so he'd be working with the newest member of the team, Isla McKenna. He'd been on leave yesterday when she'd started at the London Victoria and knew nothing about her, other than that she was a senior nurse.

He eyed the nurse in the corridor with interest. Even without the double giveaways of her name and her accent, he would've guessed that Isla McKenna was a Scot. She had that fine porcelain skin, a dusting of freckles across her nose, sharp blue eyes and, beneath her white nurse's cap, dark red hair that he'd just bet looked amazing in the sunlight. Pure Celt. It was a long time since he'd found someone so instantly attractive. Not that he was going to act on it. For all he knew, she could already be involved with someone; the lack of a ring on her left hand meant nothing. 'Isla McKenna, I presume?' he asked.

She nodded.

'Harry Gardiner. Nice to meet you. How are you settling in to the ward?' he asked as they walked down to the cubicles together.

'Fine, thanks. The team seems very nice.'

'They're a good bunch,' he said. 'So where were you before you moved here?'

'Scotland,' she said, her face suddenly shuttering.

Clearly she thought he was prying and she'd given him as vague an answer as she could without being openly rude. 'Uh-huh,' he said, lightly. 'Just making polite conversation—as you would with any new colleague.'

She blushed, and her skin clashed spectacularly with her hair. 'Sorry. I didn't mean to be rude,' she muttered.

'Then let's pretend we've never spoken and start again.' He held out his hand. 'Harry Gardiner, special reg. Nice to meet you, and welcome to the London Victoria.'

'Isla McKenna, sister. Thank you, and nice to meet you, too,' she said.

Her handshake was firm, and Harry was surprised to discover that his skin actually tingled where it touched hers.

Not good.

He normally tried not to date colleagues within his own department. It made things less complicated if his date turned out to have greater expectations than he wanted to fulfil—which they usually did. And instant attraction to the newest member of their team definitely wasn't a good idea.

'So who's next?' he asked. Hopefully focussing on work would get his common sense back to where it should be—firmly in control of his libido.

'Arthur Kemp, aged seventy-three, suspected stroke,' Isla said, filling him in. 'The paramedics did a FAST assessment—' the Face Arm Speech Test was used in cases of suspected stroke to check whether the patient's face seemed to fall on one side or if they could smile, whether they could hold both arms above their head, or if their speech was slurred '—and they gave him some aspirin on the way here. I've done an initial assessment.'

'ROSIER?' Harry asked. Recognition of Stroke in the Emergency Room was a standard protocol.

She nodded. 'His score pretty much confirms it's a stroke. I checked ABCD2 as well, and the good news is that his score is nil on the D—he's not diabetic. His blood sugar is fine.'

Harry picked up immediately what she was telling him—there was only one section of the test with a nil score. 'So the rest of it's a full house?'

'I'm afraid so,' she said. 'He's over sixty, he has high blood pressure and residual weakness on his left side, and the incident happened over an hour ago now.'

'Which puts him at higher risk of having a second stroke in the next two days,' Harry said. 'OK. Does he live on his own, or is he in any kind of residential care?'

'He has a flat where there's a warden on duty three days a week, and a care team comes in three times a day to sort out his meals and medication,' Isla told him. 'They're the ones who called the ambulance for him this morning.'

'So if he did have a second stroke and the warden wasn't on duty or it happened between the care team's visits, the chances are he wouldn't be found for a few hours, or maybe not even overnight.' Harry wrinkled his nose. 'I'm really not happy with that. I think we need to admit him to the acute unit for the next couple of days, so we can keep an eye on him.'

'I agree with you. His speech is a little bit slurred and I'm not happy about his ability to swallow,' Isla added. 'He said he was thirsty and I gave him a couple of sips of water, but I'd recommend putting him on a drip to prevent dehydration, and keep him nil by mouth for the next two or three hours. Nobody's going to be able to sit with him while he drinks and then for a few minutes afterwards to make sure he's OK—there just won't be the time.'

'Good points, and noted.'

Mr Kemp was sitting on a bed, waiting to be seen.

Isla introduced him quickly. 'Mr Kemp, this is Dr Gardiner.'

'Everyone calls me Harry,' Harry said with a smile. 'So can you tell me about what happened this morning, Mr Kemp?'

'I had a bit of a headache, then I tripped and fell and I couldn't get up again,' Mr Kemp said. 'My carer found me when she came in to give me my tablets and my breakfast.'

Isla noticed that Harry sat on the chair and held the old man's hand, encouraging him to talk. He was kind and waited for an answer, rather than rushing the patient or pressuring him to stop rambling and hurry up. Lorraine had been spot on about his skills as a doctor, she thought. 'Can you remember, either before or after you fell, did you black out at all?' Harry asked. 'Or did you hit your head?'

Arthur looked confused. 'I'm not sure. I don't think I blacked out and I don't remember hitting my head. It's hard to say.' He grimaced. 'Sorry, Doctor. I'm not much use. My daughter's husband says I'm an old fool.'

So there were family tensions, too. The chances were, if they suggested that he went to stay with his family for a few days, the answer would be no—even if they had the room to let the old man stay. 'Don't worry, it's fine,' Harry reassured him. 'I'm just going to do a couple of checks now to see how you're doing. Is that OK?'

'Yes, Doctor. And I'm sorry I'm such a nuisance.'

Either the old man was used to being made to feel as if he was a problem, or he was habitually anxious. Or maybe a bit of both, Harry thought. He checked Mr Kemp's visual fields and encouraged him to raise his arms; the residual weakness on Mr Kemp's left side that

Isla had mentioned early was very clear. And there was a walking frame next to the bed, he noticed. 'Do you normally walk with a frame?'

'Yes, though I hate the wretched thing.' Arthur grimaced. 'It always trips me up. It did that this morning. That's why I fell. Useless thing.'

Harry guessed that Mr Kemp did what a lot of elderly people did with a walking frame—he lifted it and carried it a couple of centimetres above the ground, rather than leaving the feet on the floor and pushing it along and letting it support him. Maybe he could arrange some support to help the old man use the frame properly, so it helped him rather than hindered him.

'Can you see if you can walk a little bit with me?' he asked.

He helped Mr Kemp to his feet, then walked into the corridor with him, encouraged him to turn round and then walk back to the cubicle. Harry noticed that his patient was shuffling. He was also leaning slightly to the left—the same as when he was sitting up—and leaning back slightly when he walked. Harry would need to put that on Mr Kemp's notes to be passed on to any carers, so they could help guide him with a hand resting just behind his back, and stop him as soon as he started shuffling and encourage him to take bigger steps.

Once Mr Kemp was seated safely again, Harry said, 'I'm going to send you for an MRI scan, because you had a headache and I want to rule out anything nasty, but I think Sister McKenna here is right and you've had a small stroke.'

'A stroke?' Arthur looked as if he couldn't quite take it in. 'How could I have had a stroke?'

'The most likely cause is a blood clot that stopped the blood supply to your brain for a little while,' Harry explained. 'It should be cleared by now because you're able to walk and talk and move your arms, but I'm going to admit you to the acute medical unit so we can keep an eye on you for a day or two.' He decided not to tell Mr Kemp that his risk of a second stroke was higher over the next day or two; there was no point in worrying the poor man sick. Though his family would definitely need to know. 'Has anyone been in touch with your family?'

'Sharon, my carer—she should have rung my daughter, but Becky'll be at work and won't be able to come right away.' He grimaced. 'I feel bad about taking her away from her job. Her work is so important.'

'And I bet she'll think her dad is just as important as her job,' Isla said reassuringly.

'Too right,' Harry said. Even though he didn't quite feel that about his own father. Then again, Bertie Gardiner was more than capable of looking after himself—that, or his wife-to-be Trixie, who was a couple of years younger than Harry, could look out for him.

He shook himself. Not now. He wasn't going to think about the upcoming wedding. Or the fact that his father was still trying to talk him into being his best man, and Harry had done that job twice already—did he really need to do it all over again for his father's *seventh* wedding? 'We'll have had your scan done by the time your daughter comes to see you,' Harry said, 'and we'll be able to give her a better idea of your treatment plan.'

'Treatment?' Mr Kemp asked.

'The stroke has affected your left side, so you'll need a little bit of help from a physiotherapist to get you back to how you were before the stroke,' Harry said. 'I'm also going to write you up for some medication which you can take after your scan.'

'Is there anything you'd like to ask us?' Isla asked.

'Well, I'd really like a nice cup of tea,' Mr Kemp said wistfully. 'If it wouldn't be too much trouble.'

'We can sort that out in a few minutes, after you've had your scan,' Isla said. 'At the moment you're finding it hard to swallow and I don't want you to choke or burn yourself on a hot drink, but we'll try again in half an hour and you might be able to swallow better by then. And I'll make sure you get your cup of tea, even if I have to make it myself.'

'Seconded,' Harry said, 'though I'll admit my tea isn't the best and you'd be better off with coffee if I'm the one who ends up making it.' He smiled at the old man. 'We'll get things sorted out and make sure your daughter finds you.' He shook the old man's hand and stood up. 'Try not to worry. We'll make sure you get looked after properly.'

'I'll be back with you in a second, Mr Kemp,' Isla said, and followed Harry out of the cubicles.

'Can you organise a scan and then transfer him to the acute unit?' he asked quietly when they were outside the cubicle.

She smiled at him. 'Sure, no problem.'

Her smile transformed her face completely. Harry felt the lick of desire deep inside his gut and had to remind himself that his new colleague might be gorgeous, but she was also off limits. 'Thanks,' he said. 'I'll write everything up.'

It was a busy morning, with the usual falls and sprains and strains, and a six-month-old baby with a temperature that wouldn't go down and had then started having a fit. The baby's mother had panicked and asked a neighbour to drive them in rather than waiting for an ambulance, and the triage team had rushed her straight into the department.

The baby's jaws were clenched firmly together, so Harry looked at Isla and said quietly, 'Naso-pharyngeal, I think.'

Almost as soon as he'd finished talking, she had an appropriately sized tube in her hand and was lubricating the end. Between them, they secured the baby's airway and gave her oxygen, and Isla was already drawing up a phial of diazepam.

Clearly she'd come across convulsions in babies before.

Between them, they checked the baby's blood glucose and temperature.

'Pyrexia,' Harry said softly. 'I'm pretty sure this is a febrile convulsion.'

'So we need to cool her down and check for infection,' Isla said. At his nod, Isla deftly took off the baby's sleep-suit and sponged her skin with tepid water while Harry checked with the baby's distraught mother when she'd last given the baby liquid paracetamol. Once the fit had stopped and the baby's temperature spike had cooled, Isla prepared everything for an infection screen.

'I've never seen anything like that before. Is Erin going to be all right?' the baby's mother asked.

'She's in the best place and you did the right thing to bring her in,' Harry reassured her. 'I think the fit was caused by her high temperature, but we need to find out what's causing that—if it's a virus or a bacterial infection—and then we can treat her properly.'

'Will she have any more fits?' Erin's mother asked.

'Very possibly,' Isla said, 'but that doesn't mean that she'll develop epilepsy. Having a high temperature is the most common cause of fits in children between

Erin's age and school age. We see this sort of thing a lot, so try not to worry.'

Worry, Harry thought. Parents always worried themselves sick over small children. And so did their older siblings—especially when they were supposed to be taking care of them and things went badly wrong.

He pushed the thought away. It was years ago, now, and he was older and wiser. Plus nowadays Tasha would give him very short shrift if he fussed over her too much; she was fiercely independent. And you couldn't change the past; all you could do was learn from it. Harry had most definitely learned. He never, ever wanted to be responsible for a child in that way again.

'I'm going to admit her,' Harry said, 'purely because she's so young and it's the first time she's had a fit. Plus I want to find out what's causing the infection. We'll keep an eye on her in case she has more convulsions. But you can stay with her.'

'I'll take you both up to the ward and introduce you to the team,' Isla said.

'And she's going to be all right?' the baby's mother asked again.

'Yes,' Harry said, and patted her arm. 'I know it's scary, but try not to worry.'

Ha. And what a hypocrite he was. He knew that panicky feeling all too well. *Would the baby be all right?* The overwhelming relief when you knew that the baby would survive. And then the guilt later on when you discovered that, actually, there was a problem after all... Harry's mistake had come back to haunt him big time.

'Is there anyone we can call for you?' Isla asked.

'My mum.' Erin's mother dragged in a breath. 'My husband's working away.'

'OK. As soon as Erin's settled on the ward, we'll get in touch with your mum,' Isla promised.

Harry worked with Isla on most of his list of patients that morning, and he liked the fact that his new colleague was incredibly calm, had a sharp eye, and her quiet and gentle manner stopped patients or their parents panicking. The perfect emergency nurse. He had no idea where she'd trained or where she'd worked before—Scotland was a pretty big area—but he'd just bet that she was sorely missed. She'd certainly be appreciated at the London Victoria.

They hadn't had time for a coffee break all morning and Harry was thirsty and ravenous by the time he took his lunch break—late, and he knew he'd end up grabbing something fast in the canteen so he could be back on the ward in time. When he walked into the staffroom, Isla was there.

'Hi, there. Do you want to come and grab some lunch with me?' he asked.

She gave him a cool smile. 'Thanks, but I don't think so.'

He frowned. 'Why not?'

Her expression said quite clearly, *do you really have to ask?* But she was polite as she said, 'It's nice of you to ask me, but I don't think we're each other's type.'

He blinked, not quite following. 'What?'

She looked uncomfortable. 'I, um, might be new here, but that doesn't make me an instant addition to a little black book.'

Then the penny dropped. She thought he was asking her out? Some of the other staff teased him about being a heartbreaker and a serial dater, but that was far from true. He always made sure that whoever he dated knew it was for fun, not for ever. And he hadn't been asking her out on a date anyway. Obviously someone had been gossiping about him and she'd listened to the tittle-tattle rather than waiting to see for herself. 'Actually,' he said quietly, 'as you're new to the team, I was guessing that you hadn't had time to find your way around the hospital that well yet and you might not have anyone to sit with at lunchtime, that's all.'

Her face flamed, clashing with that spectacular hair. 'I—um—sorry. I'd just heard…' She broke off. 'Sorry. I'm putting my foot in it even more.'

'Heard what?' The words were out before he could stop them.

'You have, um, a bit of a reputation for, um, dating a lot.'

He sighed. 'Honestly, where the hospital grapevine's concerned, you can't win. If you don't date, then either you're gay or you've got some tragic past; and if you do date but make it clear you're not looking for a serious relationship, then you're at the mercy of everyone who wants to be the exception to the rule and you get called a heartbreaker. Not everyone's desperate to pair off and settle down.'

'I know.' She bit her lip. 'Sorry.'

But he noticed that she still hadn't accepted his invitation to join him for lunch. Which stung. Was his reputation really that bad?

Pushing down his exasperation at the hospital grapevine, Harry gave Isla his sweetest smile. 'OK, but I give you fair warning—if you try and eat a sandwich in here, you'll be lucky to finish half of it before someone calls you to help out with something.'

'I guess it's all part of working in a hospital environment,' she said lightly.

OK. He could take a hint. 'See you later,' he said.

In the canteen, Harry saw a crowd he recognised from the maternity ward and joined them. But all the while he was thinking about Isla. Why had their new nurse been so guarded? Was it just because of whatever nonsense she'd heard about him on the hospital grapevine? Or was she like that with everyone?

Just as Harry had predicted, Isla was halfway through her sandwich when someone came into the rest room and asked her to help out.

She didn't mind—it was all part and parcel of being part of a team on the busiest department in the hospital.

But she did feel bad about the way she'd reacted to Harry the Heartbreaker. Especially after he'd explained why he'd asked her to lunch; it was just what she would've done herself if a new team member had joined the practice where she'd worked on the island. She'd been unfair to him. And, even though she'd apologised, she'd felt too awkward to join him and ended up making things worse. He probably thought she was standoffish and rude. But how could she explain without telling him about the past she was trying to put well and truly behind her?

It didn't help that she found him so attractive.

Common sense told Isla that she needed to keep her distance. Apart from the fact that she'd seen a few working relationships turn really awkward and sour after the personal relationship had ended, she wasn't in the market for a relationship anyway. Particularly with someone who had the reputation of being a charmer.

Professional only, she reminded herself. She'd apologise again for the sake for their working relationship. And that would be that.

* * *

Isla was rostered on cubicles again with Josie and Harry in the afternoon. Harry had just finished with a patient who'd been brought in with a degloving injury; when he came out of the cubicle, she asked quietly, 'Can we have a quick word?'

'Sure.'

Isla took a deep breath. 'I wanted to apologise about earlier.'

He looked blank. 'About what?'

'I was rude and standoffish when you asked me to go to lunch with you.'

His eyes crinkled at the corners. 'Oh, that. Don't worry about it. Blame it on the hospital grapevine blowing everything out of proportion.'

She felt the betraying colour seep into her face. This would be the easy option because there was some truth in it, but he'd been kind and he didn't deserve it. 'Should've known better because hospital gossip likes to embroider things,' she said. Not just hospitals: any small community. Like an island off the coast of Scotland where everybody knew practically everything about everyone. And she of all people knew how it felt to be gossiped about unfairly. 'I was rude. And I apologise. And maybe I can buy you a cup of tea later to make up for being so horrible.'

'You weren't horrible, just a bit…well, offish. Apology and offer of tea accepted. We can have Mr Kemp as our chaperone, if you like,' he suggested.

How could he be so good-natured about it? It made her feel even more guilty. 'I guess it's a good excuse to see how he's getting on.'

'Great. It's a non-date,' Harry said.

And oh, that smile. It could light up a room. He really was gorgeous. And nice with it. And he had a sense of humour.

It would be all too easy to let Harry Gardiner tempt her. But this nurse wasn't for tempting.

They spent their afternoon break in the Acute Medical Unit with Mr Kemp.

'Thank you for the tea,' he said.

'Our pleasure,' Isla told him with a smile.

'You won't get into trouble for being here, will you?' he checked.

This time, Harry smiled. 'It's our afternoon break. We're allowed to take it outside our own ward if we want to.'

'I'm such a trouble to you,' Mr Kemp said.

'It's fine,' Isla reassured him. 'Has your daughter been able to visit, yet?'

'She's coming straight after work. I do feel bad about it. She's had to get someone to pick up the kids.'

'All the working mums I know are great at juggling,' Harry said. 'I bet you she's picked up her friend's children before now. It won't be a problem. Everyone mucks in to help their friends. How are you feeling?'

'Well enough to go home,' Mr Kemp said. 'If I was home, I wouldn't be a burden to everyone.'

He was able to swallow again, Isla thought, but he definitely wasn't quite ready to go home. And he'd be far more of a worry to his family if he was on his own in his flat. 'I'm sure the team here will sort things out for you,' she said brightly.

And she discovered that Lorraine had been absolutely on the ball about Harry being great with patients, because he somehow managed to find out that Mr Kemp loved dogs and got him chatting about that, distracting him from his worries about being a burden.

'You were brilliant with Mr Kemp,' she said on their way back to the Emergency Department.

Harry gave a dismissive wave of his hand. 'Just chatting. And I noticed you were watching him drinking and assessing him.'

She nodded. 'I'm happier with his swallowing, but I think he'll be in for a couple more days yet. They'll want to assess him for a water infection or a chest infection, in case that contributed to the fall as well as the stroke. And they'll need to get social services in to look at his care plan as well as talk to his family. I'm guessing that he's not so good with accepting help, and from what he said to us earlier it sounded as if his son-in-law doesn't have much patience.'

'Very true.' Harry gave her a sidelong look. 'Though I know a few people caught between caring for their kids and caring for their elderly parents. It can be hard to juggle, and—well, not all parents are easy.'

'And some are brilliant.' Isla's own parents had been wonderful—they'd never believed Andrew's accusations right from the start, and they'd encouraged her to retrain in Glasgow and then move to London and start again.

'Yes, some are brilliant.' Harry was looking curiously at her.

'It takes all sorts to make a world,' she said brightly. Why on earth hadn't she moved him away from the subject of parents? Why had she had to open her mouth? 'And we have patients to see.'

'Yes, we do. Well, Sister McKenna.' He opened the door for her. 'Shall we?'

CHAPTER TWO

'Is ISLA NOT coming tonight?' Harry asked Lorraine at the bowling alley, keeping his tone casual.

'No.'

Lorraine wasn't forthcoming with a reason and Harry knew better than to ask, because it would be the quickest way to fuel gossip. Not that Lorraine was one to promote the hospital rumour mill, but she might let slip to Isla that she thought Harry might be interested in her, and that would make things awkward between them at work. She'd already got the wrong idea about him.

All the same, this was the third team night out in a fortnight that Isla had missed. On the ward, she was an excellent colleague; she was good with patients and relatives, quick to offer sensible suggestions to clinical problems, and she got on well with everyone. The fact that she didn't come to any of the team nights out seemed odd, especially as she was new to the department and going out with the team would be a good chance for her to get to know her colleagues better.

Maybe Isla was a single parent or caring for an elderly relative, and it was difficult for her to arrange someone to sit with her child or whoever in the evenings. But he could hardly ask her about it without it seeming as if he was prying.

And he wasn't; though he was intrigued by her. Then again, if it turned out that she was a single parent, that'd be a deal-breaker for him. He really didn't want to be back in the position of having parental type responsibilities for a child. OK, so lightning rarely struck twice—but he didn't want to take the risk.

'Shame,' he said lightly, and switched the conversation round to who was going to be in which team.

Two days later, it was one of the worst days in the department Harry had had in months. He, Isla and Josie were in Resus together, trying to save a motorcyclist who'd been involved in a head-on crash—but the man's injuries were just too severe. Just when Harry had thought they were getting somewhere and the outcome might be bearable after all, the man had arrested and they just hadn't been able to get him back.

'I'm calling it,' Harry said when his last attempt with the defibrillator produced no change. 'It's been twenty minutes now. He's not responding. Is everyone agreed that we should stop?'

Isla and Josie both looked miserable, but voiced their agreement.

'OK. Time of death, one fifty-three,' he said softly, and pulled the sheet up to cover their patient's face. 'Thank you, team. You all worked really well.'

But it hadn't been enough, and they all knew it.

'OK. Once we've moved him out of Resus and cleaned him up, I'll go and find out if Reception managed to get hold of a next of kin and if anyone's here,' he said.

'If they have, I'll come with you, if you like,' Isla offered.

'Thank you.' He hated breaking bad news. Having

someone there would make it a little easier. And maybe she'd know what to say when he ran out of words.

The motorcyclist, Jonathan Pryor, was only twenty-seven, and his next of kin were his parents. The receptionist had already sent a message to Resus that Jonathan's mum was waiting in the relatives' room.

'I hate this bit so much,' he said softly as he and Isla walked towards the relatives' room.

'We did everything we possibly could,' she reminded him.

'I know.' It didn't make him feel any better. But the sympathy in her blue, blue eyes made his heart feel just a fraction less empty.

Mrs Pryor looked up hopefully as they knocked on the door and walked in. 'Jonathan? He's all right? He's out of Theatre or whatever and I can go and see him?'

Harry could see the very second that she realised the horrible truth—that her son was very far from being all right—and her face crumpled.

'I'm so sorry, Mrs Pryor,' he said softly, taking her hand. 'We did everything we could to save him, but he arrested on the table—he had a heart attack, and we just couldn't get him back.'

Sobs racked her body. 'I always hated him riding that wretched motorcycle. I worried myself sick every time he went out on it because I *knew* that something like this would happen. I can't bear it.' Her voice was a wail of distress. 'And now I'll never see him again. My boy. My little boy.'

Harry knew there was nothing he could do or say to make this better. He just sat down next to Mrs Pryor and kept holding her hand, letting her talk about her son.

Isla went to the vending machine. Harry knew without having to ask that she was making a cup of hot, sweet tea for Mrs Pryor. He could've done with one himself, but he wasn't going to be that selfish. The only thing he could do now for his patient was to comfort his grieving mother.

'Thank you, but I don't want it,' Mrs Pryor said when Isla offered her the paper cup. 'It won't bring my son back.'

'I know,' Isla said gently, 'but you've just had a horrible shock and this will help. Just a little bit, but it will help.'

Mrs Pryor looked as if she didn't believe the nurse, but she took the paper cup and sipped from it.

'Is there anyone we can call for you?' Harry asked.

'My—my husband.' She shook her head blankly. 'Oh, God. How am I going to tell him?'

'I can do that for you,' Harry said gently. 'It might be easier on both of you if I tell him.' Even though he hated breaking bad news.

Mrs Pryor dragged in a breath. 'All right—thank you.'

'And you can come and see Jonathan whenever you feel ready,' Isla said. 'I'll come with you, and you can spend some time alone with him, too. I can call the hospital chaplain to come and see you, if you'd like me to.'

Mrs Pryor shook her head. 'I've never been the religious type. Talking to the chaplain's not going to help. It's not going to bring Jonathan back, is it?''

'I understand,' Isla said, 'but if you change your mind just tell me. Anything we can do to help, we will.'

'He was only twenty-seven. That's way too young to die.' Mrs Pryor shut her eyes very tightly. 'And that's a stupid thing to say. I know children younger than that get killed in accidents every day.'

Yeah, Harry thought. Or, if not killed, left with life-changing injuries, even if they weren't picked up at first. His own little sister was proof of that. He pushed the thought and the guilt away. *Not now.* He needed to concentrate on his patient's bereaved mother.

'It's just...you never think it's going to happen to your own. You hope and you pray it never will.' She sighed. 'I know he was a grown man, but he'll always be my little boy.'

Harry went out to his office to call Mr Pryor to break the bad news, while Isla took over his job of holding Mrs Pryor's hand and letting her talk. On the way to his office, Harry asked one of the team to clean Jonathan's face and prepare him so his parents wouldn't have to see the full damage caused to their son by the crash. And then he went back to the relatives' room to join Isla and Mrs Pryor, staying there until Mr Pryor arrived, twenty minutes later. The Pryors clung together in their grief, clearly having trouble taking it all in. But finally, Mr Pryor asked brokenly, 'Can we see him?'

'Of course,' Harry said.

He and Isla took the Pryors through to the side room where Jonathan's body had been taken so they could see their son in private. They stayed for a few minutes in case the Pryors had any questions; then Isla caught Harry's eye and he gave the tiniest nod of agreement, knowing what she was going to say.

Then Isla said gently to the Pryors, 'We'll be just outside if you need us for anything.'

'Thank you,' Mrs Pryor said, her voice full of tears.

Outside the side room, Isla said to Harry, 'I'll finish up here—you'll be needed back in Resus.'

'Are you sure?' he asked. He was needed back in Resus; but at the same time he didn't think it was fair to leave Isla to deal with grieving parents all on her own.

She nodded. 'I'm sure.'

He reached out and squeezed her hand, trying to ignore the tingle that spread through his skin at her touch—now really wasn't an appropriate time. 'Thank you. You were brilliant. And even though I know you're more than capable of answering any questions the Pryors might have, if you need backup or want me to come and talk to them about anything, you know where to find me.'

'Yes. Those poor people,' she said softly.

'This is the bit of our job I really wish didn't exist,' Harry said.

'I know. But it does, and we have to do our best.' She squeezed his hand back, and loosened it. 'Off you go.'

He wrote up the paperwork, and headed back to Resus. To his relief, the next case was one that he could actually fix. The patient had collapsed, and all the tests showed Harry that it was a case of undiagnosed diabetes. The patient was in diabetic ketoacidosis; Harry was able to start treatment, and then explain to the patient's very relieved wife that her husband would be fine but they'd need to see a specialist about diabetes and learn how to monitor his blood sugar, plus in future they'd have to keep an eye on his diet to suit his medical condition.

Mid-afternoon, Harry actually had a chance to take his break. He hadn't seen Isla back in Resus since leaving her with the Pryors, so he went in search of her; he discovered that she was doing paperwork.

'Hey. I'm pulling rank,' he said.

She looked up. 'What?'

'Right now, I really need some cake. And I think, after the day you've had, so do you. So I prescribe the hospital canteen for both of us.'

'What about Josie?'

Harry smiled. 'She's already had her break and is in cubicles right now, but I'm going to bring her some cake back. You can help me pick what she'd like.'

For a moment, he thought Isla was going to balk at being alone with him; then she smiled. 'Thanks. I'd like that.'

'Let's go,' he said. 'We have fifteen minutes. Which is just about enough time to walk to the canteen, grab cake, and chuck back a mug of coffee.'

She rolled her eyes, but stood up to join him.

'How were the Pryors?' he asked softly when they were sitting at the table in the canteen with a massive slice of carrot cake and a mug of good, strong coffee each.

'Devastated,' she said. 'But they got to spend time with their son and I explained that he didn't suffer in Resus—that the end was quick.'

'Yeah,' he said with a sigh. 'I hate cases like that. The guy still had his whole life before him.' And something else had been bugging him. 'He was only five years younger than I am.' The exact same age as one of his siblings. And he'd had to fight the urge to text every single one of his siblings who was old enough to drive to say that they were never, ever, *ever* to ride a motorbike.

'He was three years younger than me,' Isla said.

It was first time she'd offered any personal information, and it encouraged him enough to say, 'You were brilliant with the Pryors and I really appreciate it. I assume you had a fair bit of experience with bereaved relatives when you worked in your last emergency department?'

'Actually, no.'

He blinked at her. 'How come?'

'I wasn't in an emergency department, as such—I was a nurse practitioner in a GP surgery. I retrained in Glasgow and then came here,' she said.

Something else he hadn't known about her. 'You retrained to give you better opportunities for promotion?' he asked.

'Something like that.'

She was clearly regretting sharing as much as she had, and he could tell that she was giving him back-off signals. OK. He'd take the hint. He smiled at her. 'Sorry. We're a nosey bunch at the London Victoria—and I talk way too much. Blame it on the sugar rush from the cake.'

'And on having a rough day,' she added. 'So you've always worked in the emergency department?'

'Pretty much. I trained in London; I did my foundation years here, with stints in Paediatrics and Gastroenterology.' Because of what had happened to Tasha, his first choice had been Paediatrics. He'd been so sure that it was his future. 'But, as soon as I started in the Emergency Department, I knew I'd found the right place for me. So I stayed and I worked my way up,' he said.

'Thirty-two's not that old for a special reg,' she said thoughtfully. 'Though I've already seen for myself that you're good at what you do.'

Funny how much her words warmed him. He inclined his head briefly. 'Thank you, kind madam.'

'It wasn't meant to be a compliment. It was a statement of fact,' she said crisply.

He grinned. 'I like you, Isla. You're good for my ego. Keeping it in check.'

She actually smiled back, and his heart missed a beat. When she smiled, she really was beautiful.

'I've known worse egos in my time,' she said.

'And you gave them just as short shrift?'

'Something like that.'

He looked at her. 'Can I ask you something?'

'That depends,' she said.

'Why haven't you come to any of the departmental nights out?'

'Because they're not really my thing,' she said.

'So you don't like ten-pin bowling, pub quizzes or pizza.' He paused. 'What kind of things do you like, Isla?'

'Why?'

'Because you've only been at the London Victoria for a couple of weeks, you've told me that you retrained to come here, and I'm assuming that you don't really know anyone around here. It must be a bit lonely.'

Yes, she was lonely. She still missed her family and her friends in the Western Isles hugely. And, even though she was trying to put her past behind her, part of her worried about socialising with her new colleagues. It would be too easy to let something slip. And then their reaction to her might change. Some would pity her; others would think there was no smoke without fire. And neither reaction was one she wanted to face.

She didn't think Harry was asking her out—he'd already made it clear he thought his reputation wasn't deserved—but it wouldn't hurt to make things clear. 'You're right—I don't know many people in London,' she said softly. 'And I could use a friend. *Just* a friend,' she added. 'Because I'm concentrating on my career right now.'

'That works for me,' Harry said. 'So can we be friends?'

'I'd like that,' she said. Even if his smile did make

her weak at the knees. Friendship was all she was prepared to offer.

'Friends,' he said, and reached over to shake her hand.

And Isla really had to ignore the tingle that went through her at the touch of his skin. Nothing was going to happen between them. They were colleagues—about to be friends—and that was all.

CHAPTER THREE

WHEN ISLA WENT into the staffroom that morning for a mug of tea, Harry was the only one there. He was staring into his mug of coffee as if he was trying to lose himself in it. She knew that feeling well—she'd been there herself only a few months ago, when her life had turned into a living nightmare—and her heart went out to him.

'Tough shift so far?' she asked, gently placing her hand on his arm for a moment.

'No—yes,' he admitted. Then he grimaced. 'Never mind. Forget I said anything.'

It wasn't like Harry Gardiner to be brusque. The doctor she'd got to know over the last month was full of smiles, always seeing the good in the world.

He also hadn't quite lived up to his heartbreaker reputation, because since Isla had known Harry he hadn't actually dated anyone. He'd even turned down a couple of offers, which was hardly the act of the Lothario that the hospital rumour mill made him out to be. Maybe he'd told her the truth when he'd said he wasn't a heartbreaker.

Right now, something had clearly upset him. Though she understood about keeping things to yourself. Since the day that Andrew Gillespie had made that awful ac-

cusation and her fiancé had actually believed him, she'd
done the same. Keeping your feelings to yourself was
the safest way. 'OK,' she said. 'But if you want to talk,
you know where I am.'

'Thanks.' But Harry still seemed sunk in the depths
of gloom. He was still serious when he was working in
minors with her, not even summoning up his store of
terrible jokes to distract a little boy whose knee he had
to suture after Isla had cleaned up the bad cut.

By mid-afternoon, she was really worried about him.
To the point of being bossy. 'Right. I'm pulling rank,'
she said. 'You need cake, so I'm dragging you off to
the canteen.'

'Yes, Sister McKenna,' he said. But his eyes were
dull rather than gleaming with amusement. And that
worried her even more.

Once they were sitting in the canteen—where she'd
insisted on buying lemon cake for him—she asked, 'So
are you going to tell me what's wrong?'

He said nothing; but she waited, knowing that if you
gave someone enough space and time they'd start talking.

Except he didn't.

'Harry, either you've suddenly become a monk and
taken a vow of silence as well as chastity, or something's wrong.'

He looked at her. 'How do you know I'm chaste?'

She met his gaze. 'According to the hospital rumour
mill, you haven't dated in a month and everyone thinks
you must be ill.'

'They ought to mind their own business.' He scowled.
'I'm not ill. I just don't want to date.'

Fair enough. She could understand that; it was how
she felt, too.

'And the silence?' she asked.

He sighed. 'I don't want to talk about it here.'

So there *was* something wrong. And she liked Harry. She hated to think of him being miserable. And maybe talking to her would help him. 'After work, then? Somewhere else, somewhere that people from round here aren't likely to be hanging round to overhear what you're saying?'

There was a gleam of interest in his eyes. 'Are you asking me on a date, Sister McKenna?'

'That I'm most definitely not,' she said crisply. But then she softened. 'We're friends, Harry, and friends support each other. You look upset about something and you've been a bit serious at work lately, so something's obviously wrong. If you want to go for a drink with me after work or something and talk, then the offer's there.'

'I could use a friend,' he said. 'But you never socialise outside work, Isla. And isn't someone waiting at home for you?'

'I'm single, as well you know.'

He wrinkled his nose. 'I didn't mean that.'

'I don't follow.'

'Maybe you have a child,' he explained, 'or a relative you're caring for.'

'Is that what people are saying about me? That because I don't go on team nights out, I must be a single parent with babysitting problems?'

He winced. 'People get curious. But I haven't been gossiping about you.'

Given what he'd said about the hospital rumour mill, she believed him. 'Just for the record, I don't have a child, and I don't look after anyone. There's just me. And that's fine.'

'Not even a goldfish or a cat?'

'No.' She would've loved a dog, but it wouldn't be fair to leave a dog alone all day. Hospital shifts and pets didn't mix that well, unless you were in a family where you could share the care. Not to mention the clause in the lease of her flat saying that she couldn't have pets. 'You know what the old song says about not being able to take a goldfish for a walk.'

'I guess.' He paused. 'Thank you, Isla. I'll think of somewhere and text you. Shall we meet there?'

She knew exactly what he wasn't saying. Because, if they travelled to the pub or café together, someone was likely to see them and start speculating about whether they were seeing each other. Harry obviously didn't want to be the centre of gossip, and neither did she. 'Deal,' she said.

After his shift finished, Harry texted Isla the address of the wine bar and directions on how to find it.

Funny, she was the last person he'd expected to take him under her wing. She didn't date, whereas he had the not-quite-deserved reputation of dating hundreds of women and breaking their hearts. He'd been at the London Victoria for years and she'd been working there for just under a month. And yet she'd been the only one in the department who'd picked up his dark mood; and she'd been the only one who'd offered him a listening ear.

Harry didn't tend to talk about his family.

But maybe talking to someone who didn't know him that well—and most certainly didn't know any of the other people involved—might help. A fresh pair of eyes to help him see the right course of action. Because this wedding was really getting under his skin and Harry didn't have a clue why it was upsetting him so much.

It wasn't as if his father hadn't got remarried before. So why, why, *why* had it got to him so much this time?

Harry was already halfway through his glass of Merlot when Isla walked into the wine bar, looked round and came over to his table. 'Hi.'

'Hi. You look lovely. I've never seen you wearing normal clothes instead of your nurse's uniform.' The words were out before he could stop them and he grimaced. 'Sorry. I wasn't hitting on you.'

Much.

Because he had to admit that he was attracted to Isla McKenna. That gorgeous creamy skin, her dark red hair, the curve of her mouth that made her look like the proverbial princess just waiting to be woken from her sleep by love's first kiss...

He shook himself mentally.

Not now.

If he told Isla what was going through his head right now, she'd walk straight out of the bar. And it would take God knew how long to get their easy working relationship back in place. He didn't want that to happen.

'You look odd without a white coat, too,' she said, to his relief; clearly she hadn't picked up on his attraction to her and was just responding to his words at face value.

'Let me get you a drink. What would you like?' he asked.

'I'll join you in whatever you're having.' She gestured to his glass.

'Australian Merlot. OK. Back in a tick.'

Ordering a drink gave him enough time to compose himself. He bought her a glass of wine and walked back to their table, where she looked as if she was checking messages on her phone. 'Everything OK?' he asked.

'Yes.' She smiled at him. 'I'm just texting my mum, my sister and my brother to tell them I've had a good day.'

'You miss your family?' he asked.

She nodded. 'Sometimes the islands feel as far away as Australia.'

'The islands?' he asked, not sure what she meant.

'The Western Isles,' she said.

So she was from the Outer Hebrides? You couldn't get much more different from London, he thought: mountains, pretty little villages and the sea, compared to the capital's urban sprawl and the constant noise of traffic.

'It isn't that bad really,' she said. 'I can fly from here to Glasgow and then get a flight to Lewis, or get the train from Glasgow to Oban and catch the ferry home.'

But the wistfulness in her tone told him how much she missed her family. Something he couldn't quite get his head round, because he often felt so disconnected from his own. And how ironic that was, considering the size of his family. Eight siblings, with another one on the way. OK, so he didn't have much in common with his two youngest half-brothers; but he wasn't that close to the ones nearest his own age, either. And he always seemed to clash with his middle sister. Guilt made him overprotective, and she ended up rowing with him.

'But we're not talking about me,' she said before he could ask anything else. 'What's wrong?'

'You're very direct,' he said, playing for time.

'I find direct is the best way.'

He sighed. 'Considering how much you clearly miss your family, if I tell you what's bugging me you're going to think I'm the most selfish person in the universe.'

She smiled. 'Apart from the fact that there are usually two sides to every story, I very much doubt you're the most selfish person I've ever met.'

There was a tiny flicker in her expression, as if she was remembering something truly painful. And that made Harry feel bad about bringing those memories back to her.

'I'm sorry,' he said. 'Look, never mind. Let's just have a drink and talk about—oh, I dunno, the weather.' Something very English, and very safe.

She laughed. 'Nice try. Iain—my brother—squirms just like you do if we talk about anything remotely personal.'

'I guess it's a guy thing,' he said, trying to make light of it and wishing he hadn't started this.

'But sometimes,' she said gently, 'it's better out than in. A problem shared is a problem halved. And—' she wrinkled her nose. 'No, I can't think of any more clichés right now. Over to you.'

Despite his dark mood, Harry found himself smiling. He liked this woman. Really, really liked her. Which was another reason why he had to suppress his attraction to her. He wanted to keep her in his life instead of having to put up barriers, the way he normally did. 'I can't, either.' He blew out a breath. 'I hate talking about emotional stuff. And it's easier to talk when you're stuffed with carbs. They do fantastic pies here, and the butteriest, loveliest mashed potato in the world. Can we talk over dinner?'

'Pie and mash.' She groaned. 'Don't tell me you're planning to make me eat jellied eels or mushy peas as well.'

'Traditional London fare?' He laughed. 'No. For vegetables here I'd recommend the spinach. It's gloriously garlicky.'

'Provided we go halves,' she said, 'then yes. Let's have dinner. As friends, not as a date.'

Why was she so adamant about not dating? He guessed that maybe someone had hurt her. But he also had the strongest feeling that if he tried to focus on her or asked about her past, she'd shut the conversation down. 'Deal.'

Ordering food gave him a little more wriggle room.

But, once their food had been served and she'd agreed with him that the pie was to die for, he was back on the spot.

Eventually, he gave in and told her. Because hadn't that been the point of meeting her this evening, anyway? 'My dad's getting remarried,' he said.

'Uh-huh. And it's a problem why exactly?'

'Speaking like that makes you sound like Yoda.'

She gave him a narrow-eyed look. 'Don't try to change the subject.'

'You're a bossy lot, north of the border,' he muttered.

'And you Sassenachs have no staying power,' she said with a grin. 'Seriously, Harry, what's wrong? Don't you like his new wife-to-be?'

Harry shrugged. 'I don't really know her that well.'

'So what is it?'

'This is going to stay with you?' he checked.

She rolled her eyes. 'Of course it is.'

'Sorry. I didn't mean to accuse you of being a gossip. I know you're not. I don't...' He blew out a breath. 'Well, I don't tend to talk about my personal life.'

'And I appreciate that you're talking to me about it now,' she said softly.

He sighed. 'Dad wants me to be his best man.'

'And you don't want to do it?'

'No. It'd be for the third time,' Harry said. 'And I

really don't see the point of making such a big song and dance about the wedding, considering that in five years' time we'll be going through the exactly same thing all over again.'

She said nothing, just waited for him to finish.

He sighed again. 'My father—I don't know. Maybe it's a triumph of hope over experience. But this will be his seventh marriage, and this time his fiancée is younger than I am.'

His father's seventh marriage? Seeing that many relationships go wrong would make anyone wary of settling down, Isla thought. 'Maybe,' she said softly, 'your father hasn't found the right woman for him yet.'

'So this will be seventh time lucky? That'd go down really well in my best man's speech. Not.' He blew out a breath. 'Sorry. I didn't mean to be rude to you or take it out on you.' He grimaced. 'My father's charming—that is, he can be when it suits him. He can be great company. But he has a seriously low boredom threshold. And I can't understand why none of his wives has ever been able to see the pattern before she actually married him. Well, obviously not my mum, because she was the first. But every single one after that. Get married, have a baby, get bored, have an affair, move on. Nothing lasts for Dad for more than five years—well, his last one was almost seven years, but I think Julie was the one to end it instead of Dad. Or maybe he's slowing down a bit now he's in his mid-fifties.' Harry sighed. 'I really liked Fliss, his third wife. Considering she had to deal with me as a teenager...' He shrugged. 'She was really patient.'

'Did you live with your dad when you were growing up?' Isla asked.

Harry shook his head. 'I stayed with him for the occasional weekends, plus a week or so in the long school holidays. I lived with my mum and my three half-sisters. My mum also has a marriage habit, though at least she's kept husband number four.' He paused. 'Maybe that's it. Dad only has sons—six of us. Maybe he's hoping that his new wife is carrying his daughter.'

Isla added it up swiftly. Harry was one of nine children, soon about to be ten? And he'd said something about his mum being his father's first wife. 'I take it you're the oldest?'

He nodded. 'Don't get me wrong. I like my brothers and sisters well enough, but there's a whole generation between me and the littlest ones, so we have absolutely nothing in common. I feel more like an uncle than a brother.' He gave her a thin smile. 'And let's just say the best contraception ever is to get a teenager babysitting for their younger siblings. I definitely don't want kids of my own. Ever.'

'Remind me to tell my brother Iain how lucky he is that he only had me and Mags tagging around after him,' she said.

'You're the baby of the family?' he asked.

'Yes, and I'm thoroughly spoiled.'

He scoffed. 'You're far too sensible to be spoiled.'

'Thank you. I think.' She paused. 'Right. So you don't want to be the best man and you don't want to go to the wedding. I'm assuming you're trying not to hurt anyone's feelings, so you could always say you can't make the wedding due to pressure of work. That we're really short-staffed and you just can't get the time off.'

'I've already tried that one,' Harry said. 'Dad says my annual leave is part of my contract—he's a lawyer, by the way, so I can't flannel him—and he says they

can always find a locum or call in an agency worker
to fill in for me. Plus he gave me enough notice that
I should've been able to swap off-duty with someone
months ago to make sure I could be there.'

'How about a last-minute illness? Say we had norovirus on the ward and you came down with it?' she
suggested.

'Norovirus in the middle of summer?' He wrinkled
his nose. 'Nope. That one's not going to fly.'

'You have other medics in your family, then?' she
asked.

'One of my sisters is a trainee audiologist. But everyone knows that norovirus tends to be at its worst in the
winter. All the newspapers make a big song and dance
about emergency departments being on black alert at the
peak of the winter vomiting virus season.' He sighed.
'I've thought about practically nothing else for weeks,
and there just isn't a nice way to let everyone down.'

'So the kind approach isn't going to work. Have you
tried telling any of your brothers that you don't want
to go?'

He nodded. 'Jack—he's the next one down from me.'

'What did he say?'

'He thinks I should be there to support the old man.
So does Fin—he's the next one down from Jack.'

'And how old are they?'

'Dad's kids are all spaced five years apart. So Jack
and Fin are twenty-seven and twenty-two, respectively,'
he explained. 'The odd one out will be the new baby,
who'll be seven years younger than Evan—he's the
youngest.'

'OK. So you have to go to the wedding. But what
about this best man business? Isn't there anyone else
who could do it? Does your dad have a best friend,

a brother—or, hey, he could always be different and have a woman as his best man if he has a sister,' she suggested.

To her relief, that actually made Harry crack a smile. 'Best woman? I can't see Auntie Val agreeing to that. She says Dad's the male equivalent of a serial Bridezilla.' He took another sip of Merlot. 'Uncle Jeff—Dad's brother—has done the duty twice, and so has Marty, his best friend.'

'So if the three of you have all done it twice, what about your next brother down? Or the youngest one? Could it be their turn?'

'I could suggest it.' He paused. 'But even if I can be just a normal wedding guest instead of the best man, it still means running the gauntlet of everyone asking me how come I'm not married yet, and saying how I ought to get a move on and settle down because I'm ten years older now than Dad was when he got married the first time, and that means I'm totally on the shelf.'

'Apart from the fact that men are never described as being on the shelf, you would still've been a student medic at twenty-two,' Isla pointed out. 'And, with the crazy hours that junior doctors work, you wouldn't have had the time to get married or even spend that much time with your new wife back then.'

'But I'm not a student or a junior doctor now. In their view, I have no excuses not to settle down.'

'Maybe you could take a date to the wedding?' she suggested.

That would be Harry's worst nightmare. Taking a date to a family wedding implied that you were serious about taking the relationship further; then, when it was clear you didn't want to do that, someone would get hurt. But

Isla clearly meant well. 'I guess it would be a start—but it wouldn't stop the questions for long. They'd want to know how we met, how long we'd been dating, how serious it was, when we were planning to get engaged...' He rolled his eyes. 'They never stop.'

'So what would stop the questions?' she asked. 'What if you told them you're gay?'

'Nope. They'd still want to meet my partner. It's not the gender of my partner that's the issue—it's the non-existence.' He sighed. 'What would stop them? A hurricane, if it started raining fishes and frogs... No, that still wouldn't stop the questions for more than five minutes.' He blew out a breath. 'Or maybe I could invent a fiancée. And she isn't coming to the wedding with me because...' He wrinkled his nose. 'Why wouldn't she be with me?'

'She's working?' Isla suggested.

He shook his head. 'They'd never believe it. Same as the norovirus idea. The only way they'd believe I was engaged was if I turned up with my fiancée in tow.'

'And I'm assuming that you don't have anyone in your life who's even close to being a fiancée?'

No.

But, now he thought of it, that wasn't such a bad idea. If there was someone he could convince to go with him. Someone safe. Someone who wouldn't get the wrong idea. Someone *sensible*.

'That's a good point,' he said. 'She wouldn't have to be a real fiancée.' He smiled as he warmed to his theme. 'Just someone who'd go to the wedding with me and stop all the endless questions. Enough to keep everyone happy and nobody gets hurt.'

'Lying is never a good idea,' Isla said, grimacing.

'Hey—you suggested it.'

'Forget it. I was being flippant. It's a stupid idea.'

'Actually, I think it's a great one. And it won't be a lie. Just a teensy, tiny fib to shut everyone up. Not even a fib, really: it'd be more of an exaggeration,' Harry said. 'And if anyone asks me afterwards about setting a date, I can say that my fiancée and I realised we were making a mistake, had a long talk about it and agreed to call it all off.' He smiled. 'And my fake fiancée will know all this up front, so it'll be just fine. She won't be expecting me to marry her.'

'Do you have someone in mind?'

Someone safe. Who wouldn't get the wrong idea. Who didn't have a partner to make things complicated. And the person who ticked all those boxes just so happened to be sitting right opposite him.

Would she do it?

There was only one way to find out.

He looked straight at her. 'What are you doing, the weekend after next?'

CHAPTER FOUR

'LET ME GET this straight.' Isla's eyes were the most piercing shade of blue Harry had ever seen. 'You want me to go to this wedding with you—as your fake fiancée?'

It was the perfect solution to his problem. And she'd sort of suggested it in the first place. 'Yes.'

'No.'

'Why not? Because you're on duty and it'd be awkward to swap shifts with someone without explaining why and setting the hospital rumour mill going?'

'No, actually, I'm off duty that weekend.'

'Then what's the problem?' He frowned. 'You're exactly the right person to ask.'

'How?' she scoffed.

'Because if I ask anyone else to come to the wedding and meet my family, they'll have expectations,' he explained. 'They'll think that meeting my family means that I want a relationship with them. But you—you're different. You don't date. So you'll understand that I'm only asking you to come with me to the wedding to take the heat off me and stop my family nagging me to death about settling down, not because I'm secretly in love with you and want to spend the rest of my life with you.'

'That's crazy, Harry.' She shook her head. 'As I said, I was being flippant when I suggested it. You can't possibly go to a wedding and pretend you're with someone when you're not.'

'Why not?'

'Because you'll be lying to your family.'

'No, I'll just be distracting them a little,' he corrected. 'Isla, I'm asking you because I'm desperate.'

'Did you hear what you just said?' Her voice was so soft; and yet at the same time there was an edge to it.

And he could see why. He could've phrased it a lot better. He winced. 'I don't mean desperate as in...' He shook his head to clear it. 'I'm digging myself an even deeper hole, here. What I mean, Isla, is that I need a friend to support me through a day I'm really not looking forward to. A friend I can trust not to misinterpret my intentions.'

'We barely know each other,' she pointed out. 'For all you know, I could be a psychopath.'

'Ah, now that I *am* clear about,' he said. 'I've spent a month working with you. I've seen you with patients. You're kind—you're tough when you need to be and you don't shy away from difficult situations, but overall you're kind and you're sensible and you're...' He floundered for the right word. 'Well, you're nice.'

'Nice.' She sounded as if he'd just insulted her.

'I like you. Enormously. Which is why I'm asking you—because I can trust you,' he said. 'You're safe.'

'We'd still be lying to your family.'

'A white lie. Something to keep them all happy, so their attention stays on the wedding instead of on me.'

'Nobody's ever going to believe I'm your fiancée.'

'Of course they are. If we keep the story to as near the truth as possible, it'll be convincing. We work together—

and as far as they're concerned I fell in love with you as soon as I met you. You're a…what's the Scottish equivalent of an English rose?'

'I have no idea. A thistle?'

Hmm. She definitely sounded prickly right now.

'They won't buy it.' She rolled her eyes. 'I bet you normally date glamorous women. And I'm hardly the type who'd be scouted for a modelling agency.'

'You're a bit too short to be a model,' he agreed. 'But if you were six inches taller, you could be.'

She scoffed. 'It's not just my height. I'm not thin enough, either.'

'You're not fat by any stretch of the imagination. You have curves. Which isn't a bad thing.' Apart from the fact that now he was wondering what it would be like to touch said curves. How soft her skin would be under his fingertips. And she was strictly off limits, so he couldn't allow himself to think about that. 'Any of my family would take one look at you and think, yes, she's exactly the type Harry would fall for. Beautiful hair, beautiful skin, beautiful eyes, a kissable mouth.'

And now he'd said way too much. She was looking thoroughly insulted.

'It's not just about looks,' he said, guessing that was the problem—he knew his sisters hated being judged on what they looked like rather than who they were. 'As soon as they talked to you they'd think, yes, she's bright and sparky and not afraid to speak her mind, so she's perfect for Harry. He's not going to get bored with her. You've got the whole package, so it's totally believable that I'd fall for you.'

She lifted her chin. 'I'm not looking for a relationship.'

'I know, and neither am I. What I'm looking for right

now is a friend who'll help me out of a hole and humour my family for a weekend.'

'So it's suddenly gone from a day to a weekend?' she asked, sounding horrified.

'It's in Cornwall, which means it's a five-hour drive from here—and that's provided we don't get any hold-ups on the motorway. The wedding's on Saturday afternoon. We can drive up first thing in the morning, stay overnight in the hotel, and then drive back on Sunday at our leisure. Which is far better than spending at least ten hours stuck in a car, as well as going to a wedding.' He blew out a breath. 'And I know it's a bit of a cheek, asking you for two days of your precious off-duty. I wouldn't ask unless I was...'

'Desperate?' Her voice was very crisp and her accent was pronounced.

'Unless I could think of any other way out of it,' he corrected. 'Or if I could think of someone else who was single but who wouldn't misunderstand my motivation for asking her to be my plus-one for the wedding.' He sighed. 'Look, forget I asked. I don't want to ruin our working relationship. I like you and respect you too much for that, and I haven't meant to insult you. This whole thing about the wedding has temporarily scrambled my brains. You're right. It's crazy. Let's pretend we never had this conversation.' He gave her a grim smile. 'I'll just man up, go to the wedding, and do what I always do about the nagging—ignore it.' He looked away. 'My next brother down is married, and the brother below him is engaged. Maybe that'll be enough to distract them all.' Though, more likely, it would give everyone more ammunition. If Jack and Fin could find someone and settle down, why couldn't he?

Though he knew the answer to that. He didn't believe

in love. Not with the number of divorces he'd seen. The first one had been his parents, when he was five; then two more for his mum, and five more for his dad. That was all the proof Harry needed that marriage and settling down didn't work out for his family.

Isla looked at Harry. He'd said he didn't want to go to his father's wedding. Was it really that unreasonable of him to want someone to go with him—someone who wouldn't give him a hard time about his marital status? And to ask someone who he knew wouldn't misinterpret the request as his way of suggesting a serious relationship?

Then again, he was asking her to lie. Something she really didn't agree with. But she hadn't told Harry why she had such a thing about lying. About what had happened on the island: that her fiancé's stepfather ruined her life. He'd made a totally untrue complaint about her to her boss, which of course had been investigated. Any complaint against a member of the practice—even if it wasn't true—had to be considered seriously.

Even though she'd been completely exonerated of any wrong-doing, half the island had still believed that it must've been a cover-up. Andrew Gillespie was charming, popular, and employed a lot of people locally. What possible reason would he have had to lie?

She knew the answer to that. And if she'd told the full truth it would've blown his life apart—and there would've been collateral damage, too. People she really cared about would've been badly hurt. The gossip would have spread like wildfire, and done just as much damage.

But what had really hurt her was that Stewart had believed Andrew's lie. The one man she'd expected to be on her side… And he'd let her down. He hadn't backed her. At all.

She took a deep breath. 'Let me think about it.'

Harry's face brightened. 'You'll do it?'

'I said I'll *think* about it,' she corrected. And maybe she could find a compromise. Something that meant Harry could have her company at the wedding but without lying about it.

'Thank you. I appreciate it. And, if you do decide to go with me, I'd be more than happy to buy you a dress or whatever.'

'That's nice of you,' she said, 'but it really won't be necessary. Apart from the fact that I can afford to buy my own clothes, thank you very much, my wardrobe consists of a wee bit more than just my uniform and jeans.'

He laughed. 'That's what I like about you. You always tell it straight.'

'There's no point in doing otherwise.'

He smiled. 'Agreed.'

'So now can we change the subject?'

Isla thought about it late into the evening when she got home to her flat. She liked Harry's company; and weddings usually meant good food, good company and dancing, all of which she enjoyed. She was seriously tempted to go with him.

And that was exactly the reason why she should say no.

It would be all too easy to get involved with Harry, and she didn't want a relationship. Neither did he. And she really felt for him. Why did his family put so much pressure on him to settle down? Why couldn't they see him for who he was—a gifted doctor who was fantastic with patients?

Her own family had always supported her and valued her. They'd stuck up for her and done their best to squash the rumours that Andrew Gillespie had started. And, when it was clear that the whispers weren't going to go away and she was going to have to leave, they'd backed her. So Isla found it hard to understand why Harry's family didn't support him.

Or was it that he didn't let them close enough to support him? Had his determination to avoid his parents' mistakes and string of broken marriages made him push them away?

She decided to sleep on it.

And she was still mulling it over on her way to work, the next morning.

Not that she had a chance to discuss it with Harry during the day. He was rostered on cubicles while she was busy in Resus, spending the morning helping to stabilise a teenage girl who'd been knocked over crossing the road while she was so busy texting her boyfriend that she didn't see the car coming. The girl had a broken pelvis, her left leg and arm were broken in several places, she had internal bleeding, and the team had to fight hard to control it before she was able to go up to the operating theatre and have the bones fixed by the orthopaedics team. The afternoon was equally busy, with two heart attacks and a suspected stroke, though Isla was really glad that in all three cases there was a positive outcome and the patients were all admitted to the wards to recover.

By the time her shift was over, Harry had already left the hospital, though he'd also left a text message on her phone asking her to call him or text him when she'd come to a decision.

If she said no, she'd feel guilty about tossing him to the wolves.

If she said yes, she'd be lying. Something she didn't want to do. Someone else's lies had wrecked her engagement, and then she'd ended up leaving the job she loved and moving hundreds of miles away to make a new start.

But Harry was trying to keep his family happy, not trying to get his own way and prove how much power he had. Which was a very different category of lying from Andrew Gillespie's. It still wasn't good, but it wasn't meant maliciously. It meant Harry could let his family down gently.

Or maybe just having someone go with him to the wedding would be enough. They didn't necessarily have to pretend to be a couple, did they?

She picked up her phone and called him.

The line rang once, twice, three times—and then the voicemail message kicked in. Not even a personalised one, she noticed: Harry had left it as the standard bland recorded message saying that his number was unavailable right now, so please leave a message or send a text.

'It's Isla,' she said. 'Call me when you're free.'

It was another hour and a half before he returned the call.

'Hi. Sorry I didn't pick up—I was playing squash,' he said. 'How was Resus today?'

She liked the fact that he'd thought enough to ask her about her day rather than going straight in to asking whether she'd made a decision. 'Full-on,' she said, 'but all my patients survived, so it was a good day. How was cubicles?'

'Good, thanks.' He paused. 'I take it you were calling about my message?'

'Yes.' She took a deep breath. 'I've thought about it. A lot. I don't like lying, Harry. I can't go to the wedding with you as your fiancée.'

'Uh-huh.' His tone was perfectly composed and so bland that she didn't have a clue what he was thinking. 'I understand. And thank you for at least considering it. I appreciate that.'

Then she realised he thought she was turning him down. 'No, I'll go with you, Harry,' she said.

'So you've just changed your mind?' He sounded confused.

'No. I mean I'll go to the wedding with you, but as your friend—not as your fiancée.' She paused. 'That'll be enough to keep the heat off you, without us having to lie.'

'You'll actually go with me? Really?' He sounded faintly shocked, and then thrilled. 'Isla—thank you. I really appreciate it. And if there's ever a favour you want from me in return, just name it and it's yours.'

'It's fine,' she said.

'And I meant what I said about buying you an outfit for the wedding.'

'Really, there's no need. Though I could do with knowing the dress code.'

'The usual wedding stuff,' he said. 'It's a civil do. Just wear something pretty. Oh, and comfortable shoes.'

'Comfortable shoes don't normally go with pretty dresses,' she pointed out.

'They need to, in this case. The reception involves a barn dance.'

'A barn dance?'

'Don't worry if you've never done that kind of thing

before—they have a guy who calls out the steps. Actually, it's a good idea because it makes everyone mix, and you get to dance with absolutely everyone in the room.'

Did he really think she'd never been to that sort of thing before? 'I'm Scottish,' she reminded him with a smile. 'In the village where I lived back on the island, we used to have a ceilidh every third Friday of the month.'

'That,' he said, 'sounds like enormous fun.'

'It was.' And she'd missed it. But the last couple she'd gone to had been miserable, with people staring at her and whispering. In the end she'd made excuses not to go. 'Is there anything else I need to know? What about a wedding present?'

'I've already got that sorted,' he said. 'So I guess it's just timing. I thought we could wear something comfortable for the journey—just in case we get stuck in traffic, with it being a summer Saturday—and get changed at the hotel.'

And that was another issue. If he'd been expecting to take her to the wedding as his fake fiancée, did that mean he expected her to share a room with him? 'Won't all the rooms already be booked? So I might have to stay at a different hotel.'

'Dad block-booked the hotel. You'll have your own room,' he said.

'Thank you.' So at least there wouldn't be any misunderstandings there. That was a relief. She'd had enough misunderstandings to last her a lifetime.

'All I need now is your address, so I know where to pick you up,' he said.

She gave him the address to her flat.

'Excellent. And thank you for coming with me, Isla. I really appreciate it,' he said.

The next evening, just as Isla got home from work, her neighbour's door opened.

'There was a delivery for you while you were at work,' she said, handing Isla the most gorgeous bouquet. 'Is it your birthday or a special occasion?'

Isla smiled and shook her head. 'They're probably from my family in Scotland.'

'Because you've been in London for over a month now and they're missing you? I know how they feel.' The neighbour smiled ruefully. 'I really miss my daughter, now she's moved to Oxford. I send her a parcel every week so she knows I'm thinking of her. She works so hard and it's nice to be able to spoil her, even if it is at a distance.'

'And I bet she appreciates it just as much as I appreciate these,' Isla said. 'Thanks for taking them in for me.'

'Any time, love.' The neighbour smiled at her and went back to her own flat.

Once Isla had unlocked the door and put the flowers on the table, she looked at the card. The flowers weren't from her family; they were from Harry. His message was short, to the point, and written in handwriting she didn't recognise, so clearly he'd ordered them online or by phone.

I just wanted to say thank you for helping me. H x.

How lovely. She couldn't even remember the last time she'd had flowers delivered to her. And these were utterly beautiful—roses, gerberas, irises and gypsophila.

She called him. 'Thank you for the flowers, Harry.

They're lovely. You didn't need to do that, but they're gorgeous.'

'My pleasure. I hope it was OK to send them to your flat? I didn't want to give them to you at work in case it started any gossip.'

Which was really thoughtful of him. 'It's fine. My neighbour took them in for me.'

'And thank you about the best man stuff, too,' he said. 'I spoke to Dad at lunchtime and he loves the idea of Evan being his best man. Julie—Evan's mum—called me to say she thinks it's a good idea, too. It makes him feel important and that his dad isn't going to forget him, even though he no longer lives with him and Julie.'

'That's good. I'm glad.' She paused. 'That sounds like personal experience.'

'I guess it is,' he said. 'I was a bit younger than Evan when my parents split up, but I can still remember worrying that Dad would forget me if he didn't live with me, because he'd have a new family to look after.' He gave a wry chuckle. 'To Dad's credit, though, he tried to keep seeing us. Even when he was going through the screaming row stage of his marriages, Saturday mornings were reserved for his boys.'

'All of you? Or did you take turns?' she asked.

'All of us, until we'd pretty much flown the nest and were off at uni somewhere.' He gave a small huff of laughter. 'Though when I look back I was always in charge of getting us all to play football at the park, because Dad would be busy flirting with someone on the sidelines. That's how he is. Be warned, he'll probably flirt with you at the wedding.'

A cold shiver ran down Isla's spine. Andrew had flirted with her, too.

Almost as if Harry was reading her thoughts—which

was ridiculous, because of course he couldn't do that—he added, 'Just take it with a pinch of salt. He doesn't mean any harm by it. He just likes flirting.'

'Right.'

'Anyway. Thanks again,' Harry said. 'See you tomorrow.'

'See you tomorrow,' she said.

CHAPTER FIVE

THE NEXT WEEK and a bit flew by. At the crack of dawn on Saturday morning, Isla packed a small overnight case; she was glad she'd kept her packing to a minimum when Harry arrived, because she discovered that there wasn't much room for luggage in his bright red sports car.

'Do they know about this car on the ward?' she asked.

'Oh, yes.' He grinned. 'And they're torn between teasing me about it and pure envy because it's such a beautiful car.' He paused. 'Do you drive?'

'Yes, though I don't have a car in London because there's no point, not with the Tube being so good.'

His grin broadened. 'I'd never drive this to work because it's much more sensible to use the Tube, but on days off… Sometimes it's nice just to go wherever the mood takes you without having to worry about changing Tube lines or how far away the train station is from wherever you want to go.' He indicated the car. 'Do you want to drive?'

'Me?' She was faintly shocked. Weren't men usually possessive about their cars? And Stewart had always hated being driven by anyone else, so she'd always been the passenger when she'd been in the car with him.

'If you'd rather not drive through London, I'll do the first bit; but, if you'd like to get behind the wheel at any point, all you have to do is tell me,' Harry said. 'She's a dream to drive.'

'You're a walking cliché, Harry Gardiner,' she said, laughing. 'The hospital heartbreaker with his little red sports car.'

He just laughed back. 'Wait until you've driven her and then tell me I'm a cliché. Come on, let's go.'

The car was surprisingly comfortable. And Isla was highly amused to discover that the stereo system in the car was voice controlled. 'Boys and their toys,' she teased.

'It's so much better than faffing around trying to find what you want to listen to, or sitting through songs you're not in the mood for,' he said. 'By the way, if you'd rather connect your phone to the stereo and play something you prefer, that's fine by me.'

'Actually, I quite like this sort of stuff,' she admitted.

'Classic rock you can sing along to.' He gave her a sidelong glance. 'Now, Sister McKenna, that begs a question—can you sing?'

'You'd never get me doing karaoke,' she prevaricated.

'I won't tell anyone at work if you sing out of key,' he promised with a grin. 'Let's do it.'

'Seriously?'

'It'll take my mind off the wedding,' he said.

'So you're still dreading it?'

'A bit,' he admitted. 'Though I guess it'll be nice to see all my brothers. We don't get together that often nowadays.' He shrugged. 'Obviously the girls won't be there, because they're not Dad's, so you'll be saved from Maisie interrogating you.'

'Maisie?'

'My oldest sister,' he explained. 'Then there's Tasha and Bibi.' He gave her a wry smile. 'There are rather a lot of us, altogether.'

'It's nice that you all get on.'

'The siblings do, though the ex-wives are all a bit wary with each other,' he said. 'Obviously there have been some seriously sticky patches around all the divorces, but things settled down again after a while. The only one of his ex-wives coming to the wedding is Julie, and that's only because Evan's too little to come on his own.'

'Uh-huh,' she said. 'OK. Put on something we can sing to.'

'A girl after my own heart,' he said with a smile, and did exactly that.

Isla thoroughly enjoyed the journey; and, after they'd stopped for a rest break at a motorway service station, she actually drove his car for a while.

'Well?' he asked when they'd stopped and he'd taken the wheel again for the final bit of the journey.

'It's great,' she said. 'I can see why you love it.'

'Told you so,' he said with a grin.

Though he stopped singing along to the music as they drew nearer to the hotel where the wedding was being held. By the time he parked the car, he looked positively grim.

She reached over and squeezed his hand. 'Hey. It's going to be fine. The sun's shining and it's going to be better than you think.'

'Uh-huh.' He didn't sound convinced, but he returned the squeeze of her hand and gave her a half-smile. 'Thank you, Isla.'

'That's what friends are for. You'd do the same for me.' And she tried to ignore the fact that her skin was tingling where it touched his. It was a completely inappropriate reaction. Even if she wanted to start a relationship with someone—which she didn't—this definitely wasn't the place or the time. 'Let's do this,' she said.

He nodded, climbed out of the car, and insisted on carrying her luggage into the hotel as well as his own.

When they reached the desk to book in, the receptionist smiled at them. 'Dr Harry Gardiner? Welcome to Pentremain Hotel. Here's your key. You're in room 217. Second floor, then turn left when you get out of the lift.'

'There should be two rooms,' Harry said. 'Harry Gardiner and Isla McKenna.'

'I'm afraid there's only one room booked,' the receptionist said. 'But it *is* a double.'

'There must be a mistake,' Harry said. 'Dad definitely said we had two rooms.'

'I'm afraid there's only one.' The receptionist bit her lip. 'I'm so sorry. We're fully booked, so I can't offer you an alternative.'

'It's fine,' Isla said, seeing how awkward the receptionist looked and not wanting to make a fuss. 'We can sort this out later. Thank you for your help.' She forced a smile she didn't feel.

Going to the wedding with Harry was one thing; sharing a room with him was quite another. And he didn't look exactly thrilled about the situation, either.

They went to the lift and found their room in silence.

'I'm so sorry about this. I did say that we were just friends and we needed two rooms. I hope my father isn't making assumptions,' Harry said. 'Look, I'll ring round and see if I can find myself a room somewhere nearby.'

'Harry, this is your family. You ought to be the one to stay here,' Isla pointed out.

'I'm really sorry about this. Dad definitely said we

had two rooms. Give me a moment and I'll find an alternative,' he said, grabbing his phone to check the Internet for numbers of nearby hotels and guest houses.

Several phone calls later, he'd established that there were no rooms available anywhere near. 'Absolutely everywhere is fully booked with holidaymakers. Which I guess you'd expect on a weekend at this time of year.' He sighed. 'OK. I'll sleep in the car.'

'You can't possibly do that!' Isla frowned at him. 'Look, it's just for one night. We can share the room.'

'In that case, I'll take the couch.'

'You're too tall, your back will feel like murder tomorrow morning.' She took a deep breath. 'Look, we're adults. We can share a bed without...' She stopped before she said the words. Even thinking them made a slow burn start at the base of her spine. *Making love. With Harry.*

Any woman with a pulse would find Harry Gardiner attractive, and of course it would cross her mind to wonder what it would be like to be in his arms. She'd just have to make sure she didn't act on that impulse. 'Well,' she finished lamely.

'You're right. It's not as if we're teenagers,' he said. And at least he hadn't seemed to pick up on what was going through her head.

'Exactly. Now, we need to get changed,' she said briskly. 'Do you want to change in here or in the bathroom?'

'You pick,' he said.

'Bathroom,' she said, and escaped there with her dress and make-up bag.

Sharing a room with Isla McKenna.

It was the sensible solution, Harry knew.

The problem was, he didn't feel sensible. He was already on edge about the wedding, and if they shared a bed it would be all too easy to seek comfort in her.

She's your colleague, he reminded himself. Off limits. She wants a relationship just as little as you do. Keep your distance.

He'd just about got himself under control by the time he'd changed into the tailcoat, wing-collared shirt and cravat his father had asked him to wear. He left the top hat on the bed for the time being, took a deep breath and knocked on the bathroom door. 'Isla, I'm ready whenever you are,' he said, 'but don't take that as me rushing you. There's plenty of time. I just didn't want you to feel that you had to be stuck in there while I was faffing about in the other room.'

She opened the door. 'I'm ready,' she said softly.

Harry had never seen Isla dressed up before. He'd seen her wearing jeans and a T-shirt, and he'd seen her in her uniform at the hospital. On every occasion she'd worn her hair pinned back and no make-up, not even a touch of lipstick.

Today, she was wearing a simple blue dress that emphasised the colour of her eyes, a touch of mascara, the lightest shimmer of lipstick—and she looked stunning. Desire rushed through him, taking his breath away. How had he ever thought that Isla would be *safe*? He needed to get himself under control. Now.

'You look lovely,' he said, hearing the slight croak in his voice and feeling cross with himself for letting his emotions show.

'Thank you. You don't scrub up so badly yourself, Dr Gardiner,' she said.

Exactly the right words to help him keep his burgeoning feelings under control, and he was grateful for them. 'Shall we?' he asked and gestured to the door.

'Sure.' She gave him a cheeky grin. 'Don't forget your hat.'

'No.' He glanced at her high-heeled shoes and did a double-take. 'Isla, are you going to be able to dance in those?'

'I'm Scottish. Of course I can.' She grinned. 'And if I can't I'll just take them off.'

He really, really wished she hadn't said those words. Because now there was a picture on his head that he couldn't shift. Isla, all barefoot and beguiling, standing before him and looking up with her eyes full of laughter. And himself taking off every piece of her clothing, one by one...

Get a grip, Harry Gardiner, and keep your hands and your eyes to yourself, he warned himself. He pinned his best smile to his face, and opened the door.

'Isla, this is my father, Robert Gardiner,' Harry said formally when they joined the wedding party in the hotel gardens. 'Dad, this is my friend Isla McKenna.'

Isla could see the family resemblance. Although Bertie's hair was liberally streaked with grey, clearly once it had been as dark as Harry's, and if it hadn't been cut so short it would've been as curly as Harry's, too. Bertie had the same dark eyes and same sweet smile as his son, though Harry hadn't inherited his dimples.

'It's lovely to meet you, Mr Gardiner,' she said.

'Everyone calls me Bertie,' he corrected with a smile. 'It's lovely to meet you, too, Isla—I can call you Isla?'

'Yes, of course.'

'Good.' His eyes twinkled at her. 'I believe I have

you to thank for persuading Harry to be here at all, and I hear it was your idea for Evan to be my best man.'

She winced. 'Sorry, that sounds horribly like interference on my part.'

He smiled and clapped her shoulder. 'Sweetheart, it was an inspired suggestion, and you talked Harry into coming so I most definitely owe you champagne.'

For a moment, she froze. Andrew Gillespie had been just as charming and flirtatious, but he'd hidden a serpent under the smile. Then she remembered Harry's warning that his father would flirt with her but meant nothing by it. And he was right. There was nothing remotely assessing in the way Bertie looked at her. No hidden agendas. He wasn't a carbon copy of Andrew.

'Now, has my boy here introduced you to everyone?' Bertie asked.

'We've hardly had time, Dad—remember, we drove up this morning from London and we had to get changed.'

'You could've come last night and had dinner with us,' Bertie pointed out. 'But you said you were on a late shift and couldn't get anyone to swap with you.'

'Exactly.' Harry gave him a tight smile. 'I happen to work in the busiest department at the hospital, you know.'

'Hmm.' Bertie rolled his eyes. 'Come with me, sweetheart, and I'll introduce you.'

'Where's Trixie?' Harry asked.

Bertie smiled. 'Now, son, you've been to enough of my weddings to know that it's bad luck for the groom to see the bride before the ceremony.'

And then Isla finally relaxed, liking the way Harry's father was able to poke fun at himself.

The next thing she knew, she'd been introduced to a dozen or more of Harry's family, including most of his brothers. The twelve-year-old looked as if he'd rather not be there and she made a mental note to go and chat to him later; the seventeen-year-old looked a little awkward. The two oldest, Jack and Fin, seemed to be assessing her suitability for Harry.

'Sorry about that,' Harry said softly as soon as they were alone again. 'Clearly they were under instructions from Maisie. Jack's only a year and a bit older than her, and they see things pretty much the same way.'

'It's fine,' Isla said with a smile.

The wedding ceremony was held under a canopy on the clifftop, and the views were breathtaking. And seeing the sea made Isla feel suddenly homesick.

'Are you OK?' Harry asked.

'Sure. It's just been a while since I've seen the sea properly.'

'Before we go back to London,' he promised, 'we'll go for a walk on the beach.'

'I'll hold you to that. It's the one thing I regret about London—there's no sea. And I miss walking by the waves.'

'There's a beach of sorts on the Thames. I'll show you some time, if you like.'

'Thank you.'

The wedding itself was lovely. Harry's youngest brother was indeed the best man, and he handed the rings to Bertie at the altar.

Trixie and Bertie's vows were very simple and heartfelt. Isla guessed that Harry was going to find this bit the hardest, so she slipped her hand into his and squeezed his fingers. He squeezed back and then didn't let her hand go.

* * *

After the wedding, the photographer had everyone clustering together in groups. Isla particularly liked the one of Bertie with his six sons, all of them wearing top hats and then a second shot with them all throwing their hats into the air. She took a couple of snaps on her phone for posterity.

And then the photographer called her and Harry over. 'Now, you two. Stand together here.' He posed them, then shook his head. 'I want you closer than that,' he said.

Oh, help. He was clearly under the misapprehension that she and Harry were a proper couple. Just as she had a nasty feeling that Harry's family thought that, too—even though Harry had made it clear they were just friends.

'That's it. Arms round each other,' the photographer said.

They'd have to go along with it. Making a fuss now would make everything awkward and embarrassing.

'Look into each other's eyes,' the photographer said. 'That's it. I want to see the love. As if you're just about to kiss each other.'

Isla's mouth went dry.

Kissing Harry.

The worst thing was, she could just imagine it. Putting her hand up to stroke his cheek, then sliding her hand round his neck and drawing his head down to hers. Parting her lips. Seeing his pupils widen with desire. Feeling his lips brush against hers, all light and teasing and promising; and then he'd pull her closer, jam his mouth properly against hers and deepen the kiss…

'That's *exactly* what I'm talking about!' the photographer crowed.

Isla focussed again and saw the shock in Harry's eyes.

Had she given herself away? Or was he shocked because the same feelings had been coursing through him?

She didn't dare ask, but she made some excuse to dive back into the crowd. And please, please, let her libido be back under control before Harry could guess what she'd been thinking.

Trixie—who turned out to be a primary school teacher—clearly understood how bored the younger members of the family would find things, so she'd arranged a duck race on the stream running through the hotel grounds for them. Evan insisted on making a team with Harry, and made their duck into a pirate.

Harry was such a sweetheart, Isla thought; he was as patient with all the children here as he was in the emergency department. And yet he'd been so adamant about not wanting children of his own. She couldn't quite work it out.

'He's very good with children,' Bertie said, joining her.

'They love him at work—he has this stock of terrible jokes to distract them,' Isla said with a smile.

'I can imagine. Half of them come from his brothers.' Bertie paused. 'So you met when you started working together?'

Isla had half expected an inquisition. And the best way to stop the misconception being uncovered and making things really awkward would be to stick as closely to the truth as possible. 'Yes—a couple of months ago.'

'And you're a doctor, too?'

'No, I'm a nurse,' Isla said.

'Senior nurse, actually.' Harry came up and slung one arm casually around Isla's shoulders, clearly having worked out what was going on. 'Let's have the inquisition over now, please, Dad.'

'If you actually told me things, Harry,' Bertie grumbled good-naturedly, 'then I wouldn't have to pump other people for information, would I?'

'I'm a doctor. I'm used to keeping things confidential,' Harry said with a grin.

'You're impossible,' Bertie said with a sigh.

'Like father, like son,' Harry said with a broad wink. 'Isla's my friend. End of story. Come on, Isla—it's time for food and I'm starving,' he added, and shepherded her into the large marquee on the lawn.

The food was wonderful: Cornish crab terrine followed by roast beef and all the trimmings, then a rich pavlova with clotted cream and raspberries, and finally a selection of traditional Cornish cheeses and crackers.

The waiters topped up everyone's glasses with champagne, ready for the speeches.

The father of the bride gave the first speech. Sticking with tradition, he welcomed the guests, thanked everyone for coming, spoke a little bit about Bertie and Trixie, and then toasted the bride and groom.

Harry murmured in her ear, 'Excuse me—I'm going to have to leave you for a minute or two.'

She realised why when little Evan stood up on his chair, with Harry crouched beside him.

'I'm Evan and I'm my daddy's best man,' Evan said proudly. 'My big brother Harry says my speech has to be funny, so I'm going to tell you my favourite joke. What did the banana say to the monkey?' He waited for a moment before delivering the punchline. 'Nothing— bananas can't talk!'

Everyone laughed.

'Harry says the speech has got to be short as well as funny, so I'll stop now. Happy wedding day, Daddy and Trixie.'

Everyone echoed, 'Bertie and Trixie.'

Harry whispered something in Evan's ear and the little boy's eyes went wide. 'Harry, I forgot!'

Harry smiled at him and patted his shoulder, and mouthed, 'Go on.'

'Um, I'm sorry, everyone, I forgot the other bit. The bridesmaids look really pretty and they did a good job. You have to drink to the bridesmaids now.'

There were amused and indulgent laughs, and everyone chorused, 'The bridesmaids.'

Bertie stood up last. 'And I must say thank you to my best man, who did a fabulous job.'

'And Harry,' Evan chipped in.

Bertie grinned. 'I gather it was a bit of a team effort between my youngest and my oldest sons. But that's what family's all about. Pitching in together.' He raised his glass. 'I'd like to make a toast to my beautiful bride, Trixie, and to my wonderful family—thank you all for coming here to celebrate with us.'

Harry quietly came back to join their table at that point. Isla reached for his hand under the table and squeezed it.

After the speeches, it was time to cut the cake. 'The middle layer is chocolate,' Trixie said, 'so that should make all the men in my new family happy.'

'As sweet as you are,' Bertie said, and kissed her. 'And I believe the band is ready for us. Perhaps we could all move in to the other marquee?'

The band was set up at one end, and there were chairs lining the edges of the floor. For the first dance, the band played a slow dance; Bertie and Trixie started things off, followed by the bride and groom's parents, and then the bridesmaids and best man.

Isla wondered if Harry was going to suggest dancing with her, but at the end of the song the singer announced, 'And now it's time for you all you to dance off that cake—I want everybody up on the floor, and there's no excuse for not dancing because we're going to call the steps for you.'

There were protests from the younger members of the wedding party, but they were roundly ignored—and, by the middle of the first dance, everyone was laughing and thoroughly enjoying themselves. Isla knew most of the steps from the ceilidhs she'd been to back on the island. Her own wedding reception would've been just like this. But she pushed away the sadness; now wasn't the time or place, and she wasn't going to let the shadow of Andrew Gillespie spoil this weekend.

Harry watched Isla dancing while he was on the other side of the room. Her glorious hair flew out behind her, and she'd been telling the truth about being able to dance in high heels. Before today, he hadn't had a clue how well his colleague could dance. If the rest of the staff could see their quiet, capable, almost shy senior nurse right now...

She was sparkling, and she fitted in well with everyone. And he noticed that Isla had even managed to get his two middle brothers to join in the dancing, rather than sitting on the edge of the room, mired in teenage awkwardness. She'd actually got them laughing as they danced together. Harry already knew from working with her that she had great people skills, but this was something else. She wasn't just coping with his extended family, she was actually joining in with them.

He had a nasty feeling that Isla McKenna was the one woman who could tempt him to break his 'no serious relationships' rule. So much for asking her to come here with him because she was safe: she was nothing of the kind. And he would need to be careful, especially as they were sharing a room tonight.

And almost everyone in his family had something to say about her to him. Fin said it was about time he found someone like her; Jack pointed out how well she was getting on with everyone and how nice she was with the teenagers; Julie came over to say how much little Evan liked her and so did she.

If his family had their way, they'd be getting married next week, Harry thought moodily. And he hoped Isla wouldn't take any of it to heart. He'd told them the truth. They just didn't want to believe it, and wanted him to have the happy-ever-after.

Marriage wasn't an option he would ever seriously consider. In his world, the happiness from marriage was brief and the heartache lasted an awful lot longer.

The band had a break when the canapés and sandwiches appeared, and he managed to snatch some time with Isla.

'Oh, look at this—miniature Cornish pasties, and miniature scones with clotted cream and strawberry jam!' she exclaimed in delight. She tried a scone. 'Oh, you really have to try this, Harry,' she said, and popped a bite of scone into his mouth.

His lips tingled where her fingers had touched them.

Oh, help. He was going to have to keep himself under strict control. It would be all too easy to do something stupid—like catch her hand and kiss the back of her fingers, and then turn her hand over so his mouth could linger over the pulse at her wrist.

'This is one of the nicest weddings I've been to,' she said.

Harry pulled himself together with an effort. 'I guess it's better than I thought it would be.' The real reason that it was better for him was because she was there, but he was wary of telling her that because he didn't want her to take it the wrong way. Especially as he had a nasty feeling that it meant more to him than just the support of a friend—and, despite the fact they'd just celebrated a wedding, he knew this wouldn't last. It never did.

But he pushed the thoughts away and forced himself to smile and be sociable.

After the break, the band switched from the barn dance to more traditional wedding music. Isla danced with his two oldest brothers and Bertie, and then Harry reclaimed her.

Just as the band segued into a slow dance.

It was too late to back out now, because she was already in his arms.

Now he knew what it was like to hold her close. She was warm and soft and sweet. And it scared him, how right this felt—like the perfect fit.

He could see his father smiling approval at him. His brothers did likewise.

Oh, help. They all thought that he and Isla had been fibbing about their relationship and were a real couple—and, even though he'd originally intended that they believe that, he realised now that Isla had been right and it made things way too complicated.

They really ought to sit out the next dance. Go and talk to other people. Distract his family.

But he couldn't let her go. The next song was another slow dance, and he ended up drawing her closer and dancing cheek to cheek with her instead. He could smell her perfume, all soft and beguiling—much like Isla herself. He closed his eyes. All he had to do was turn his head towards her, just the tiniest fraction, and he'd be able to kiss the corner of her mouth. And then he'd find out if her lips were as sweet as the rest of her.

He felt almost giddy with need. It had been a long time since he'd wanted to kiss someone as much as he wanted to kiss Isla McKenna.

Giddy was about right. The mood of the wedding had clearly got to him and he needed to start being sensible, and that meant right now, before he did something they'd both regret.

He pulled away from her slightly.

'Are you OK?' she asked, her blue eyes dark with concern.

He nodded. 'I just need some fresh air.'

'I'll come with you if you like.'

He ought to say no. He really, really ought to make an excuse to put some distance between them. Not walk outside with her in the gardens under the light of a full moon.

But, despite his best intentions, he found himself saying yes, holding her hand and walking out of the marquee with her.

CHAPTER SIX

THE SKY WAS darkening and the first stars were appearing; they were so much brighter out here in the countryside than they were in London. Harry could hear the gentle, regular swish of the waves against the sand at the bottom of the cliffs and it was hypnotic, soothing his soul. He sat down on the grass next to Isla, looking out at the sea, and slid his arm round her shoulders. For a moment he felt the tiniest bit of resistance from her; then she leaned into him and slid her arm round his waist.

Funny how right it felt. Not that he was going to let himself think about that. Because he didn't do serious relationships and he valued Isla too much to mess things up between them.

They sat in companionable silence together for a while. Eventually, she was the one to break it. 'So are you really OK, Harry?' she asked softly.

'Yeah. I'm OK.' He blew out a breath. 'It's just... This whole wedding thing. It's good to see my brothers, but when I look at them I can't help remembering the times they've cried on my shoulder, convinced it was the end of the world because their mum and dad were fighting all the time, or had just split up and they had to move house and start at a new school. Every divorce caused so much damage. It uprooted the kids and made them so miserable.'

'They all seem pretty well adjusted now.'

Except him, perhaps. Not that he intended to discuss that. 'But they've still been hurt.' He sighed. 'Ten marriages between my parents. It's a bit excessive.'

'Your dad seems happy.'

'For the moment—but you can see the pattern, Isla. It's meant to be a seven-year itch, but Dad only seems to make it to four or five years before he's had enough and misses the thrill of the chase.' He shook his head. 'And I don't want to be like that, Isla. If I'm like my parents and I can't settle down... I don't want to hurt anyone.'

'And that's why you isolate yourself?' she asked.

He'd never thought about it in that way. He'd always thought about it as saving others from him repeating his parents' mistakes. 'I guess.'

She rubbed her thumb in a comforting movement against his back. 'You're pretty hard on yourself, Harry. From what I've seen today, your family loves you. Your brothers all look up to you.'

He gave her a wry smile. 'Maybe.'

She twisted her head to kiss his cheek, and heat zinged through him at the touch of her mouth against his skin. Just as much as it had when the photographer had suggested they should look in love with each other, as if they were just about to kiss.

Right at that moment he'd really wanted to kiss Isla, to see if her mouth was as soft and as sweet as it looked. Her eyes had been wide and dark, and it would've been oh, so easy to lean forward and do it. Just as he wanted to kiss her, right now.

This was a bad idea.

He knew he ought to take his arm from her shoulders, move away from her, and suggest that they go back to the marquee and join the dancing.

But he couldn't move. It felt as if they were held together by some magnetic force. Something he couldn't break—and, if he was honest with himself, something he didn't want to break.

'You're a good man, Harry Gardiner,' Isla said. 'I can understand why you avoid connecting with anyone—but you're really not being fair to yourself. You're loyal and you're kind, and I think you more than have the capacity within you to make a relationship work. To really love someone.'

He groaned. 'You sound like my mother. And my sisters.'

'If that's what they say, then I agree with them,' she said.

'Can we change the subject?' he asked plaintively.

'Because you're too chicken?'

Yes. 'No, because the sky's beautiful and I don't want to talk about something that makes me antsy.'

'Fair enough,' she said.

'You looked as if you were enjoying the dancing earlier.'

'The barn dance? Yes—it's very similar to the ceilidhs we had on the island. That's what we were going to have for our wedding.'

Wedding?

Isla had been going to get married?

The fact that she was single—and had made it clear she intended to stay that way—meant that something must have gone badly wrong. Was that the reason that had made her leave the island? And why she'd reacted so badly to the idea of being a fake fiancée—because she'd once been a real one?

'Were?' he asked softly.

She shook her head. 'Don't worry about it. It's a long story.'

'Right now I have all the time in the world.' His arm tightened round her shoulders. 'It's not going any further than me—you've kept my confidence and I'll keep yours. Plus someone very wise once told me it's good to talk because it's better out than in. A problem shared is a problem halved, and all that.'

'Before I ran out of clichés, you mean?' she asked wryly, clearly remembering that conversation.

'What happened? Your fiancé died?' he asked quietly. It was the only reason he could think of why Isla hadn't got married.

'Stewart? No. He's still alive and perfectly healthy, as far as I know.' She blew out a breath. 'We'd known each other since we were children. I guess it all goes with the territory of living in a small community. You end up settling down with someone you've known for ever.'

He waited, giving her the space to talk.

'We started dating a couple of years ago. He asked me to marry him and I said yes. My family liked him and I thought his liked me.'

So that had been the problem? Her ex's family hadn't liked her? And yet she'd still been prepared to meet his own family today. His respect for her went up another notch.

'But then Stewart's mum asked me for a favour,' she said softly. 'According to Bridie, Andrew—Stewart's stepfather—had bit of a drink problem. She wanted me to talk to him and see if I could persuade him to get some help to stop drinking, before he ended up with cirrhosis of the liver.' She looked away. 'I was trying to help.'

'And he didn't like you interfering?'

'Partly, but Andrew got the wrong end of the stick when I asked to talk to him privately. He assumed I was interested in him and he made a pass at me.' She sighed. 'I should've handled it better. I just hadn't expected him to react in that way. I always thought his marriage to Bridie was rock-solid and he would never even think about looking at another woman.'

'It wasn't your fault, Isla. Besides, any decent man understands that if a woman says no, it means no.' Harry had a nasty feeling where this might be going. 'So he wouldn't take no for an answer?'

'Oh, he did,' she said grimly. 'But Andrew Gillespie was used to getting his own way. He really didn't like the fact that I'd said no to him. So he called the head of the practice and said that I'd behaved unprofessionally. He claimed that I'd asked to see him privately under the guise of talking about his health, and then made a pass at him.'

'What? That's appalling. I hope your boss sent him away with a flea in his ear.'

'My boss,' she said, 'had to investigate. Exactly as he was bound to do if any patient made a complaint about any of the staff at the practice.'

'But it obviously wasn't true.'

'And I was exonerated.' She blew out a breath. 'But you know all the clichés. There's no smoke without fire. Mud sticks.'

He blinked. 'Other people believed him?'

She nodded. 'I lived in a village. Everyone knew me; but everyone also knew Andrew. He was popular with the locals—partly because he employed a lot of them, and partly because he could be very charming indeed.'

'But surely your fiancé and his mum knew the truth?'

'Andrew could be persuasive as well as charming.'

Harry really didn't get this. 'But his wife asked you to have a quiet word with him and help him with his drinking problem. She knew there was more to him than met the eye. Surely she must've known that he wasn't telling the truth?'

'And there's another cliché for you: stand by your man. Even if it means upholding a lie.'

'That's…that's…' He didn't have the words. 'I don't know what to say.' But there was one thing he could do. He shifted her on to his lap and held her close. 'Best I can do right now is give you a hug.'

'Gratefully accepted.'

And, oh, he wanted to kiss her. Except that would be totally inappropriate. He couldn't suggest that they lose their worries in each other. Much as he felt that it might help them both tonight, tomorrow they'd have to face up to their actions and it would all get way too messy. So he just held her. 'I'm really sorry that you had to go through something so horrible. And I don't see how anyone who'd known you for more than ten minutes could believe that you'd ever be unprofessional, much less try it on with your fiancé's stepfather.'

'Thank you for the vote of confidence,' she said.

'I still can't get over the fact that people you'd lived with and worked with and treated thought that you were capable of that kind of behaviour. Much less your ex. And right now I don't know what to say,' he said. 'Other than wanting to punch this Andrew Gillespie guy very hard—and I know exactly where to hit him to do the most damage—and wanting to shake your ex until his teeth rattle for being such an idiot and not seeing straight away that you weren't the one telling lies.'

'Violence doesn't solve anything,' she pointed out.

'Look at all the drunks we have to patch up on a Friday and Saturday night.'

'I know, but it would make me feel better,' he said.

She smiled. 'You're not a caveman, Harry.'

'Right now I'd quite like to be. Being civilised can be overrated.'

She stroked his cheek. 'Thank you for taking my part.'

'Isla, anybody who knows you would realise the truth without having to be told. You're honest, dependable and sincere.'

'Thank you. Though I wasn't fishing for compliments.'

'I know. I'm just telling you, that's all. And I'm sorry that you had to go through such a horrible situation. Though I'm glad you chose to work at the London Victoria. And I'm also very glad you're here with me right now.' And he really understood now why she wasn't in the market for a relationship—why she'd been wary even of joining in with the team outside work. She'd been let down so badly. It would be hard to take the risk of trusting someone again.

If anyone had told Isla a month ago that she'd be sitting on Harry's lap with their arms wrapped round each other, she would've scoffed.

And yet here they were. Doing exactly that.

And she'd just spilled her heart out to him.

Odd that Stewart had known her for years and years, and yet he'd got her totally wrong; whereas Harry had known her only a few weeks and he knew her for exactly who she was. *Honest, dependable and sincere.* It warmed her heart to know that was what he thought of her.

'I'm glad I'm here, too,' she said. And, even though she knew she was skating on very thin ice indeed, she gave in to the impulse to lean forward and kiss his cheek. 'Thank you for believing in me.'

His eyes went even darker. 'Isla.' He was looking at her mouth.

Just as she was looking at his.

Was he wondering the same as she was, right now? What it would be like if their lips actually touched? Did his mouth tingle with longing, the same way that hers did—the same way she'd felt when the photographer had posed them, except this time it was just the two of them in the starlight, and it felt so much more intense?

Clearly yes, because he leaned forward and touched his mouth to hers. And it felt as if the sky had lit up with a meteor shower. His mouth was warm and soft and sweet, promising and enticing rather than demanding, and she wanted more.

She slid her hands into his hair; his curls were silky under her fingertips. And he drew her closer so he could deepen the kiss.

'We wondered if you two lovebirds would be out here,' a voice said, and they broke apart.

She felt colour flare through her cheeks as she looked up at Harry's father and new stepmother. What on earth did she think she was doing, kissing Harry like that in the middle of the garden where anyone could see them?

'Don't say a single word,' Harry said, dragging a hand through his hair and looking as guilty as Isla felt.

'It's my wedding day and it's Cornwall, so it's meant to be romantic,' Bertie said. 'Though you weren't quite telling the truth about being just friends, were you?'

Harry groaned. 'Dad. Not now.'

'We came out to find you because Evan is supposed

to be going to bed and he refuses to go without saying goodnight to you—and that's both of you, actually,' Trixie said, including Isla. She grinned. 'He likes you. We all do, Isla.'

'OK, OK, we're coming,' Harry said, and exchanged a glance with Isla. She climbed off his lap and they headed in to the marquee to say goodnight to Evan. The little boy did his best to persuade them to read him a couple of stories each, but Julie whisked him away with a promise of 'later'.

'You're a natural with kids, Isla,' Harry remarked when Evan had gone.

'Because of my job,' she said. 'And so are you.'

He laughed. 'It's my job—and probably because I have so many siblings.'

'And yet you say you don't want kids of your own, even though you're so good with them. I don't get it.'

'I just don't,' Harry said. 'And I'd rather not talk about it.'

'Fair enough.' And she hadn't told him everything about Stewart, so she was hardly in a position to nag about keeping secrets.

'Come on—they're playing your song,' Harry said as the band started playing Abba's 'Dancing Queen'.

It was a deliberate distraction, and Isla knew it, but at the same time she didn't want to push him. He'd looked as if he'd had enough soul-baring for today.

'I'm a little bit older than seventeen, you know.'

'You can still dance,' he said, and led her onto the floor.

What else could she do but join in? Especially as this part of the band's set was cover versions of all the kind of songs that got everyone on the floor at weddings, from the youngest to the oldest.

Though Harry avoided the slow dances that were played every so often to change the mood and the tempo, she noticed. Which was probably just as well, given what had happened outside in the garden. If they'd been in each other's arms again, holding each other close, the temptation to repeat that kiss might've been too much for both of them.

At the end of the evening, they headed for their room.

'I really ought to take the couch,' Harry said.

'Because we kissed in the garden?' She took a deep breath. 'Let's blame it on the moonlight and Cornwall being romantic.'

'I guess.'

'Harry, we're adults. We've got a long drive back to London tomorrow. We both need sleep. It's not as if I'm planning to pounce on you.' Even though part of her really wanted to.

'Of course. And you're right.' He gave her a smile, but she could see that he had to make the effort. 'Do you want to use the bathroom first?'

'Thank you.'

She lingered as long as she dared, hoping to give herself a little time to calm down. Once she'd cleaned her teeth and changed into her pyjamas, she went back into the bedroom. Harry was still dressed. 'Do you have a preferred side of the bed?' she asked.

'Whichever you don't want,' he said.

'Thanks. I like to sleep by the window,' she said. 'See you in a bit.'

When Harry came out of the bathroom, he was wearing pyjamas and Isla was in bed. It was all very civilised and proper, but underneath everything there was an undercurrent. Her mouth was still tingling in memory of that kiss. Plus this was the first time she'd shared a bed with anyone since she'd broken up with Stewart. Even though they'd both made it clear that this was going to be completely chaste, it still felt unnerving.

Particularly as part of her didn't want this to be chaste at all. And, from the way Harry had kissed her under the stars, she had a feeling that it was the same for him. Wanting the ultimate closeness—but scared it would all go wrong, and not wanting to have to deal with the resultant carnage.

'Goodnight,' he said, climbed in beside her and turned his back.

Which was the most sensible way of dealing with it, she thought. Keeping temptation well at bay. 'Goodnight,' she echoed, and turned her own back.

Isla was very aware of his closeness and it took her a while before she could relax enough to sleep. She woke briefly in the night to discover that Harry was spooned against her, one arm wrapped round her waist and holding her close. She'd really missed this kind of closeness. It would be oh, so easy to turn round and kiss him awake; but that would change everything and it wouldn't be fair to either of them. She knew he didn't want a relationship; she didn't want one either.

Even if Harry Gardiner did kiss like an angel.

She'd just have to put it out of her mind. They were colleagues and friends, and that was that.

The next morning, Harry woke to find himself spooned against Isla, with his arm wrapped round her. Her hand was resting lightly over his, as if she welcomed the closeness.

He could tell from her slow, even breathing that she was still asleep.

Oh, help.

She was all warm and soft and sweet. It would be so easy to brush that glorious hair away from her shoulder and kiss the nape of her neck, his mouth brushing against her bare skin until she woke.

And he knew she'd respond to him, the way she'd responded to his kiss in the garden last night. If his father hadn't interrupted them, he had a nasty feeling that he might've carried Isla to the bed they shared right now and taken things a whole lot further.

As in all the way further.

He took a deep breath. She'd told him about what had happened to her in Scotland, though he had a feeling that she'd left a fair bit out. Why on earth hadn't her fiancé believed in her? Surely he'd realised that his stepfather hadn't been telling the truth? Although Isla hadn't said which of them had broken off the engagement, Harry knew it had shattered her faith in relationships.

So he needed to ignore his body's urging. He had to do the right thing.

Carefully, he disentangled himself from her without waking her, took a shower and dressed. It was still relatively early for a Sunday morning after a wedding reception, but they had a long way to drive and it would be sensible to leave earlier rather than later. He made them both a cup of tea from the hospitality tray on the dresser, set hers on the table next to her side of the bed, and touched her shoulder. 'Isla.'

Her eyes fluttered open. For a moment, she looked confused, as if she wasn't sure where she was or why someone was sharing her bedroom. Then her eyes widened. 'Oh. Harry.'

'Good morning. I made you a cup of tea.'

'Thank you,' she said, sounding almost shy. 'What time is it?'

'Eight. I know it's a bit early.'

'But we have a long drive.'

He was relieved that she understood. 'I thought I might go for a walk before breakfast. It'll give you a chance to shower and get changed.'

She looked grateful. 'I appreciate that.'

'See you in half an hour?'

'I'll be ready and packed,' she promised.

'Yeah.' He smiled at her. So there wasn't any collateral damage from last night, then—either from the kiss or from her telling him about her past. She still looked a little shy with him, but he knew she'd won her trust. Just as she'd won his.

And, back in London, everything would be just fine.

CHAPTER SEVEN

AT BREAKFAST, LITTLE Evan was there and insisted that they join him and his mother. Isla was amused to note that he copied Harry exactly in everything he ate; clearly the little boy had a serious case of hero-worship where his big brother was concerned.

When they'd finished, they said goodbye to Harry's family, then drove back to London. It was much quieter on the way back; there wasn't quite an awkward silence between them, but this time Harry was playing classical music rather than something they could both sing along to, and Isla didn't really know what to say. They probably ought to discuss what had happened yesterday and reset the ground rules, but she had the distinct impression that Harry didn't want to discuss it and would change the subject if she raised it.

Although they stopped for lunch, Harry suggested that they grabbed a burger at the motorway service station—and she noticed that this time he didn't offer to let her drive.

She'd always been good with people, but the way Harry was stonewalling her was unlike anything she'd ever known.

'Are you OK?' she asked.

'Sure. Just thinking about work.'

And there wasn't really an answer to that.

'Do you want to come in for coffee?' she asked when he parked outside her flat, even though she was pretty sure he'd say no.

'Thanks, but I've already taken up enough of your time this weekend,' he said, equally politely.

Isla felt as if somehow she'd done something wrong; but, if she tried to clear the air, would it make things even worse between them?

She was beginning to see what the hospital grapevine meant about Harry the Heartbreaker. He was already withdrawing from her and they'd gone to the wedding just as friends, not as part of a date. Was he really that wary of emotional involvement?

'Thank you for coming with me this weekend,' he said.

'Hey, that's what friends are for,' she said lightly. Though she had a nasty feeling that their burgeoning friendship had just hit an iceberg, one that could totally sink it.

Harry was still in scrupulously polite mode as he took her bag from the car and saw her to her door. 'See you at work tomorrow, then,' he said.

'Yes, see you tomorrow.'

And he really couldn't escape fast enough, she noticed. Back inside her flat, she kept herself busy by catching up with her chores, but it wasn't quite enough to occupy her full attention. She couldn't help wondering if what had almost happened between them in the moonlit garden would affect their relationship at work. Tomorrow, would Harry be his usual self with her, or would he have withdrawn even further?

She had no answer the next morning, because they

weren't rostered on together; he was in Resus and she was on triage duty.

But, in the middle of the morning, a woman came in carrying a toddler who rested limply against her. She sounded utterly distraught as she begged, 'Please help me—it's my grandson. I think he's dying!'

Isla signalled to the receptionist that she'd take the case.

She swiftly introduced herself. 'I can see that you're worried, but I need you to take a deep breath and answer some questions for me so I can help your grandson,' she said gently. 'What's his name and how old is he?'

The woman's voice was quavery but her answers were clear. 'Peter Jacobs, and he's two.'

'Can you tell me what's happened, Mrs Jacobs?'

'He started being sick and his vomit was a weird colour, a kind of greyish-black. And he's drowsy—at this time of the morning he's usually really lively. I called the ambulance, but they said they'd be a while before they could get to us, so I asked my neighbour to drive us in.'

Greyish-black vomit. It flagged up alarm signals in Isla's brain. 'Do you know if he's eaten anything he shouldn't have?' she asked.

'He said something about sweeties and tasting nasty. I couldn't think what he might have eaten, at first— I always keep any tablets in the medicine cabinet on the wall in the bathroom, and it has a child lock on it even though he can't reach it yet—but my husband's been taking iron tablets. He has arthritis in his hands so he can't use a childproof cap on his tablets. I didn't realise he'd left them in our bedroom instead of putting them back in the medicine cabinet. It has to be those—Peter hasn't been in the garden, so I can't think of anything else.'

'Do you have any idea how many tablets he might have eaten?'

Mrs Jacobs shook her head, and rummaged in her bag to produce a packet of iron supplement tablets. 'I brought these in case they'd help you. My husband can't remember how many he's taken, but it wasn't completely full. Please help us.' Her face was anguished. 'My son's never going to forgive me if anything happens to Peter.' She swallowed hard. 'If he—if he dies. I can't...'

'He's not going to die,' Isla soothed, though she knew that iron poisoning could be fatal in children. 'You did the right thing by bringing him straight here. Do you have any idea how long ago he might have taken the tablets?'

'It must have been in the last hour or two.' She bit her lip. 'Lee dropped him off just before he went to work. My daughter-in-law's away on business and Lee had to go in. I was only supposed to be minding Peter for the morning. And now...' She broke off, shuddering.

Isla squeezed her hand. 'Try not to worry. Let's go in to the department now because I need to discuss something very quickly with the doctor and then we'll treat your grandson.' She took Mrs Jacobs into Resus and beckoned Harry over.

'This is Mrs Jacobs and her grandson Peter, who's two and we think he might have accidentally eaten some iron tablets,' she said. 'Mrs Jacobs, would you like to sit here and give Peter a cuddle while I fill Dr Gardiner in on all the details?'

Mrs Jacobs looked grey with anxiety, but she did as Isla directed and sat on the bed with Peter on her lap.

'Mrs Jacobs doesn't know how many tablets he took, but she thinks it happened in the last couple of hours. The symptoms sound like iron poisoning.' She gave him a rundown of what Mrs Jacobs had told her.

'I agree—it sounds like iron poisoning.' Harry said. 'OK, we need serum iron, full blood count and glucose. Iron tablets are radio-opaque, so let's do an X-ray to find out how many tablets he took, and then we'll do gastric lavage or even whole bowel irrigation.'

Isla knew that activated charcoal couldn't absorb iron, so bowel irrigation was the most effective treatment, but it was going to be an unpleasant experience for the little boy and even worse for his grandmother. 'I know she's going to be worried about her grandson, but I think we should advise her to stay in the relatives' room while we treat him.'

'Agreed. Let her go with you to the X-ray,' Harry said, 'but then it's hot sweet tea and wait for us to finish.'

They went over to the bed where Mrs Jacobs was sitting with her grandson. 'Peter, I'm Dr Harry and I'm going to try and make you better,' Harry said.

The little boy clearly felt too ill to smile, let alone respond verbally.

Harry turned to the boy's grandmother. 'Mrs Jacobs, we're going to run some blood tests and give him an X-ray to see if we can get a better idea of how many iron tablets he's taken; then we'll be able to treat him. I know this is going to be hard for you, but while we're treating him I'd like you to wait in the relatives' room.'

'Why can't I stay with him? He doesn't know anyone here and he'll be frightened,' Mrs Jacobs said.

'It'll upset you more to see the treatment than it'll upset Peter to be with us, especially as he's quite groggy,'

Harry explained. 'I promise we'll do our best for him, and we'll come and get you so you can be with him again as soon as he's stable.'

She looked distraught. 'My son's never going to forgive me.'

Forgiveness. Yeah. Harry knew all about that. His mother and Tasha had forgiven him for that awful afternoon, but he'd never been able to forgive himself. Even now he still woke up in a cold sweat, having relived the whole thing in his dreams. Seeing his little sister tumble all the way down the stairs, and everything felt as if it was in super-slow motion—and, whatever he did, he just couldn't stop it happening. And then she lay there on the floor, not moving...

Except his dream was always that bit worse than real life. The worst and ultimate might-have-been. In his dream, Tasha never woke up. In real life, thank God, she had.

Mrs Jacobs bit her lip. 'I thought I'd been so careful. I've got cupboard locks and those things you put on the door to stop it slamming on their little fingers. I never thought he'd go into our bedroom and take those tablets.'

Just as Harry had never thought that Tasha would follow him up the stairs. He gave her a rueful smile. 'You can never predict anything with toddlers—and I'm sure your son will forgive you. You'd be surprised what children will forgive their parents.' *And their brothers*.

Mrs Jacobs didn't look convinced.

'You made a mistake, and you'll know in future to keep everything locked away,' Isla said. 'We'll do our best to make sure he's going to be absolutely fine. Do you want someone in the department to call your son for you?'

Mrs Jacobs shook her head. 'No, that wouldn't be fair on him. I'll do it.'

'OK,' Harry said, and squeezed her hand. 'Try not to worry too much, and this will take a while.'

'You can come with me to the X-ray department, so he won't be scared,' Isla said, 'and then I'll show you to the waiting room. Peter, sweetheart, I'm Nurse Isla, and I'm going to help Dr Harry look after you and make you better.'

She took Peter and Mrs Jacobs to the X-ray department, then showed the older woman where to wait. By the time Isla came back to Resus, Harry already had the X-ray up on his screen.

'There seem to be a dozen tablets,' he said. 'So we'll need to do a whole bowel irrigation.'

It was an unpleasant and lengthy procedure, but between them they managed to get rid of the iron tablets and stabilise Peter's condition.

'Shall I go and fetch his grandmother now?' Isla asked as they transferred the little boy to the recovery room.

'Good idea,' Harry said. 'The poor woman must be worried sick.'

Isla went into the relatives' room to see Mrs Jacobs. There was a man with her who bore enough family resemblance for Isla to guess that he was Peter's father.

They both looked up as she walked in. 'Is he all right?' they asked in unison.

'He's going to be absolutely fine,' Isla said, 'and you can come in to the recovery room to see him and have a word with Dr Gardiner.' She looked at the man. 'I assume you're Peter's father?'

'Yes. I couldn't believe it when Mum called me.'

'I'm sorry,' Mrs Jacobs said. 'And I promise you

nothing like this will ever happen again while I'm looking after him.'

'He could've *died*,' Mr Jacobs said, his voice cracking.

'But he didn't,' Isla said gently, resting her hand on his arm for a moment in sympathy, 'and accidents happen. The most important thing is that Peter's all right—and the scariest part is over now.'

She took them through to the recovery room, where Mr Jacobs put his arms round his son and held him tightly. The little boy was still groggy, but mumbled, 'Daddy, Peter got poorly tummy.'

'I know, baby. I love you,' Mr Jacobs said, 'and you're going to be all right.'

'Want Mummy,' Peter said tearfully.

'Mummy will be home soon,' Mr Jacobs said, 'and I'm not going to leave you until she's back. You're safe.'

The little boy snuggled against his father. And oh, how Harry never wanted to be in that position again. Worried sick about a small child whose injuries could've been fatal.

'Mr Jacobs, this is Dr Gardiner,' Isla said.

'Peter's going to be fine,' Harry said. 'I assume your mum already told you that he accidentally ate some iron tablets.'

'Dad should never have left his tablets where Peter could see them,' Mr Jacobs said, his voice tight. 'I can't believe he was so stupid.'

'Peter isn't the first toddler who's eaten tablets thinking that they were sweets and he won't be the last,' Harry said calmly. 'No matter how careful you are, accidents happen, and your mother did exactly the right thing in getting Peter straight here.'

What a hypocrite he was, telling this man that accidents happened and to forgive his mother. Because Harry had never been able to forgive himself for Tash's accident. Not after they discovered that the damage was more permanent than concussion and a broken arm. 'We irrigated his bowel to get rid of the tablets.'

'Oh, my God—that sounds horrific!' Mr Jacobs said, looking shocked.

'It's more effective at getting rid of the tablets than giving him an emetic, and it's also less risky,' Isla said.

'But he'll have nightmares about it.' Mr Jacobs bit his lip. 'My poor boy, having to go through all that.'

'He probably won't remember any of it. He's very young and was quite groggy when he came in,' Harry reassured him.

'So can I take him home now?' Mr Jacobs asked.

'No—because he's so young we want to admit him to the children's ward for the next twenty-four hours, so we can keep an eye on him,' Isla explained.

'So he could get worse?' Mrs Jacobs asked, her face full of fear.

'The early symptoms have settled now, but they sometimes come back the day after, so we always play it safe with young children and keep an eye on them,' Harry said. 'We can take you up to the children's ward and introduce you to the team, and they have facilities for parents or grandparents to stay overnight.'

'I can't believe...' Mr Jacobs shook his head as if to clear it. 'Oh, my God. If I'd lost him...'

'He's going to be fine,' Isla reassured him. 'I know it's easy for me to say, but try not to worry.'

Harry was glad she'd been the one to say it. Those particular words always felt like ashes in his mouth when the patient was a child.

She took the Jacobs family up to the children's ward

and helped them settle in, then headed back down to the Emergency Department. She'd missed her lunch break, so she grabbed a coffee in the staff kitchen and topped it up with cold water so she could drink it more quickly. She knew she could grab a chocolate bar from the vending machine on the way back to the triage team, and that would keep her going to the end of her shift.

Isla was halfway through her coffee when Harry walked in, holding two packets of sandwiches and two cans of fizzy drink. 'I guessed you wouldn't have time for lunch, either, so I nipped out to the sandwich stall by the hospital shop and grabbed these for us. They didn't have a huge choice but there's tuna mayo or chicken salad. You get first pick.'

'Thank you,' she said, feeling a huge surge of relief. Harry was behaving just as he had before they'd gone to Cornwall—which meant that the weekend hadn't damaged their working relationship after all. She hadn't realised quite how worried she'd been about it until she felt the weight leaving her shoulders. 'Why don't we split them and have one of each?'

'Sounds good to me,' he said.

'The kettle's hot. Do you want a coffee?'

He indicated the drinks. 'I'll get a quicker caffeine hit from this. I bet you put cold water in that coffee, didn't you?'

'Yes,' she admitted.

He grimaced. 'I prefer my coffee hot, thanks all the same. Do you want one of these cold drinks?'

'I'll stick with my half-cold coffee, but thanks for thinking of me,' she said. 'How much do I owe you for the sandwich?'

He flapped a dismissive hand. 'It's your shout, next time. That was a good call with young Peter.'

'I feel for his grandmother,' Isla said. 'She was trying her best, and accidents happen. Her son was so angry with her.'

'His dad probably feels guilty because he wasn't there to stop it happening, and that's why he was so angry,' Harry said. He blew out a breath. 'And that's another reason why I don't ever want to settle down and have children. You can't do a job like this and give enough attention to your kids.'

Plenty of other hospital staff managed it, Isla thought. Harry was letting his family background colour his judgement. But it wasn't her place to argue with him. 'Mmm,' she said noncommittally, and ate her sandwich. 'I'd better get back to the triage team.'

'And me to Resus. See you later.'

'Yeah.' She smiled at him. 'Thanks again for the sandwich.'

It was a busy week in the department. Isla wasn't looking forward to being rostered on cubicles on Saturday night; she hated having to pacify the more aggressive drunks, who seemed to take the hospital's zero tolerance policy personally and it made them even more aggressive with the staff.

She knew that having to deal with aggressive patients was par for the course for the shift, but her heart sank when she saw her patient at one o'clock in the morning; the guy had clearly been in a fight. As well as the black eye and lacerations to his face, there was what looked like a bite on his hand; either he'd hit the other man very hard on the mouth, in which case there might well be a tooth embedded within the bite, or the other guy had just bitten him anyway.

Damping down her dismay, she reminded herself that she was a professional.

'How long ago did this happen, Mr Bourne?' she asked.

'I've been waiting here for hours, so you tell me,' he asked, curling his lip.

Great. Drunk and aggressive, and not in the mood for giving information. She suppressed a sigh.

'I thought you lot had to see us within a certain time?'

'We have targets,' she said, 'but we have to treat the more urgent cases first. That's why we explain to patients that they might have to wait, and someone who came in after them might be seen first because their condition is more urgent.'

'Huh.' He swore enough to make his opinions about that very clear.

'I need to examine your hand, Mr Bourne. May I?'

He held his hand out for her to take a look. Thankfully, she couldn't see any foreign bodies in the wound. 'The good news is your hand isn't broken,' she said when she'd finished examining his hand, 'and there doesn't seem to be any joint involvement. As it's a puncture wound, there's more risk of it developing a bacterial infection, so I need to clean it thoroughly before you go. But it won't hurt because I'll do it under local anaesthetic. Can you remember the last time you had a tetanus injection?'

He shrugged and pulled a face. 'Dunno. Maybe when I was at school.'

'OK. I'll play it safe and give you a tetanus shot as well.'

He took one look at the needle before she anaesthetised his hand and was promptly sick.

''S not the drink. 'M not good with needles,' he slurred.

'It's OK,' she said. 'I'll clean it up when I've finished treating you.' She numbed the skin around the bite, irrigated it thoroughly, and had just turned away to get scalpel from the trolley to debride the ragged edges of the wound when she felt her bottom being roughly squeezed.

Unbelievable.

She turned round and glared at him. 'That's not appropriate behaviour, Mr Bourne. Don't do it again. And may I remind you that we have a zero tolerance policy here?'

'Oh, come on, love.' He leered at her. 'Everyone knows what you naughty nurses are like beneath that starched uniform.'

'You're here as my patient,' she said firmly, 'and nothing else. Just to make it very clear, Mr Bourne, I'm not interested, and I don't want you to touch me like that again. Got it?'

'You don't mean that. You know you want—'

But the man broke off his blustering when the curtain suddenly swished open.

Harry stood there, his arms folded and his face grim. 'Problem, Sister McKenna?'

She just nodded towards the patient.

'There's no problem, Doc,' Mr Bourne slurred. 'She's just being a tease, that's all. Playing hard to get.'

Isla had been here before, thanks to Andrew Gillespie. Another drunk, though he'd had more of a civilised veneer. Anger flashed through her; she was half tempted to be totally unprofessional and smack the guy over the head with one of the stainless steel bowls on the trolley.

But then she went ice cold. She'd told Harry some of what had happened with Andrew back on the island. And this case was oh, so similar. Would he think that Isla had been lying to him, and her two accusers were telling the truth after all? That she was a tease and she'd asked for it? Would he, like Stewart, refuse to back her?

'Playing hard to get? Absolutely not,' Harry said, his voice filled with contempt. 'That's complete and utter rubbish.'

Relief flooded through her. It wasn't going to be like before, then. Harry was going to back her. And she was shocked by how much she'd wanted him to believe her.

'We have a zero tolerance policy in this department,' Harry said, 'and that includes both verbal and physical abuse of the staff. Sister McKenna is here to treat you—and if you continue abusing her and touching her without her consent, then you'll leave the hospital without any treatment.'

Mr Bourne clenched his fists. 'And you'll make me, will you?'

'You're drunk,' Harry said. 'You've thrown up everywhere and you're barely capable of standing, so it wouldn't be hard for security to escort you out.'

'Too scared to do it yourself?' Mr Bourne taunted.

'No, too busy tending to people who need help,' Harry said. 'Don't try and play the tough nut, because I'm not interested. I'm here to do a job, not to bolster your ego. By the look of your hand, if we don't treat you, it'll be infected by the morning and it's going to hurt like hell—so it's your choice. You can apologise and let us do our job, or you can leave now and risk a serious infection. Your call.'

'I could sue you.'

'You could try,' Harry said, 'but who is a judge going to believe? Two professional medics, or someone who's too drunk to use his judgement?'

This could escalate very quickly, Isla thought. And if that comment about needles had been the truth rather than bravado, maybe there was a quick way of stopping Mr Bourne in his tracks. 'You'll need antibiotics,' she said, and took the largest syringe from the trolley.

The drunk went white when he saw it.

She quickly put a bowl into his hands. 'If you're going to throw up again, please try and aim for this. If you're sick over your hand, I'll have to clean it out again.'

He retched, but thankfully the bowl remained empty.

'Is there something you'd like to say to Sister McKenna?' Harry asked coolly.

'Sorry,' Mr Bourne mumbled.

'Good. And I don't want another word out of you unless it's to answer a question.' Harry turned to Isla. 'Sister McKenna, I'll stay with you to make sure this man doesn't make a nuisance of himself.'

'Thank you,' she said. 'And now I can get on with my job.' She finished debriding the wound. 'Because this is a bite wound, Mr Bourne,' she said, 'I can't put stitches in it straight away as there's a greater risk of infection. You'll need to go and see your family doctor or come back here in three or four days and we'll stitch it—then.' She put a sterile non-sticky dressing over it and looked at Harry. 'Given that it's a hand wound involving a human bite, should we use prophylactic antibiotics?'

'Good idea,' he said. 'I'll prepare the syringe for you.'

'And a tetanus shot, please,' she said.

'But you're the doctor,' the drunk man mumbled, staring at Harry as he drew up the medication. 'Not supposed to take orders from a nurse.'

'I told you I didn't want another word out of you,' Harry reminded him, 'and for your information Sister McKenna is a senior nurse and is more than qualified to do all of this. I'm only here as a chaperone because you were behaving like an idiot. I suggest you treat the staff here with the respect they deserve.'

'Sharp scratch,' Isla said cheerfully, and administered the tetanus shot.

Mr Bourne whimpered.

'And another,' she said, and gave him the antibiotics. 'I don't expect you'll remember what I say to you right now,' she said, 'so I'll give you a leaflet to back it up. Go to your family doctor or come back here in three or four days to have that wound stitched. If the skin around the wound goes red, swollen and tender, or you get a temperature, then you need to see someone straight away as it means you have an infection. But hopefully the antibiotics should prevent that happening in the first place.' She handed him the leaflet. 'Is anyone waiting for you outside?'

'Nah. The mate who brought me here will've gone home by now or his missis'll be in a snit with him, snotty cow that she is.'

'Then I'll leave you to make your own way out of the department,' she said.

He grimaced, got to his feet and lumbered off.

'I'm pulling rank,' Harry said. 'Staff kitchen, right now.'

Isla shook her head. 'I need to clean this place up first.'

'Then I'll help you,' he said, and did exactly as he promised.

When all the vomit had been cleaned up and the cubicle was fit for use again, he said softly, 'No more arguments. Staff kitchen.'

She nodded and went with him in silence.

He put the kettle on. 'I'm making you some hot, sweet tea. Are you all right?' he asked.

'Thanks, but I really don't need tea. I'm fine.'

'Sure? Apart from the fact that his behaviour was totally unacceptable, that must've brought back—'

'I'm fine,' she cut in, not wanting to hear the rest of it. Memories. Yeah. It had brought them back. But she wasn't going to let it throw her. 'And thank you for coming to the rescue.'

'Which any of us would do if any colleague was dealing with a difficult patient. You don't have to put up with behaviour like that.'

'Not just that,' she said softly, 'you believed me. You backed me.'

He smiled. 'Isla, apart from the fact that I know you well enough to be absolutely sure you'd never do anything unprofessional or encourage patients to grope you, the guy stank of stale booze and vomit—not exactly female fantasy material, was he?'

'I guess.'

Harry grimaced. 'And his attitude to women stank even more.'

She nodded. 'Just a bit.'

'Are you really sure you're OK?' he asked.

'Yes. But thank you for asking.'

He patted her shoulder. 'Any time.'

Heat zinged through her at his touch; and how inappropriate was that? Especially given that he'd just had to rescue her, and he'd said that she would never do anything unprofessional.

She could do with a cold shower.

Or an injection of common sense.

'I really don't need any tea, and it's heaving out there. We'd better get back to work. See you later,' she said. And she walked away before she said something needy or stupid. Harry Gardiner had made it very clear that he was off limits, and she'd promised herself she wouldn't get involved with anyone again.

And that was non-negotiable.

CHAPTER EIGHT

HARRY WAS WAITING for Isla when she came off duty after the handover.

'I'm seeing you home,' he said.

'Thank you, but there's no need,' she said.

'Actually, there is. You had a rotten shift.' He paused. 'And I'd just feel a bit happier if I saw you home and made you a bacon sandwich.'

'Tough. I don't have any bacon.'

'Then we'll do plan B,' he said. 'I know a very nice café not far from here where they do the best bacon sandwiches ever. And a bacon sandwich with a mug of tea is the best answer to a rubbish shift.'

'You're not going to give up, are you?' she asked.

He smiled. 'Nope.'

'A bacon sandwich would be nice,' she admitted, 'but I'm buying. To say thanks for rescuing me earlier.'

'Am I allowed to buy us a mug of tea, then?'

'I guess so.' She smiled at him.

They walked to the café together, where they ordered bacon sandwiches and a large pot of tea with two mugs.

'Thanks again for rescuing me,' she said.

'I'd do the same for any colleague who was being hassled by a patient,' he said.

'I don't mean just that—we'd all step in—but the fact that you believed me.'

'Of course I did,' he said softly. 'But that's why I wanted to have breakfast with you this morning. Because I don't want the behaviour of a stupid, thoughtless patient ripping open some fairly recent scars.'

'It did, a bit,' she admitted. 'It made me remember the look on Andrew's face when I turned him down, and then how my life suddenly went into quicksand mode.' And it was still her biggest fear: that someone would make another false accusation against her, that even though she was exonerated people would still think she'd done something wrong, and she'd have to pick up the wreckage of her life all over again.

Harry reached across the table and squeezed her hand. 'I know you had a tough time on the island, but that's not going to be repeated here,' he reassured her. 'Apart from the fact that every single person in our department knows you're totally professional, the guy was drunk and obnoxious.' He paused. 'There's more to it than that, isn't there?'

She sighed, suddenly too tired to hold it in any more. 'I was so scared you wouldn't back me.'

'Of course I'd back you! You're my colleague and my friend.' He frowned, as if remembering something. 'But you said your ex didn't back you when his stepfather lied about you. Why not?'

She sighed. 'I guess for him there were only two possibilities. One was that I was a faithless liar who was trying to cheat on him with his stepfather and was lying even more about it to save my own skin when I'd been found out. The other was that I was telling the truth, and the man who'd brought him up since he was two and treated him as if Stewart was his biological son rather than his adopted son was capable of cheating on Stewart's mother.'

'But surely he knew you well enough to know that you'd never cheat on him—that you weren't the liar?'

'That's what I'd hoped, but I was wrong,' she said sadly. 'I suppose he went for the lesser of two evils. For him, it was better to think that he'd made a mistake and picked the wrong person than to think that his mother had made a bad choice and could end up being hurt. Bridie had already had enough unhappiness in her life, with Stewart's dad being killed at sea when Stewart was only six months old. Andrew had made everything all right again. Stewart needed to believe that it was still going to be all right.'

'Even though that meant not believing you?'

'As I said, it was the lesser of two evils.' She bit her lip. 'I had hoped that, once he'd got over the shock, he'd see I was telling the truth and we'd work it out. But it was obvious he didn't want to see it. Then again, even if he had seen it, I'm not sure I would ever have managed to get past the feelings of being betrayed. How could I spend the rest of my life with someone who didn't believe me? What would happen the next time we had a difference of opinion—would he take my part, or would he assume that I was lying?' She looked away. 'So I broke it off.'

'Did Stewart know that Andrew had a drink problem?'

'I don't know. I guess Andrew could be very plausible and, if Bridie was colluding with him to keep the situation from everyone...' She sighed. 'Probably not.

'And you didn't tell Stewart the truth?'

'How could I? Breaching patient confidentiality is totally unprofessional—and doing that would've meant that Andrew's accusations were true, at least in part. Plus Bridie and Andrew could've denied that he had a drink problem. And that in turn would make Stewart and everyone else think that either I was lying to save myself, or that I was perfectly happy to gossip about something that a patient had told me in strictest confidence.'

'So whatever you did, you couldn't fix the situation—someone would end up being hurt. That's a horrible situation to be in.'

'It wasn't much fun at the time,' she said wryly. 'At least my family and close friends believed me.'

'But the gossip still drove you away from the island?'

'I was going to tough it out. But every day I had to face the same kind of speculation. Every day I had patients who didn't want to see me because they'd lost their trust in me. Every day I found I couldn't do my job properly because all the lies and the gossip were getting in the way. After three months of it, I wasn't sleeping or eating properly because I was so miserable. Which is when my parents, my brother and my sister sat me down, told me they loved me and they believed in me. They said basically I could stay on the island and let my soul wither away a little more every day, or I could leave and retrain and recapture the joy in what I did for a living.'

'And that's why you chose to work in the emergency department? Because you'd still be helping people, but they wouldn't know you and you wouldn't know them, and there wouldn't be any cradle-to-the-grave stuff?'

'Which is ironically why I became a nurse practitioner in the first place,' she said. 'But yes. And I like my job in the emergency department. I do.'

'But you miss your family.'

'I'm a big girl. I'll cope. And,' she added sadly, 'you might want to have it all, but in the end I guess you have to make some sacrifices and learn to compromise. That's life.'

'I guess,' he said. 'But in your shoes I'd be really angry about it.'

'I was,' she said, 'but I'm pretty much over the anger now. I'm just sad it worked out that way.'

'And then some idiot who's drunk out of their mind starts behaving in the same way towards you.'

'There is that,' she admitted.

'And because the guy had beer goggles on, he clearly assumed everyone else did, too.'

'Beer goggles?' She wasn't with him.

'When you've drunk enough beer to think that whoever you see is more attractive than they are. Except in this case he was right about you and wrong about himself,' Harry explained.

'Even sober and not covered in his own vomit, he wouldn't have been my type,' Isla said with a grimace.

'That's a cue to ask what your type is,' Harry said, 'except I wouldn't quite dare.'

'And I wouldn't answer,' Isla said crisply. Because she wouldn't dare tell Harry Gardiner that he was exactly her type. Not just because he was easy on the eyes, but because he was a genuinely nice guy and she liked the way he treated other people. She just wished he'd be a bit kinder to himself.

He laughed. 'And that's my cue to top up our mugs of tea.' He released her hand. 'Seriously, though, I was worried about you. We all have things in our career that make us flinch when we come across a similar case later on.' He always hated dealing with toddler falls. Especially serious ones. Not that he planned to tell Isla about that. Instead, he said, 'For me, it's a ruptured abdominal aortic aneurysm.'

'You lost the patient?' she asked.

'Yup. On my very first day in the emergency department. It was very nearly my last,' Harry said. 'I mean, I know statistically we lose more patients in our department than any other, simply because of the nature of the job. But I wasn't prepared to lose someone on my first day. She was the same age as my grandmother—in fact, she even looked like my grandmother. Masses of fluffy grey curls, carrying a little bit too much weight. She came in with back pain.' He blew out a breath. 'She was sweating, tachycardic and hypotensive. I thought it might be a ruptured abdominal aortic aneurysm, but she didn't have any mottled skin on her lower body and, because she was overweight, when I examined her I couldn't be sure that there was a pulsatile abdominal mass. I went to see my special reg to ask for a second opinion and some advice on what I should do next, but by the time we got back to my patient she'd collapsed and the nurse was calling for the crash team. And then we lost her. I went home after my shift and cried my eyes out, then I rang my grandmother and begged her to get herself checked out properly and go on a diet.'

'Oh, Harry.' Her sympathy showed in her expression, too.

'Going in to work the next day was awful. How did I know I wouldn't kill off any more patients?' He shrugged. 'I seriously thought about giving up medicine.'

'Harry, you didn't kill your patient. You were young and inexperienced, and you did the right thing—you knew you were in over your head and you went to get help rather than blundering on.'

'I still should've thought harder about what I was doing. I should've had a much lower threshold of suspicion and got the portable ultrasound.'

'Even then, you probably couldn't have saved her,' Isla pointed out. 'You know as well as I do that a ruptured aortic aneurysm has a really high mortality rate and a lot of patients don't even make it to hospital.'

'I knew that with my head,' Harry said, 'but my heart told me otherwise.'

'But you got through your next shift?'

'Yes. Actually, the senior sister on the ward was a real sweetheart. She gave me a hug when I came in, told me that I'd been unlucky to have such a bad first day in the department, and that I was to put it out of my head. And then she said I was rostered in Resus.' He blew out a breath. 'I was terrified that I'd kill another patient. But I saved someone. A toddler who'd had a severe allergic reaction to eggs. The paramedics had already given her adrenaline, but she got worse on the way to the emergency department and I had to intubate her and stabilise her. And that's when I realised what our job was all about. You do your very best to save someone. Sometimes you can't, and some patients are very difficult to help—but as long as you know you've done your very best then that's enough.'

That was true. But he hadn't done his best with Tasha, had he? He'd left the stair gate open and assumed she wouldn't follow him. And he wasn't going to put himself back in a situation where so much would be at risk—not ever, ever again.

When they'd finished their breakfast, Harry insisted on walking Isla home.

She paused at her front door. 'I guess that bacon

sandwich revived me a bit. Would you like to come in for a coffee?'

Part of Harry wanted to back away. After all, he'd told Isla some pretty personal stuff in the café. Plus he had a nasty feeling that this thing between them was drawing nearer and nearer towards a proper relationship, the one thing he'd always sworn to avoid—and actually going in to her flat was another step towards that.

But his mouth clearly wasn't working in sync with his brain, because he found himself saying, 'Thanks, I'd like that.'

'Come and sit down and I'll put the kettle on. Decaf?'

'If I'm to get any sleep this morning, then yes please,' he said with a smile.

She ushered him into her living room and bustled off to the kitchen. Her flat was neat and tidy, just as he'd expected.

The mantelpiece in her living room was full of framed photographs. There was one of Isla on her graduation day with two people who were obviously her parents, as he could see the resemblance to both of them; a couple of weddings that he guessed were her older sister and her brother, given that Isla was the bridesmaid and again he could see a resemblance; and others which were obviously christening photographs.

And the look of sheer love on her face as she was holding the babies told him everything: Isla was the sort who wanted to settle down and have a family. Right now she was still getting over the way her ex had let her down, but Harry thought that these photos were a warning sign that he really shouldn't start anything with her because they wanted completely different things out of life. Things that weren't compatible.

They'd talked about compromising, but this was one

area where he just couldn't compromise. He didn't want to be responsible for a child. Given his genes, if he tried to make a go of it with Isla and actually got married, there was a fair chance they'd end up divorced—and if they'd had a child, that would mean shattering another life. He didn't want to put a child through the kind of hurt he'd been through when he was smaller. And he didn't want to hurt Isla, either.

So he needed to back off.

Right now.

Which was exactly what he'd been doing since the wedding…until that drunk had groped Isla and claimed that she'd started it. Harry really couldn't have left her to deal with that on her own, especially because he knew it had happened to her before. And he'd been thinking with his heart rather than his head when he'd taken her for breakfast and seen her safely back here.

He was just about to stand up, go to the kitchen and make some excuse to leave when Isla came through with two mugs of coffee and a tin of biscuits, which she put down on the small coffee table in the centre of the room.

Too late.

He'd have to stay long enough to drink his coffee, or it'd be rude and he'd upset her. And he wanted to let her down *gently*.

Small talk. That was what would save the situation. 'Nice flat,' he said.

'I like it,' she said. 'It's light and airy, and although it's a bit on the small side it's convenient for work.'

He managed to keep the small talk going for just long enough to let him gulp down his coffee. Then he yawned and said, 'I really ought to leave and let you get some sleep. I need some myself or I'll be nodding off all through my shift tonight.'

'I know what you mean,' she said with a smile. 'See you later. And thanks again.'

'No problem,' he said.

And when he left her flat, he gave himself a pep talk all the way home. Back off. Keep your distance. And stop wanting something you definitely can't have.

CHAPTER NINE

HARRY WAS DISTANT with Isla that night at work; she would've put it down to them both being busy, but he didn't ask her to eat with him or have coffee together at their break.

They didn't see each other while they were off duty on Monday and Tuesday, but he was distant with her for the next couple shifts they worked together.

Something had obviously happened, but Isla couldn't work out what she'd said or done to upset him. He'd been so lovely with her when the drunk had upset her; he'd backed her on the ward, and then he'd made her feel safe and secure by having breakfast with her and walking her home. But, now she thought about it, he'd started going distant on her when she'd made him a mug of coffee, back at her flat.

She really needed to clear the air and find out what she'd done so she didn't repeat it. She valued him as a friend and a colleague and she didn't want anything spoiling that.

Was it the shadow of Andrew Gillespie? Harry had said he believed her, but was he having second thoughts now, the way so many people on the island had back then?

At the end of their shift on Friday, Isla waited to

catch Harry. 'Hey. I was thinking, maybe we could go for a drink somewhere.'

'Sorry, I can't.' He gave her an apologetic smile. 'I'm supposed to be playing squash. League match.'

Why did that feel like a made-up excuse? she wondered. 'Harry, I think we need to talk,' she said quietly. 'I've obviously done something to upset you and I'd like to clear the air. Can we meet after your squash game, maybe?'

He didn't look her in the eye and his tone was a little too breezy for her liking when he said, 'You haven't upset me at all.'

'So why have you been keeping as much distance as you can between us, this last week?' she asked.

Harry looked away. 'Have I?'

She sighed. He still couldn't look her in the eye? Oh, this was bad. 'Yes, and we both know it. I thought we were friends.'

'We are.'

'So what's happening?' she asked.

He shrugged. 'I've no idea what you mean.'

'Then come round for a drink when you've finished your squash match.'

'Sorry, I can't. We're all going out for a pizza afterwards.'

She gave up. 'OK, have it your way. Clearly I'm making a massive fuss over nothing. Enjoy your squash match.'

Harry watched her walk away, feeling guilty. After all, she was right: he had been lying to her. He wasn't playing squash at all this evening, much less going out for a meal afterwards with friends.

He lasted another two hours before the guilt got the better of him and he texted her. Isla, are you at home?

It was a while before she replied. Why? I thought you were playing squash. League match, you said.

He squirmed, practically hearing the tones of Scottish disdain and knowing he deserved it. But she had been right earlier: they did need to clear the air. Is that offer of a drink still open?

For a nasty five minutes, he thought she was going to say no. And he'd deserve that, too.

Then his phone pinged. Sure.

Relief flooded through him. See you in an hour?

He stopped off at the supermarket and bought an armful of the nicest flowers he could find, a mix of sweet-smelling white and lilac stocks. By the time he stood on her doorstep after ringing the bell, he felt ridiculously nervous.

'For you,' he said, thrusting the flowers at her when she opened the door.

'Thank you—that's very kind of you. But what's the occasion?' she asked.

She deserved the truth. 'No occasion. It's guilt and an apology,' he said.

She looked puzzled. 'I'm not with you, but come in. Do you prefer red or white wine?'

'Whatever you've got open.'

'There's a bottle of pinot grigio in the fridge. Perhaps you'd like to open it for me while I put these gorgeous flowers in water,' she suggested. 'The glasses are in the cupboard above the kettle.'

He found the glasses and the wine, opened the bottle, and poured them both a drink while she arranged the flowers in a vase, then put the bottle back in the fridge.

She ushered him through to the living room and he put the glasses down on the coffee table.

'So what's all this about, Harry?'

'You're right,' he said, 'about all of it. I *have* been avoiding you all week.'

'Why?'

He took a deep breath. 'Because we're supposed to be friends.'

She frowned. 'I thought we were.'

'We are.'

'Then…' Her frown deepened. 'Harry, you're not making any sense at all.'

'I know,' he said miserably. 'You were supposed to be safe.'

'And I'm not?'

'Far from it,' he said.

'Why?'

He sighed. 'Because I kissed you in Cornwall. Every time I see you, I want to do it again. And I know I'm rubbish at relationships and you've been hurt before, so the only thing I could do was stay out of your way,' he finished. 'Give me a few more days to get my head straight, and then hopefully I can look at you again without wanting to…' His mouth went dry as his imagination supplied the rest of it. Without wanting to pick her up, carry her to bed, and make love with her until they both saw stars.

'Without wanting to what, Harry?' she persisted.

'It doesn't matter,' he said, 'and I'm not going to make a nuisance of myself. But I thought you deserved an explanation and an apology.'

'Thank you.' She paused. 'But just supposing,' she asked softly, 'I've been thinking about Cornwall, too?'

'Then you're as crazy as I am,' he said, equally softly,

'because we can't do this. You've been badly hurt, and the last thing you need is to get mixed up with someone like me.'

'And how would you define someone like you?'

'You know what they call me at the hospital.' He shrugged. 'Harry the Heartbreaker. The man who won't date you more than three or four times because he doesn't do commitment.'

'That isn't the man I see,' she said. 'The man I see is kind, decent and caring. He notices the little things and he does his best to make everything right without making a huge song and dance about it all.'

'They're right about one thing. I don't do commitment,' he repeated. 'Come on, Isla. You've met my family.'

'And they're lovely.'

'They're lovely,' he agreed, 'but they're no good at commitment. My parents have ten marriages between them, including the one to each other. *Ten*. So it's in my genes to make a mess of things.'

'Or maybe,' she said, 'you could learn from your parents' mistakes.'

'I already have,' he said, 'and for me that means not getting involved in a serious relationship.' He looked at the glass of wine he hadn't even touched. 'I'd better go.'

'Why?'

'You know why, Isla. Because I don't want to give in to temptation and do something that'll hurt us both.'

'You curled around me in your sleep,' she said.

Yeah. He knew. He'd woken with her in his arms, all warm and soft and sweet. It had taken every single bit of his strength to climb out of that bed instead of waking her with a kiss. 'So?' he asked, trying his best to drawl the word and sound totally uninterested.

'So,' she said, 'maybe I woke before you did and I didn't move away.'

'Seriously?' That had never occurred to him. And now she'd said it, he could hardly breathe.

'Seriously,' she said. 'And maybe I've been thinking about it every single morning since when I've woken up. And maybe the bed's felt way too big.'

He went very still. 'Are you saying…?' He couldn't get the words out. Couldn't think straight. Was this really possible? Could they…?

'Maybe,' she said, 'I've been remembering how it felt when you kissed me.' She paused. 'And maybe I'd like you to do that again.'

'You'd actually risk a relationship with me?' he asked, wanting to make it clear.

'My head says no, that I should be sensible.'

'Fair enough.' He agreed with her completely.

'But there's another bit of me that thinks, maybe I shouldn't let what happened with Stewart wreck the rest of my life. Maybe it's time I was brave and took the risk.'

He could hardly breathe. She was choosing him? 'With me? But I'm about as high-risk as you could get.'

'I like you, Harry,' she said softly, 'and I think you like me, too. And I don't mean just as friends.'

'But what if it all goes wrong?' he asked. 'I can't promise you that this is going to work out. I can't promise you for ever.'

'I'm not expecting for ever. We're both adults. If it doesn't work out, then we'll be sensible about it and put our patients and the team first at work, just as we do now,' she said. 'But consider this, Harry—what if it goes right?'

His mouth went dry at the thought.

Risking a relationship with Isla McKenna.

Dating her.

Kissing her.

Making love with her.

He knew she'd been hurt. But if she was prepared to take the risk, then he'd have to step up to the plate and be brave, too.

'We need to set some ground rules,' he said.

She nodded. 'Ground rules sound fine to me.'

'Firstly, this is between you and me—as far as work is concerned, we're just colleagues.'

'That's sensible,' she said. 'Agreed.'

'Secondly, we're honest with each other—if we're uncomfortable with anything, then we say so.'

'Again, I don't have a problem with that.'

'Thirdly…' He couldn't think of anything else because his brain had turned to mush.

'Thirdly,' she said softly, 'why don't you just shut up and kiss me, Harry?'

Something he'd been aching to do ever since Cornwall—ever since he'd first found out how sweet and soft her mouth was.

'That,' he said, 'is the best idea I've heard all day.' He took her hand and drew it to his lips.

He could feel the shiver run through her as he kissed the back of each finger in turn, keeping his gaze firmly fixed on hers. Yeah. Me, too, he thought. He ached with wanting her. He turned her hand over and brushed his mouth against her wrist, and she shivered again. Still keeping eye contact, he found her pulse point with his lips; he could feel it beating strong and hard.

And then he drew her into his arms and kissed her properly.

And it felt as if the sun had just come out and made everything shimmery and sparkling.

He ended up sitting on her sofa, with Isla on his lap, her head pillowed against his shoulder and their arms wrapped round each other.

'OK?' he asked softly.

'Very OK,' she said, stroked his face.

'I'm on an early shift tomorrow. You?'

'Same,' she said.

'Are you busy afterwards? Or can I see you?'

'I'm not busy. I'd like to see you,' she said.

'Dinner,' he said. 'And dress up. Because we're actually going to go on a proper date.'

She laughed. 'Why does that make me feel as if I'm eighteen years old again?'

'Me, too. Which is crazy.' He kissed her lightly. 'Right now I want to do all kinds of things, but I'm going to keep myself in check because I think we need to take this slowly. Get used to the idea.' He stole another kiss. 'I don't date. But for you I'm going to try to change. I don't know if I can,' he warned, 'but I'm going to try. That's the best I can promise.'

'And that's enough for me,' she said.

'Hmm.' He kissed her again. 'I'll see you at work tomorrow. And then I'll meet you here at seven.'

'Sounds perfect.' She wriggled off his lap, letting him stand up, then walked him to the door and stole a kiss. 'Good night, Harry. Sweet dreams.'

'They will be,' he said softly. 'You, too.'

Isla managed to concentrate on her patients for the whole of Saturday—it helped that she and Harry were rostered on different sections of the departments and their breaks didn't coincide—but anticipation prickled through her once she was back at her flat.

A proper date.

And he wanted her to dress up.

So it ought to be a little black dress.

She dug out her favourite dress from her wardrobe, and took time with her hair and make-up. Her efforts were rewarded when she opened the door to Harry and his eyes widened.

'You look stunning,' he said.

'Thank you. And so do you.' She'd seen him wearing a suit before, but she was so used to seeing him in a white coat at work that she'd forgotten how sexy he looked in formal dress.

He reached out to twirl the end of her hair round one forefinger. 'Your hair is glorious,' he said, his voice catching.

'Thank you.' She smiled. 'It gets in the way at work. That's why I wear it pinned back.'

'I like it both ways—when you're being a starchy matron and when you're being a siren.'

She laughed. 'I'm not a matron—and I am so not starchy.'

'No, but you don't put up with any nonsense. Which is a good thing.'

'And I'm not a siren.'

'I beg to differ,' he said. 'You're the walking definition of sexy.'

She laughed again. 'Flatterer.'

'Nope. Statement of fact. And I can't wait to take you to dinner, Ms McKenna.' He glanced at her high heels. 'Can you walk in those?'

She rolled her eyes. 'I'm a nurse. I walk miles every day.'

'In flats.'

She took pity on him. 'Yes.'

'Good. Because it's a nice evening and I wanted to stroll hand in hand with you.'

'Works for me,' she said with a smile, and locked the door behind her.

They walked hand in hand to the tube station. Harry didn't say where they were going, but she also noted that he didn't have to stop and look up directions. Was it because he usually took his dates to wherever he'd booked a table, or did he just know London really well?

'This might be a bit cheesy,' he warned when they got to the West End. 'I've never been to this place before, but it's always on the list of the most romantic restaurants in London and the reviews are good. And I wanted to take you somewhere a bit special for our first date.'

So there she had her answers: he knew London well, and he'd never taken anyone else to this particular restaurant. Warmth spread through her and she found herself relaxing. And she fell in love with the restaurant on sight: the ceiling had been made into a canopy covered in white blossom and fairy lights, there were tealight candles on the tables casting a soft glow, the seats were all covered in red velvet, and the tablecloths were pure white damask.

'I can see exactly why this place tops the list,' she said. 'It's lovely.'

And the menu was equally good; she couldn't resist the hand-dived Scottish scallops, then corn-fed spring chicken with potato gnocchi, green beans and baby carrots. Harry joined her; it tasted every bit as good as it sounded, and he insisted on sharing a bottle of champagne.

'This is fabulous,' she said, 'but remember we're going halves.'

'Absolutely not,' he told her, his dark eyes sincere.

'This is our first official date, so I am most definitely picking up the bill, but...'

Anticipation tightened in her stomach. Was he saying there were strings attached to dinner?

'If you want to buy me lunch tomorrow, I won't be offended,' he finished. 'Or just a chocolate brownie and some coffee in the hospital canteen, if you're working.'

'I'm off duty tomorrow. If you are, too, then it's a date for lunch,' she said.

'And a walk first,' he said. 'There's something I want to show you.'

'What?' she asked, intrigued.

'If I tell you now, it won't be a surprise tomorrow,' he said, tapping his nose and laughing.

She liked this side of Harry—the fun, charming, relaxed man.

And she enjoyed sharing a pudding with him, even if he did eat more of the chocolate mille-feuille than she did.

'I've had a really lovely evening,' she said when he walked her back to her front door. 'Thank you.'

'My pleasure.'

'Do you want to come in?'

He stole a kiss. 'Yes. But I'm not going to. We're going to take this slowly.'

So neither of them would get afraid and back away? 'Works for me,' she said softly, and kissed him good-night. 'I'll see you tomorrow.'

CHAPTER TEN

ON SUNDAY MORNING Harry woke, smiling, because he knew he was seeing Isla. He texted her to let her know he was on the way to meet her.

'So where are we going?' she asked when they left her flat.

'I thought we'd have a wander through the city.'

She smiled. 'Sounds good.'

When they emerged from the Tube station, Isla looked around and said, 'Isn't that Big Ben? So we're doing the touristy places?'

'Not especially,' he said, 'though if you want me to take a picture of you with Big Ben or the statue of Boudicca in the background, we can go up to the bridge.'

'No, I'm happy to go wherever you had in mind.'

He took her along the south bank, then groaned when they stopped. 'Sorry, I should've checked the tides.'

'Tides?' she asked.

'The Thames is a tidal river, so sometimes you see the beach just here and I thought you might like that. I guess it's the nearest you'll get to the sea in London.'

'Maybe another time,' she said.

They walked over the Millennium Bridge to St Paul's; then Harry led her through little side streets and a park to a part of Clerkenwell that was full of upscale clothes shops, jewellers, art shops and cafés.

'I thought we could have lunch here,' he said.

'This is lovely.' Most of the cafés had tables outside with umbrellas to shield their patrons from the sun; it made the place feel almost Mediterranean. 'Do you recommend anywhere in particular?' she asked.

'I haven't been here before,' Harry admitted. 'So pick one that takes your fancy.'

They browsed the menus on the boards outside; Isla chose a café with a French influence and they ordered a croque monsieur with freshly squeezed orange juice, then shared a brownie.

'Good choice,' Harry said. 'The food's great here.'

'And it's really nice exploring London with someone who actually knows the place,' Isla said.

'I've lived in London since I was eighteen. Obviously I don't know every single street, but I know a few nice out-of-the-way places,' he said, 'and it's always good to find somewhere new. I saw a write-up of this area in a magazine.' And he couldn't think of anyone he wanted to share this with more.

Funny, now he'd actually made the decision to start a proper relationship, it felt easy. Natural. The wariness he usually felt when dating someone had gone.

Or maybe it was because he'd found the right person.

Not that he was going to pressure Isla by telling her that. It was way too soon even to be thinking about it. They'd keep this low-key and fun, and see where it took them both.

At work, Harry and Isla managed to be professional with each other and treated each other strictly as colleagues. They were careful never to leave the hospital together unless it was as part of a group. Harry had persuaded Isla to open up a little more and come to one of the team nights out. He noticed that she thoroughly enjoyed the ten pin bowling, and went pink when one of the others told her they were all glad she'd come along because it was nice to get to know her outside work.

Later that evening, she told him, 'I'm glad you made me go. I really feel part of the team now.'

'Good. Welcome to London,' he said, and kissed her.

He saw Isla most days after work; one of them would cook, or they'd grab a takeaway, or if they'd gone into the city they'd find some nice little bistro. He felt they were getting closer, more and more in tune; the more he got to know her, the more he discovered they had in common. He actually felt in tune with her. There wasn't that antsy feeling that she'd expect more than he could give and it would all go spectacularly wrong. With her, he could relax and be himself—something he'd never experienced before. At the end of the evening it was getting harder to kiss her goodbye on her doorstep.

And it was harder to keep everything to himself at work, too. Whenever he saw Isla, it made him feel as if the sun had just come out. He found himself making excuses just so that their paths would cross in the department. And surely someone at the hospital would notice that he smiled more when she was around and start asking questions?

One Wednesday night when he'd walked her home after the cinema, she said to him, 'How brave are you feeling?'

'Why?' he asked.

'As we've made it way past your proverbial fourth

date,' she said, 'I thought maybe we could, um, run a repeat of a certain garden in Cornwall. Except it won't be in a garden and we're not going to be interrupted. And this time we don't have to stop and be sensible.'

Heat rose through him. 'Are you saying...?'

'Yes.' She lifted her chin. 'I'm ready.'

The heat turned up a notch. 'Me, too,' he said softly. 'You have no idea how much I want you.'

'I think, Dr Gardiner, that might be mutual.' And the huskiness in her tone told him that she meant it.

Once she'd closed the front door behind them, he pulled her into his arms and kissed her. He nibbled her lower lip until she opened her mouth, letting him deepen the kiss. It was intoxicating; but it still wasn't enough. He needed the ultimate closeness.

He broke the kiss, whispering her name, and drew a trail of open-mouthed kisses all the way down her throat. She tipped her head back and gave a breathy little moan.

So she was as turned on as he was? Good—though he had no intention of stopping yet.

The thin strap of her top was no obstacle to him. He nuzzled along her shoulder, then along the line of her collarbones. 'I want you so much, Isla,' he whispered. 'Your skin's so soft, and I want to touch you. See you.'

'Do it,' she said, her voice shaky.

'Not here.' He picked her up.

'Troglodyte,' she teased.

'Yeah.' He stole another kiss. 'So where am I going?'

'Harry, my flat has four rooms and you've seen three of them. I hardly think you need directions or a map.'

He laughed. 'Sister McKenna, with her scathing Scottish common sense.' He carried her across the hallway to the one doorway he hadn't walked through. 'Are you sure about this, Isla?' he asked.

'Very sure.' She paused. 'Though do you have protection?'

'Yes.' He stole a kiss. 'And that's not because I'm taking you for granted or because I sleep around.'

'I know. You're being practical.'

'Exactly.' He wanted to make love with her but he didn't want to make a baby with her. He didn't want children. Ever. He'd already had that responsibility way too young in his life, and it had gone badly wrong. He wanted to keep life simple. *Safe*. None of that gut-wrenching fear.

He pushed the thoughts away, opened the door while balancing Isla in his arms, carried her over to the bed and then set her on her feet again. He let her slide down his body so she could feel how much she turned him on.

'Well, now, Dr Gardiner,' she said, but her voice was all breathy and her face was all pink and her eyes were all wide.

'Well, now, Sister McKenna,' he said, and his voice was as husky as hers. 'What next?'

'Your move,' she said.

'Good.' He slid his fingers under the hem of her top, stroked along the flat planes of her abdomen. 'May I?' he asked softly.

She nodded, and let him peel the soft jersey material over her head.

She was wearing a strapless bra; he traced the edges of the material with his fingertips, then slid one hand behind her back, stroked along her spine and unhooked her bra.

'You're beautiful,' he whispered as the garment fell to the floor.

Colour heated her face. 'And I feel very overdressed.'

'Your move,' he said.

She was almost shy in the way she undid his shirt and slid the soft cotton off his shoulders. 'Very nice pectorals, Dr Gardiner.' She smiled and slid her hands across his chest, then down over his abdomen. 'And that's a proper six-pack.'

'So we're touching as well as looking now, are we?' He cupped her breasts and rubbed the pad of his thumbs across her hardening nipples.

She shivered. 'Oh, yes, we're touching.'

'Touching isn't enough. I want to taste you, Isla. Explore you.' He dropped to his knees and took one nipple into his mouth. She slid her hands into his hair; he could feel the slight tremor in her hands as he teased her with his lips and his tongue.

She followed his lead, dropping to her knees and undoing the button of his jeans.

He did the same with hers, then leaned his forehead against her bare shoulder and chuckled.

'What's so funny?' she asked.

'We didn't think this through.' He gestured to their positions. 'Right now I'll be able to pull your jeans down as far as your knees, and that's about it.'

She looked at him. 'And we're on the floor, when there's a nice soft bed right next to us. How old are we, sixteen?'

He stole a kiss. 'You make me feel like a teenager. In a good way, though; there's none of the angst and fear that the first time's going to be a disaster instead of perfect.' He nibbled her earlobe. 'Because we're both old enough to know it's not going to be perfect or a disaster.'

'What is it going to be, then?' she asked.

'An exploration. Discovering what each other likes. Where and how we like to be touched. Kissed.' He punctuated his words with kisses, then got to his feet, took her hands and drew her to her feet beside him.

'Starting here,' he said, and finished undoing her jeans. He stooped to slide the denim down over her curves and helped her step out of them. 'Your move, I think.'

She did the same with him, then grinned. 'You're wearing odd socks.'

'It's a London thing. A trend. The ultimate in sophistication,' he said.

She laughed. 'Is it, hell.'

'Busted.' He kissed her. 'I wasn't paying attention last time I did my laundry. I was thinking of you. Fantasising.'

'Oh, yes?'

'Definitely yes.'

He got rid of the rest of their clothes, pushed the duvet to one side, then picked her up and laid her against the pillows. 'You look like a mermaid,' he said, kneeling down beside her.

'A mermaid?'

'With that glorious hair spread out like that—definitely a mermaid. Or maybe a Victorian model for some supersultry goddess,' he mused.

'Compliment accepted.' She reached up to stroke his face. 'And you're as beautiful as a Michelangelo statue.'

'Why, thank you.' He leaned forward to steal a kiss. 'And your skin's like alabaster, except you're warm and you smell of peaches.'

He nuzzled his way down her sternum, then paid attention to the soft underside of her breasts. 'You're incredibly lovely,' he said.

'Just like you fantasised when you were doing your laundry?'

'Way better,' he said. He rocked back on his haunches. 'I want to explore you,' he said softly.

Colour bloomed again in her cheeks. 'I'm all yours.'

He started at the hollows of her anklebones, stroking and kissing his way up to the back of her knees. Her breathing had grown shallow by the time he parted her thighs, and she slid her hands into his hair to urge him on. She shivered when he drew his tongue along her sex, dragged in a breathy moan when he did it again, and when he started teasing her clitoris he heard her murmured 'oh' of pleasure.

Harry was really looking forward to watching Isla fall apart under his touch. He loved the idea that he could turn all that sharp common sense to mush, just for a little while.

Her body tensed, and he felt the moment that her climax hit.

'Harry,' she whispered, and he shifted up the bed so he could hold her tightly.

'OK?' he asked when she'd stopped shaking.

'Very OK—I wasn't expecting that,' she said. 'I thought you said this wasn't going to be perfect?'

He smiled and stroked her face. 'I'm not finished yet, not by a long way.'

'No—I think it's my turn to make you fall apart,' she said. Her hands were warm and sure as she explored him.

Harry loved the way she made him feel, the way his blood heated with desire as she stroked and caressed him. Then she dipped her head so that glorious hair brushed against his skin, and desire surged through him.

'Isla,' he said softly, 'I love what you're doing to me and you feel like heaven—but right now I really, *really* need to be inside you.'

'Your wish is my command,' she teased. 'Condom?'

'In my wallet—in my jeans pocket.'

She climbed off the bed, fished his wallet out of his jeans and threw it to him. He caught it and took out the condom. 'Are you really sure about this?'

'Really sure,' she said, her voice husky, and took the little foil packet from him. She opened it, rolled it over his shaft and leaned over him to kiss him. 'Do you have any idea how sexy you look, lying there on my bed?'

'Not as sexy as you'll look with your hair spread over the pillow like a mermaid,' he replied.

'Hmm, so the man has a thing about mermaids?'

He drew her down to him, shifted so that she was lying beneath him and knelt between her thighs. 'Yeah,' he said, and eased into her.

It was very far from the first time that he'd ever made love, but it was the first time that Harry had ever felt this kind of completeness, this kind of bond.

Which made Isla McKenna dangerous to his peace of mind.

But she drew him so much that he couldn't resist her. Didn't want to resist her.

She held him tightly as his climax burst through him.

CHAPTER ELEVEN

WHEN HARRY HAD floated back to earth, he moved carefully. 'Help yourself to anything you need in the bathroom,' Isla said. 'The linen cupboard's in there with fresh towels.'

'Thanks.'

Isla lay curled in bed while Harry was in the bathroom, feeling warm and comfortable and that all was right with the world. She didn't bother getting up and dressing; Harry hadn't taken his clothes with him to the bathroom, and she was pretty sure that he'd come back to bed with her. Like Cornwall all over again, except this time they wouldn't be falling asleep on opposite sides of the bed, trying to keep a careful distance between them. This time, they'd fall asleep in each other's arms.

When Harry came back, his skin was still damp from the shower and he looked utterly gorgeous.

'I'm afraid I smell of flowers,' he said. 'Your shower gel's a bit, um, girly.'

She laughed. 'Actually, in Regency times, there was very little difference between the scents men and women used. Lots of them were floral—based on rose, lavender or orange flower water.'

He looked intrigued. 'How do you know that?'

'I read a lot of Regency romances,' she said, 'and I

was interested in all the social history side of things. I looked up a few things on the Internet—according to one of the really long-established London perfume houses, Beau Brummell's favourite scent involved lavender.'

'Beau Brummell? Hmm. So you like Regency dandies, do you?'

'And Scottish lairds—and I dare you to say it's girly for a man to wear a kilt.'

He laughed. 'Can you imagine me in a kilt?'

'Oh yes—especially if you let your hair grow a bit.'

'My hair?'

'You know your mermaid thing? Well, that's me and period drama. It's the sort of thing I love watching on telly. And you'd be the perfect period drama hero,' she said. 'I can imagine you riding horseback and wearing a tricorn hat.'

'We could always play the lady and the highwayman,' he said with a grin. 'I think I'd like that. Hands up, my lady.'

'Now, you need a domino mask to do that properly, and maybe a white silk scarf over your face, otherwise I could tell the local magistrate what you look like and you'd get arrested.' She laughed. 'Come back to bed.'

He shook his head. 'Sorry, I really need to go. I'm on an early shift tomorrow.'

'I have an alarm clock.'

'Even so. I don't have a change of clothes or a toothbrush.'

'I can always put your stuff through the washing machine, and I'm pretty sure I have a spare toothbrush in the bathroom cabinet.'

But he wouldn't be swayed. And the carefree, laughing man who'd just teased her about her highwayman fantasy had suddenly gone distant on her.

He got dressed in about ten seconds flat.

And Isla felt wrong-footed, unsure what to do next. Should she get dressed and see him out? Or just grab her dressing gown?

But when she moved to get out of bed, he said, 'Stay there. You look comfortable. I'll see myself out.'

'OK.'

'See you tomorrow,' he said.

'Sure,' she said, masking the flood of hurt that he could walk away so easily. And she noticed that he didn't even kiss her goodbye before he left. How could he switch from being so sexy and dishevelled to so cool and dispassionate, so very fast?

She'd thought they were both ready for the next step, but had this been an intimacy too far? Was Harry having second thoughts about their relationship? And would he revert to being the heartbreaker that the hospital grapevine said he was? Was he right when he said he wasn't capable of committing to a relationship?

Bottom line: had she just made a really, really stupid mistake?

The questions went round and round in her head. And she had no answers at all.

Harry knew he'd behaved badly.

He'd seen the hurt in Isla's face, even though she'd masked it quickly.

And he'd bet right now that she was feeling used. That he'd basically had his way with her and walked away.

Ah, hell.

This was a mess.

Maybe he needed to be honest with her and tell her that he was running scared. Panicking. But that would mean admitting that his feelings about her were changing. That he thought he might be falling in love with her—her warmth, shot through with common sense and humour that he found irresistible.

He didn't get involved. He'd never wanted to get involved. He'd seen the carnage it left behind every time his parents divorced their current partner—and, even though everyone eventually managed to be civil for the children's sake, he knew from first-hand experience what it felt like in the early days. When your world crumbled round you and you thought it was your fault, that you'd done something bad that made it impossible for your parents to live together. When you didn't understand what was going on.

And so he'd always kept his relationships light. Walked away before things started getting serious.

Except this time it was too late. It was already serious between him and Isla. And he didn't know when or how that had happened. They'd started off as friends; then, little by little, he'd fallen in love with her. Everything from her dry, slightly scathing sense of humour through to the way she smiled. From the cool, capable way she handled every crisis at work through to her sensual delight in eating out.

The blood seemed to rush out of his head as it hit home: he was in love with her.

Which left him stuck between a rock and a hard place.

Either he walked away from Isla—which would hurt; or he let their relationship move forward, risking being hurt even more when it went wrong. Because it *would* go wrong: he'd learned that from his parents. Love didn't last.

Isla had said at his father's wedding that she thought he had the capacity to make a relationship work—that he was isolating himself, and it was wrong because he was loyal and kind and loving.

But he wasn't so sure. Did he really have that capacity?

He'd already hurt her. Guilt prickled at him. He knew she'd wanted him to stay, and yet he'd walked away. Rejected her. Let his own fears get in the way. He hadn't been fair to her. At all.

And he slept badly enough that night that he texted her first thing in the morning.

I'm sorry. I was an idiot last night.

Her reply was suitably crisp: Yes, you were.

I don't have any excuses.

But he wasn't quite ready to admit the truth—that he'd never felt like this about anyone before and it left him in a flat spin.

But can you forgive me?

It was a big ask, and he knew it.

I'll think about it, she replied. See you at work.

Would things have changed between them at work? It was the one constant in his life, the place where he was sure of himself and knew he belonged. He didn't want that to change. And he was antsy all the way to the hospital.

But Sister McKenna was as calm and professional as she always was, treating Harry just like she treated every other member of the team. It helped that they weren't rostered on together; and Harry was able to relax and sort out his patients' problems.

Isla didn't reply to his text suggesting dinner. She also hadn't said anything about any other arrangements, so he bought flowers and chocolates and headed over to her flat. If she wasn't in, then he'd leave his apology with a neighbour.

Thankfully, she was in.

And she frowned when she saw the flowers and chocolates. 'Harry, what is this?'

'An apology,' he said.

She raised an eyebrow. 'Would you be repeating your father's mistakes, by any chance?'

It had never occurred to him before: but, yes, he was. Now he thought about it, Bertie was always sending flowers or chocolates to apologise for behaving badly. 'Ah,' he said, and grimaced. 'I think the penny might just have dropped.'

'I don't want you to give me flowers or chocolates when we fall out,' she said.

No. He knew that she wanted something that would cost him far more. She wanted him to talk to her. To open his heart.

He blew out a breath. 'I'm really not good at this sort of stuff, Isla.'

'Would a mug of tea help?'

Even though he knew it had strings attached, he nodded. Because he knew she was making more of a concession than he deserved.

'Come in. And thank you for the flowers. Though

if you ever buy me flowers again,' she warned, 'then I might hit you over the head with them.'

'Noted. Though I guess at least they'd be soft,' he said, trying for humour.

To his relief, she laughed.

Taking heart from her reaction, he walked forward and put his arms round her. 'I'm sorry. It's just…'

'You don't do relationships, and I asked you to stay the night. Which is tantamount to proposing to you with a megaphone while standing on a table in the middle of the hospital canteen.'

'In a nutshell,' he agreed. 'Isla—I did warn you I was rubbish at relationships.'

'And you're using your parents as an excuse,' she said.

He winced. 'You don't pull your punches.'

'You're the one who set the ground rules,' she reminded him. 'Honesty.'

'You want honesty?' He leaned his forehead against hers. 'OK. I want to be with you. I want to make a go of this. The way I feel… I…' He blew out a breath. 'I'm never this inarticulate. Sorry. I'm making a mess of this. But I don't want to hurt you, and I don't want to end up hurt either.'

'Then you need to make a leap of faith. Is it really so hard to stay the night?'

'Last time I did that…' His voice faded. 'Actually, the last time I spent the night with anyone was with you. But the time before that—my girlfriend assumed that our relationship meant more to me than it did. And it got messy.'

'Spending the night,' she said, 'means both of us get

a little more sleep before work, the next day. But I guess you didn't bring a change of clothes or a toothbrush.'

'No. Can you be a little bit patient with me?' he asked.

'I can, but there's a string attached.'

He wasn't sure he wanted to know the answer, but he knew he had to ask the question. 'Which is?'

'As long as you promise to talk to me in future,' she said.

He remembered something that gave him a way out. 'I thought you liked brooding Regency rakes?'

'In period dramas on screen or in books, yes,' she said. 'In real life, they'd be a pain in the neck. I'd rather have openness and the truth, even if it hurts.' She gave him a wry smile. 'Because the alternative is leaving me to guess what's in your head. And I'm not a mind-reader. What I imagine can hurt me far more than the truth.'

'I'm sorry,' he said. 'I...have feelings for you.' There, it was out. The best he could say for now, anyway. He wasn't ready to say the L-word; he was still trying to come to terms with his feelings.

Odd. At work, he could always find the right words. Here, when it really mattered, he found himself silent. He couldn't even quote a song or poetry at her. His mind had gone completely blank. He felt numb and stupid and awkward.

She stroked his face. 'I have feelings for you, too, Harry. One of them's exasperation.'

He knew he deserved it. But he took a tiny risk and stole a kiss. 'I'm trying, Isla. This isn't easy for me.'

'I know.' She kissed him back. 'But we'll get there. We'll just have to work on it a bit harder. Together.'

She had more faith in him that than he did, he thought wryly.

* * *

Harry still hadn't quite managed to spend the whole night with Isla when she went back to the Western Isles to see her family for four days, the week before her birthday. She didn't ask him to go with her, and he wasn't sure if he was more relieved or disappointed.

He was shocked to discover just how much he missed her during those four days. Even though there was a team night out and a squash match to keep him busy on two of those evenings, he still missed her. The odd text and snatched phone call just weren't enough.

And if he put it all together, it was obvious. He was ready to move on. To take the next step. To take a risk. With her.

Surreptitiously, he checked out her off-duty for the week of her birthday and changed his own off-duty to match. He didn't want to take the next step in London; it would be better on neutral ground. If he took her away for her birthday, he'd be able to relax instead of panicking that it was all going to go wrong. He spent the evening researching, and found what he hoped would be the perfect place.

He knew which flight she was catching back to London, and met her at the airport with an armful of flowers.

'They're soft ones,' he said, 'because I remember what you said you'd do next time I bought you flowers.' Hit him over the head with them.

She laughed, clearly remembering. 'I meant if you gave me apology flowers instead of talking things through,' she said. 'These are different. They're romantic. Welcome-home flowers. I love them.'

He knew she wanted the words. And he was half-surprised that he was ready to say them. 'I missed you,' he said. 'A lot.'

'I missed you, too.'

'Did you have a good time?'

She nodded. 'It was lovely. It made me realise how much I miss the island. The sky and the mountains and the freshness of the air. And most of all, the sea.'

Then there was a fair chance that she'd really love what he'd arranged for her birthday. Though a nasty thought struck him. If she was homesick… 'Do you miss it enough to want to go back?'

'I've moved on,' she said softly, 'and they replaced me at the practice, so if I went back now…' She shrugged. 'I wouldn't have a place, really.'

'But you've retrained. You're an emergency nurse. I assume there are hospitals on the islands?'

'I could work in the emergency department in Benbecula, or in the GP acute department in Stornoway,' she said.

'But?'

She shook her head. 'Not right now. Maybe some time in the future.'

So she did want to go back. Then what was stopping her? He remembered what she'd told him about the way people had behaved towards her after the whole thing blew up with her fiancé's stepfather. 'Are people still giving you a hard time about Gillespie?'

'No, but I did see Stewart while I was there.'

He went cold. That night after their fight and he'd admitted to his feelings… She'd said she had feelings for him, too. But had seeing her ex again changed that? Maybe the surprise he'd planned for her birthday was a bad idea after all.

'He's engaged to another lass,' she said, 'someone we both went to school with, and I wish them both well.'

'And you're OK about that?' he asked softly.

She nodded. 'I've moved on. I've met someone else. Someone I really like.'

He smiled and kissed her. 'I like you, too.' More than liked, if he was honest about it, but he wasn't quite ready to say it yet. 'So it's your birthday on Monday.'

'Yes. I assume it's standard practice to bring in cake for everyone in the department?'

'And chocolate bars for those off duty,' he confirmed. 'And birthdays are always celebrated at the local pizza place with the team, so I'm afraid I can't take you out to dinner on your actual birthday.'

'Because otherwise people will work it out that we're an item.'

He knew that hurt her, but he still wasn't quite ready to go public. 'However,' he said, 'you're off duty two days later—that's when I'm taking you out to dinner.' He paused. 'And you'll need to pack.'

'Pack?' She looked surprised, then wary.

Did she think that he was asking her to stay at his place? 'For two days,' he said. 'It's part of your birthday present. You'll need casual stuff for walking, and something nice to dress up in. I'll pick you up at your place after your shift.'

It was good to be back in London. Isla had a feeling that Harry had missed her as much as she'd missed him—his lovemaking that evening was even more tender—but she noticed that he still didn't stay overnight.

Though he was planning to take her away for her birthday, the following week. But then a nasty thought struck her: were they sharing a room, or had he booked separate rooms?

On her birthday, she was touched to discover that banners and balloons had been put up in the staffroom, and the team had clubbed together to buy her some gorgeous earrings. She thoroughly enjoyed the team night out at the pizza place, especially as someone had arranged for a birthday cake with candles and everyone sang 'Happy birthday' to her.

Harry saw her home afterwards, and gave her a beautifully wrapped parcel. 'It's the first bit of your present,' he said. It was a beautiful bangle, inlaid with precious stones, and he'd clearly paid attention to the kind of things she liked. But again, he didn't stay the night. Not even on her birthday. And it hurt. Would he ever be ready to spend the night with her—to make a move towards a greater commitment?

Isla was rushed off her feet on the early shift on the Tuesday. Harry still hadn't told her where they were going, but after their shift he picked her up in his little red sports car and drove her down to the Dorset coast, down a tiny track to a lighthouse.

'We're staying here?' she asked, surprised. 'That's just lovely.'

'For two nights,' he said. 'I know you miss the sea and I thought you'd like it here.'

It was incredibly romantic; there was a four-poster bed against one wall, opposite picture windows that overlooking the sea. She walked over to the window and gazed out. 'Harry, this is so perfect. Thank you.'

And he'd booked only one room. She knew that for him spending the whole night together was a huge turning point. For the first time, she really started to hope that he could get past his fear of falling in love and they had a future.

'I got it right, then?' For a moment, he looked really vulnerable.

'More than right,' she said, kissing him. 'However did you find this place?'

'Just did a bit of research,' he said. 'Luckily, because it's midweek, they had a vacancy.'

Dinner was fabulous: locally caught fish, followed by local ice cream on Dorset apple cake. But better still was afterwards, when Harry carried her over the threshold to the four-poster bed. It felt almost like a honeymoon, Isla thought.

In the next morning, she woke in his arms. And, unlike their trip to Cornwall, Harry made love with her before breakfast.

The morning was bright; they went to Lyme Regis and walked along the famous harbour wall of the Cobb, then headed for the cliffs and looked among the loose stones for fossils. Harry was the first one to find an ammonite and presented it to Isla with a bow. Then they headed for the boulders; they were marvelling over the massive ammonites embedded in the rock bed when they heard a scream from the shallows.

A small girl was holding her foot up and crying, while her mother was clearly trying to calm her down and find out what had just happened.

'Maybe the poor kid's trodden on something sharp,' Harry suggested.

'Do you think we ought to go and offer to help?' Isla asked.

'Yes,' Harry said, and took her hand.

'We're medics,' he said to the little girl's mum, who

was sitting on the sand next to her daughter, looking at the little girl's foot. 'Can we help?'

'Abbie said she trod on something and it hurt—I can't see anything but I wondered if she'd trodden on some glass,' the mum said.

'Abbie, I'm Dr Harry,' he said to the little girl, 'and this is Nurse Isla. Can we look at your foot?'

The little girl was still crying, but nodded shyly.

'I can't see any glass or any blood like you'd get with a cut,' Harry said, 'but I think she might have stood on a weever fish. They bury themselves in the sand under shallow water; the spines on their back and gills are laced with venom, and it feels like a sting if you step on them.' He showed the woman the swollen and reddening spot on Abbie's foot. 'We'd better get her over to the lifeguards' hut. We need some tweezers so we can take the spine out, clean the area with soap and water and rinse it with fresh water, then put Abbie's foot in hot water so it'll "cook" the protein in the venom and stop it hurting. And hopefully they'll have some infant paracetamol.'

'I've got the paracetamol,' Abbie's mum said.

'Good. I'll carry her over for you,' he said.

'I'll go ahead and talk to them so they can put the kettle on and get the first aid kit out,' Isla said.

Harry carried Abbie to the hut where the lifeguards were working. Isla had already explained their theory, and the first aid kit was out already.

He set Abbie gently on the bed so he could crouch down and examine her foot again, this time with a torch illuminating the area. 'I can get one of the spines out, but there's another one near the joint of her big toe, so I'd like that one looked at in the nearest emergency department,' he said.

One of the lifeguards called the ambulance while Harry took out the weever fish spine he could see easily, and the other provided a deep bowl of hot water.

'Ow, it's hot!' Abbie said, crying again.

'I know, sweetheart, but you need to put your foot in to stop it hurting,' Harry said. 'If you can do that for me, I'll tell you a story.'

'All right,' Abbie said bravely.

He'd just finished telling her a long-drawn-out version of the Three Little Pigs—where he had everyone in the lifeguards' hut booming out the wolf's threat to huff and puff and blow the house down—when the ambulance arrived. Harry gave a quick rundown to the paramedics.

'Thank you so much for looking after us,' Abbie's mum said. 'And I'm so sorry we took up your time on your holiday.'

'It's fine,' he said with a smile. 'Hope Abbie feels better soon.'

He was so good with children, Isla thought. So why was he so adamant he didn't want children of his own? What had happened in his past? Had he dated someone with a child and it had all gone wrong? But she couldn't think of a way to ask him without it seeming like prying. She'd have to wait until he was ready to open up to her and talk about it. But Harry was stubborn. Would he ever be ready?

'Well, Dr Gardiner, I think you earned a pot of tea and a scone with jam and clotted cream,' she said lightly.

'Sounds good to me,' Harry said, and looped his arm round her shoulders.

They ended up spending the rest of the day at the coast, eating fish and chips on the cliff-top and watching the setting sun. The spectacular flares of red and orange faded to yellow at the horizon, and the colours were reflected across the sea.

'Definitely a selfie moment,' Harry said, and took a picture of them on his phone with the sunset behind them.

This was perfect, Isla thought. It couldn't have been a nicer day.

The next day, they went exploring again; they stopped to walk up the hill and view the famous natural limestone arch of Durdle Door, and discovered the enormous chalk-cut figure of the Cerne Giant looming across another hill. And just being together was so good.

Back in London, this time Harry stayed overnight at Isla's flat.

They'd definitely taken a step forward, she thought. And maybe, just maybe, this was going to work out.

CHAPTER TWELVE

OVER THE NEXT couple of months, Harry and Isla grew closer still. They both kept a change of clothes and toiletries at each other's flat, though they were careful not to arrive at work together when they were on the same shift, and they hadn't made a big deal of letting people know that they were an item.

But one morning Isla felt really rough when she got out of bed.

'Are you all right?' Harry asked.

'I feel a bit queasy,' Isla admitted. 'I think maybe I'm coming down with that bug that's hit the department.' Which probably explained why she seemed to have gone off coffee, the last few days.

'Maybe you ought to stay home and call in sick,' Harry said. 'If you've got the lurgy, you don't want to spread it to the rest of the team or the patients.'

Normally it took a lot more than a bug to stop Isla working her shift, but right at that moment she felt absolutely terrible. 'Yes, I think you're right,' she said.

Harry made her some toast and a mug of hot lemon and honey; he also brought a jug of iced water in to the bedroom and put it by her bedside. 'Can I get you anything else to make you comfortable? A book or a magazine?'

'I'll be fine. But thank you.' She smiled. 'You have a lovely bedside manner. Anyone would think you were a doctor.'

'Yeah, yeah.' He grinned back. 'Text me later to let me know how you're feeling, OK?'

'Yes—though I was thinking, maybe you'd better not come back here after work today. I don't want you to pick it up.'

'I've got the constitution of an ox,' he claimed. 'Look, I'll call you when I leave work and see how you're doing, and then you can tell me if you want me to pick up anything from the shops for you.' He kissed her forehead. 'For now, get some rest.'

Isla lay curled up in bed with a magazine for the rest of the morning. She was feeling considerably better by lunchtime, and she felt a bit guilty about being off sick when she was clearly fine. Or maybe she'd been lucky and had the super-mild version of the bug and it was over now. She texted Harry to say she felt better and was just going out to get a bit of fresh air. But, when she went to the corner shop to buy some milk, the woman in the queue in front of Isla was wearing some really strong perfume which made her feel queasy again; and the smell of greasy food wafting from the fast food place next door to the corner shop made her feel even worse.

When she got back home, it slammed into her. Nausea first thing, a heightened sense of smell, an aversion to coffee... If a patient had described those symptoms to her, she would've suggested doing a pregnancy test. But she couldn't be pregnant—could she?

They'd always been really careful to use condoms.

Although, the night of her birthday, they'd got carried away with the sheer romance of having a bedroom in a lighthouse, and maybe that night they hadn't been as careful then as they should've been.

She thought back. Her last period had been really light, and she knew that women sometimes had break-through bleeding during early pregnancy. Could she be pregnant?

It niggled at her for the next hour.

In the end, she went to the local supermarket and picked up a pregnancy test. This would prove once and for all that she was making a fuss about nothing.

She did the test and stared at the little window, will-ing the words 'not pregnant' to appear. Although she hoped that Harry was revising his views on the 'never settling down' question, she was pretty sure that his stance on never having children of his own hadn't changed. She knew he was dead set against it.

She kept staring at the window. Then, to her hor-ror, the word 'pregnant' appeared. Followed by '3+'—meaning that she was more than three weeks pregnant.

What?

She couldn't be.

Maybe the test was faulty. Maybe there was a prob-lem with the pixels or something in the area on the screen that should've said 'not', and that was why it was blank. Just as well there were two kits in the box.

She did the second one, just to reassure herself that the first one was a mistake.

Except the result was the same: Pregnant. More than three weeks.

Oh, no. She was going to have to tell Harry.

But how? How, when she knew that he didn't want children? When he was practically phobic about it?

She still hadn't found the words by the time he called her.

'I've just finished my shift now, so I'm on my way to see you,' he said. 'Do you want me to pick up anything from the shops?'

'No, thanks—it's fine.'

'How are you feeling?' he asked.

Panicky. 'Better,' she lied. 'But I think maybe it'd be best if you didn't come over, just in case I'm still incubating this bug.'

And that would give her time to work out how to tell him the news, wouldn't it?

Except she still hadn't come up with anything by the next morning. She felt even queasier than she had the previous morning and only just made it to the bathroom before she was sick.

Grimly, she washed her face and cleaned her teeth.

She definitely couldn't let Harry stay over—or stay with him—until she'd told him the news, because she didn't want him to work it out for himself. Which of course he would, if she dashed out of bed and threw up every morning.

She just hoped that none of her patients that day would be wearing particularly strong perfume or aftershave, and that she could either avoid the hospital canteen completely or they'd have totally bland foods on the menu with no smell.

Thankfully, she wasn't rostered on with Harry. But he caught up with her at her break. 'Are you sure you should be in? How are you feeling?' he asked, his dark eyes filled with concern.

'Fine,' she fibbed, and sipped her glass of water in the hope that it would stop her reacting to the smell of his coffee. 'How was your morning?'

'Rushed off my feet.' He grimaced. 'I had one mum bringing in a sick baby, but she had two more children with her under school age, both of them with rotten colds. Clearly she hadn't been able to get anyone to babysit them while she brought the baby in to us. It was total chaos, with both of the toddlers wanting their mum's attention, and she was trying to explain the baby's symptoms to me at the same time. I couldn't hear myself think.'

'Was the baby OK?'

'She had bronchiolitis,' he said. 'Classic intercostal recession. I sent her up to the children's ward. I took a sample of mucus from her nose, but I'm pretty sure it'll be RSV positive. It's the beginning of the RSV season,' he said with a sigh, 'where they'll have two bays of the children's ward full of babies on oxygen therapy, and every single member of staff up there will have the cold from hell.' He rolled his eyes. 'And people wonder why I never want to have kids.'

She flinched inwardly, knowing that he was just exaggerating a bit to make his morning sound dramatic—or was he? He was always brilliant with any sick children who came into the department, and at the wedding he'd been so good with his youngest brother. Yet he'd always been adamant that he didn't want kids of his own and he'd never really explained why. When she'd tried to ask him, he'd simply changed the subject.

So she really wasn't looking forward to telling him the news that, actually, he was going to be a dad. She had to find a way to soften the blow for him, but she had no idea how.

'Do you want to come over for dinner tonight?' he asked.

'I'm still feeling a bit fragile, so I think I'd better pass and have an early night with a hot water bottle,' she said. She knew she was being a coward, but she really needed to work out the right way to tell him. A way that wouldn't hurt him. Just... How?

Was it his imagination, Harry wondered a couple of days later, or was Isla trying to avoid him? Ever since she'd gone down with that bug, she'd been acting strangely. Had she changed her mind about their relationship? He'd been seriously thinking about it himself; he'd never felt like this about anyone else before in his life. And she made him feel that the world was a better place. Just being with her made his heart feel lighter. He'd started to think about asking her to move in with him, maybe even take the next step and get engaged. Take the risk he'd always avoided in the past, so sure it would go wrong because he'd seen it go wrong so often for both his parents.

But now Isla seemed to be going distant on him, he was having doubts about it again. Did he have it all wrong? Did she not feel the same as he did, any more? Or was he so messed up about the idea of commitment that he couldn't see straight?

By the end of the week he was really concerned. They hadn't spent any time together for more than a week, so something was definitely wrong. All he could do was persuade Isla to go somewhere quiet with him, and then maybe he could talk to her and find out what the problem was. And then he could solve it. He hoped.

They had a busy shift in Resus that morning, and Harry was about to suggest that they went for a break between patients when the paramedics brought in in a woman who'd been in an RTA.

'Mrs Paulette Freeman,' the paramedic said. 'A bicycle courier cut in front of her; she had to swerve to avoid him, and crashed into the car on her right-hand side, which made her air bag go off. She's thirty years old, and twelve weeks pregnant with her first baby. There haven't been any problems so far in the pregnancy, and when we examined her there was no sign of bleeding. Her blood group is A positive.'

Harry and Isla exchanged a glance of relief at the news about the blood group. At least there wouldn't be a risk to the fetus from rhesus antibodies.

'Can you remember, did you bang your head at all, Mrs Freeman?' Harry asked.

'No, but the airbag went straight into my stomach.' Mrs Freeman looked anxious. 'Is my baby all right? Maybe I shouldn't have worn my seat belt.'

'Seat belts really do reduce the risk of serious injury in pregnancy,' Harry reassured her, 'so you did the right thing. Now, I'm going to examine you—just let me know if any area feels a bit tender.'

'My stomach's a bit sore,' she said, 'but that's probably from the airbag. It doesn't matter about me. What about the baby?'

'The baby's pretty well cushioned in there but of course you're worried. My job now is to see how you both are,' Harry said. 'Try and relax for me.' He added quietly to Isla, 'Call the maternity department and get Theo Petrakis down here, please. I always play it supersafe with pregnant patients.' He turned back to Mrs Freeman. 'Is there someone we can call for you?'

'My husband,' she said.

'I'll do that. Can you tell me his number?' Isla asked, then wrote the number down as Mrs Freeman said it. 'I'll call him straight away and ask him to come in,' she said.

'I'm going to examine your stomach now, Mrs Freeman,' Harry said. 'Tell me if anything hurts.'

She was white-faced and tight-lipped, and didn't say a word. He couldn't feel any uterine contractions, but the uterus felt firmer than he'd like.

A pelvic examination showed no sign of bleeding, which he hoped was a good thing. But he was starting to get a bad feeling about this case.

'I'm just going to listen to the baby's heartbeat,' he said, and set up the Doppler probe. But instead of the nice fast clop-clop he was expecting to hear, there was silence. He couldn't pick up the baby's heartbeat.

'What's wrong?' Mrs Freeman asked. 'Why can't we hear the baby's heartbeat?'

'I'm sure there's nothing to worry about,' Harry reassured her. 'Often this particular machine doesn't work very well in the first trimester. I'll try the old-fashioned way—obviously you won't be able to hear it, but I will.' He picked up a horn-shaped Pinard stethoscope; but, to his dismay, he still couldn't hear anything.

Isla came back in. 'I've spoken to your husband, Mrs Freeman, and he's on his way in. Dr Gardiner, Mr Petrakis is on his way down right now.'

'Good. I just want to get the portable ultrasound. I'll be back in a tick,' Harry said, doing his best to sound calm and breezy.

Isla had clearly seen the Doppler and the Pinard next to the bed and obviously worked out that he hadn't been able to pick up the baby's heartbeat, because when he brought the machine back she was sitting next to the bed, holding Mrs Freeman's hand.

Harry's bad feeling suddenly got a whole lot worse.

He knew that pregnant women could lose a lot of blood before they started showing any sign of hypovolaemic shock. In a case like this, with blunt force trauma, there was a high risk of placental abruption—

where the placenta separated from the uterus before the baby was born—and the fetus was likely to suffer. Worst-case scenario, the baby wouldn't survive. Although there was no sign of bleeding, with a concealed placental abruption the blood remained in the uterus. It was the more severe form of abruption and if his fears were correct the baby had already died.

'I'm going to do an ultrasound now to see what's going on,' he said. 'It's very like the machine they used when they did your dating scan, Mrs Freeman. Can you bare your stomach again for me so I can put some gel on it? I'm afraid our gel down here tends to be a bit cold.'

'I don't care if it's like ice, as long as my baby's OK,' she said, and pulled the hem of her top up so he could smear the radio-conductive gel over her abdomen.

He ran the transceiver head over her abdomen and begged silently, oh, please let the baby be kicking away.

The ultrasound didn't show any sign of a blood clot, but it did show him the thing he'd been dreading: the baby wasn't moving and there was no heartbeat.

Oh, hell. He was going to have to deliver the worst possible news. This was the bit of his job he really, really hated.

Theo arrived just before Harry could open his mouth. 'You asked to see me, Dr Gardiner?'

'Yes. Thank you for coming. Excuse me a second,' Harry said to Mrs Freeman. 'I just want to have a quick word with Mr Petrakis, our senior obstetric consultant. I'll introduce you properly in a moment.'

He walked away and said to Theo in a low voice, 'I couldn't pick up the fetal heartbeat. I know that's common in the first trimester, but also there's no movement or heartbeat showing on the ultrasound. The mum's not bleeding and I couldn't see a clot, and there's no sign right at this moment of hypovolaemic shock—but, given that it was blunt trauma and what's happened to the fetus, I think we're looking at a concealed placental abruption.'

'Sounds like it,' Theo said. 'Poor woman. In that case we need to restore her blood volume before she goes into shock and we'll have to deliver the baby PV—it's the only way to stop the bleeding from the abruption. And I'll want to admit her to the ward for monitoring in case she goes into DIC.'

Harry went back over to Mrs Freeman with Theo and introduced the specialist to her. Theo looked at the ultrasound and from the expression in the consultant's eyes Harry could tell that his original diagnosis was indeed correct. They wouldn't have time to wait for her husband to arrive to break the news; they needed to treat her now, before she went into shock.

He sat down beside her on the opposite side from Isla and held her other hand. 'Mrs Freeman, I'm so sorry. There is no nice way to tell you this, but I'm afraid the accident caused what we call a placental abruption. Basically it means that the force of the accident made your placenta detach from the uterus.'

'What about my baby?'

'I'm so sorry,' he said. 'We still need to treat you, but I'm afraid there's nothing we can do for the baby.'

She stared at him in horror. 'My baby's dead?' she whispered.

'I'm so sorry,' he said again. If only he could make this right. But there was nothing that anyone could do.

Mrs Freeman was shaking. Fat tears were rolling down her cheeks, but she made no sound. What he was seeing was total desolation. And it wasn't fixable.

Isla had her arm round Mrs Freeman's shoulders, doing her best to comfort her.

Feeling helpless, Harry explained what they were going to do next and that they needed to keep her in for a little while to keep an eye on her.

Halfway through treatment her husband arrived and Harry had to break the bad news all over again.

'I'm so sorry, Mr Freeman,' he finished.

Mr Freeman looked dazed. 'Our baby's dead? And Paulette?'

'We're treating her now, but we want to keep her in for monitoring. Would you like to come and be with her?'

'Yes—I— Is she going to be all right?'

'She's going to be fine,' Harry reassured him. 'I'm just so sorry I can't give you better news.'

By the time Harry's shift finished, he was completely drained. The last thing he felt like doing was talking to Isla to find out what was wrong, but he knew it had to be done. Maybe he could arrange to see her tomorrow and they could sort it out then. When they'd both had time to recover from their rough day.

But when he saw her outside the staff kitchen, he could see that she'd been crying.

'Are you all right?' he asked softly, even though he knew it was a stupid question; it was obvious that she wasn't OK at all.

'Rough shift,' she said. 'You should know. You were there.'

'Yeah.' He closed his eyes for a moment. 'I hate breaking that kind of news to people. I hate seeing their dreams shatter like that.' He opened his eyes again. 'I don't know about you, but I can't face going anywhere and talking tonight. Shall we just get a pizza and go back to my place?'

'I…' She dragged in a breath. 'Harry, we really need to talk.'

He went cold. The way she was talking sounded horribly final. Just like the way he'd always broken the news to whoever he was dating that it wasn't really working and he'd rather they just stayed as friends.

Was Isla going to end it between them?

But surely not right now—not after the day they'd both had.

Not feeling up to talking, he asked, 'Can this wait until tomorrow?'

She shook her head. 'It's already been dragging on too long.'

He really didn't like the sound of that. He had a nasty feeling that he knew why she'd been distant, these last few days: because she was ending it.

'Is that café round the corner still open?' she asked.

He guessed that she meant the one where he'd taken her for a bacon sandwich, the morning after the night shift where the drunk had come on to her. 'We can take a look,' he said. 'Is that where you want to go?'

'It'll be a lot more private than the hospital canteen. It means we can talk.'

'OK.'

They walked to the café in silence. Harry could feel himself getting more and more tense, the nearer they got to the café; and, even though he was trying to prepare himself for being dumped, it just hurt too damn much. He didn't want it to end between them. He wanted to take it forward. Take the risk.

'Tea and a bacon sandwich?' he asked outside the door to the café.

She shook her head. 'Just a glass of water for me, thanks.'

'OK. If you find us a table, I'll sort out the drinks.' He ordered himself a mug of tea, to put off the moment that little bit longer.

When the waitress sorted out the drinks, Harry discovered that Isla had found them a quiet table out of the way. Good.

Well, he wasn't going to be weak and wait to be dumped. He was going to initiate the discussion and ask up front. 'So are you going to tell me what I've done wrong?' he asked as he sat down.

'Wrong? What do you mean, wrong?'

'It feels as if you've been avoiding me for the last few days,' he said. And he was aware how ironic it was that they'd had this conversation before—except, last time, he'd been the one doing the avoiding.

'That's because I have,' she said softly.

Pain lanced through him. He hadn't been imagining it, then. She was going to end it—and she'd been working out how to tell him, the last few days. While he, being a fool, had been thinking about moving their relationship on to the next step.

'So what did I do wrong?' he repeated.

'Nothing.'

He didn't get it. 'So why were you avoiding me?'

She took a deep breath. 'There isn't an easy way to say this.'

So she was definitely ending it—and he was shocked to realise how much it hurt. How much she meant to him and how empty his life was going to be without her.

* * *

This was one of the hardest things Isla had ever done. She hated the fact that her words were going to blow Harry's world apart. She was just about to make his worst nightmare come true.

But he'd clearly already worked out that something wasn't right.

Even though her timing wasn't brilliant—he was already feeling low after a rotten shift—she couldn't keep it from him any longer.

'I'm pregnant,' she said.

He looked at her, saying absolutely nothing—and she couldn't tell a thing from his expression. How he was feeling, what he was thinking…nothing.

'With our baby,' she clarified. Not that there could be any mistake. They'd both been faithful to each other.

Still he said nothing. He just stared at her as if he couldn't believe what he was hearing. He looked shocked to the core.

Well, what had she expected? That he'd throw his arms round her and tell her how thrilled he was?

He'd made it clear enough that he never wanted children, and she was telling him that he was going to be a father—exactly what he didn't want.

The fact that he'd said nothing at all made it very obvious that he hadn't changed his mind. He just didn't know how to tell her without hurting her.

So she was going to have to be brave and be the one to walk away.

'It's all right,' she said, even though it wasn't and it left her feeling bone-deep tired and unutterably sad. 'I know you don't want children. I'm not expecting anything from you, and I understand that it's the end between us.'

And it was clear what she needed to do next. This was Harry's patch. He'd lived in London since he was a student; he'd trained and worked in the same hospital for twelve years. She'd been in the emergency department at the London Victoria for only a few months. It was obvious which of the two of them would have to leave.

'I'm going home to Scotland,' she said. 'To the island. But I didn't want to leave without telling you why. I'm sorry, Harry.'

And she got up to leave.

CHAPTER THIRTEEN

SHOCK RADIATED THROUGH HARRY.

He couldn't believe what he was hearing.

Isla was pregnant?

With his baby?

Well, of *course* his baby—she wasn't the sort to have an affair. He knew that without having to ask.

But he couldn't quite process the idea of being a father. He couldn't say a word. It felt as if his mouth had been filled with glue. And someone had glued him to his seat, too, because Isla was walking away from him and he was still stuck here, watching her leave.

This had to be a nightmare. One of those hyper-real dreams where the situation was so close to real life that it could really be happening, but there was something out of kilter that would tell you it was all a figment of your imagination.

Like being stuck to your seat. Like there being no sound at all, even though they were in a café and there would usually be the hiss of steam from a coffee machine and the sound of a spoon clinking against a mug as sugar was stirred in, the low buzz of other people talking.

He'd wake up in a second. It'd be stupid o'clock in the morning, and he'd be in either his own bed or Isla's, spooned round her body. He'd hear her soft, regular breathing and he'd know that this was just a dream and all was right with the world.

Any second now.

Any second now.

But then the door closed behind her and the sound all seemed to rush back in—like the moment when a tube train arrived at the station, and all the noise echoed everywhere. Hissing steam, clinking spoons and mugs, the hum of conversation.

Oh, dear God.

This wasn't a nightmare.

Isla was pregnant, she was planning to leave London, and...

No, no, no.

He couldn't let her leave.

He needed to talk to her. Tell her how he felt about her. Ask her to stay. Beg her to stay. On his knees, if he had to.

He could do with someone tipping a bucket of ice-cold water over him to shock his brain back into working again, so he could find the right words to ask her to stay. Failing that, he'd just have to hope that he could muddle his way through it.

Ignoring the startled looks of the other customers in the café, he left his unfinished mug of tea where it was and rushed out after Isla.

He looked out either side of the door in the street. He thought he caught sight of her walking away and called out, 'Isla, wait!'

Either she hadn't heard him or the woman wasn't actually Isla. Inwardly praying that it was the former, he ran after her and finally caught up with her.

Thank God. It was her.

'Isla, wait,' he said again.

She stopped and stared at him. 'Why? You made it perfectly clear just now that you didn't want to know.'

'Did I, hell.'

'I told you the news and you didn't say a word.'

'You didn't exactly give me a chance!' he protested.

'I did,' she said. 'I sat there like a lemon, staring at you and waiting for you to say something.'

'I was too shocked to think straight, let alone for my mouth to work. I needed a few seconds for the news to sink in. And now it has. I think.'

She blinked back the tears. 'Harry, you've told me often enough that you don't want kids and you don't want to settle down. I'm not expecting you to change for me.'

'What if I want to change?' he asked.

She shook her head. 'I can't ask you to do that.'

'You're not asking me. I'm offering.'

'No. Don't make any sacrifices, because you'll regret it later. Anything you decide has to be because you really, really want it. You can't live your life to please other people.'

'I don't want you to leave,' he said. 'Stay.'

'If I go home to Scotland, at least I'll have my family round me to help with the baby. If I stay here, I'll be struggling on my own,' she pointed out. 'It makes sense to leave.'

'So you want to keep the baby?'

She dragged in a breath. 'You can actually ask me that after what happened at work today, when that poor woman lost a baby she clearly wanted very much?'

He winced. 'Sorry, that came out wrong. I don't mean that at all. Just—we didn't plan this, did we? Either of us. We haven't talked properly about what we want out of life. We've been taking this thing between us one step at a time.' He dragged a hand through his hair. 'I'm making a mess of this, but we need to talk about it, and I can't let you just walk away from me— and the street really isn't the right place to discuss this. Your place or mine?'

'I guess yours is nearer,' she said.

'Mine it is, then—and there's no pressure. We'll just talk things through, and then, if you want me to drive you back to yours afterwards, I will.' He blew out a breath. 'Just talk to me, Isla. You once said to me that you weren't a mind-reader. Neither am I. And I really need to know what's going on in your head.'

She looked at him, and for a nasty moment he thought she was going to refuse; but then she nodded.

They walked back to his place in uneasy silence. He tried letting his hand accidentally brush against hers, but she didn't let her fingers curl round his, so he gave up. Maybe she was right. Maybe they needed to do this with a clear head, not let the attraction between them get in the way and muddle things up.

'Can I get you a drink?' he asked once they were in his living room.

'No, thanks.'

Were they really reduced to cool politeness? But then he found himself lapsing into it, too. 'Please, have a seat.'

He noticed that she picked one of the chairs rather than the sofa, making it clear that she didn't want him right next to her. He pushed the hurt aside. OK. He could deal with this. He needed to give her a little bit of space. Clearly she was upset and worried, and all the hormonal changes of pregnancy weren't helping the situation one little bit.

Hoping that she wouldn't misinterpret where he sat, he chose a seat on the sofa opposite her. All he wanted to do was to hold her and tell her that everything was going to be all right. But how could he promise her that, when he didn't know that it would be anywhere near all right?

What a mess.

He didn't even know where to start. Emotionally, this was a total minefield and it was way outside his experience. So he fell back on the thing he knew he was good at. Being a doctor. Maybe that would be the best place to start. 'Are you all right?' he asked. 'I mean, are you having morning sickness or headaches?'

'It's not been brilliant,' she admitted.

'How long have you known?'

She took a deep breath. 'I did the test nearly a week ago.'

So she'd had a week to get used to the idea and work out how she felt about it, whereas he'd only had a few scant minutes—and it wasn't anywhere near enough. 'When you thought you had the bug that was going round?' he asked.

'Except it wasn't that.'

Now he was beginning to understand why she'd backed off from him—because she'd discovered she was pregnant and she'd been scared of his reaction. Because he'd told her often enough that he didn't want kids. He just hadn't told her why. And maybe it was time he explained. 'I'm sorry,' he said. 'You should've been able to tell me. And I feel bad that I'm not approachable enough for you to have said anything before.'

'We didn't exactly plan this, did we?' She bit her lip. 'And we were careful.'

Not careful enough. The only guaranteed form of

conception was abstinence. 'Do you know how pregnant you are?'

'The test said more than three weeks. My last period was very light, but I thought…' She shrugged. 'Well, obviously I was wrong.'

'Isla, I don't know what to say,' he admitted. 'I really wasn't expecting this.' He raked a hand through his hair. 'And, after a day like today…'

'I couldn't keep it to myself any longer,' she said. 'Not after today. Because what happened to that poor woman made me think, what if it had been me? I hadn't really let myself think too much about the baby and what options I had. But after sitting there, holding her hand while you told her the bad news, it became really clear to me what I wanted.'

To keep the baby. She'd already told him that. But what else? Did she want to bring up the baby on her own, or with him?

And what did he want?

He'd had no time to think about it, to weigh up the options. He'd always been so sure that he didn't want children. So very sure. But now he was going to be a dad, and he didn't have a clue what to say.

'I've been trying to work out for the last week how to tell you. I knew it was your worst nightmare,' she said, almost as if she could read his mind. But then she frowned. 'But what I really don't understand, Harry, is why you're so sure you don't want kids. You're so good with them at work—and at the wedding, you were great with little Evan. And when we went away, you were lovely with that little girl on the beach who stood on the weever fish—you told her a story to keep her mind off how much her foot hurt. You'd make such a great father. I don't understand why you'd cut yourself off from all that potential love. Is it because you have so many brothers and sisters, but you didn't grow up with most of them?'

'No.' He blew out a breath. Maybe if he told her the misery that had haunted him for years, she'd get it. 'Do you remember the little boy who'd eaten his grandfather's iron tablets?'

'Yes.' She looked puzzled. 'Why?'

'And you remember I told his grandmother that toddlers were unpredictable?'

'Yes.'

'And I know that's true, because I've walked in her shoes,' he said softly.

She stared at him. 'What, you had a toddler who accidentally ate iron tablets—one who died?'

'Not my toddler and not iron tablets and no death, but something bad happened, something that's haunted me ever since,' he said. 'I was eleven. Mum had just popped out to the shops and she asked me to keep an eye on my sisters. Maisie was five, Tasha was two, and Bibi was a baby. I thought it'd be all right. I put Maisie and Tasha in front of the telly—there was some cartoon on they both liked—and I was doing my homework at the dining room table. French, I remember. Then Bibi started crying. Maisie came and told me the baby was all stinky, so I knew I had to change her nappy—I couldn't just leave her crying until Mum got home. I thought the others would be fine in front of the telly while I took the baby upstairs and changed her.'

'What happened?' she asked softly.

'I forgot to close the stair gate,' he said. 'Tasha got bored with the telly and decided to come and find me. I had the baby in my arms, and I saw Tasha get to the top of the stairs. She was smiling and so pleased with herself. Then she wobbled and fell backwards. Right down the whole flight of stairs. Before I could get to her. Everything happened in slow motion—I could see it happening, but I couldn't do a thing about it. And then she was just lying there at the bottom of the stairs and she wasn't making a sound. I thought she was dead and it was all my fault.'

'This is your middle sister, yes? And she wasn't…?'

He shook his head. 'She survived.' Though she hadn't made a complete recovery.

'Harry, just about anyone would struggle to look after three children under five, and you were only eleven years old at the time,' Isla pointed out. 'You were doing your best. You were busy changing the baby. You weren't to know that your two-year-old sister would fall down the stairs.'

'I know—but if I'd closed the stair gate it wouldn't have happened.'

'Or she might have gone into the kitchen or the garden and hurt herself there instead,' Isla said. 'You're right about toddlers being unpredictable, and you can't blame yourself—plus it's so easy to see things differently with hindsight. It's not fair to blame yourself. What did your mum say?'

'She came home to find an ambulance outside our house with a flashing blue light,' Harry said, 'so she was pretty shocked—and her first words to me were that she'd trusted me to look after the girls while she went to get some bread and some milk, and why hadn't I kept a proper eye on them?'

Isla winced. 'That to me sounds like a panicky mum who isn't thinking straight.'

'She apologised later,' Harry said. 'She told me that it wasn't my fault.' He paused. 'But we both knew it was, and she never asked me to look after the girls again on my own after that.'

'I bet she was feeling just as guilty—she was the adult, and she'd left you in charge of three young children, when you were still only a child yourself,' Isla pointed out. 'And how far away were the shops?'

'A fifteen-minute walk,' Harry said. 'Not far—but it was long enough for me to nearly kill Tasha. I had bad dreams for months about it. I saw my little sister lying at the bottom of the stairs, her face white, and I couldn't see her breathing. I never wanted to go through fear like that again, and that was when I vowed that I'd never have kids of my own. I didn't want that responsibility—or to let another child down.'

Isla left her seat, came over to him and hugged him fiercely. 'You were a child yourself, Harry, and having that kind of a responsibility as a child is completely different from having it as an adult. And she was fine, wasn't she?'

That was the big question. 'The hospital said it was concussion and a broken arm.' He bit his lip. 'We thought she'd recovered just fine over the next few weeks. But over the months, Mum noticed that Tasha was always off in a dream world. When she got a bit older, if she was reading, you had to take the book out of her hands to get her to realise you'd been calling her.'

'Because she lost herself in the book?'

He shook his head. 'Mum talked to the health visitor about it. They thought she might have glue ear. But when the audiology department at the hospital tested her, they found out that actually, her hearing was damaged permanently.' This was the crunch bit. 'According to the audiogram, what was wrong was impact damage—so it had been caused by the fall. Because I didn't look after her properly, Tasha's on the border of being severely deaf, and for certain pitches she's profoundly deaf—she can't hear really deep voices.'

'Plenty of people cope with deafness,' Isla pointed out gently, 'and I get the impression from what you've told me about your sisters that they're all very independent.'

'They are,' he admitted. 'But don't you see? Her deafness was caused by the fall. It shouldn't have happened. And I feel bad that she's always had to struggle and work harder than everyone else. She was bright enough to pick things up from books, but half the time she couldn't actually hear what the teachers were saying. Even with hearing aids, it's difficult—when she's in noisy surroundings, it's hard to pick up what people are saying, especially if they have quiet voices or they're in her difficult range and she can't see their faces to lip-read. She has to concentrate so much harder to pick up all the social stuff as well as cope with work.'

'Is that how she sees it?' Isla asked.

'Well—no. We fight about it,' Harry admitted. 'She refuses to be defined by her hearing. She says I'm over-protective and it drives her crazy.'

'Have you tried putting yourself in her shoes?' Isla asked softly.

'Yes. And I still blame myself. And I'll always remember how I felt, seeing her lying there on the floor, not moving. That choking feeling of panic.' He dragged in a breath. 'I see parents most weeks who are panicking as much as I did back then. Parents who are worried sick about a baby or a toddler with a virus or a severe allergic reaction. I think the fear's the same, however old or however experienced you are.' He paused. 'And I guess that's part of why I didn't want to get involved with anyone. I didn't want to risk things going wrong. I told myself that getting involved with someone, getting married and having kids…that wasn't for me.'

Isla swallowed hard. 'And then I came along.'

'And you changed everything,' he said. 'You made me see that things might be different to what I always thought they were. That, just because my parents had made mistakes, it didn't mean that I was necessarily going to repeat them.' He took a deep breath. 'So if I was wrong about that, maybe I'm wrong about other things, too. Like not wanting children.'

'So what are you saying?'

'I'm saying,' he said, 'that I need a little time to let it sink in and to come to terms with it. Right now, I'm still shocked and I feel as if someone's smacked me over the head with a frying pan. But give me a little time to think about it and get used to the idea. You've had a week, and I've only had a few minutes. I can't adjust that fast, Isla, no matter how much I want to. I'm only human.'

'I'm sorry. I'm being selfish.' Her eyes misted with tears.

She looked as if she was going to pull away from him, but he wrapped his arms round her and hauled her onto his lap. 'Isla. These last couple of weeks, I've been doing a lot of thinking myself. And this week I thought that you were avoiding me because you were working out how to dump me—'

'Dump you?' she interrupted.

'Dump me,' he repeated. 'I'd been thinking about us. About how I like being with you. About how my world's a better place when I wake up in your arms in the morning. About how you make me want to be brave and take the risk of a real grown-up relationship.' He paused. 'I had been thinking about asking you to move in with me.' He paused again. 'This is probably too little, too late. But I'm going to tell you anyway, because you can't read what I'm thinking. I was going to ask you to get engaged.' He swallowed hard. 'To take the really big risk and get married.'

'What? *You* want to get married?' She looked at him in utter shock.

'Yes.' He gave her a wry smile. 'I didn't believe it either, at first. But the thing is, I met someone. Someone I really like. Someone I really believe in and who seems to believe in me, too. Someone who told me that I was capable of really loving someone. She made me think about it properly for the first time ever.' He paused. 'And you were right. I am capable of loving someone. I love you, Isla McKenna. And, if you'll have me, I'd very much like to marry you.'

'Uh…' She stared at him. 'I think it's my turn to have the frying pan moment. Did you just ask me to marry you?'

'I did.'

'Me *and* our baby?' she checked.

'I believe you come as a package,' he said dryly.

'But—you—me—how?' she asked plaintively.

He stroked her face. 'Now I definitely know you're pregnant. The hormones have put a gag on all that strident Scottish common sense.'

'Have they, hell. Harry, you're allergic to marriage.'

'There's no immunoglobulin reaction, as far as I can tell,' he said, starting to relax and enjoy himself.

'You said you didn't want to settle down. Ever.'

'Tsk—are you so old-fashioned that you think it's only a woman's prerogative to change her mind?'

'Harry Gardiner, you're the most impossible—'

He judged that he'd teased her enough. So he stopped

her words by the simple act of kissing her. 'I love you, Isla,' he said when he broke the kiss. 'I might even have loved you from the first day I met you. But every day I've worked with you, or dated you, or woken with you in my arms, I've got to know you a little more and I've grown to love you a little more. And although I admit I'm absolutely terrified at the idea of being a dad—and I'm even more terrified by the idea that I might let our child down, the way I let my sister down—I know I'm going to make it work because you'll be at my side. And, with you by my side, I know I can do absolutely anything. Because I can talk to you, and you can make me see sense. And you can talk to me, knowing I'll always back you and take your part. We're a team, Isla. Not just at work.'

A tear spilled over and trickled down her cheek, and he kissed it away.

'Hormones,' she said.

He coughed. 'Wrong word. The one you're looking for has one syllable, three letters, and starts with the twenty-fifth letter of the alphabet. The middle letter's a vowel. And the last letter's often used as a plural. Got it?'

'You didn't actually ask me,' she pointed out. 'You said, if I'll have you, you'd like to marry me. Which isn't the same as asking me.'

'Yes, it is.'

She just looked at him.

He sighed, shifted her off his lap, and got down on one knee before her. 'If you're being picky about it, I also don't have a ring—and am I not supposed to present you with a ring if I do it the traditional way?'

'You said you'll back me. That's enough.' She flapped a dismissive hand. 'We don't need flashy gemstones.'

He laughed. 'Ah, the Scottish tartness is reasserting

itself. Good. Isla McKenna, I love you. And I'm still terrified out of my wits about being a dad, but I know I'll love our baby just as much as I love you. Will you marry me?'

She smiled. 'Yes.'

He coughed.

'What?' she asked.

'You haven't said it,' he reminded her. 'Three little words. And I've spent the last week in a bad place, thinking that you were going to walk out on me. I need a little TLC.'

'Ah, the three little words. Tender, loving care.'

'Three *smaller* words,' he said, giving her a pained look. 'Come on. I said it first.'

'I know. And I'm glad.' She smiled. 'I love you, too, Harry Gardiner. I think I did from the second you kissed me in the moonlight in Cornwall. And I admit that I, too, am just a little bit panicky about whether I'm going to be a good enough mum. But with you by my side, I think the answer's going to be yes. It's like you said. We're a team. Things might not always go smoothly, but we'll always have each other's back.'

'You'd better believe it,' he said softly.

EPILOGUE

Three months later

'WE SHOULD'VE ELOPED,' Harry said. 'How about I go and borrow a horse and a tricorn hat, kidnap you and carry you off to my lair?'

Isla laughed. 'Are the boys giving you a hard time?'

'Not just the boys. Five best men. *Five*. It's excessive. And then the girls accused me of sexism and demanded to know why they couldn't be best women. All of them.' He groaned. 'I can't possibly have eight best men and women on my wedding day!'

'As you're only going to get married once, none of them wants to miss out, so I don't think you have much choice,' Isla said. 'And I'm surprised your father hasn't tried to make it nine.'

'He did. He said I'd been his best man so I ought to let him be one of mine. I reminded him that he's already got a role as the father of the groom,' Harry said. 'But the others... They're supposed to let the oldest sibling boss them around, not the other way round. They're impossible!'

Isla laughed again, knowing that his grumbling was more for show than anything else. Since Harry had opened his heart to her, he'd also opened his heart to his brothers and sisters—and as a result he'd become much, much closer to his whole family. 'I love your brothers and sisters. They're so like you. Totally irrepressible.'

He groaned. 'So much for a quiet wedding. We really should've disappeared to Gretna Green.'

'Scotland? Hmm. I don't think that would've been quiet, either. And you do know my family's planning on teaching yours to party the Scots way tonight, don't you?'

'We definitely need to run away,' Harry said.

'I think it's a little too late for that. We're supposed to be in church in two hours. And you're not supposed to be here, much less talking to me through a closed door.'

'You're the one who insisted that it was bad luck to see me on our wedding day before you got to the church,' he reminded her. 'That's why I'm talking to you through a closed door. Are you quite sure we can't elope?'

'Harry, stop panicking,' she said. 'Go with the flow and let your siblings enjoy your wedding. Because you're only getting married once.'

He sighed. 'Our poor baby doesn't know what he or she has in store.'

'Oh, I think he or she does,' Isla corrected, 'and I think this is going to be the most loved baby in history.'

'And definitely by his—or her—dad.' Harry had been in tears at the scan, and had been a besotted father-to-be ever since.

'See you at church,' she said softly. 'And thank you for the beautiful necklace. It goes perfectly with my dress.'

'Well, you needed a "something new" to wear. It's traditional.' He coughed. 'It's also traditional to give your husband a kiss for a gift.'

'I will. At the altar,' she promised. 'I love you, Harry. And today's going to be fun. Really.'

And it was. Right from the moment Isla walked up the aisle on her father's arm, seeing the small church absolutely bursting at the seams with all their family and their friends from work, through to seeing the love in Harry's eyes as he turned to face her at the altar, through to everyone throwing dried rose petals over them both as they walked out of the church as man and wife.

The reception was even better. And Isla really enjoyed the best-men-and-women's speeches. Harry's brothers and sisters had clearly got together before the wedding and practised, because they all lined up on the stage behind the top table.

'The best man's speech is supposed to be short,' Evan said, starting them off, 'but we all wanted to be the best man and made Harry let us all do it, and we all want to say something so the speech won't be very short. It's funny, though. And I'm going to tell you a joke. What did the banana say to the monkey?'

The others all chorused, 'Nothing, bananas can't talk!' and did a little tap-dance with jazz hands, making everyone at the reception laugh.

Harry's siblings went in age order after that, with each of them telling a Harry story that made everyone laugh, though Isla noticed that Harry's middle sister seemed to have missed her slot.

But then, when Jack had finished speaking, Tasha took the microphone. 'My Harry story isn't a funny one. But it's about the bravest, best man I know. When I was two, I fell all the way down the stairs and I broke my arm. A few months later, we worked out that the fall had made me deaf in one ear, too. Harry's always blamed himself for what happened, but there's no way he could've rescued me when he was right in the middle of changing Bibi's nappy. We all think he's a superhero, but even he can't be in two places at once.'

Isla slipped her hand into Harry's, and squeezed his fingers.

'Without him, I wouldn't be a trainee audiologist, and I wouldn't be able to understand my patients as well as I do,' Tasha continued. 'And actually, I'm kind of glad it happened, because I know it was one of the reasons why he became a doctor—and the emergency department of the London Victoria wouldn't be the same without him.'

There were loud cheers of agreement from Harry and Isla's colleagues.

'And because he's an emergency doctor, that meant that he met Isla at work. We're all so glad he did, because she's the best thing to happen to him, and it's lovely to see my big brother get the happiness he never thought he deserved—but he really *does* deserve it.' She lifted her glass. 'So the best men and women all want you to raise your glasses now for a toast—to Harry and Isla, and may their life together be full of happiness.'

Harry stole a kiss from Isla as everyone chorused the toast. 'Yes. It's never going to be quiet, but it's going to be full of happiness,' he said with a smile. 'I love you. And our baby. And our chaotic, wonderful extended family.'

'Me, too.' Isla smiled back. 'I'm with you all the way. Always.'

* * * * *

ONE NIGHT...
WITH HER BOSS

BY
ANNIE O'NEIL

Published in Great Britain 2016
By Mills & Boon, an imprint of HarperCollins*Publishers*
1 London Bridge Street, London, SE1 9GF

© 2016 Annie O'Neil

ISBN: 978-0-263-25423-5

Dear Reader,

This book was a real crackerjack for me, and an absolute hoot to write. A book full of muscly rugby players and a dreamboat of a team doc? Woo-hoo!

I am a *big* rugby fan—not that I know any of the teams or players or rules... I just love the dedication and commitment the players show to the game—and they're respectful to boot. Just like the perfect hero.

Ali is a great heroine—I really, *really* like her a lot. Mostly because she was inspired by a wonderful choreographer I know here in the South East of England. She is a fireball, and has met her match in Aidan.

I hope you enjoy reading this book—and I promise there are no horrid scenes that make you feel you need to drop and give anyone twenty of anything! It's just pure indulgence.

Enjoy!

Annie O'

This book is for my former editor, Charlotte Mursell, who first brought me on board with Mills & Boon and helped fine-tune me into the work in progress I am today…(which is better than when she got me). This was the final book we worked on together and she was pure inspiration. I was a lucky gal to have begun my writing career with her. Thank you, Charlotte!!! Annie X

Books by Annie O'Neil

Mills & Boon Medical Romance

The Surgeon's Christmas Wish
The Firefighter to Heal Her Heart
Doctor…to Duchess?

Visit the Author Profile page at
millsandboon.co.uk for more titles.

CHAPTER ONE

ALI SCRUNCHED HER eyes as tightly as she could manage, then popped them open. Nope. No good. Even the snow-capped stadium filled to the brim with cheering rugby fans couldn't help her push *That Night* back to the inaccessible recesses of her memory. Who would've thought a liaison two weeks ago at an airport hotel would still be sending heated shivers of response careering round her body?

Fourteen days on and the sensations were just as potent. She'd wanted change—and now she was virtually swimming in it. Ali rubbed at her arms as if that would help scrub the heated thoughts away. *Pah!*

"Doc!" One of the players started doing star jumps on the sidelines. "You cold? Just do some of these— they'll warm you up sharpish."

Ali tossed a smile at the player and made a little jog-in-place movement to show willing. She was "only" a locum up here, but the lads had already made her feel a welcome part of the beast that was the North Stars rugby team. She wondered what it would be like when the Chief Medical Officer got back from his holiday. She was used to running her own clinic, so being some-one's subordinate would take a bit of a mental shift. But learning from a master of sports medicine? That would be worth it. Definitely.

After that...who knew what lay ahead? Going back to En Pointe Physio didn't appeal. She wasn't sure if it ever would. The day she'd walked into her favorite coffee shop back in London and hadn't even needed to open her mouth to order her specialty mocha was the day she'd started hunting for a locum position. She didn't do predictable. She didn't do steady. The longer you stuck around somewhere, the more likely you were to get hurt. When you tried new things—like an unexpected one-night stand on the eve of your new job—suffice it to say, it shook things up a bit.

A shiver rippled up her spine, and even though it was pretty obvious the snowy weather had sent the chill she couldn't resist closing her eyes again. Letting go of that night was near impossible. Especially when her body was still responding to the memory of his caresses, smoothing and shifting along her bare skin. His name...? A mystery—and it would stay that way.

Whatever had possessed them to head up to her hotel room that night—both of them with their flights grounded for a measly three inches of snow—had been well worth it. Who was she kidding? She knew *exactly* what had possessed them. Pure as the driven snow, hot as molten lava: desire. Her first ever one-night stand and it had been about as smokin' hot as they got.

The roars and songs of the crowd blurred into white noise as she dipped and dived into the ten hours and forty-seven minutes they had spent together. And on Valentine's Day, to boot! She was normally a cynic when it came to twittering birds and love hearts. Life had shown her there was no such thing as "The One."

Even so, the universe must've had other ideas—at least for that one night.

"Cupid shot your plane down?" He had placed his drink on the bar next to her empty glass. Cheesy line—but from the quirk in his lips he'd known it.

Her attraction to him had been immediate.

"That obvious?" she'd shot back with a laugh and a smile.

The bartender had placed a fresh cocktail in front of her. One she hadn't ordered. A Cosmopolitan, complete with a twist of orange peel. Her favorite.

She wasn't normally a sucker for a well-dressed man—but this one…? No matter what had been about to play out there, she'd already known she would remember him as "The Suit."

He'd worn his as if he had been sewn into it. And she hadn't doubted for a second how delicious he would look out of it.

"Been here long?"

She'd felt him make the visual journey up from her biker-style boots, crossed at the ankle, to the bit of leg on show below the swing of fabric that had made up her wraparound dress.

"Long enough."

Already, she'd only had eyes for him, and the buzz of magnetic energy had tugged them into a cocoon of "Me and You." Another sip of Cosmo, remarkably little chit-chat, a slight lift of his eyebrow—*shall we?*—and they had headed off to the elevators.

It had been raw animal attraction. They hadn't needed to discuss it. They'd just *known*. No names. No deep and meaningful forays into the other's psyche. Just unreserved, unadulterated, lust. She'd never felt anything consume her so completely before.

The doors of the elevator had barely shut before his hands had begun exploring her, heated kisses had drawn them closer together. She'd felt reckless, wanton, and exactly where she should have been. She'd been completely under his spell, and this total stranger had made himself at home with the dips and curves of her body. Fingers had slipped along waistlines, hands had been drawn possessively along hips, lips had tasted and teased and all she'd been able to do was respond.

She didn't even remember how they'd got to her room. But Ali could distinctly recall the moment her dress had slipped to the floor, her skin shuddering with desire as she'd pressed against him, still wearing every bit of that three-piece suit. She should have felt vulnerable, exposed. But she hadn't. Far from it. She'd felt feminine, sexy, and for the very first time she'd understood the power of desire.

The need to feel him inside her had grown as his hands had begun to explore her more intimately. Her breasts, then her nipples had grown taut as she'd pressed against the wool of his suit jacket. He'd slid a hand between her legs, his fingers slipping slowly back and forth, back and forth. Her breath had caught in her throat and he'd tipped his head down to lazily tease his tongue round first one nipple, then the other.

She'd rolled her feet up onto tiptoe. Fluidly, as if she were still dancing and the accident had never happened, she'd tucked first one leg and then, with a small hop, the other around his hips. He had easily carried her across the room to the high bed. As he'd begun to lower her swiftly, almost brusquely, he had turned her around, his hands moving along the sides of her breasts. Then one hand had traced along her front and the other down her back, until he'd cupped her between her legs. Her skin had felt as though it were on fire. She had never wanted anyone more than she'd wanted The Suit.

She'd felt his thick five o'clock shadow along her cheek and, as if he reading her mind, he'd whispered into her ear, "I only have two—so you're going to have to be patient."

Two condoms. One night with a man she'd never see again.

These walls better have soundproofing, she remembered thinking. She'd met her match, and from the way his hands had taken such pleasure in exploring her body he'd felt it, too…

"Woooo-hoooo! Did you see that, Doc?"

Ali snapped out of her sexy dreamscape, eyes scanning the field to quickly connect the dots. *Must pay more attention!*

The clutch of assistant coaches she'd stationed herself next to were whooping it up as the scoreboard flickered to life with a new set of numbers. The North Stars were surging ahead of their opponents.

She grinned and pulled her knitted team skullcap down over her ears. Man, it was cold out here! A far cry from her swish and well-heated therapy center in the heart of London.

The thought pleased and stung at the same time.

Enough.

The Chief Medical Officer was due back sometime today—possibly even mid-match—and it would hardly do for her to be caught daydreaming. Especially dreams of the super-naughty kind.

She forced herself to be alert to the players on the pitch. They were, after all, her responsibility.

As play recommenced, then abruptly stopped, Ali's senses sharpened. The crunch of shoulder on shoulder, skull on skull was never a nice sound, but these rugby boys didn't do things by halves.

The howls of pain coming from the field set her into motion. Drama queens, maybe—but these men were not babies. A player was hurting.

Oblivious to the roar of the thousands of fans watching the heated North versus South trial match, Ali picked up her pace as the stretcher-bearers joined her on the snow-spackled field. A scrum combined with a slippery playing surface could easily lead to a spinal injury. She hoped for the player's sake it wasn't the case.

The huddle of sweaty, mud-covered men split open as she arrived.

"Hope you've got a strong stomach, Harty," One of the players mumbled as she made it to the center of the group.

There, lying on the ground, staring straight ahead as he fought to control his breathing, was Chris Trace—the team's hooker. To say he was a sight to behold was putting it mildly. She almost had to laugh. She'd wanted a change and this was most definitely *not* the sort of injury you saw in the Royal Ballet.

Their player had taken the full brunt of a Southern Cross player's might. Blood was pouring from a gash in his forehead, and as he swept a hand across his face to clear it from his eyes it looked as though he was going to have one heck of a shiner by the end of play.

The stadium fell into a hush as both teams stood at attention—waiting for the verdict.

"All right, Chris." Ali grabbed her run bag and pulled out some wipes. "Let's see what price you've paid for victory."

Spitting out his mouth guard, the athlete tried to grin up at her. A good sign.

"I'll be back on the field in no time, Doc. Just put a plaster or something on me and I'll be good to go." Chris couldn't stop the flinch crossing his broad face as he tried to lift his head.

"No, you don't!" Ali pressed him back down to the ground. "You're not going anywhere until I check you out. What happened to your goggles?"

She smiled down at him, admiring his determination to finish the game. The North Stars were grittily committed to being at the fore of the infamous North against South showdown in just over three months' time. The last day of her contract. Losing a player to an injury was the last thing they needed.

She began sponging the blood off his forehead to see how big a gash they were dealing with. Head injuries were big bleeders, and with all the sprawling around in the muck these guys did infection was easy to come by.

"Goggles popped off when I landed on my face—or someone's foot knocked them. Can't remember."

"Can't remember or can't think straight?" a male voice asked from behind her.

Ali froze. She knew that voice. It had whispered deliciously naughty intentions into her ear not so very long ago.

Her eyes moved along the ground from where she knelt with Chris, her breath caught tight in her chest. Blood began to thunder between her ears as a pair of leather shoes came into view and walked to the opposite side of Chris. It was all she could do not to cry out as the owner of the shoes came into view as he kneeled across from her. *Oh, she knew him, all right.* She knew him intimately. And she didn't know him at all.

As their eyes met Ali physically felt the breath being sucked out of her body.

The Suit.

Images flickered past her mind's eye, of their bodies tangled together in a series of sexual acrobatics she'd never believed possible. A wash of pleasure rippled through her and it was all she could do to keep her jaw clamped firmly shut.

She'd never asked him his real name. Nor had he of her. That had been their deal. One night only.

Someone needed to pinch her. And fast.

"Take me through it."

He was speaking to her, but looking at Chris. *What was he doing here?*

"I want to find my goggles." Chris tried to push up from the ground again.

"No, you don't!"

"No, you don't!"

Ali could barely suppress a surprised smile as she and The Suit each pressed on a shoulder, keeping Chris on the ground.

"Not until we know what else you've done to yourself. How does the socket around your eye feel?" Ali pressed him down again, this time with her hands covered in purple nitrile gloves, before she gently palpated the area.

"Fine—it's just the cut, Doc. Honestly. Dr. Tate— tell her."

For a second time Ali felt her chest constrict.

"*You're* Aidan Tate?"

Dr. Aidan Tate? The award-winning sports medicine expert whose articles on non-surgical sports injuries she'd devoured like chocolate? The North Stars' Chief Medical Officer? And...wait for it...*her new boss*?

Well. This was a bit of a pickle.

The biggest freaking pickle in the whole entire universe!

Her tummy pirouetted and heated as she stared at him—only just managing to suppress a smile. A short, sharp shake shifted the X-rated images from her mind and she rapidly went back to swabbing away the blood from Chris's forehead.

"Earth to Lockhart! *Harty?* What gives? Am I getting back into play or what? *Where are my goggles?*" he shouted to the other players, who leapt into action.

Ali looked up and caught the eyes of her new boss. His face was unreadable. Hmm… This was nothing short of awkward.

"Got 'em!" One of the Southern Cross players jogged over and handed the protective eyewear to Chris, complete with blood and a tuft of muddy grass. He plopped them on the front of his blood-smeared face and gave Ali a *See? I'm Fine* grin.

"Nice look, Chris." Ali guffawed at the gruesomely comic sight, then looked across at Aidan Tate with a mortified expression. He was her new boss. Never mind that she'd seen him naked. He'd hired her to be a *doctor*, not to snicker at the players' made-for-Halloween gruesome faces.

Way to make an impression, Lockhart.

She was surprised to see Aidan smirk his approval at her reaction to Chris. She guessed he wanted to make sure the new girly doc could play gross with the rest of the boys.

She glanced at Aidan again, and he nodded for her to proceed. She couldn't help but feel whatever she said was going to be under microscopic examination. Which was fair enough. If she'd found out the man she'd had a sizzling one-night stand with was her shiny new employee she would probably have held him to a higher standard.

"The cut doesn't look too deep. Let's do the spine and concussion drills and then get you to the sidelines for a couple of stitches." Then for good measure she added, "And maybe give your specs a bit of a bath."

Ali trained her eyes on Chris and deftly carried out a thorough inspection of his neck and upper spine to make sure it was safe to move him.

"Any tingling sensations in your arms? Burning? Stinging?" She rattled through the checklist, all too aware of Aidan's eyes on her.

"Nah," Chris answered.

"Shortness of breath?" She tapped along his lungs. A pneumothorax would be an unwelcome complication.

Chris heaved in a deep breath of air and exhaled with a lion noise. His lungs were fine. "Nope."

"Guess you've kept everything intact except your brainbox—lucky boy. Wiggle your toes."

"I'm *fine*, Harty! We're a breed apart from all your fluffy ballerinas. Made of tougher stuff, we are."

"Oh, really? And here was me thinking you were only human." She signaled to the stretcher lads. He was safe to move off the field for a more thorough consultation.

"No way!" Chris pushed himself up. "I'm walking off on my own two feet, thank you very much."

He stood up between them—weaving ever so slightly—then raised his arms in a victory move and swaggered off the field to the roar of the crowd.

Which left her face-to-face with Dr. Aidan Tate.

Her stomach gave a life-affirming heave and she almost lost her balance, which—considering she was still kneeling—was quite a feat. The man took her breath away. There was no getting away from that. Salt and pepper hair she'd run her fingers through on their way to naughtier climes, coffee-black eyes and a perfect set of cheekbones. Oh—and had she mentioned his lips? They were very, *very* nice lips.

"Go on." He pointed toward the sidelines, pushing up to a standing position. "You've got work to do."

She rose and looked into his eyes—hoping for some answers to the thousands of questions whirling round her head, well aware that every part of her body was responding to seeing him again. Hearing him. Being close enough to touch him.

"You need to leave the pitch so all that stops."

"What?" She looked around.

He lifted his chin in the direction of the stands, from where a flow of catcalls was pealing out. They were obviously aimed at Ali.

"You're fine with that?" Aidan's dark eyes crackled— the energy between them was as potent as it had been the first time they'd met.

"The shouting?"

"Yes." His face was grim.

"I can barely hear them." And it was the truth. All her senses were triangulating in one very specific direction.

"I'm not fine with it." Aidan took her by the elbow, turned her around and began to walk her off the field.

"Hey! I can walk on my own, thank you very much!" Ali protested.

"You don't need to make a bigger show of things than you already have," Aidan bit out.

"I'm sorry?" Ali bridled. "I think the only 'show' was Chris's head-bleed. Frog-marching me off the field is a pretty bad idea."

And it was. Aidan dropped her elbow instantly and strode off the field. She could make her own way.

Dr. A. Lockhart. Dance injury specialist, sports medicine MD, and surgeon, brought in for a locum position. When he'd hired her he'd thought her ream of credentials made her perfect for fine-tuning the team's training in the build-up to the final.

And now he knew she was very same woman who had slowly but surely been consuming every sane brain cell he had left since their night at the airport?

Miss Cosmopolitan.

She had actually rocked his world. Never before had a woman made such an impression on him. From the very moment he'd laid eyes on her.

She'd been sitting at the hotel bar, her eyes on the television weather report, lazily tracing a swizzle stick along her lips. He had become mesmerized by the movement as her mouth had responded to the touch of the little black straw. It had been just about the sexiest thing he'd thought he'd ever seen. Before he could give himself time to think better of it he'd sent her a drink. Ten... fifteen minutes couldn't have passed before they'd been in the elevator and he'd been tracing a finger along her lips, hungry for more. *Much* more.

No names...no attachments. It wasn't how he normally operated—had ever operated—but by the time they had been finished she had been worth every single nail scratch on his back.

He narrowed his eyes as he watched her disappear down the tunnel toward the changing rooms. Glossy black hair streaming in a thick swatch from beneath her team cap, crystal-clear blue eyes so bright they seemed lit from within, and a pair of raspberry-red lips which he could all too easily remember—

No you don't! Stop.

"Doc! Watch it!"

Aidan nearly collided with Chris, who was trying to give his face a scrub with his filthy jersey.

"Sorry, mate. Away with the fairies."

"Where's Harty?" Chris looked around the sidelines.

"Who?"

"Dr. Lockhart," Chris bit out, his tone abruptly changing.

"Chris, are you all right?" Aidan walked him over to a bench.

Ali had capably gone through the concussion test, he knew—he'd kept careful watch. But sometimes a clot could appear later, with devastating effect. He hoped that wasn't the case.

"Yeah, fine." Chris exhaled heavily as he sat. "I just want to get back out there. When's Harty going to stitch me up?"

"Don't you trust my stitches anymore?" As the words came out of his mouth Aidan knew they sat wrong, but the mention of Dr. Lockhart on such comfortable, friendly terms had riled him.

She'd been here—what?—a fortnight?—and already had a nickname? He'd been with the team five years and had barely managed to get the odd "Doc" out of the players. Then again—it wasn't exactly as if he was the easiest person to get to know. He knew if he was more open with the players they would respond in kind—but he wasn't there yet. Maybe he never would be. Maybe "closed off" was just who he was.

Either way—he didn't need to be behaving like a jealous doctor. Ali's stitches…his stitches—it didn't matter. She was a highly qualified doctor and he'd hired her for her skills. She clearly had the stomach for it. A "fluffy ballerina" type wouldn't laugh at a face covered in blood. The best thing he could do was shake it all off. It would keep things professional. Unlike his response to Ali.

Feeling envious because the players got along with the new doctor...? Ridiculous. It was what anyone would hope for. Harmony between support staff and players.

He scraped a hand along his stubbled jawline.

Harmony?

Who was he kidding? The only way he could describe his response to Ali Lockhart was Class A caveman. And that wasn't going to work. Not here. His reputation went hand in hand with the team's. Work and emotions weren't things he mixed. *Ever.* His annual fortnight of charity work in the Pacific Islands was an upfront-and-center reminder of that. Five years on and he still hadn't shed a tear. Maybe he never would.

"Are you all right for me to do the stitches?"

Ali appeared by his side with a suture kit in her hands.

"Go ahead." He nodded in Chris's direction without looking at her. Those blue eyes spoke volumes and he couldn't go there. Not now. "Do the concussion tests again before you okay him for play."

"Would you rather do it?"

"You're getting paid to look after these boys. You go on ahead."

He kept his eyes on the field, arms tightly crossed over his chest as he watched the players get into formation at the referee's whistle. It might look like mayhem to some, but he liked rugby. There was a system. A playbook. Rules.

He liked order, and Ali's presence here was bringing nothing but chaos.

* * *

Ali wished she could scrub away the crimson heat racing into her cheeks. She wasn't used to being spoken to like an underling.

The cheek! Her hands flew to her face. *Her* cheeks! *Aaaargh!*

She huffed out a sigh and started swabbing at Chris's mud- and blood-covered forehead.

Working with Britain's premier sports physician was meant to be professionally rewarding. *Trying* was more like it! On multiple levels.

"Ouch! Easy, Harty."

"I thought you were a roughtie-toughtie?" Ali gave Chris an apologetic grin and tried to lighten her touch.

She couldn't let Aidan get to her. Not on a professional front, anyway. Her job was the one thing Ali knew she excelled at, and she was not about to let some perfectly gorgeous chippy doctor from up here in the hinterlands boss her about. Even if she *had* spent several hot and steamy, never to be repeated, perfectly delicious hours of lovemaking with him.

She rubbed a numbing agent on Chris's forehead, quickly put in the stiches and gave him another run through the concussion exam. She wasn't one hundred percent convinced—not enough to prove to Aidan, anyway—so told him he'd have to sit out the rest of the game, and then she'd do the tests again.

"Safety first!" she quipped with a Doris Day grin. Or at least that was the look she was going for. Chris stuck his tongue out at her in response. Child...

Maybe coming here had been a mistake. Already she was getting attached to these big old lugheads, and that hadn't been part of the plan. Not by a long shot. Nor had sleeping with her new boss, but it seemed that had happened, too. This was all going swimmingly!

Aidan Tate was The Suit.

Who would've believed it?

She'd been a secret admirer of his expertise for years. He'd sounded so caring and professional in the medical journals he was regularly published in. And he'd been oh, so very tender and attentive at three, four *and* five in the morning, when neither of them had felt the need to sleep. Humph! *Double*-humph!

She grabbed her phone from her coat pocket and did what she always did when things started to get emotional. She bashed out a message to her former mentor from dance school.

What's the protocol on breaking my contract?

Her mentor had been wise and sage, had had hair like Einstein and—also like Einstein—he had known everything. At least about her. The one person on the planet who had. He'd helped her move on. Just as she had when her mum had died. Just as she had when she had learned she would never dance again.

Then she deleted it. He was gone now—some ten years ago—and she wasn't a quitter. Never had been. Except when life had forced her to...to alter her course. That was how she preferred to see things. Taking matters into her own hands.

She took her cap off and ran her hand through her hair. Platitudes. Handy when you needed them, trite when you didn't.

She tried to focus on the stands, the players, the flashing billboards—anything to keep her eyes from the unmoving figure of Aidan Tate. But no matter where she looked her internal camera kept imposing Aidan everywhere. On the big screens, on the looping advertising banners encircling the pitch...even the close-ups of the players showed those flashing dark eyes and that thick black hair she'd so enjoyed running her fingers through as she—*ahem*—had behaved distinctly unlike her old self.

Aidan had quite obviously been behaving out of character, as well. Caring and studious? *Ha!* Cranky control freak was more like it. It appeared looks weren't the only things that could be deceiving.

She tipped her head back and forth in the hope that some answers might fall out. If she'd learned anything in the past few years, it was that most situations were definitely *not* what they seemed to be. She needed to get out of there.

She watched as the players hurled themselves around the field.

No.

She didn't.

She owed it to these guys to stick around.

She'd made an oath. An oath to protect and care for her patients. And there they were—all cauliflower ears, biceps bulging, thigh muscles like logs, all gussied up in their unmistakable red-and-black uniforms. The North Stars.

As the cool air swirled around her play intensified and the crowd audibly kept pace with the action. She couldn't have felt further away from home. Not that she had one to go back to anyhow. Which was the whole point, wasn't it? Being here. Now.

The past is where it belongs, she reminded herself. *You're safe here.*

Ali couldn't help letting a burble of giggles escape her lips. Safe here? On the sidelines of one of Britain's most brutal games?

That'd be about right.

CHAPTER TWO

SWITCHING ON THE overhead lights to her warehouse loft flat, Ali felt the adrenaline from the day's match drain away. The adrenaline from finding out The Suit was her new boss…? *That* little nugget was keeping her pulse-rate a bit high.

She kicked off her shoes. They landed one by one with a satisfying thunk-thunk on the far side of the flat. She was giving "bachelorette pad messy" a whirl, and it was fun. More fun than watching Aidan sort out the day's steady stream of cuts, abrasions and strained muscles. She thought she'd earned some Brownie points with her treatment of Chris's cut, but he'd hardly let her so much as swab a skinned knee after that. So much for earning her keep…

Her stores of controlled breathing, counting to ten and biting her tongue had pretty much been exhausted by the time the final whistle had blown.

Where was the amazing physician she'd heard about, who took new doctors under his wing and single-handedly teased new and seemingly unreachable skills out of them? Where was the volunteer coach lauded as a hero to a rugby squad of twelve-year-old girls? Who had stolen the doctor every medical journal in Britain couldn't praise enough and replaced him with Generalissimo Grumpyhead? What was the point of being here if she wasn't going to *learn* anything?

She leaned against the closed door, well aware that her body was virtually vibrating with all the things she had learned from him—just nothing she could use in the workplace.

But honestly! Who in their right mind would turn down a guy who looked as if he could fix your car, fend off a swath of marauding invaders and pose for one of those posters of sexy guys holding tires in a garage, wearing not much more than a scrappy old pair of jeans? Scrappy jeans just slipping off his hips…right where the little notchy muscle definition bits met…

Nooooooo! Not the way this thought process was meant to go.

She felt herself soften. A little. He couldn't be *that* much of a control freak. She had just worked two weeks on her own while he'd been off swanning around in the Pacific, or wherever it was they said he'd gone. Maybe it was all part of some unknown test he set for his minions. Prove thyself—then watch and learn.

Geniuses were supposed to be arrogant, condescending, haughty and superior—but from what she'd read this guy had sounded as if he had heart. That would need some excavating. Not to mention his inability to give her a go. He should be thanking his lucky stars she had come up here at all! She had her own reams of kudos, accrued over a lifetime of—well, of avoiding everything one did in life but work.

Bah! None of this was helping.

She padded across the worn Oriental rug sprawled across the aged wood floors. It was the only thing she'd brought from her "old life" in London, and it matched the vintage feel of the building perfectly. The floor-to-ceiling windows were her favorite feature of the loft. A classic accent from the building's heyday as a thread factory. If she was really honest she could very easily fall in love with the place. An enormous loft penthouse with an enviable view overlooking the River Teal versus her two-up, two-down with a view across the street? It'd be pretty easy to get used to this.

Not that the flat was her new *home*. It was an investment. She didn't put down roots. She made investments. Easier to leave that way.

Ali slipped her keys into a red-lacquered bowl she'd found at a charity shop—the only decorative touch to her kitchen island—and pulled open the door to her enormous American-style refrigerator. The pickings were pretty sparse. The remains of a triangle of cheddar, an out of date ready-to-bake baguette and some just-about-to-wilt salad greens were the only inhabitants of the shelves. It was hardly the food of champions.

She had hit the ground running when she'd moved up here, and grocery shopping hadn't made it on to her list of things to do. After such a rough day, a hot meal would go down a treat. In London she'd already be on the phone, ordering Thai noodles or a delicious eggplant parmigiana from Casa de Luna. They made it perfectly—crispy round the edges, nice and gooey in the center. Here—well, she knew they had takeaways, up here in the wilds of the North of England, but...

It wasn't the same.

"It's *not* the same—and that's the point, you ninny," she scolded herself out loud. Onward and upward!

She was here to push her limits, to reach new horizons and blah-dee-blah-blah-blah. How many pep talks did she have to give herself before something, somewhere, felt right again?

Heaving a dramatic sigh, Ali draped her team duffel coat over one of the two kitchen bar stools, went to her bedroom, peeled off the layers of outdoor gear and put on her favorite pajama shorts with a cozy slouch-shouldered jumper.

Me, some scraps of old cheese and a bit of TV. Precisely what the doctor ordered!

The jangle of the doorbell nearly made her jump out of her skin. She hadn't had any visitors before and certainly wasn't expecting any now.

She hurriedly pulled on her woolly slipper boots and jogged to the door. When she pulled it open her stomach careened round her insides and her heart lurched into her throat all in one blood-racing moment.

Standing there, or rather filling up her doorway, eyes twinkling and a bottle of red dangling from his fingers, was The Suit.

"Hello, there, neighbor. Fancy a bit of work talk over a glass of *vino*?"

Ali's heart changed its syncopation—moving from dirge to dance mix in an instant. Pure determination kept her from unleashing a broad smile at his presence. She was a steely-gazed doctor, not a moony-eyed teenager. *Right?*

Her body's response to Aidan had absolutely nothing to do with the fact that he was the most gorgeous male specimen she'd ever seen. Clothed or otherwise. Or with the fact that his voice was about as trickle-down-your-spine scrumptious as they came. Especially when he was whispering sweet nothings into her ear as he traced his fingers across her bare belly in an endless swirl of figure-eights.

He was an arrogant know-it-all! And now he was her *neighbor*?

"What are you doing here?"

Not really a comment out of the etiquette books, but she was pretty sure they were past social niceties.

"I live a couple of buildings down in the complex and thought I'd be a bit more welcoming than I was this afternoon," he explained with an innocent smile.

"But how did you know I...?" she started, then petered out.

"Apart from the fact your contact details are listed on every emergency sheet at the stadium, who do you think sent you the recommendation you check the place out?" He held up the bottle of red. "This was my thank-you from the building committee for your decision to move in. I thought it would only be fair to share the spoils."

Aidan practically purred as he made to enter her apartment minus an invitation.

Ali stepped aside on autopilot, all too aware of the scrummy male scent of him as he swept past her into the loft. She could think of a thing or two he could do to be more welcoming—and they were definitely not in an etiquette book.

Regroup! Ali stared at the closed door and tried to come up with a plan. *Think, think, think, think.*

Kick him out. It's the only way. Time to show the upper hand.

Ali whirled around, only to see Aidan merrily nosing around her kitchen.

"What's for dinner, honey? Hope it goes with red!"

Aidan's voice was infused with the same twinkle of humor she could see in his eyes. The same rascally voice that had kidded her about how quickly she had managed to rip his clothes off. Well, not *rip* exactly— she had been aware that he might need his shirt the next day—but who knew cotton could seem such a thick barrier between a woman and The Suit's chest? The clothes had had to go!

He gave her a wink. A cute one that threatened the tightly pinched corners of her mouth. He really *did* have the most beautiful brown eyes. They somehow managed to look even more like dark chocolate now than they had the first time she'd seen them. A rich contrast to the deep maroon lambswool jumper that his shoulders filled to designer perfection. Of course. Would The Suit's shoulders do anything but?

What had happened to his suit, anyway? Probably best he didn't have it on. Too much temptation. Mind you, his earth-toned moleskin trousers didn't exactly look off the rack. Aidan was rocking a sophisticated "lad" look. Complete with ironically arched eyebrow as he scanned her flat.

It was obvious, as she watched him take in the old leather sofa, the bare walls and the small dining table without chairs, that he found her living arrangements amusing.

"I'm presuming no one told you we have furniture stores up here?"

"Look—" Ali started, then clamped her lips tight. It wasn't as if she was going to tell him she'd sold all of her furniture in a spontaneous and very thorough need to clutter-clear.

Everything she'd had before her mum died was a memory, and ever since then she didn't do rehashes of the past. She wasn't going to tell him a single thing. Not about her mother. Not about her who-knew-where-the-hell-he-was? father. Not about the accident that had ended her dance career before it had even begun. Not a word. Just like she'd said at the airport. No names. No history. Just unbridled passion.

It was obvious Aidan wasn't after a roll in the hay now. He was on a fact-finding mission.

Too bad! This was *her* space. One night stands at snowy airports were one thing. Casual drop-in dinner dates with her grouch of a boss had a whole other rulebook.

"Doesn't seem the doctor's got much in the house."

Aidan was making himself quite at home—merrily inspecting her refrigerator's stores and, having found them wanting, opening up the cupboard doors where he would see, Ali knew, absolutely no food. It was all very familiar for someone with whom she was—er—intimately familiar.

"I've been busy. I haven't really—"

"If you're going to be part of this team you've got to keep your energy up." Aidan wagged a teasing finger in her direction.

Who *was* this man? Dr. Jolly-Jekyll or Mr. Keep-Your-Hands-Off Hyde?

"Well?" Aidan looked at her expectantly.

"Sorry? I didn't catch that." Ali tugged her fingers through her hair, twisting a few dark strands round her index finger. Her stomach was in knots, so her hair might as well be, too.

"What's it short for?"

"What?" She stared at him blankly.

"Your full name—I presume it's not Ali."

"Alexis. Defender of humankind," she answered by rote, eyes suddenly locked with his.

Aidan stepped out from behind the kitchen bar, clasping her right hand between both of his. A burst of electricity shot along her spine as she found herself eye to eye with the appealing expanse of his chest.

She'd kissed that chest. Lots. A nice display of sexy man whorls of hair above a *c'mon, punch me hard* set of abs.

If she were to look up into those espresso-colored eyes of his and—

She felt her hand being rigorously shaken.

Er... Was she missing something here?

"Hello there, Alexis." He further corrected himself, "Dr. Lockhart. I think we got off to the wrong start today."

Today?

"Allow me to introduce myself. I'm Dr. Aidan Tate, Chief Medical Officer for the North Stars—at your service."

He dropped her tingling fingers, took a broad step backward and performed a half bow, then looked up at her with those incredible, endlessly dark eyes. Ali felt her knees give a little.

For heaven's sake. You've met the entire royal family and didn't act like such a ninny. Pull yourself together!

She gave him a slight head-nod. If this was his version of an apology he had yet to win her over. Well. Professionally. "Dr. Ali Lockhart—at *your* service."

There were a number of things Aidan could have said in response, but they wouldn't serve the purpose of his visit. He was here to begin afresh with Dr. Alexis Lockhart, the team's new physio-surgeon with one turn-you-green-with-envy CV.

"On paper it looks as though you've never taken a moment off to do anything other than study or practice medicine. When did you start? When you were twelve?"

"Something like that." Ali crossed her arms protectively across her chest and looked away.

There was a story there. Maybe too much time in

the science lab accounted for her wild-girl antics at
the airport.

His gaze slipped down toward Ali's feet, stopping to
note a couple of scars on her left knee. He'd not noticed
them the other night—which was pretty amazing, considering the gymnastics they had achieved. His curi-
osity was piqued, but he looked away. He wasn't being
fair. He'd come here to apologize and now he was treating her just the way he'd insisted to the coach the players would. Like chattel.

Coach Stone had been fairly terse when Aidan had
suggested they see if they could transfer her to another
team and bring in a different locum for the rest of the
tournament season. One who wasn't so easy on the eyes.

"Not a chance." That had been the unwavering reply.
The players had taken to her straight away, Stone had
said, and hiring someone else with credentials like hers
at this point in the season was going to be nigh on impossible. She was staying and that was that.

He cleared his throat and looked at Ali's reflection
in the window. *Since when were lambswool boots and
a mismatched set of pajamas so sexy?*

Maybe if he pictured Ali with an eye patch it would
help. And a hideous perm. And a hunchback.

"Earth to Aidan?" Ali was waving her hands in front
of his face, pulling him out of an embarrassingly obvious stupor.

"Yeah—sorry, I was just thinking."

"Anything you care to share?"

Might as well go for it.

"The elephant in the room."

"Which elephant would that be?" Ali smiled her
hostess smile at him.

Aidan couldn't help returning her smile. If things were

different they'd make a great pair. But they weren't—so it was best to lay his cards on the table. The man she'd met at the airport didn't exist in his everyday life. The man she'd met was an anomaly.

"Well, we could talk about the big elephant—about how we slept together—or the smaller one—how you should probably clear your spare underwear and gym kit out of my desk."

"Oh, blimey. That's *your* desk, is it?" Ali clapped her hands over her mouth.

"Who else's would it be?"

"I don't know—it didn't seem to have anything personal on it so I just thought it was free."

Good point. He didn't do personal. Especially at work. But that didn't address the issue at hand.

"The locker rooms have eyes and ears, Dr. Lockhart. Very acutely tuned, testosterone-charged cauliflower ears. I don't think it would be wise to have what happened at the airport being public knowledge. Or to be repeated."

She gulped, looked away, then began to laugh. Nervous giggles or happy memories? He knew what camp *he* was in.

"Can you imagine if the lads knew?" she asked. "About that night?" she qualified, as if he could have even begun to forget.

She lifted her gaze to his and this time he was certain they both felt the same connection. Having her standing in front of him in sexy little jim-jams wasn't strictly helping his body keep it neutral.

Her expression turned sober. "You're right. Absolutely right. The only reason I came up here was to learn, and all the…" she blew a slow breath between her lips "…other stuff would just get in the way."

They nodded at each other for a moment, as if they'd just signed a significant pact. And they had. They would be colleagues only. It was agreed.

"I know it wasn't what you planned for tonight—but what do you say we go out for a bite to eat?"

Ali gave him a dubious look.

"To talk about the team...your next three months here and what you hope to get out of it. Professionally." He weighted the word as a reminder to himself.

"I'd like that," she replied, then looked down at her skimpy outfit. "I'm guessing pajamas aren't the dress code. Smart or casual?"

He knew what he wanted to say, but picked the pragmatic response. As agreed. "Casual is fine. I know a great little Greek place—just around the corner."

"Love a bit of meze!" Her smile brightened. "Give me two minutes."

He smiled at Ali's retreating figure. The man who she'd met at the airport would have waited as long as she needed. Not that he'd tell her that. This whole situation was a matter of using his head over his...other parts. They'd had their night and it had been a one-off. Now he just had to work his way through the next one-hundred-odd days, convincing himself that all work and no play was the most sensible thing to do.

He'd made it through the past five years without so much as a fissure in his heart. Keeping Ali at arm's length couldn't be that hard. What was the worst that could happen?

Operation Pals-R-Us was officially under way.

"Are you kidding me? It came out of the *socket*?" Ali could barely contain her disbelief. She was really going to have to hone her shoulder joint skills. Knees...? She had them nailed. Shoulders...? Not so commonly injured during the *pas de deux*.

"Completely. You could've heard his screams down in London, I'll bet—but I got it back in, he's been diligent with his rehab, and now to see Mack run you'd never know otherwise."

"Amazing. To get him playing again was quite a feat." Ali didn't bother curbing her *I'm impressed* voice as she put her serviette onto her empty plate. Bodies were crazy things, and it sounded like Aidan had had his fair share of having to think outside the box to keep his players fit.

"I had to. These guys have a really short career window. If I can help make it just a little bit longer—so much the better."

She had to fight the automatic wince. *Her* career window had been just as short. *Nonexistent* was more like it. But the past was the past. The players were lucky they had someone like Aidan looking out for them.

In fact, his idea to go out to dinner had turned into a good one. Better than she'd thought when they'd first arrived at the restaurant after a virtually silent ten-minute walk. Trying to make chitchat when all you can think about is kissing your new boss was tough work.

After a bit of an awkward recitation of their professional histories, and some seriously divine moussaka with homemade pita, they had moved on to medical horror stories. The topic was inevitable between doctors, and it had definitely put the pair of them on neutral territory.

In fact, Ali discovered as the evening zipped along, it was really fun. Aidan was turning out to be everything she'd hoped when she had agreed to the locum posting. Smart, funny—and, yes, deeply gorgeous, but she hadn't known that when she'd signed on the dotted line. And now they'd agreed to keep things professional... Thank God they had medicine in common!

"I hope you don't mind—" Ali held up her hand to flag the waiter. She'd just about eaten her body weight in moussaka and was ready to crash for the night.

"Not up for a shot of ouzo?"

Ugh. The thought turned her stomach. "No, thanks— you're on your own with that one."

"No problem. I'm amazed I made it this late."

She raised an inquisitive eyebrow.

"Jet lag," he explained.

"Crikey! I totally forgot. You must be exhausted. Where was your holiday—some island in the Pacific, wasn't it?"

"It wasn't exactly a holiday." Tricky. Aidan wasn't one to lie—but he wasn't in the habit of letting anyone into his confidence either.

"Oh?"

"It's just something I do every year."

She looked at him blankly.

"For a charity."

"Oh, right! Which one?" Her eyes brightened.

"It's to do with the tropical storm that devastated the region a few years back."

"Oh, gosh. I remember that. It was horrible, wasn't it? Thousands of lives lost, weren't there?"

"Mmm. It took a lot of lives." Including one that had meant the world to him.

"That's brilliant that you go out there. I've often thought of doing some charity work in London— inner-city kids, that sort of thing—but I was always so wrapped up at the clinic."

"You really made a success of that, didn't you?"

Aidan gratefully swerved from more questions about the island. Yes, he did charity work—but the rest of it…? That was neatly locked up in his emotional no-go zone.

"I hope so," Ali began to twist the corners of her serviette into a tight coil. "Most people thought I was foolish for opening such a specialized clinic—but it's not as if the only ballerinas who injure themselves are in the Royal Ballet. We get clients from all over the world now. My 'little baby' is all grown up now."

"You were smart. Got in there before someone else thought of it and then made an art of it."

Aidan nodded his approval—not that she needed it. En Pointe was now *the* destination for anyone with a dance-related injury. Impressive for someone who'd just turned thirty-two. The only way you could get that kind of success, this early, was undiluted drive.

"So how could you leave it all behind?"

Ali looked away.

"Oh…it was time to spread my wings—let new pairs of eyes see to things."

"So you're not going back?" This time he couldn't hide the surprise in his voice. "I don't know if I could leave *my* baby as easily."

"You mean you'd never leave the North Stars?"

"No, it's not that. If something amazing tempted me I'm sure I'd go. But I'm happy enough here, and any 'wing-stretching' I need to do lands in the clinic just about every week in the form of new injuries, new techniques. I don't need to go elsewhere. Don't get me wrong—I'm delighted you're here—but to leave behind your clinic after putting all that time and energy into it… It's your calling card, surely?"

"No," Ali answered quietly, still avoiding his gaze. "I never needed to be lauded for the work we do at

En Pointe—I just wanted to make sure the resource
was there. Dancers need a place they can rely on to
specifically deal with *all* their needs when they're injured. That's why it provides a multi-level approach to
the care it gives. We don't just stick bandages on the
dancers. They receive surgery, rehab, counseling—the
whole lot."

"That sounds like the voice of experience." Aidan
leaned forward, lowering his head to see if she would
receive his inquisitive smile.

"We've all got history." Her eyes remained reso-
lutely elsewhere. "Shall we…?" Ali abruptly dropped
her knotted serviette onto the table and briskly headed
toward the waiter who'd been making up their bill.

"Hang on, Ali." Aidan jogged to catch up with her,
pulling his wallet out of his pocket. "This one's on me."

"No need," she replied with a tight smile. "I'm perfectly capable of looking after myself." A look of remorse flashed across her face. "Sorry. Thank you. That's
very kind." She shot him an apologetic grimace. "I guess
you're not the only one who's tired."

"Not to worry."

Aidan handed a couple of bills to the waiter and
waved away any change as Ali shrugged on the coat
she'd left on one of the hooks near the front door. She
was halfway out the door by the time he'd grabbed his
own. There was definitely a story there—a painful one,
from the looks of things. But he wasn't one to dig—
particularly as he'd been doing his own "artful dodg-
ing." He was no psychiatrist, but he'd put money on the
idea that Alexis Lockhart—defender of humankind—
hadn't come up North solely to expand her medical
horizons.

"Shall we go back via the river route?"

"You're the boss!" Ali quipped.

"Hopefully not a *bossy* boss," he shot back with a grin. Witty lines had never really been his forte.

"There's still time." Her face bore no trace of humor.

Aidan chose silence as the best response. He'd had enough experience with clamping his mouth shut when yet another woman he'd casually dated had expressed disappointment over things not turning more serious. Not that Ali seemed all that interested in plumbing emotional depths with him. Quite the opposite, in fact. Keeping things superficial…? Now, *that* he could do.

She rubbed her hands together in the cold winter air and huffed out a puff of breath. "Sorry. I'm sounding really narky and I don't mean to."

He pointed her toward the riverside path that would bring them to their respective homes. And he didn't mean to be superficial. Not with her. He felt a rush of desire to keep things between them on a good level— positive. He'd already seen two sides to this woman and he liked them both. Very much.

"Not to worry. It's been a long day."

"You can say that again."

CHAPTER THREE

"ALL RIGHT, LADS—let's clear some room for the lady."
The assistant coach ushered the players aside for Ali,
with her medical tote bag in hand.

"It's only *Harty*!" one of the guys shouted.

"Cheers, mate," Ali riposted.

She enjoyed being just "one of the lads." It was about
a gazillion times easier than being anywhere near Aidan,
whose mere presence insisted upon reminding her of
how very much like a woman he had made her feel.

"What did you do this time, Rory? Eyes all right?"

She knelt down on the ground next to Rory Stiles,
who was busy clutching his shoulder with his eyes
squeezed tight shut. From his expression, it looked as
though the blindside flanker had taken the full brunt of
his fellow player's might. As she peeled his hand away
from his shoulder, one glance at the tenting at his collarbone told her all she needed to know.

"Right. Let's get you off the field and into the clinic.
You've done a job on your clavicle."

The redheaded athlete cracked open his eyes and
tried to grin at her through the pain. "It's nothing, Harty.
Just get a figure-of-eight on me and I'll see out the rest
of the practice."

"No sling is going to see you through the next thirty

seconds, let alone two hours, my friend." She smiled down at him. These guys were just like dancers. Injured or not—the show must go on!

"Just give me some meds—I'll be fine."

"I'm afraid I can't give you pain meds right now. Not until we know what else you've done to yourself. We want those bones to heal properly, don't we?"

"Tate would give me meds!"

"No, he wouldn't." The familiar rich voice filled the air around them. "What's going on?"

"Rory seems to have broken his collarbone and wants to compromise his long-term health for the sake of a practice session."

"No need to be so melodramatic, Dr. Lockhart. These lads are made of sterner stuff than your tutu brigade." Aidan knelt down alongside her.

"My *what?*"

"Ah! Ha-ha-ha! Tutu brigade! Good one, Dr. Tate."

Rory laughed and Ali shot him a look. One that said, *Thanks for nothing*, and carried on with her silent and thorough inspection of Rory's neck and upper spine.

What was *that*? thought Aidan. The *fifth* time he'd stuck his foot in it today? Working with Ali was becoming progressively more difficult. Yes, he respected her professionally—but the side of him that wanted her on a completely carnal level was constantly threatening to take over his practical side. His professional side. The one he'd insisted they respect. Work. Careers. Things you could rely on. And all he could think about was taking her in his arms and having his *very* wicked way with her.

"Any tingling sensations in your arm?" Ali asked Rory.

"Nah."

"Shortness of breath?"

Rory sucked in a deep breath. "Nope."

"Guess you've kept your arteries out of the pinch zone. Lucky boy. Doesn't feel like a compound fracture—otherwise it'd be surgery for you!"

"C'mon, Rory. Up you get. I'll have a look." Aidan went to help Rory push up from the ground.

"Excuse me, I think we're good here. Aren't we, Rory?" Ali moved to Rory's other side as he rose.

"You and me are *always* good, Harty. Now...if Tate, here, would just shave a little more often—"

"Invasive surgery isn't the answer to everything." Aidan glared across the expanse of Rory's chest at her.

"I'm pretty sure I've got this one covered, Dr. Tate."

"Hey, listen, guys—no need to fight over me." Rory giggled.

"We're not fighting!" Ali and Aidan answered simultaneously.

"Uh..." Rory looked round at his teammates. "Anyone else here see Mommy and Daddy bickering again?"

"Yup."

"Sure did."

"Me too!"

"Same old, same old."

Aidan tightened his grip on Rory's elbow as the confirmations rolled in. They weren't fighting.

"Dr. Lockhart and I were merely having a professional disagreement. Over treatment. Which is a wise thing to do. Options should always be discussed before invasive action is taken. That was the reasoning behind our hiring Dr. Lockhart in the first place."

"Not because she's a hot doc?" shouted one of the boys.

Aidan threw a glance in Ali's direction, hoping for some backup. Annoyingly, she was laughing along with the rest of the lads.

ANNIE O'NEIL43

"Rory. Get a move on. We need to get some ice on you and take some X-rays."

"I'll just stay here with the boys, shall I?" Ali called after him.

"Whatever you think is best, Dr. Lockhart," Aidan called over his shoulder, hating himself as he did it.

What could he do, though? It wasn't as though he was going to *admit* he had the hots for his new colleague. Work and pleasure—they just didn't mix. If it meant he had to come across as a hard-ass some of the time—well, then, so be it. These boys had a tournament to win—and that needed to be his priority.

"What was *that* all about?"

Ali held the door open, but didn't look anywhere near issuing him an invitation to enter. She hadn't said two words to him the rest of the day at work, and he couldn't blame her. He'd gone all Cro-Magnon on her and that wasn't the best way to work together. It wasn't *any* way to work together.

"Would it help if I said you were possibly right?"

"Possibly?" Ali looked indignant.

"Well, it's a fracture. I strapped him up—figure-eight—and told him to rest and ice it tonight, and that both of us would take a look in the morning, when the swelling had gone down."

"That's very magnanimous of you." Ali fake-smiled at him, then began to close the door as she spoke. "Thank you for coming by to let me know."

"*This*—" he lifted up a two grocery sacks and stuck his foot in the doorway "—is a peace offering. Can I make you dinner?"

"What? And have you one-up me again?" Ali's hackles were well and truly raised.

"No." Aidan pressed his heels into the ground and made himself grow a couple of inches.

He knew he'd been a jerk, but he was hardly going to let Ali turn this situation into a free-for-all of notch-gathering. The North Stars' medical needs were ulti-mately his responsibility. And he knew the patients better than she did. *Fact*.

"I'm happy to have takeaway—or nothing, if you prefer—but we've got to sort this out."

"What, exactly?"

"You. Me. How we deal with things at work."

Ali rocked back in her woolly boots and he could almost see the decision-making process in her eyes.

"What were you going to make?"

"Risotto."

She pushed her lips out into a deep red moue and arched a brow.

"What kind?"

"Asparagus and lemon. My nan's recipe."

"I didn't know your nan was Italian."

"She wasn't—but I dare you to diss my nan's risotto."

"Ha!" Ali pulled open the door and let him pass. "Do you have her tucked around the corner somewhere?"

"Not tonight," Aidan mused as he carried the shop-ping to her kitchen island. "I wasn't certain if you'd offer to cook."

"That's something we both know is unlikely to hap-pen." Ali padded over to him and began to nosy through the bags.

"You want to open up that wine I brought the other day?" He scanned the counter to see if it was still there. It was.

"You go ahead." Ali slipped onto one of the bar-stools and watched as Aidan began to hunt round her kitchen for knives or chopping boards or whatever it was he needed to make risotto. "I'm 'in between' drinks right now."

"Oh, yeah?" Aidan smiled up at her. "What does that mean?"

"It happens sometimes—I just can't pick what drink I like. Right now I'm leaning toward soda and lime."

"Jumping on the wagon?"

"No—" she started, then reconsidered. "Maybe. I don't know... Just haven't felt like drinking. It's my new boss." She pulled a face at him. "He's working me so hard I need to be at the top of my game so he'll stop *questioning my expert opinion* about things. Like injured clavicles near the pinch zone."

"Ali..."

"Yes?" She drummed her fingers along the kitchen island.

She was looking forward to an explanation. She was used to being in charge. Biting her tongue in front of her patients was not familiar terrain and she didn't like it. Not one bit.

"Here." Aidan handed her a knife and a big handful of asparagus. "Chop these up, will you?"

"Tell me why you undermined me today." She stood her ground. She wasn't going to be sidetracked and pushed into a sous chef role to boot.

"Honestly?" He looked at her and about a thousand thoughts jockeyed for pole position. "I'm..." he began, then reconsidered. "You're— This is all a big change. Having you here."

"Why? Because I'm a woman or because I'm better at practicing medicine?" She gave him a sassy grin.

"Because you're different." Aidan responded tactically. "I know you would be hard-pressed to believe

it—but I don't really do change. And having you here
is one change after another, so you're going to have to
be patient with me. I hired you because I respected your
work. I'd like you to stay—but you're going to have to
get used to working *with* me. We're meant to be a team.
This isn't a one-woman chop shop, okay?"

Ali couldn't stop herself. She had to laugh. *One-
woman chop shop?* That was a good one.

"Who doesn't like a bit of surgery?"

"*Me*! It's not my area of expertise and— Oh, for
heaven's sake, Ali. Do I have to spell it out for you? I
may be the CMO of one of Britain's best rugby squads
and able to make a killer risotto, but *you* know your way
around the surgery ward. It's impressive, Ali. Truly."

Their eyes met. He was *impressed* by her? Her lips
twitched into a smile. She was tempted to do a little
victory dance, but gloating wasn't her style.

"What was it you wanted me to do with this stuff?"
She pointed at her cutting board.

"The asparagus? Small bite-sized pieces, please."

Ali began hacking away at the innocent asparagus
stems and snuck a peek at Aidan, meticulously pith-
ing a lemon. You did pith them, right? Something like
that... With big strong hands attached to some rather
lovely forearms...

He glanced across at her cutting board. "Easy there,
Doctor. I hope you don't treat your patients like your
asparagus."

"Sorry?" Talk about micromanaging! Hadn't they
just been through this?

Aidan received the full force of her crackling blue
eyes. "Don't glare at *me*! You're the one attacking
it!" He couldn't help laughing at her furrowed brow.
"Here—let me."

Aidan laid a hand on Ali's and gently guided her knife across the asparagus spears, slicing them into emerald green bite-sized pieces.

He felt her hand stiffen at his initial touch, but as they made their way through a few more of the fluid movements she began to relax. A warmth began to move from her hand to his, straight up his arm and across his shoulders. Being with her this way, doing something as familiar as cooking, was calming him. A welcome tonic after a hectic day with the North Stars. A heated memory of the night they'd shared. An unspoken suggestion of things to come.

He felt her hair brush against his cheek as she turned to face him. Her blue eyes were searching his. There was very little space between them and it would have been incredibly easy to just lean in and tease a few kisses out of her full lips. Lips he'd been aching to taste from the very moment they'd parted at the airport.

From the look on her face, she wouldn't stop him if he leaned in. He saw it in her eyes—just as he had the moment they had seen each other at the bar. Desire. Longing. But tonight it went deeper than that. If he touched her now he knew he wouldn't stop at a kiss, a simple caress. He couldn't. Not with her.

Ali reached him on a level he hadn't thought possible anymore. Not after the island, where his heart had gone numb with shock when he'd lost his grip on his childhood sweetheart's hand. He hadn't even begun to know how to mourn her. How to honor her life—the future they would never have together. But from the very moment he had laid eyes on Ali he had felt *alive*. It was intoxicating, and he knew he was going to have to fight every cell in his body to maintain control.

Abruptly, Aidan returned to the other side of the

kitchen island. He—they—had made a deal. A professional relationship. That was all he and Ali would share. He didn't look at her, but he could tell Ali felt it, too. The connection. The silent *simpatico* he couldn't quite define. It was a heated medley of disappointment, understanding, expectation and stasis. This close, he could smell her perfume—something a little citrusy? A bit of clean linen? It suited her. As did the blue top she wore. It made her sea-blue eyes that much harder to resist.

Aidan felt his controlled exterior weaken.

He glanced over at Ali, who was now sawing away at some cherry tomatoes for the salad.

"Is this another example of your technique in the operating theater?"

Ali bristled. What did he know about her? Her work? What did he know about *anything*?

One minute he was doing a sexy kitchen version of *Ghost* with her, making pulses of heat strobe throughout her body, and the next he was making narky comments about the one thing in the world she knew she excelled at.

"You know where the door is, Dr. Tate." She couldn't keep an edge from her voice. "No one's forcing you to stay."

"Easy there, pet. I was just teasing."

As quickly as he'd irked her, his gentle voice calmed her down. Aidan's Northern accent wasn't strong, but this was the first time the regional term of endearment she'd been hearing all week had made her knees turn to jelly. Good thing she was parked on a stool.

Come to think of it, no one had had that effect on her. *Ever.* Sure, she'd had boyfriends—if you could call someone you'd dated for a few months a boyfriend. Her work had always been her go-to partner. Never before had she met someone who came close to being both. Not that Aidan was. He was her colleague. Her boss. "The Suit" was someone she wouldn't meet again.

Ali squeezed her eyes tight, listening as Aidan stirred rice into a pan of frying shallots. He poured in some liquid that immediately released a heady, steamy, intoxicating scent. It smelled the way she felt when Aidan looked at her. A bit other-worldly.

She sighed, rubbing her fingers across her eyes. She didn't know if she could stand another hour of ping-ponging emotions, let alone three months of working together.

"Look." She put the knife down on the cutting board filled with asparagus and tomatoes. "Cooking is clearly not my arena. It's yours. I'll do what I'm good at and select some music."

"Is that a challenge?"

"No, it's not," she snapped. Did *everything* have to be a competition? "I just know my area of expertise is not anywhere around *this* part of the apartment." She waved her arms around the open-plan kitchen area.

"Being around the players all day must bring out the combatant in me." Aidan held his hands up in the surrender position, one hand clothed in a flowery oven mitt, the other holding a pink-handled spatula. Another internet purchase.

Ali looked at him standing there, this absolute picture of manhood, bedecked with flowery kitchen gear, and couldn't help bursting out laughing.

Aidan feigned surprise that she should find his appearance funny, and then joined in her laughter. It felt good. Relaxing.

"Truce?" He offered her the hand with the oven mitt on it.

Still giggling, Ali took the oven mitt and shook it with a somber expression.

"Truce. Not that I know what we were fighting about, but a truce sounds perfect. I need a mate up here."

Aidan's eyes widened.

"A friend—a *friend*!" Ali covered, quickly busying herself with her music collection. *Nice one, Ali.* That's some top Freudian slippage, right there.

Aidan's expression turned serious as he returned to the risotto, giving it an occasional stir, visibly trying to formulate what he was going to say next.

"Ali, I want you to know I'm glad you're here. That you're part of the team."

She held her breath, a little nervous that there was a *however* attached to this kind statement.

Aidan poured in another dollop of stock, waited for the sizzle and whoosh of steam then looked up at her. He took a thoughtful sip of wine, swished it around a bit and then swallowed. He reminded Ali of one of those annoying wine critics on TV.

"Your CV is flawless and the team couldn't ask for anyone better. Apart from—"

"Apart from...?" Ali tried to tease the rest of his sentence out of him without exploding in fury.

"Me, of course." And then he released another one of those perfectly gorgeous smiles.

Unable to help herself, Ali fell apart with an enormous belly laugh. You didn't get as good as this man was rumored to be without a healthy splash of arrogance.

She raised an invisible glass to him, "Touché, Dr. Tate. Touché."

"Let's put that asparagus in, then. We need to get some food into you—then it's straight to bed. Tomorrow's another big day."

Ali felt heat creep into her cheeks for the second time that night and hid her face in her hands.

It was all too easy to imagine Aidan carrying her into her sparsely decorated bedroom and having his manly way with her. *Again.*

She peered at Aidan through her fingers. She had come up here to shake things up a bit, and there was no contesting the fact that meeting him again had done that to a tee!

"Asparagus, please, chef."

Aidan's voice broke into her thoughts, sending another disconcerting tangle of heat twirling round her stomach.

"It's tender enough that it can just steam in amongst the rice."

She slid the cutting board across the island and watched as he fluidly cascaded the delicate spears into the creamy risotto. He gave the mixture a few swift turns, then pulled a couple of plates out of the oven.

She raised an eyebrow.

"You didn't expect your risotto on a *cold* plate, did you?"

From you it's hard to know what to expect.

Aidan joined Ali on the spare stool at the kitchen bar as her dining room chairs were nonexistent.

They ate heartily and silently.

Aidan frowned at his risotto. Not because it wasn't good. It was excellent and he knew it. He was confused as to why Ali was living like a Buddhist monk.

"So, is this what you Southerners call 'Extreme Living'?" He tried to keep his voice light, but saw that his comment had chafed. Her eyes had clouded over with something he couldn't quite put a finger on. Loneliness? Sorrow?

That was it. Sorrow.

Nice one, Aidan. Seemed he just couldn't keep his foot out of his mouth tonight.

"Call it what you please, but I like it this way."

Her tone was curt and there was defiance in her expression, daring him to suggest that her home should be otherwise.

"I think it suits you."

"What's *that* supposed to mean?"

He could see she didn't know whether to smile or be insulted. "It looks like the home of someone who has something to hide."

A flash of anger crossed her face.

"Why would you think I have something to hide?"

He took another mouthful of rice, pretty certain he wasn't meant to answer. Her lips parted as she took in a deep breath, then began speaking again, using her fork to visibly accent her key points.

"So I wanted to try something new! What's so bad about that?" She raised an attitude-filled eyebrow at him—if such a thing was possible.

"Not a thing."

"Damn tootin' right! I suppose *your* flat is stuffed to the gills with furniture? Or is it more magazine-spread-ready, in case you're chosen to be the centerfold for *Physio Monthly*?"

Ali smiled broadly as that picture fleshed itself out in her mind. *Uh-oh. Wait a minute.* He was naked in her mental picture. Not so very professional. She looked over at Aidan—*fully clothed* Aidan—to see if she could shake the image from her head.

The only things in her line of vision were his perfect lips. There was a bit of a five o'clock shadow in her sightline—the kind that made him appear just the opposite of scruffy.

Rugged. Male. Kissable.

If she thought she'd had butterflies before, her stomach went into full flip-flop overdrive mode now, when he reached for her hand, as if to say, *It's okay. I'm not attacking you.*

Ali nearly fell backward off the stool as her mobile phone began a little dance on the counter, the vibration and ringtone breaking through the thick atmosphere.

"Sorry," she mumbled, abruptly pulling her hand away from his.

Grabbing her phone, she walked to the far end of the large loft.

"Hello?" Ali knew her voice sounded unnaturally high, and she forced a slow breath between her lips to try to steady herself.

She held the telephone close to her ear, willing it to stop the roar of blood racing through her entire system. She could feel Aidan's eyes on her, but she refused to turn around, focusing instead on the twinkling lights of the city reflected in the wide river steadily flowing past. She wished her nerves were a tenth as calm.

"Doc? It's Rory."

"Hi, Rory. How's the collarbone? Is everything all right?"

Ali struggled to control her breath. She was really going to have to get a grip. Three more months of "friendship" with Aidan Tate was going to be much harder than she thought. She knew how moody and defensive she was coming across to him, but for some reason he brought out the extremes of all her emotions!

"Not really."

Ali's emotions sobered quickly, her years of medical training coming to the fore.

"You're not feeling light-headed, are you? Finding it hard to breathe?"

"No, Doc. Nothing like that." She heard him inhale sharply before continuing in a tight voice, "It's just that I was practicing with the resistance bands and—"

"What?" Ali felt her eyebrows fly up and couldn't help raising her voice. "You were meant to be resting it tonight. Icing it!"

"Yeah, I know." She heard the remorse in Rory's voice as he continued, "I thought I'd get a head start on rehab, so I'd be ready for the match, but I think I've made it worse."

"Rory, I need you to lie down on the floor if you're not already. I'm going to call an ambulance."

"Don't be ridiculous."

Before she could continue with Rory, she felt the phone being taken from her hand.

Blood rushed to her face. How *dared* he? She was consulting with her patient. Aidan had already undermined her once today—and now he had the cheek to grab her phone from her in her own home?

Wheeling around to retrieve the phone, she saw Aidan holding out an arm as if to keep her at bay.

Unbelievable. He was so insecure he couldn't even let her speak to one of "their" patients. *This was going to have to stop.*

"Rory—it's Aidan here. Are you able to get to the clinic, mate?" He paused, looking intently into Ali's eyes.

She felt her cheeks burn, ashamed that the heat came from a mix of frustration and attraction. The whole situation was ridiculous. She leaned her head against the cool window to try to regain some levity. If this was how the next few months were going to be, it was never going to work. She was too advanced in her career to be treated like a junior doctor.

Taking a deep breath, Ali reached out and took back her phone. "Rory, it's Dr. Lockhart again. I'm going to put you on speaker so we can get you the best treatment straight away, all right?"

This time she kept her gaze steady, noting Aidan's eyebrows rising a fraction, while the rest of his face remained neutral.

"Hi, Docs." Rory couldn't keep the confusion as to why they were together out of his voice, "I'm not sure, exactly, but when I was working with the resistance bands I think I dislodged my clavicle, and it seems to be in a weirder place than it was before."

Ali glanced over to Aidan. Reading those darkening eyes of his was virtually impossible.

Pulling her eyes away, she continued. "Rory, you could've just dislocated it again, and I can fix that pretty quickly, but from what you're saying there's a chance the fracture has become compounded. The bone could move and pinch your carotid artery. We definitely don't want *that* to happen. Are you alone?"

"Uh...not exactly."

"Mate." Aidan redirected his gaze to the phone, "Ali is right. You need to get on the floor immediately and have your guest get some ice, or frozen peas—whatever you have in the house—on that shoulder now. We'll be over as soon as possible. Got it?"

"Sure, Doc," Rory's voice was sounding a bit weaker now.

"Hang in there, Rory. We won't be long. If you begin to feel short of breath, or if any extremely sharp pains run down your arm, have your—erm—*friend* call an ambulance immediately."

Ali ended the call and started scrolling through her address book for Rory's details. She'd entered all of the players' numbers and addresses into her mobile phone the previous week, just in case anything like this happened. She just hadn't expected "anything" to pop up so quickly.

"I'll drive." Aidan's voice sounded commanding. *Surprise, surprise.*

"Look, Dr. Tate—"

"Oh, we're back to formal titles now, are we?" Aidan taunted as he strode across her apartment to the door, not even bothering to look at her as he spoke.

Wow. This man really knew how to rankle. The *arrogance*!

"Yes. This is a professional situation and I'm not going to spend the next few months begging you for permission to treat a patient. I don't think I need to remind you who it was he rang."

Ali kept her voice steady, but knew if she let go of the kitchen counter she was clenching her knees might betray the wobble they felt.

"And I don't think I need to remind *you* who knows their way around the city."

"Fine. You drive. But when we get there—he's my patient." Ali's eyes sparked brightly as she spoke.

Aidan noted with a sense of admiration that she had managed to keep her voice level, even though he was pretty certain she was fuming. Truth be told, if someone had treated *him* as he'd just treated her...for a second time... Well, it wouldn't have been pretty.

"Meet you in the garage in five?"

"Fine."

Aidan took the stairs to his own apartment. How had he managed to make such a hash of their new "working relationship" so quickly?

He slipped the key into his door.

Simple. Rory had called Ali and not him. It rankled. He had always been the go-to man for the team. The only consistent medic in their lives. Despite having to be available round the clock, and forsaking what little social life he had, he had enjoyed having the team's trust. He'd been their medical point man. And now, in just one short fortnight Ali had become their first port of call.

His mind raced with the things he could've done wrong with Rory. Had he set the figure-eight brace incorrectly this afternoon? He'd followed the usual checklist, hadn't he? Or had he been too concerned with getting back out on the field and asserting his control over Ali?

Aidan shook his head clear, knowing he was going to have to face some hard truths. And soon. He kept trying to control her because she brought out a side in him he'd thought was long gone.

A few strides into his loft and a quick look to the right revealed that his medical bag was where he always left it—in the unused contemporary fireplace. Medicine. That was what got him charged. Sent fire through his veins.

Romantic evenings by the fireside weren't really his thing.

Perhaps it was time to reconsider. He didn't like the way he was treating this perfectly innocent woman who'd appeared in his life, rattled his cage and given him a good old-fashioned dose of reality. But romantic evenings by the fireside...? Not really appropriate.

He wondered if she'd ever been to kickboxing...

He grabbed his bag and shut the door behind him. *Work*. That was what he needed to focus on. Not one hundred and one ways to spend time with Ali Lockhart. She was his colleague and that was it.

CHAPTER FOUR

A TWENTYSOMETHING BLONDE woman pulled open the front door to Rory's palatial modern house when they arrived before shrinking into the corner of the well-appointed room, from where she silently watched as Ali and Aidan knelt on either side of the player.

The moment Ali saw Rory's ashen face she knew he'd done more than dislocate his collarbone joint. A separated shoulder wouldn't tent like this. He'd compounded the fracture.

"Pulse is up. Too high." Aidan's voice was professional, efficient, as he took the player's obs.

"Rory, don't try to move. Are you able to follow my finger with your eyes?" Ali raised her index finger a few inches above Rory's pale face and watched as he tried to follow her moving it slowly in an arc. His breath started to come in short, sharp bursts.

"Shuuurrre, Doc…" Rory's speech was barely audible, and decidedly slurred.

"I think he's compounded the clavicle and pinched the carotid. He'll need surgery."

"You're sure?"

"As sure as I can be without an X-ray, but we don't have that luxury." Ali was relieved to hear that Aidan's question hadn't been laced with doubt. It had been just one professional confirming a course of action with another. "Call an ambulance. He'll need to get this plated and he shouldn't be moved without a proper stretcher."

"On it."

Ali's energies were entirely on Rory. If his carotid artery was pinched for much longer it could lead to a stroke, changing the young man's life forever. Time was of the essence.

"This isn't going to feel good, Rory. I need you to try your best to focus, all right?"

Glancing up at the young woman in the corner, Ali motioned toward a cushion on the long white leather sofa.

"Could you bring that cushion over for him?" The girl didn't move. "It's all right," Ali reassured her, "This will help him."

Two quick strides and Aidan was at Rory's side, cushion in hand, phone cradled between his shoulder and ear, holding on to the player's hand.

"As big a breath as you can muster, mate—ready?"

Aidan looked up at Ali and gave her a quick nod of assent. Time was against them and she needed to act now.

Placing her hands on Rory's neck and clavicle, Ali deftly felt for what was surely a compound fracture and realigned the bones as quickly and adroitly as she could.

Rory howled in pain and there was a rush of blood to his face. A welcome sight after the ghostly pallor he had worn when they'd first arrived.

"Hold him—he needs to stay stationary. This relocation isn't permanent."

Aidan responded quickly, placing a knee on the player's good shoulder as Ali pressed down the best she could on his injured side with the melting packet of frozen peas and what looked to be a sirloin steak she'd found lying by Rory's side.

She looked up again at the woman in the corner and gave her a reassuring smile. "You did well to keep him flat and have his shoulder iced. What's your name?"

"Amber."

Her voice was so soft Ali strained to hear her. She seemed nice.

"Amber. That's a lovely name." She offered her another smile and then tipped her head in the direction she assumed was the kitchen. "Would you be able to get together a bag or a tea towel filled with as much ice as you can find?

Looking back at Rory, who had his eyes clenched tight with pain but was breathing more regularly, Ali kept her voice low and steady.

"Rory? You've bashed yourself up a bit more than we thought, so we're going to have to go to hospital, all right?" His eyes fluttered open in acknowledgment. "We're most likely going to put a plate on your clavicle, which will give you a sexy little scar, but hopefully it will get you playing for the final."

Rory smiled and made a move as if to sit up.

"Oh, no, you don't!" Aidan removed his knee from the player's shoulder and quickly pressed down on it with one of his hands.

"Stay down, Ror— Ali's got you covered on this one."

Ali looked up, sensing Aidan's eyes upon her. She caught her breath as their eyes met. Felt her teeth bite into her lower lip. He hadn't deemed her capable of taking a phone call half an hour ago, but now he was happy to let her take the proverbial driver's seat and bring Rory into surgery. Would wonders never cease?

"Do you know who's on the surgical staff at Teal-side?"

"Why? You're not up to it?"

Ali thinned her eyes, to assess if he was taunting her. His look was open, curious. It was not an attempt to catch her out. It was just a question.

Releasing Rory's shoulder, she gave herself a mental shake. She was going to have to stop being so distrustful. Keeping Aidan at arm's length was only going to be tough if she made it that way. She took a deep breath and decided to go with trust. It was the only way this "relationship" was going to work.

"I just thought we'd better see who was on at the hospital to make sure I don't push any noses out of joint. If they've got a shoulder specialist they'd be better placed to do the op. But I'm happy to do it if no one else is available."

"I'm not sure, but the paramedics can find out en route. They should be here any minute."

Aidan was impressed that Ali knew where to start and stop with her levels of treatment. It was clear her patient's health was paramount. Other surgeons liked the glory. Who *wouldn't* want to add award-winning North Stars player Rory Stiles to their tick-list of surgeries? Particularly when his place on the team could mean a win or lose in the final.

A thick lock of shimmering black hair had come loose from her ponytail and now hung across her right eye. He had to fight the distinctly unprofessional urge to reach up and brush it behind her ear. Just slip it back

into place before running his finger along her jawline.
Just like every colleague did for another. *Not!*

"Well, I'd prefer it if you do the surgery." His voice
was huskier than he'd hoped, but he continued anyway.
"It'll be better in the long run as you'll know exactly
what to do for follow-up. Let's get him stabilized at the
hospital and hope you can put the plate in tomorrow."

"We should probably see what the preliminary X-rays
show. The last thing Rory needs is inflammation pressuring the carotid."

"Absolutely—let's check everything. But regardless
of who's on staff at Tealside, I think you're the best
man—*woman*—for the job."

"You're positive you'd be happy for me to run with
this?"

"He's sure!" Rory croaked up at them, cracking a
crooked smile. "And would you two stop flirting over
me? It reminds me of the night I'm *not* going to be having with Amber."

Aidan resisted an urge to punch Rory in the arm.
They hadn't been flirting. They'd been speaking professionally. Cordially. Respectfully. Like workmates.

He chanced a glance at Ali, whose cheeks had
flushed crimson and who was busily chewing on her
exquisite apple-red lips. She didn't look happy.

Fine. Hands up! He'd been flirting.

In a professional manner.

It was about as close to flirting as he got, and Rory—
the team's king of leaving broken hearts in his wake—
ought to know.

It seemed everyone in the room was holding their
breath. Could the tension in the room get any higher?

Aidan felt a sigh of relief escape his lips as Amber

ran into the room, lugging a pillowcase filled nearly to the brim with ice cubes.

"I found an ice machine in the games room. Is this enough?"

If ever there was a time to be grateful to ride in the back of an ambulance it was now. Ali kept her hand on Rory's shoulder as a paramedic took his obs and gave him a couple of milligrams of painkiller. She'd asked him not to dose him up to the hilt before they knew what procedures they would need to carry out tonight.

An unfortunate side effect of feeling better was that Rory had got chatty. *Real* chatty.

"Yeah, he's definitely into you, Harty."

"Who?" She could play dumb for a bit, right?

"Tate! I've never seen him so weird. Man, earlier on the field I thought he was going to have a fit!"

Ali stiffened. "Because a woman was treating you?"

"No, Doc. You got it all wrong." Rory waved for her to come closer, even though he didn't lower the decibel level of his voice an iota. "He *fancies* you."

"Don't be daft!" She swatted at him, feeling not a little mortified that the paramedic was quite merrily enjoying their conversation.

"You know," Rory continued, clearly enjoying the topic, "you could always take on The Monk as a special project..."

"The Monk? And that is..." She chanced a glance over at the paramedic, who was feigning deafness. It must make the earwigging easier.

"Dr. *Taaaaaaaate*..." Rory drawled, the meds taking him swinging toward Sleepyville.

The Monk, huh? Interesting... She had pegged Aidan for one of those "girl at every away game" types. With

looks like his and that bobby-dazzler of a smile...
Hmm... Maybe being judgmental didn't suit her either.

"We've been trying to set him up for *aaaaages*.
Never takes, though."

"Never takes what?"

Rory's lids began a losing war to stay open.

For heaven's sake. Don't fall asleep on me now!

Ali pressed her hands to the bench of the ambulance
to steady herself as it slowed and turned into what must
be the hospital forecourt.

Her mind flicked back into work mode. Exactly
where it should have been for the ten-minute ride. She'd
need to get X-rays, make some quick decisions about
how quickly Rory did or didn't need surgery, and then
try to grab some sleep if she was going to be in theater
in a few hours' time.

The ambulance pulled to a stop and the back doors
virtually burst open to reveal none other than a grinning Aidan Tate.

"Hey, look! It's Beauty and the Beast!"

Ali's jaw dropped open, then clapped shut as Rory
gave her a heavy-lidded *I told you so* wink.

Aidan gave Ali a sidelong glance. The X-rays were
looking the opposite of good. She'd been right all along.
A preventative op would have prevented the fracture
compound and the carotid arterial pinch. It might easily
have been fatal. In practice, he preferred to steer clear
of surgery unless it was necessary, but in this case he
should've known Rory would push the boundaries. This
year's final meant the world to the team.

Ali's profile was giving nothing away. Nor was she.
She had been tight-lipped since their arrival at the
hospital.

"Fancy a coffee?"

"I think some sleep might be in order." Ali continued to frown at the X-rays, then asked, "What time did you say the theater is booked?

"Six a.m."

They both glanced at the clock hanging above the X-ray light board. Just gone midnight.

"Right. I'd better head home. Is there a taxi rank anywhere?"

She looked around the room as if it might offer her an answer. Anywhere but at him. What had he done now?

"Oh, didn't I say?"

Ali looked at him blankly.

"I took the liberty of organizing one of the on-call surgeons' rooms for you here. Unless the idea of a resident's room makes you run for the hills?"

"No, that sounds fine." Her expression was inscrutable. "I'm not fussy. So long as they've got a toothbrush and some scrubs I could borrow."

"Great. I've already popped some things in there for us."

"Us?" Her tone spoke volumes. The not-a-chance-in-hell variety.

"Yes. Us. I was hoping to watch the master at work." He crossed his heart and gave her a silly grin. "I'm not being a control freak, if that's what you're worried about—honest!"

She quirked an eyebrow, unconvinced. He had to admit the idea of spending a night in such close proximity to Ali had set off blaring sirens, warning that staying in the Pal Zone would be tough. He mentally crossed his fingers.

"I'll be on my best behavior. Scout's Honor."

"Well…" She eyed him suspiciously, arms firmly crossed. "How high did you get in the Scouts?"

"Explorer." Actually, he'd been a nerd, and had stayed on as part of the Scout Network for a long time, but she didn't need to know that.

"That's *it*? My cousin made it to Scout Network, and he was a city boy. No deal."

"Fine—you got me. I stayed on until I started med school. Three years of Scout Network. You can trust me." He made the Scout's Honor sign again for good measure.

"Dr. Tate?" Ali's lips began to shift into a grin. "Were you trying to look *cool* by saying you stopped at Explorer?"

"Maybe." He returned the grin, then pointed toward the wall clock. "T-minus six hours, Doctor. It's time to start counting sheep."

Aidan swung his arm in a dramatic *This way, madam*, gesture and felt his lips thin as she passed him. Staying in his own bunk when all the others had been filled with scouts was easy. Doing the same with Ali not a meter above him…?

Maybe the visitor's chair in Rory's room would be a better choice.

"And we're ready to close."

Ali stepped back from the surgical table, grateful that it had been a straightforward op. The plate and screw fixation were in, and would hopefully allow for early mobilization. If Rory had listened to them he would've been looking at four to six weeks' recovery for the fracture— now he was looking at closer to three months, but with a better guarantee of proper bone union.

The big North v South match was barely beyond

the three-month marker. When he was up for it she was going to give him one meaty lecture. As the surgical team moved in to close she glanced over at the observation room, where Aidan was giving her a quick thumbs-up and a grin.

Despite her best intentions to totally block him out, she felt like warm sunbeams were shooting out from her chest. Good grief! Since when did she need a thumbs-up approval rating on a simple plate-and-screw surgery?

"Do you think Dr. Tate's going to wait for Rory in Recovery?" a nurse asked quietly.

"You'll have to ask him yourself. I'm not his keeper."

Ali hoped her words hadn't sounded as sharp as they had in her head. Keeping tabs on Aidan was most definitely not on her "to-do" list. Especially now, after she'd gone into the bunkroom he'd booked for them and then he had never shown up. Not that sleeping would've come easily if he *had* been in the same room. But even so she had felt the loss of not being with him.

Getting up for surgery had been the only way to clear herself of the growing realization that Aidan Tate was making an impact on her. A big one.

Surgery was the one zone where she was able to shut everything else out—thank God. But one thumbs-up and a rakish smile later here she was, back in the land of reminding her knees that the rest of her body would like to remain upright.

"Sorry," the nurse continued. "It's just that he's never stayed with a patient overnight before, so I assumed…"

The poor woman's voice petered out as Ali's eyes widened. Then the nurse carried on, as if Ali had told her talking about Aidan was her absolute favorite thing in the whole wide world. Maybe it was. Was it…?

"For a little while we all thought he was going to stay in the surgeon's bunk with *you*!"

"Oh?" Ali replied non-committally.

"Don't worry!" The nurse laughed. "We've all tried to break the impenetrable veneer of 'The Monk.' No one's managed. Keeps himself to himself. But he's about as dishy as they come, don't you think?"

Ali kept her eyes on the vacant spot in the observation room where he had been. *Yes. Yes, she did think.* Not that she was going to tell the nurse. "I hadn't really noticed. He's all yours!"

Ali left the theater quickly, heading back to the locker room where she'd hung her clothes. She needed to change, check on Rory in Recovery and then get back to Aidan. *No!* That wasn't right. Get back to work. *Work.* Where she was learning new things. From Aidan. Like finding out that she could reach a ridiculously divine orgasm when he did those soft kisses and silky-smooth caresses all along her—

"Lockhart?"

Speak of the devil.

"Coming!" Ali tugged her jumper down, grabbed her bag and careened out the door, narrowly avoiding colliding into one very familiar chest.

Aidan steadied her, his brown eyes seeking an explanation for her frenetic behavior. She shrugged herself out of his hold and headed for Recovery. Minimal contact meant minimal heat detonations in her erogenous zones, right?

"Lockhart…?"

She stopped and gave Aidan a pointed look. He was interrupting her No Touching pep talk to herself.

"You all right?" He leaned against the doorframe in that really annoying I'm-a-deeply-sexy-supermodel way. "Want to come to the gym with me later? You look like you've got some energy to burn."

A flash of white teeth and a wink followed the statement.

Ali looked Aiden straight in the eye and blew a steadying breath between her lips. Gym buddy or not—he was asking for it. Her fingers were curled into tight fists and she could feel adrenaline begin to charge her. Four weeks into her time Up North and she'd managed to avoid this sort of confrontation with Aidan, but here they were, face-to-face, and she was on the attack.

You can do this. Piece of cake. She wriggled her fingers into new fists and did a couple of quick hops back and forth. *You will do this.* She would be ready to go in just...three, two, one—and in an explosive shift of her weight she began to kick as if her life depended on it.

"Is that it?" Aidan grinned back at her, completely unfazed by her power moves. "That's all you're good for? C'mon. You're worse than last week. Give it to me, Harty. Harder."

He wanted hard? She could do hard. Ali shifted her weight again and gave the punching bag all she had.

Aidan barely blinked. "C'mon, Lockhart! You call those stitches on Mack's forehead today *butterfly*? Dr. Frankenstein could have done a better job!"

"Oh, you want to play dirty, do you?" *Bam!* She gave the punching bag a satisfying whack.

"A double specialty in physio and orthopedic surgery? Peanuts. A chimpanzee could've topped that."

Bash!

"And I had to rewrap Jonesey's wrist today—twice!"

Biff! That was a lie and he knew it. This was getting to be fun!

"You kiss like a girl."

What?

She hadn't really heard him above the blare of the music. Was he dissing her kissing? Ali went still, leveled her gaze at him and shook her head slowly.

Now that was *low*. They'd both been very diligent about avoiding any mention of "That Night…" But if that was how he wanted to play it—

"I kiss like a *woman*." The depth of her assertion surprised even herself. She watched Aidan's eyes widen as hers narrowed. She twisted her body into an almighty whirling dervish spin and kicked the bag with all her might. *"Don't mock my kissing!"*

Ali was flat on her back before she could say *boo*. The rest of the kickboxing class fell silent, the air thick with the thump-pump of dance tracks blaring out from the speakers.

Had she said *kissing*? Aidan dropped to Ali's side, horrified. Her footing must have gone wrong in the kick and she'd ended up flat on her back. Everything slipped into a horror-film-style slow motion. *This was his fault.* He had pushed her. Just like he'd pushed his girlfriend to go snorkeling all those years ago. *Try new things! Reach for new limits!* What the hell was wrong with him?

Someone turned off the music and flicked on the overhead lights. Ali was out cold.

This isn't happening…this isn't happening!

His mouth went dry as he tried to gather his wits. No blood pooling at the back of her head. Good. He felt along her neck and the back of her head for any obvious injuries. Ali's pure blue eyes remained firmly shut.

He cupped her face in his hands, frantically repeating her name again and again, his thumb caressing her forehead, her cheek. He'd totally been lying when he'd told her she meant nothing to him. He'd come to rely on her these past few weeks. More than that. He couldn't get enough of her. Every minute of every day he wanted to be with Ali and find out more. More about what made her tick. More about what she liked...didn't like.

All of his medical skills seemed to abandon him. He was a *doctor*, for God's sake. Shouldn't he be checking her eyes? Her obs? Doing something medical?

This sort of injury happened in team practice and in games often enough—a person being knocked to the ground so hard the brain's electrical patterns were disrupted—and they always treated head injuries with intense scrutiny. The ramifications of a bad blow were huge. There could be a rupture to the brain's membrane or to the brain tissue, which could lead to arterial damage, which in turn could lead to brain damage or a fatal blood clot.

She could die.

Aidan lifted his eyes up to the ceiling as if it would give him some answers. *What had he done?* Critically injured the one person who was beginning to make him feel alive again?

"Aidan?"

Ali's voice was a low croak, her eyes slowly working their way open, making an immediate connection with his own. There had never been a pair of eyes he was more happy to see.

"Ali! Can you hear me? Don't move your head."

He didn't care if she saw the gloss of tears in his eyes. She was okay! Maybe he would tell her how his feelings were changing. How spending time with her made him feel like being a whole person again. A whole person who felt every single minute of the past few weeks had been supercharged with vitality…life.

"Follow my finger. Just follow the arc of my finger."

Ali's eyes didn't move. They stayed locked with his. A wash of emotion sent his heart lurching into his throat.

"You're right," Ali whispered.

"About what?" Aidan ran his fingers through her hair—he couldn't help it. Every pore in his body wanted to look after this woman, to care for each intensely passionate, über-talented and deeply sexy cell of her.

"My kicking could do with some improvement!" Ali flashed him a cheeky grin and popped up from the floor, her hands already in sparring position, feet hopping back and forth. *Float like a butterfly…sting like an Ali.*

"Alexis Lockhart! Were you *faking* being knocked out?"

Another broad smile met his indignant question.

"You're lucky I don't pop you one in the kisser."

He pushed himself up from the floor, his chest burning with a whole new mix of feelings. Indignation was winning the battle, but she had properly frightened him. And made him realize something very clearly. *He cared.* He cared about Alexis Lockhart. This was much more than a professional relationship to him. That didn't sit well. Not one teeny, tiny speck.

"C'mon, Tate." Ali jiggled her head from side to side, oblivious to the turmoil she'd created in his heart. "What did you expect? You've been doing this for years and I've been doing it for a few weeks. I've got to work with my assets, and tonight I aced psyching you *right* out of the park! *Ha!* You should see yourself. You're white as a ghost!"

"And your point is…?" Aidan knew hands on hips

wasn't his best look, but he had to restrain himself from shaking her—or, more to the point, from pulling her into his arms and telling her never to do such a stupid thing again.

He'd been nanoseconds away from smothering her in kisses and sweet nothings when she'd opened her eyes. Heaven had been merciful and saved him that embarrassment. These were playground tricks. He should've seen it coming a mile away—particularly having witnessed how easily she could spar verbally with the lads. He couldn't *believe* he'd been on the brink of telling her he *cared*. Lucky break.

"No point—just saying. A girl's gotta do…" Ali stopped herself, suddenly very aware that there was a lot more going on in Aidan's eyes than superficial concern. Her prank had really shaken him.

What was *that* all about? She'd thought their whole joshing, jokey mates thing had been working pretty well in terms of keeping the sexual tension at bay. At the very least it had meant they could spend more time together without constantly being under threat of being arrested by the kissing police. Maybe she'd pushed too hard. It didn't feel right to know she'd hurt him.

"Let's say we even out the playing field, seeing as you're obviously the kickboxing master." Ali began unraveling the tape he'd strapped her into at the beginning of class. "I've done your kickboxing malarkey for quite a few weeks now. I think it's time you did something *I'm* good at." She sized him up, hoping her heavy-lidded, high-browed gaze would make him a bit nervous.

Nope. Steady as they came. The "Great Wall of Tate" face.

It was time to pull out the big guns. "Let's just see if you're up to matching a bit of girl power."

"And that would be what, exactly?" He crossed his arms, visibly dubious that she could come up with anything that would get her one up on him.

"Apart from dance injury medicine, which I already know you stink at?" She didn't really—but they were still sparring. Just a little…

"And cooking, which we know *you* stink at?" Aidan added, beginning to enjoy their tête-à-tête.

She spread her hands out in front of him as if presenting him with a sign. "Ninety continuous minutes of hot yoga."

The smug expression immediately dropped from his face. "Hot what?"

"You heard me. You wouldn't be afraid of leaving your comfort zone, would you? Hot yoga. You and me." She made the *I see you* gesture with her fingers. "After practice tomorrow. No more of this namby-pamby kickboxery."

She spun toward the door with a small sniff, rubbed the back of her head—which she *had* actually conked a bit—and flounced away the best she could in her trainers and sweat-soaked gym gear. *Hot yoga. That'll separate the boys from the men.*

Ten minutes later, in the privacy of the men's locker room shower, Aidan let the shakes he knew he needed to purge begin. He pressed his hands against the tile wall and let the water stream down his head and back. Seeing Ali lying on the floor like that had been a knife in the heart. Nothing short of pure bravura had helped him keep up their light-hearted banter.

He'd never even had the chance to see Mary's body. Nor had he had a chance to propose. Sensible as ever, he'd wanted to wait until toward the end of their holiday, to make sure they got on in every type of scenario. They'd made it through school, then uni—separate ones, she'd wanted to teach—and she'd waited patiently for him when he'd gone off to medical school. She had been his steady-as-they-came girl. The ring and her body had both been washed away, along with God knew what or who else, when the storm had struck.

Aidan lifted his face up into the stream of water, willing the shower to flush away the sting of tears teasing at his nostrils. This was the closest he'd come to crying about that day, and he didn't know if he could handle opening that particular door. It had been well over five years ago, but the shock he'd felt at seeing Ali lying there today had brought it all back to the fore. He couldn't lose another person—not one that he cared about.

He pulled his head out of the steaming water, blinked away the droplets and looked around the stall, as if the tiles might start explaining the situation to him.

Was this real? Was he really beginning to care about Ali? Had their being together developed into something deeper than the raw attraction he knew they felt for one another?

His body reminded him of their physical connection every time he saw her afresh. There was no getting away from that. But they had sensibly and proactively reshaped the sexy tension between them into the perfect cocktail of—in turn—ignoring each other, taking jabs at one another's medical practices and spending just about every waking minute they had together. As if it were a means of constant checking that the other person wasn't going back on their deal to keep things professional.

They hadn't so much as shared a goodnight kiss. It was hardly as if he was falling in love with her.

His breath caught in his throat.

Was he?

Nah. She was a good-time girl. Of course he respected her professionally, but it was easy enough to see that the girl didn't do long-term anything. Just like him. A perfect match.

Aidan blew a raspberry into the stream of water and loaded his hand with a good-sized squirt of shower gel. She'd just given him a bit of a fright. Served him right for pushing her so hard.

Hot yoga, eh? *Bring it on, Lockhart!*

CHAPTER FIVE

AIDAN WASN'T ENTIRELY sure he'd be able to unfold his legs out of the pretzel shape he'd somehow cajoled them into. Ali hadn't been kidding when she'd said ninety minutes of hot yoga would be a challenge. Walking out upright would be a feat at this juncture. And she had upped the potential for humiliation stakes by inviting as many lads from the team as she could. *Cross-training, my eye!*

He looked round at the players who'd agreed to come along and saw similar expressions of consternation on their faces. It was impossible to stop a smile from forming when his eyes landed on her. There in the center of the class, looking as Buddha-calm as could be, her legs folded into a perfect lotus position, rail-straight spine and gently bowed head, was his ebony-haired colleague.

The class might have been meant to center him, but ever since Ali had arrived in his life he felt as if the earth's surface had shifted into a wobble board. She was shaking some cast-in-stone positions he'd held. Like not mixing business and pleasure, for one. And that was a *big* one.

"You still lining things up with your chi, there, Tatey?"

Aidan looked up at Mack—one of the players—who was offering him a hand to get up. He grabbed it gratefully.

"Or were you in the Lockhart Zone?"

"What?" Aidan dropped the young player's hand as if it was a burning coal, making a quick check to see if anyone had been listening.

"Tate, you transparent slice of manhood!" Mack's eyes were bright with delight.

Aidan steered them toward the changing room—thankfully on the opposite side of the studio from the women's.

"I don't have the slightest clue what you're talking about, Mack."

"You're joshing me, aren't you, Doc?" Mack punched him playfully in the arm with one of his meat-cleaver-sized fists. That would bruise. "As one of the Inseparables, you don't have a clue?"

"The Inseparables?" Now Aidan actually *didn't* know what Mack was talking about.

"You and Harty. Do you think the rest of us are blind?"

Mack waited for him to catch up but Aidan refused to play along, giving him a blank look in return as he pushed through the doors into the changing room.

"Always with each other? At training? Out of training? You don't get one without the other? C'mon, Doc. You and your last assistant never hung out that much. Just how many 'work dinners' does a guy need?"

"It's the lead-up to the finals." Aidan pressed his lips together. He wasn't so sure he liked where this was going.

"Ali and Aidan, sitting on a tree…" Mack was really getting into the swing of things now.

"All right! I get your point! Go take a shower, you rank beast."

"Hey, Aidan!" another player shouted from the doorway. "Harty wants to know if she should wait for you after to grab some dinner?"

Mack shot Aidan a knowing look, snapped him with a towel and ran toward the showers, hooting with triumphant glee.

Cringeworthy didn't even *begin* to cover it. The half dozen or so players who'd joined them for the class all turned to him, waiting for his answer.

Of *course* he wanted to meet her for dinner. And pudding. And every single meal in between now and the end of her three-month contract. Not that he'd tell them— or her. But blowing her off in front of the guys...? That wasn't cool.

He scanned their expectant faces. This truly was a no-win situation. Blow her off and retain his 'The Monk' moniker, or accept the invitation and open himself up to some top-rate razzing.

He was man enough. He could do this.

"Tell her I'll meet her outside in fifteen. I need to talk over some of your body fat charts with her." *Good cover, Aidan.*

Whoops of delight mingled with some not so subtle catcalls as Aidan elbowed his way to his locker to grab a towel. Insufferable, these lads. Couldn't a fellow go out for an entirely innocent meal with a colleague?

As he tugged off his T-shirt he thought of Ali doing the same thing on that faraway night at the airport hotel, her eyes alive with desire. His body responding to her every move.

Maybe his thoughts weren't so innocent. He'd have to put a stop to their after-hours "mates" thing. And soon.

"You're acting weird tonight." Ali twisted her fork through her clam *spaghettini* and waggled the noodles at Aidan accusingly.

"*You're* acting weird," he retorted.

"Aidan." She put on her best schoolmarm voice. "I am not going to play *No, you are* with you all night. What's going on, weirdo?" She popped the forkful of food into her mouth with a smirk.

Aidan sighed and pushed back from the table. He wasn't hungry, and that meant only one thing. He was about to do something he didn't feel right about. The only way he could keep this relationship verging on anything close to professional was to put a halt to these out-of-work get-togethers. They could cloak them in any guise they wanted—exercise, going over notes, getting a bite to eat, watching replays of the game—but at the end of the day he and Ali were spending time together because they liked it. *He liked it.*

Even watching television seemed an empty experience if she wasn't there, wondering aloud why on earth he had to keep flicking the channels so much or have the volume on "so freakin' loud." How this had come to pass in a few short weeks was beyond him, but if the team was calling them The Inseparables they weren't far off base.

"Hey, what's wrong?" Ali's expression was genuinely concerned now, nothing remaining of her goofy grin.

"You want it straight up or watered down?"

A small crease formed between her eyes. He didn't blame her. He was being elusive, and the only person his behavior was protecting was himself.

Nipping this thing with Ali in the bud was the kindest way to go. She might as well go forward with her eyes wide open.

"It's nothing, really..." He dove in, avoiding eye contact by rearranging his ravioli into a poor recreation of a St. George's Cross. "The guys were just giving me some guff after our 'cross-training' and they seem to think we're a couple. I just don't want them to get the wrong idea—you know...with the final coming up and all. *Focus.* They need to focus. *I* need to focus—make sure they don't get injured—and *you* need—"

Quit talking.

She put her fork down quietly. "I see."

"None of this hanging out together has been romantic, right?" He raised his eyes hopefully.

"Of course not!" She huffed away the very idea. "What on earth would make them think I fancy you?"

Ali regretted the words the moment they were out of her mouth. There were about five gabillion things that would make the team, let alone Aidan, think she fancied him—but she really didn't need to put them in outline form for him to analyze.

"That came out wrong."

"You think?" Aidan's voice was dryer than the Sauvignon Blanc he'd just taken a sip of.

"Soooo..." She folded her serviette and laid it on the table. Her appetite had been properly stemmed. No wine, and now no pudding. "What exactly do you propose we do to set them right?"

She glared at Aidan. This was completely his fault. If he hadn't sent her that Cosmopolitan all those weeks ago none of this would be happening. Right?

Wrong.

It most likely wouldn't have mattered *where* she'd met Aidan Tate. He knocked her for six on or off the field. They had chemistry, and trying to ignore it was going to be a Herculean task.

"Well, we can't exactly stop working together—Coach is insisting you stay." Aidan frowned.

"Wow. Thanks for the vote of confidence," Ali snapped back.

Unexpectedly, Aidan laughed. "I suppose this sort of thing isn't really a problem at your clinic, with all those girlies floating about in their tutus."

"*Nothing* at my clinic is like being here," Ali grumbled.

"Hey." Aidan reached across and gave her hand a squeeze. "It's not *all* bad up here, is it?"

"Better watch it. What if someone from the team sees you?"

Ali pulled her hand back, knowing she was milliseconds away from weaving her fingers through his, finding comfort in the warmth of his hand. But comfort was the last thing she could expect from Aidan. He was making sure she knew that—loud and clear.

"C'mon, Ali. Don't be like that."

"Like what? There's obviously nothing going on between us—so we're good." She gave him a cheery smile. "I'll get the bill. Or do you want to go Dutch so no one gets the wrong idea?"

"Now you're just being childish."

"Childish? Really? I'm trying to play this game by your ever-changing rulebook, Aidan. Apologies if I'm not managing to keep up."

"I'm just trying to make this easy."

Aidan gave her a pointed look with those dark brown eyes of his. Eyes that were just far too close to those deliciously strong cheekbones, so prominent you could trace them oh-so-easily straight down to his mouth. She felt her focus narrowing. He really had a lovely mouth...

An unwelcome warmth started to make itself known between her legs. She shifted in her seat. And all of a sudden it came to her—clear as day. She had the perfect solution. "I've got it."

"What?"

"How we fix this 'thing.'" Her fingers hung in the air in quotes as her heart began to race with excitement. This could *really* work! She looked him square in the eye. "The easiest thing to do would be to start having sex again, so we can quit pretending that being pals is what we both want. I like working with you—but this whole buddy thing is a farce. We should be... I don't know... booty call buddies instead."

Ali clapped her hand over her mouth, astonished she'd said the words out loud.

Aidan sat silently for a moment, just watching her. He looked down at his hands, then back up at her, his face a picture of sobriety.

"All right, then."

"What?" Ali's heart-rate took off. "What *exactly* are you saying all right to?"

She couldn't tear her eyes away from Aidan as she waited for him to answer. Had she—*they*—gone completely raving mad? Were they going to *do* this? Give being a couple a try? *No.* Booty call buddies. Having secret assignations in the night. This wasn't part of the plan. But feeling alive was, and if there was one thing she knew it was that being in Aidan's arms made her feel ridiculously alive. So...since that was the case... some regular sex might make it easier to ignore him at work. *Maybe.*

"Let's do it." He nodded his head decisively. "On one condition."

"Of course there's a condition." It was all Ali could do not to slap the table in frustration. "Jeez Louise, Aidan! Is *nothing* straightforward with you?"

He started laughing. *"Jeez Louise?"*

"Yeah—Jeez Louise." She started to giggle along

with him. "Now, stop your laughing and tell me what your stupid condition is."

"How do you know it's stupid?"

"Because it's a condition on having yours truly as a friend with benefits—and with half the team proposing to me on a regular basis that's just stupid. Like you."

Maybe she should poke him in the arm for good measure. She was enjoying this now. *Friends with benefits.* She'd never done that before. Tick! An unexpected add-on to her list of new activities. Would she regret this later? Most likely. Then again—nothing ventured...

"We keep it like it was at the airport."

"What? No names? I think we're a bit late for that."

"I was thinking more along the lines of what goes on on the road stays..." He let her fill in the blanks.

Hmm... She could see where he was coming from. Getting non-stop shtick from the team could be tricky if they went public about things.

"Not even my gal pals Down South?" Not that she really had anyone to fit that role—but being a sort-of couple with the sexiest man alive...? She needed to tell *someone*!

"Not even them. Loose lips and all that..."

"Until when?"

"The end of your contract."

"Then this 'friendship' ends?" She indicated the two of them with a quick flick of her hand.

"Precisely."

Now Aidan was smiling, as well. One of those sultry come-hither numbers. Tingles of anticipation began to slow-dance across her nerve endings. She needed to get this show on the road, *stat*.

"Do you want it in writing?"

"I can think of quite a few other ways we can seal the deal." Aidan gave her a decidedly saucy look.

Ali tucked her lips in, then pushed them out decisively. If she'd thought she was numb to the world's delights before she'd come Up North, she was swinging giddily straight to the other side of the pendulum.

"Very well, then." She extended her hand across the table to shake on it. "I'm ready when you are, Suit."

"Miss Cosmopolitan."

He took her hand carefully, almost studiously in his, bent and pressed his lips upon it before looking up from her fingers with a naughty, naughty, grin.

"Waiter! Check, please."

To have said the walk back to Aidan's flat was fraught with sexual tension would have been putting it mildly. She'd never had such an openly agreed upon fling without strings. Then again, she had never physically ached to be with someone as much as she desired Aidan. *Never.*

After her mum had died she'd pretty much perfected being one of life's cooler customers. A few dates here. A few dates there. By choice she'd never had anything to really dig her teeth into. Not to say that she hadn't bitten Aidan's shoulder, trying to stop herself from unleashing a non-hotel-friendly howl of rapture. Or scratched his back with her nails. Maybe just a little. And he had groaned with pleasure.

Oh, she was in trouble. If her all-over body tingling was anything to go by, the veneer was threatening to crack.

No. No it wasn't. This was just overdue, right? A sexy encounter. It would make everything easier. More relaxed.

Aidan brushed his hand against the back of hers,

then wove his fingers through hers as they virtually race-walked through the narrow brick passage leading to their riverside complex. A whoosh of electricity shot through her.

Long, long overdue.

She snuck a peek at him. Blimey, he was good-looking. Would it be acceptable to just jump on him right now? There weren't that many people walking along the river on this cold March night. Maybe here, in the dark of the passageway? A perfect place for secret lovers to share a kiss. Or a thousand. Not that they *were* lovers. They were— Well... She didn't know what they were. She couldn't remember ever wanting someone as much as she had ached for Aidan's touch. And then to have to put it on hold for the past few weeks... She'd needed every single one of those kickboxing classes. Aidan had been right. She had energy to burn.

"Everything all right?" He gave her hand a quick squeeze before letting go of it to dig a key out of his pocket.

Ali felt her entire body tingling with desire. She watched as he put the key in the door and licked her lips in anticipation of what was to come.

They were here. Outside the door of his flat. In a manner of microseconds she could start ripping off his clothes and sating the hunger she hadn't appreciated just how much she'd been stemming. Everything was more than all right. Everything was set to just get better and better. As long as she could keep her heart in check everything would be perfect.

"Wow." Ali wasn't sure if she'd whispered the word or just mouthed it.

"You can say that again." Aidan nuzzled into her

neck and threw in some kisses along her shoulder for good measure. *Yum.*

"Woooooowwwwuhhh!" She whooshed the sound into his ear, gave him a few kiss-nibbles along his jawline, then turned her head toward the starlit view. "Do you think people can see in?"

Aidan was still holding her up against his floor-to-ceiling windows, her legs wrapped around his waist, her body as bare as the day she'd come into the world. Just like his. She felt as if they'd just had naughty hotel sex, minus the hotel.

"Not at three in the morning."

Ali unfolded her legs and started gathering up her erratically scattered clothes.

"Is that what time it is? I had no idea. What time do we have to be at the stadium?"

"Cool your jets. Coach Stone called me yesterday, and as it's Saturday they're doing some sort of cross-country run in the morning, then meeting with their nutritionist and calling it a day at lunchtime. We're just on call tomorrow. Today." He corrected.

"Thanks for telling, boss." She glared at him, did a quick calculation and dropped her clothes back on the floor. "Sooooo..." She sauntered back over to him with a sexual confidence she'd never known she possessed. "We've got time for a snooze."

"We've got time for a lot of things."

Aidan grabbed her by the hand and pulled her over to his big ol' Man Bed, complete with dark navy duvet and sheets in that weird Merlot color men always seemed to like. His interior décor skills, however, were the least of her concerns. Everyone had to have a flaw. Let that be his.

She snuggled into his arms as if she'd been doing it

every day for the past five years. What a sea change! She would never have dreamed it was possible to have such open and trusting sex with someone—let alone hanging around for a snuggle...

Ali tugged Aidan's top arm more snugly round her waist and wove her fingers through his. Safe and secure. That was how she felt. Which was hilarious, considering it was the last thing she should be feeling with this obvious commitment-phobe. The hours they'd just shared had definitely topped their time at the airport. Aidan seemed to know her body better than she did. Intimacy with him was— *Rewind!* This wasn't intimacy. It was what they'd agreed on: a couple of months of blissful commitment-free sex. And then—and then what?

Then you move on to something else, like you always do.

Besides, who knew what the world would be waiting to throw on her plate next week, let alone in a few months' time?

Aidan's breath slowed and with it the cadence of her own breathing steadied. *Right now*, she thought as she felt herself slipping off to sleep... *Right now is good.*

"It's a gorgeous day out there." Aidan took a slurp of Ali's thick-as-tar version of coffee and winced. Blimey. If he judged her coffee in the same vein as her lovemaking there didn't seem to be a single thing this woman didn't do by halves. "What do you say I take you on a tour of the River Teal?"

"Are there footpaths?" Ali raised an interested eyebrow and took a deep drink from her coffee mug without a trace of a flinch. She was clearly made of tougher stuff than he was.

"Miles of them. So I thought it would be more fun

if we went by bike. There's a rental shop just round the corner—or, if you like, you could go wild and buy one."

"Ah..." Ali's enthusiastic expression cooled.

"There's a really nice gastropub about ten or fifteen miles down from here—straight along the river. We could earn ourselves a really nice lunch."

"Anything we could *walk* to? I'm game for a hike!"

"It's flat, if that's what's got you all frowny."

"I'm not worried about not being able to make it, Aidan. I just wondered if there were any good walks instead."

Aidan hesitated. There was something going on here that wasn't about foot or cycle paths.

"There are loads of walks, but the White Hart is a really special place—I'd love to take you there. It's great to approach it from the riverside."

"Maybe another time." Ali peered out the window and pointed out some nonexistent clouds. "Looks like the weather could turn at any time. We wouldn't want to be stuck out in bad weather in March."

"Dr. Ali Lockhart—if I didn't know better I would think you didn't know how to ride a bike."

From the wounded expression that immediately appeared on her face Aidan guessed he'd hit the nail on the head. He reached across and gave her arm a reassuring rub.

"Not to worry. I can teach you how to ride. With all of your yoga panache you should pick it up easily."

"No." Her voice was brittle and she gave him a look laced with nothing less than gritty ire. "I know how to ride a bike, thanks. I just don't *want* to ride a bike."

"Hey, you." Aidan came out from behind the kitchen island and gave her arm a gentle squeeze. "We don't have to do anything you don't want to, but from what

I've seen you're game for just about anything. What's so off-putting about jumping on a bicycle?"

Ali fought the urge to turn away from him and pressed her lips tightly shut. It was her go-to reaction whenever anyone tried to get closer—to "talk things out." She didn't do close. How could Aidan come anywhere near understanding how utterly hollowed out she'd felt when her mum had been taken from her? She trusted Aidan implicitly on an intimate sexual level. Could she trust him to understand the workings of her heart?

She pressed her eyes shut for a count of three, then opened them up. Yup. He was still there, a gentle smile of encouragement playing on his lips. Maybe it would be good for her. Part of the go-on-the-road psychological reboot she was trying to give herself. If she told Aidan, perhaps she could leave all of the grief she felt behind when she went back home. Not to mention the fact she felt a really overwhelming urge to tell him.

"My mum and I..." She paused and took a deep, steadying breath.

She shouldn't have gulped her coffee down so quickly. Then again, maybe the caffeine would help get everything out. Quickly.

She stared into her mug and began again. "I was raised by my mum. My dad turned out not to be 'The One' she thought he was, but she didn't let it get her down. She was a champion. An amazing woman who worked her socks off to make sure my dreams of becoming a dancer could be fulfilled."

She looked up at Aidan, who nodded at her to continue. He pulled over a chair and plonked himself in it. The gesture said: *I'm not going anywhere. I'm here for you.*

Ali fought the tingling prick of tears and continued.

In for a penny… "Anyway, my mum died of cancer when I was sixteen and—" She stopped, desperate to stem the sob that came with the memory. She swigged back a couple gulps of coffee and went on. "A few days after she died… As you can imagine, I wasn't really operating in the real world, but she'd made me promise that no matter what I would continue with my dancing. She believed in me and was convinced I'd be a prima ballerina one day. So, a few days after she died I was riding my bike to rehearsal—I was attending the British Ballet School on scholarship—and—"

"What happened?" Aidan nodded for her to continue, giving her elbow a quick squeeze. He was there for her. He would help her carry the load.

"A couple of streets—" Ali grabbed the counter edge and dug her nails in until they went white from the pressure. "A couple of streets away from the school I was sideswiped by a lorry."

Aidan clapped a hand over his mouth. She could see he knew what was next, but she pointed to the scars on her knee anyhow.

"No more ballet for Ali." Her eyes met his.

"Oh, Ali, I am *so* sorry for your loss." And he looked as though he truly meant it."

"I just wish for my mum's sake I had become a dancer. Made her dream come true!"

"Wasn't it your dream, as well?"

"Yes, but—" She stopped, realizing she'd never really bothered to look at from that angle before. "I suppose once I found medicine I found something else I loved."

"Isn't that enough? Don't you think your mother would be bursting with pride to know her daughter not only overcame her accident but had the strength to be a—no, *the* leading specialist in dance injuries?"

"I hadn't really thought of it like that." Despite her best efforts, she felt tears fill her eyes. "I just miss her so much."

She abruptly cleared her throat and swiped at her eyes. This was all too close to the bone. Too much like opening up your heart to someone who was going to stick around. Neither she nor Aidan were going down that road, so she'd be best to cut this conversation off now.

"So. In answer to the question, Do I think a bike ride would be a fun thing to do? No, I really, *really* don't."

He gave her a sad smile and nodded his understanding, before putting a hand on her knee and rubbing his thumb along one of her scars.

Her gut instinct was to bridle. And then something inside her shifted. In a good way. For the first time it felt as though she was just *saying* the words she'd repeated again and again after losing so much. *I don't want to ride a bicycle.* Had she really meant them this time? Was she ready to tackle this demon?

Aidan leaned back against the counter with a studied look. "I can't even imagine how horrible that must've been, but I've got to ask—are you not bike-riding because you blame yourself for having the accident in the first place, or because you're scared?"

"How do you *do* that?" Ali couldn't believe her ears. "What?"

"Take something that's been gnawing me up from the inside out for a long time and boil it down to two simple questions?"

It was difficult to tell if she felt angry or relieved. As she sought answers in his eyes Ali felt her chest release its tight grip on her lungs and her shoulders dropped a little. Relaxed back into place.

"Probably because I'm not living it," Aidan replied. "Perspective is a whole lot easier if you're not the one busy slaying dragons."

Good point.

"Is that the voice of experience talking?"

"Perhaps." He shrugged. "We've all got demons stuffed in our closets, don't we?" He looked away for a moment, his eyes fixed on an invisible horizon, then turned back to her with a bright smile. "But I bet you'd look damn hot in dragon-slaying getup." He gave her a wink, grabbed her empty mug and moved to the sink to wash up.

Ali couldn't help herself. She smiled. A picture of herself in a warrior-princess outfit—or maybe a slinky chainmail number—flashed across her mind's eye. Sword in hand, fire-breathing dragon backing down as she fearlessly approached.

Her eyebrows moved closer together as she concentrated on Aidan's questions. *Yes.* Yes, she supposed she *did* blame herself, to an extent. Her mentor at the dance academy had spent countless hours assuring her that her mother would never have minded a jot. Her only goal had been to make sure Ali was happy. And yet here she was, still slaying dragons all by herself. No mum. No one she felt brave enough to open up her heart to.

She looked over at Aidan, giving the mugs a good scrub. Maybe she had a little help now. Could she go forward and let go of her unfulfilled dreams? Perhaps create some new ones?

Maybe.

Would never riding a bike again change the fact that

the plan they had spoken about again and again as her mother's health had failed would never be a reality?

Ali traced a figure-eight pattern along the tabletop. "Are these paths completely closed to traffic?"

"Completely," Aidan replied solidly, popping the clean mugs one by one onto the draining board. "And I've got two very large, deeply unattractive helmets and reflective vests we will *both* wear. At all times. Even at lunch."

"And does this gastropub you're talking about have sticky toffee pudding?" She had to hold out just a little bit. Didn't she?

"With honeycomb ice cream on the side."

"Now you're talking!"

Ali slid off of her stool and walked over to Aidan. She couldn't help it. She needed a hug. As if reading her mind, he turned away from the sink, slipped his arms around her waist and popped a little kiss on her forehead. She nestled up against his chest and let herself breathe him in. Friends gave each other a cuddle every now and again, right? Even friends who had spent the bulk of the night exploring one another's bodies in just about the most erotic way possible?

She stilled her own breathing. If you took away the physical attraction she had for him, she was still left with a huge mountain of respect. Professionally and— the more she was getting to know him—personally. Aidan's chin rested lightly on the top of her head and in the quiet of the morning she could hear his heartbeat.

Even though she knew this whole thing—whatever it was—was just "matey," she felt safe, cared for. Protected. Was this what it felt like to let someone in? Of course, there was a time limit with Aidan. They'd shaken hands on it. That kind of deal was binding. Just a couple of months. Just enough time to get ready to move on.

"Want to run over to yours and change?" Aidan moved his chin off of her head and took a glance at his watch. "I'll meet you by the river in ten minutes."

"And if after two minutes I decide I want to back out and come home...?"

"I've got a few unopened box sets waiting to be watched." He rubbed his palms together gleefully.

"What kind?"

"Zombies, intergalactic warzones and old Westerns."

Ali couldn't help the crinkle of dismay from appearing on her face. *Yuck!* Not her genres in any way. Okay. Deep breath. She could do this. Bike-riding it was.

"See you in ten."

CHAPTER SIX

"Do you see those swans up ahead? Lovely, aren't they?"

"Sure are!" Ali was laughing now.

Aidan had been playing the distraction game non-stop since they'd hit the bicycle path, and by this point he knew his psychological tactics were well and truly transparent.

He was proud of her. Seriously, right into the marrow of his bones proud. When they'd started out, just wheeling the bikes across the street at a traffic crossing, she had looked whiter than a ghost. Rosy cheeks and glittering blue eyes wouldn't even begin to describe the energy pouring from her now. He would like to think he'd had a small part in helping her, but she was a strong woman. She would've reached this place on her own eventually.

Sometimes getting a small push in the right direction was all you needed. Too bad *he* couldn't take a dose of the same medicine. Maybe then he'd be open to the possibility of love again. Too bad life just hadn't handed him the right cards.

He glanced across at Ali. She was grinning away at the swans circling at the river's edge. It was going to be hard to say goodbye when the time came.

"Pub's not too far beyond them."

"Aidan Tate! That's exactly what you said after the locks, after the chestnut trees, and after the ducks! I'm beginning to think this pub is a bit of fiction on your part."

Aidan looked at her as if he were aghast she could suggest such a thing. "I have done no such thing! Look." He pointed ahead as a gabled roof just started to become visible in the distance. "I can smell the sticky toffee from here. Race you?"

"You're on."

Ali would know if he let her win, so the only fair thing to do would be to give her a run for her money. Head bent, stomach muscles tightened, he began to press the pedals of his bike with all the welly he could muster.

"This has to be the gooiest pudding I've ever had." Ali put the spoon back in her mouth, knowing that until she had devoured every last drop of toffee she just wouldn't, in good conscience, be able to leave the table. It would be rude to the chef not to lick the plate absolutely clean. Fifteen miles on a bike—not ten!—was worth every calorie-loaded morsel.

"You could always eat the plate." Aidan's voice was ripe with sarcasm.

"Hey, mister!" Ali waggled the shiny clean spoon at him. "This whole thing was your idea. You should feel proud all of your brainwashing worked. The dragon has been slayed."

As she spoke the words she realized there just might be some truth in them. She would always miss her mother. Deeply so. But burying herself in her work would never bring her back, no matter how hard she tried. Nor would moving on every time she felt as if she just might be getting a friend—or in this case a lover. But she wasn't quite ready to go there yet. This "friends with benefits" thing would do for now. Even so, today felt like a bit of a breakthrough—almost as if she was looking at the world through a fresh lens.

"I'm delighted to hear it, O Warrior Princess." Aidan gave her a wink before trying to steal a bit more pudding. Unsuccessfully.

"Thank you." Ali locked eyes with him.

"For what? Letting you eat all of my pudding as well as your own?"

"Don't be coy. You know as well as I do I might never have ridden a bike again if it weren't for you."

Aidan leaned his elbows on the table, resting his chin on the weave of his fingers. "As much as I would love to bask in the glory of your leap forward in the cycling world, I am quite convinced the bulk of the credit lies on your side of the table."

"How do you work that out? You're the one who suggested the bike ride."

"You're the one who got on the bike."

Ali felt her lips stretch into a huge grin. "I did, didn't I?" She swiped the spoon in a Zorro-esque X gesture, scooped up the last bite of pudding and then airplaned it over to Aidan. "I suppose it'll still be a wait-and-see-what-happens when I get back to London...not so sure about the busy streets there. But I still think I owe you a thank-you."

"Well, this will do nicely." Aidan took the spoon from her hand and consumed the enormous mouthful in one fell swoop, eyes staying with hers as he finished

it with a satisfied cartoon gulp. "Are you looking forward to going back?"

Not really. Best dodge that one.

"It'll be interesting to see what my colleague has
done to my practice."

"That's a lot of trust to put into someone."

"Cole Manning is my Old Reliable in the friend department. We went to med school together."

"Surely you've got a stack of those?"

"No."

Aidan leaned back in his chair. "You sound pretty
certain about that."

Ali sighed and tipped her head into her hands, taking her time to run her thumbs along her temples before looking back up. This man was intent on digging
up all her old baggage today, wasn't he? She was in a
great mood, feeling proud, and churning up those dark
days, when she'd shut just about everyone who cared for
her out of her life... *Ugh*. She'd done enough dragon-
slaying for the day.

"I think I've done more than enough baring of my
soul today. Maybe it's time I turned the tables?" She
shot him an impish grin.

"Fancy some banoffee pie before we hit the road?
Potassium is good fuel!"

Ali laughed. "Nice conversation-changer, Tate!"

Fair enough. Maybe he didn't have any old baggage.
Then again...that was unlikely. Everyone had baggage—
it just came in different shapes and sizes. She'd play
along and give Aidan a break. She owed him one for
today. Big-time.

"I think I've probably eaten more than the entire ballet company at this one sitting! Ballerinas don't really

do puddings. Nor do gymnasts. It's been great being around people who eat!"

"What made you pick dance injuries as your specialty?"

"It sort of evolved, I guess. No. That's not right. I'd made my mum a promise. She dedicated her life to helping me reach *my* dream, so I thought it was only right that I help other dancers reach theirs. A karma balancer, I guess."

He nodded, eyebrows lifted with approval.

"So, you're totally on your own now?"

"Yup. That about sums it up! What about you?"

Now she really *did* need to switch the tables. Ali felt a fresh sting of tears tickling at the back of her throat. Their day together had been so great—it'd be a shame to mess it up now.

"Oh, you know…" Aidan looked off toward the fire burning in the far corner of the pub.

"No, I don't. That's why I asked you." Ali tried to be playful with her taunt but could see there was a lot of hidden history in those eyes of his. Not from anything she'd caused, but there was hurt lurking in there somewhere.

There was definitely more to this man than being an über-confident charm machine who picked up girls at airports. She'd learned that over and over again from the team. They respected him. Why on earth someone so talented, not to mention big and bouncy-balloon-gorgeous was single was beyond her.

"What do you say we race home, get back into bed and watch one of those box sets?" Aidan crumpled up his paper serviette and popped it on to the table.

And the crowd goes wild at yet another artful dodge by Dr. Aidan Tate!

"I think I'll leave the zombies to you. I've got a couple of exciting loads of laundry to catch up on." She reached across the table and gave his hand a squeeze. If she was going to keep her heart sewed up tight, twenty-four-seven with Aidan Tate was simply not an option. "But, Aidan, seriously, I want to thank you for today. I didn't think I'd ever be on a bike saddle again, and you've just helped me tick off one of my New Year's resolutions!"

"Which one was that?"

"'Poke Your Demons in the Eye'—number seventeen," she answered without a moment's hesitation.

Aidan laughed heartily. It was nice to see the smile back on his face. Maybe one day he'd rate her as someone he could confide in in the same way he'd been there for her.

He pushed his chair back and grabbed his bicycle helmet off of the adjacent chair. Today obviously wasn't going to be "one day."

"Just how many of these resolutions do you have to get through?"

Ali felt a light flush color her cheeks. She might just possibly have gone a bit overboard in the resolutions department.

"Seventy-three."

"Ha!" Aidan hooted to the ceiling. "And you've done one? Harty—you've got a lot of work to do."

"Oh, I've done at least two!" she shot back, before she thought better of it.

"Oh, reeeeally?"

He drew out the second word, making it all smoky... sexy. Sheeesh. Did the man do anything that didn't make her want to rip his clothes off?

"Yes," she responded primly.

"And what exactly was this other resolution?"

"Well, it wasn't 'Have a One-Night Stand at the Airport With the Man Who is Your New Boss.'" She popped on her helmet and snapped the straps together with a flourish. "It was 'Try New Things.'"

Aidan put his hand in the small of her back as they headed toward the riverside exit to the pub. "I see. So, what new things did you try?"

"I had a one-night stand at the airport with the man who it turned out was my new boss."

Would he take that hand off the small of her back? She was feeling sassy. *Super*-sassy. She made a bee-line for her bicycle, which was chained to a railing at the river's edge.

"Sounds exciting." Aidan was right behind her, his breath teasing along the length of her neck.

"It was."

He turned her around to face him. *Heavenly bodies*, he knew how to unleash the butterflies. His fingers brushed her cheek as he unclipped her helmet, removed it and pulled her close to him in one incredibly fluid move. Didn't this kind of thing only happen in movies?

"The guy must've been something special. To catch the eye of a girl like you."

He tipped her chin up with a finger and her eyes caught the hungry look in his.

"Oh, he was all right…" she managed to whisper. Whimper was more like it.

"Sounds like he had room for improvement." Aidan's mouth began a torturously slow descent toward her own.

"Like I said, he's all right…" Her voice faded away.

When their lips finally met Ali felt a rush of desire surge through her so powerfully she could hardly believe it was real. The kiss was soft, tender, and then passionately loaded with all the triumph and depth of feeling she'd experienced that day. And yet—it was just a kiss.

Just a kiss? That'd be like calling Rudolph Nureyev *just* a chap who wore tights. If they hadn't been in public she probably would've torn Aidan's fleece and everything else off him right then and there. Not that he brought out the wild animal in her or anything. Or that it was part of their "deal."

"Well, then!" Ali pulled back from Aidan, using the railing as ballast. "Guess we better get you back to your box sets!"

Aidan dropped another one of those flirty winks in her direction. "I'd hate to keep you from your laundry."

Oh, we're getting to the laundry, all right! Just the emotional kind. And it feels an awful lot like the spin cycle!

CHAPTER SEVEN

"So, HAVE THINGS improved with Tate?"

In a manner of speaking...

"They're going all right." Ali crossed her fingers, relieved that her friend and new head of En Pointe couldn't see her face. She was a terrible liar. They were having their weekly "clinic catch-up" chat, and keeping Aidan off of the topic list was getting harder.

"When I worked with him he was definitely a hard nut to crack—definitely keeps himself to himself—but I thought you two would hit it off."

That's one way to put it.

Better stay on safer territory. "So, what have you done to my practice? How has the team taken to your new-fangled American ways?"

"Oh, I'd say I've been dragging this little house that Ali built into the twenty-first century!"

"What?" Ali sat bolt-upright. She had a Class A clinic and knew as well as her former classmate did that it was miles ahead of other clinics in the city, let alone the country. He was lucky she trusted him so much.

"Chillax, Lockhart. Don't worry. I've actually dragged it back a few centuries. One of the girls—the Russian one—"

"Which Russian one? There are heaps of them!" Ali couldn't help but laugh.

"I don't know—Katarina, Alexandra, Olga—*any-hooooow...*" Cole Manning drew out the word in his usual leisurely Southern drawl. The man sure could drag out a story. "I got an acupuncturist in to help her with some of the tendonitis. Seems to have made a difference."

"That's great! It's probably Alexandra—the ballet doesn't have many Olgas. At least not the way you say it."

"How *do* I say it?" Cole was laughing now, too.

"Like anyone called Olga is a troll. Does she have long blond hair?"

"What do you want from me, Ali? They've all either got long blond or long black hair. The least you could've done was color-code them a bit more for me!"

"Listen, mister!" Ali cried, despite the laughter burbling away in her throat. "If you mess with my clinic—"

"Hold on, girl. Don't you mean *my* clinic? That was the deal, wasn't it? I get you a top locum position Up North and you keep your mitts off while I have my wicked way with En Pointe—Britain's number one destination for ballerinas and gymnasts on the mend."

"Cole Manning—you just remember I have put my life's work into that place. If you—"

"Easy, there, tiger. I'm only messing with you. Everything's fine. The clients are fine—the list is growing, in fact."

"What? Who?" Ali sat up straight. She loved a new challenge as much as the next doctor, but equally she knew all of the local prima ballerinas personally—and a new client meant a new injury. An injury that could spell the end of a career.

"Erm—let me have a look."

She could hear papers being shuffled across a desk. "You haven't made my—*your*—desk a complete pigsty, have you, Cole?"

Ali grinned at the phone as she spoke the words. Of course he had. The man was a certified genius—but he scored in the negatives when it came to tidiness. So much for the "tidy desk, tidy mind" adage.

"Look, Little Miss Everything Has Its Correct Time and Place, I thought this whole switcheroo was to shake things up a bit?"

"Yeah, but—"

"Yeah, but nothin'." Now Cole was serious. "You did *not* trek up to the far North of England and surround yourself with a bunch of testosterone-laden menfolk just to keep everything clinical and perfect like you always do."

"I hardly think—"

"That's precisely your problem, Ali. You think too much. Stop it. Live a little, why don'tcha?"

If only he knew.

"You're lucky you said all that with your cute Southern accent, Cole. Otherwise, I might have half a mind to come down and clean up my—*your*—desk right now," she playfully sniped back.

But his words had the sting of truth about them. Then again, one-night stands, kickboxing and having a time and date-stamped affair were all pretty big steps in the Leaping Emotional Hurdles department, right?

Aidan couldn't resist. He lightly traced his finger along the lock of hair shading Ali's sleeping face and tucked it back behind her ear. Fourteen. That was the number of light freckles that made up a tiny constellation across her nose. Two. The number of nibbly, kissable, lush lips he was currently trying to resist. Two. The number felt leaden now. The number of weeks left in Ali's contract.

He gave her cheek a stroke with the back of his hand and rolled onto his back, his arm still trapped by her head.

She was a snuggler. And he had to admit he was loving every wiggly, cuddly, close-as-you-can-get moment of being with her. And it wasn't just the sex. Make no mistake—the sex was good. Ridiculously good. But Ali was the whole package, and as the days wore on—or ran out—he was feeling less and less like this whole "what goes on the road, stays on the road" affair was fair.

Ali deserved more. Someone who would—*could*—open up his heart and giftwrap her in lashings of love. Deep, full-bodied love.

Two weeks. That was all they had left. Two weeks until the big North-South match. It was something he had never thought he'd dread.

If what he'd had with Ali had only been that one extraordinary night at the hotel, then saying goodbye would have been much easier. She would definitely have been etched on his mind forever, and heaven knew going to the airport would never be a straightforward business again, but one night with this amazing woman would have been survivable.

Now, with the few dozen nights they'd already notched up... Total annihilation. She'd nabbed him— hook, line and sinker. Getting over Ali at this juncture was going to be near on impossible. Which was why he had to start closing the doors.

"Are you watching me sleep?" Ali cracked a single eye open, her fingers taking a lazy journey across his chest.

"Hardly!" He protested with a grin. "That would be creepy."

"Yes." She nodded in sleepy agreement. "That would. It's not like you'd be falling for me, or anything daft like that."

Okay, mind reader. Enough of that.

"Got it in one," he replied lightly, as if feigning falling in love would hide the reality.

"Yeah, right." She replied with a cheeky grin. "As if The Monk would fall for his fluffy ballerina locum."

"Stranger things have happened." He was straining to keep his voice bright. "What are you up to today?"

"I was thinking of going into town to buy a lamp." She pushed herself up on an elbow and began to thoughtfully trace a finger along his shoulder. "I only have the one, and I have to keep dragging it from the lounge into the bedroom when I want to read in bed."

Aidan laughed. "It's a bit late in the game to be making yourself at home, isn't it?"

"That's rich, coming from you." She gave him a poke in the chest.

"What's *that* supposed to mean?" He knew what it meant, but it'd be interesting to have Ali's take on his rather sparse décor.

"You had the gall to come to my place when I'd been there all of two weeks and mock my one-sofa, two-chair existence, only for me to discover you lived virtually the same way after—how many years has it been, Dr. Tate?"

"Five terribly busy years."

"Five years. And you have…let's see…two more lamps than I do and a better-stocked larder. Oh, and more throw pillows than you can shake a stick at," Ali teased, then fell back onto her pile of pillows. "If you like, I'll give you my new lamp when I go."

Aidan rolled over onto his back. He didn't want to think about that. Or discuss his own "bare bones" decorating style. Staring at the ceiling suddenly seemed less like being under the microscope.

"It's easier to clean. Easier to not get attached."

"And what are you not getting attached to? Bookshelves? Sets of drawers?" Ali's voice was still warm with humor, but he definitely felt the conversation train taking a different route.

"Things I can't have."

"Like what?"

"Oh, I don't know."

You, for one.

He bought himself some more time. "Settling in just always seemed too much hassle. My life is out there—" he pointed out the window in the direction of the stadium "—not in here. Why waste time on home furnishings when my real investment is with the team? When I initially signed on this job was the promise of something more permanent than anything I'd have with a patient in hospital. I'd really get to know the team. Learn and grow with them. Help them."

"It's a bit like that at my clinic."

"Yes, I suppose it would be. But with the team—I don't know. I guess I felt I was signing on for something bigger. Something lasting. And then one player gets transferred, another signs off with injuries, coaches switch teams…" He trailed off. This was all getting a bit heavy for a Sunday morning. "And before you know it, your second-in-command leaves and is replaced by a nymphomaniac from the South."

"Hey! I don't ever hear you saying no!" A full smile

lit up Ali's eyes before she pulled Aidan's arm around her shoulder and plopped back down on to the pillow.

"Very true. Then again—you'll just be another thing to replace when you swan off back to the magical land of London." Aidan traced his fingers along Ali's arm.

"You'd better not replace me!"

"You're the one with the contract."

"You know what I mean. It will be strange—going back…"

Aidan bit back the urge to ask her to stay. To say she was welcome to extend their "deal" as long as she wanted.

"Don't be crazy—you can have anything you want back there."

"Not anything." All the playfulness had drained from Ali's voice.

"Of course." Aidan slapped his forehead. *What an idiot.* "Your mum."

"My mum…" Ali repeated softly. "I miss her more than anything in the world."

"I can imagine."

"Poor little me!" Ali's voice came out louder than she'd intended. This conversation had definitely veered toward Gloomsville. "All alone in the world!"

"You've got friends down South, right?"

Ali barked out a quick laugh, then put on a singsong voice. "The valuable resource of hindsight has allowed me to see that I have been a great boss—but not necessarily so good in the social skills department."

"And why is that, then?" Aidan kept his eyes trained on the ceiling. Having this conversation with Ali's naked body semi-nestled into his was not familiar territory for him. Actually, having any sort of conversation with a naked woman beside him was relatively new. *Ali* new.

"Oh... I just couldn't count on..."

"Couldn't count on what?" Aidan pressed gently.

It was like a light bulb being pinged on. Ali suddenly saw the situation as clear as a bell. "I had friends, and a teacher-cum-mentor who took care of me after my mum died. Then he died when I was in uni, and I guess I just short-circuited. I didn't want friends anymore. I just wanted a family."

As the words came out of her mouth she wished she could reel them back in. What a thing to say in front of Mr. Can't-and-Won't-Commit!

"Which is why I've come Up North to work with a bunch of testosterone-laden athletes."

Aidan threw her a bemused look. "Does working with rugby players put you off having a family?"

"No!" She waved away his theory. "It pushes me out of my comfort zone. Reminds me there's no one to depend upon but myself."

"You've got me!" Aidan remonstrated.

"Ha!" Ali snorted. "For about two more weeks!" Had he not remembered the conditions surrounding their "friendship"? Work and play—two very separate things, with one very solid deadline.

"And then what? London?"

"Hmm. I'm not so sure about London. I guess I pack up my new lamp—if I ever get to the shops and buy one—or give it to you and see what's next."

"You wouldn't stick around? Stay Up North?" He made a stab at lifting his eyebrows with black-and-white movie star panache. "It'd be satisfying to know someone finally figured out things up here are better than in the big smoke."

"Who knows? What is this, anyway? The Northern Inquisition?" Ali filled the quiet space after her question with a laugh, wanting to escape the taut atmosphere their conversation had enshrouded them in.

She didn't want to leave. Not one bit. She was genuinely enjoying her work with the team and could easily see herself staying. But in two weeks the clock would run out and her days as medical practitioner to the North Stars would be over. More to the point, her days with Aidan would be over. She was dreading saying goodbye, so ignoring it seemed the easiest way to go. Why play twenty questions?

"No, it's not an inquisition," Aidan drawled. "But I was wondering…"

"Wondering what?" Ali couldn't stop her heart from skipping a beat. Would he ask her to stay?

"I was actually wondering how I could pull my arm out from underneath your dead weight of a head so I could go meet my girls."

Ali's eyes popped wide open, and quickly she pushed herself upright and away from him. "*Excuse* me?"

"My girls. Didn't I tell you about them?"

Ali grabbed an armful of duvet and covered herself up, an expression of shock playing across her face. "I'm pretty sure I would've remembered if you'd told me about your *children*."

It was Aidan's turn to pop his eyes wide open. And then he started laughing. Hard.

"Not my children, silly! Well, I mean—yes—in a way…"

He didn't stop laughing and it was now officially irritating.

"This hasn't really come out the way I meant it to."

"*What* hasn't come out the way you meant it to, Aidan?"

Ali's steely-eyed gaze was hilarious. Aidan knew he could fix it right now if he wanted to—help her grimace relax into a smile. *So why wasn't he fixing it?* The silence between them was humming with emotion and with a blast of clarity he realized how easy it was to imagine having children...having a family with Ali. The two of them and one, two, three—however many didn't matter. But that sort of idyllic future wasn't meant for him. History had been all too clear about that one. Best put on the brakes. All this talk of family, putting down roots, had clearly unbalanced him. Best return to firmer ground. Get real.

"I coach a girls' rugby team. Twelve and under."

Ali's shoulders dropped back into place and—as he'd hoped—there was that smile of hers. The one that worked its way straight into his heart.

"But it's probably best you go on ahead with your lamp-shopping. You can't come along to practice as my g—" He stopped himself before he finished the sentence, knowing it was already too late.

"Come as your what?"

Ali's voice had turned investigative. He was making one hell of a hash of this.

"Nothing—don't worry. I don't really know what I was saying."

"Were you going to say *girlfriend*?"

She said the word as if it tasted of moldy cheese. Or, more accurately, as if the idea of her being his girlfriend was about as preposterous as things could get.

"No." *Uh, yes*—he had been going to say that.

"Aidan Tate! You were going to say *girlfriend*!"

"I was not!"

"What?" Ali changed tack and stuck out her lower lip, trying her best to make a monster face. "Is the idea so unappealing?"

He laughed, but couldn't stop the curl of uneasiness shifting around his gut. Of course it would be great—better than great—to have Ali as his girlfriend, but that wasn't how things worked. How *this* worked. They'd agreed. They'd shaken hands on it!

Ali's laughter broke through the silence. "I'm just messing with you, Tate. I know you didn't mean that."

I did. I do. I can't.

"'Course not—I just meant I'm their coach, so you can't take the mick out of me in front of the girls. You're more than welcome to come, or you can wander off into town and lamp-shop to your heart's content. Your choice."

"Sure thing, ding-a-ling."

Ali pushed herself out of the bed and pulled on a T-shirt and some tracksuit bottoms. Aidan let himself get lost in the graceful flow of her movements. He started when she spoke again.

"I think I'll take a raincheck on judging your coaching skills."

"You know—I'd love for you to meet the girls. It's just…well… They're used to it just being me and them."

"Right. Fine."

Aidan was smart enough to know that when a woman said "fine" the situation was anything but. He was pretty sure he'd just stuck his foot in it. Big-time.

"I'll see you tomorrow at work." She gave him a wave and turned to go.

"Great. Or see you later?" Aidan gave a wave to her disappearing figure, before deflating against the bed's headboard and smacking himself on the head.

Girlfriend.

He hadn't let himself call any of the women he'd seen over the years a girlfriend. In truth, none of his "relationships" had warranted it. He'd made it clear as day that he wasn't one for long-term. And now here he was, tables turned, trying to convince himself—no, to convince Ali—that he didn't want her to be his girlfriend, when he knew deep in his heart that was all he wanted. All he wanted and more.

Ali stared at the recipe she'd ripped out of the Sunday paper. What was *braising* steak anyway? Could you get that at a butchers? Were butchers even open on a Sunday? How long did one "reduce" stock? Why weren't there more *details*? *Disasterville.* This was never going to happen.

She flicked the paper over to see what another option might be.

Super Simple Pizza.

Pizza! Perfect. She could do that. Easy-peasy.

She'd already cleaned her flat, done all the laundry and folded her clothes. Three times. Then she'd gone out shopping, totally forgetting what it was she'd left home for in the first place, and returned home empty-handed. To the darkness. When she'd remembered she had gone out for a lamp. Oh, and then she'd gone for a run by the river. A long one.

She was still buzzing with excess energy and needed to take things down a notch. Aidan always looked so relaxed when he cooked, so she thought she'd give it a whirl. Not that he was her go-to resource for how to fix a problem.

Urrrrrgh!

She was tense. Shoulders-up-in-her-ears tense. The

whole debacle that morning with Aidan over the word *girlfriend* just made her cringe.

She didn't know why she'd said it. Well—she *did* know why she'd said it. It was ruddy obvious Aidan was laying down the ground rules. He didn't want her involved in his personal life. They weren't "a thing."

Which she *knew*! Of *course* she knew… Even though that little-girl, pink-clothes-wearing, dreaming-of-princesses part of her occasionally slipped through the chinks of her armor and let herself imagine…*what if?*

No. There was no "what if?" about it. They'd made a deal, shaken hands and agreed. They were "Colleagues Who Canoodled." Some mighty fine canoodling to boot. The type of canoodling that had sunbeams shooting out of her ears and little sighs of contentment slipping past her lips like a happy, sexy kitten.

Well. A mature kitten. A tigress? Maybe the whole cat analogy was a bad one. At this juncture *any* analogy was a bad one, because she didn't know if she'd just blown the lid off of what they had by—by what, exactly? Daring to dream of something more?

Ali began yanking open the kitchen cupboards on a quest for some zero-zero flour, as per the so-called "super-simple" recipe. She knew she didn't have any, and suddenly the fact that any old flour wouldn't do was a further source of irritation. The contents of her culinary arsenal hadn't really changed from when she'd moved in.

Aidan generally cooked when they were at his place, and they'd have takeaway when they were at hers. And they'd had a fair few away games, too. Away games when, given the chance, she and Aidan would send each other a drink with a wink and a bar mat complete with a hastily scribbled room number. And then… *Bah!*

This whole thing was a disaster. She didn't know why she'd thought she'd be able to rein her heart in and just see Aidan as a bit of edible eye candy when they weren't at work. He was so much more to her. Smart, thoughtful, funny, generous, with about the best head of hair she'd ever run her fingers through in—well, forever. Not to mention the possessor of a bagful of exceedingly sensual moves that had released more than one cry of rapture from her.

Surprise! She'd never known she was a screamer.

She stomped to the kitchen counter and stared at the recipe some more, as if the ingredients would magically fly out of the piece of paper and assemble themselves into a mushroom and mascarpone pizza before her very eyes.

Nope. No good. All she could see was Aidan, giving her his come-hither man winks. *Urrrgh!* They were so *good* together, and as every minute passed it was getting harder and harder to contain her willful heart. She flopped down on the sofa and grabbed the remote. She wasn't really hungry anyway. Perhaps a bit of culture would stem her appetite.

She clicked on the television. Her stomach gurgled. *Terrific.*

The buzz of her phone had her launching herself across the flat to answer it. Cole was the only one who ever rang "out of hours," and she could do with a dose of her pal right now.

She didn't bother to check the number before answering, "Oh, Lordy, I need to hear your voice!"

"Five hours too long for you, then?"

Ah. Not the person she'd expected.

"Sorry, Aidan. I thought you were someone else."

"Oh, so it wasn't *my* voice you were missing?"

Not just your voice...

"What's up? How did your training session go?"

"I was just calling to see if you had anything in that pathetic excuse of a kitchen of yours."

Mind reader.

"I'm cool."

"I know that, Ali, but I'm guessing you don't have anything for your dinner. How does pizza grab you?"

Spooky.

"Mushroom and mascarpone?"

"Just picked it up from the shop. Put your oven on. See you in twenty."

Ali practically skipped to the oven to flick it on to a high heat—they both liked their pizza super-crispy, and it always needed a top-up sear after its journey. And there'd be a huge green salad with peppers and tomatoes tossed in. Not that they were beginning to know each other's preferences or anything. Like a boyfriend and girlfriend would. No...nothing like that at all. Just a couple of colleagues sharing a companionable pizza...

Just two more weeks. She could *do* this.

It was like a litmus test on how mature she was. Sophisticated city girl, coming up to the wilds of the North of England and having a free-spirited love affair...a free-spirited *affair*...with a man who was so ridiculously attractive it was *insane* that he was single.

She needed to keep her cool. There were only a few more nights when she would be able to be held by him, touch him, make the most of those delicious kisses. Just a teeny-tiny handful of days until the final match and then life would return to normal. Ali would be on her own somewhere out there in the world. A warrior princess, standing her ground. Alone. Just the way she liked it.

* * *

"Maybe I should've bought two." Aidan was looking incredulously at Ali. For a slender woman, she could pack it away.

"I went for a run today," she mumbled through her fifth slice of pizza.

"Burning off excess energy?"

"Something like that."

"Ali, I—"

"Yeah?"

She looked at him over the edge of her pizza. She'd been pretty quiet all night. Unusually so. Normally she talked through whatever they watched on television and tonight they'd just watched television. The atmosphere was all wrong. He wanted relaxed and happy Ali back.

"We're all right? The two of us?"

"Of course—what do you mean?" She put on an expression of pure wide-eyed innocence.

"C'mon, Ali. You know what I mean. The 'girlfriend' gaffe. I'm sorry about that."

"Not to worry." She started picking at a piece of mushroom on her pizza, then sent it somersaulting into the empty box between them on the sofa. "It was as much my fault as yours. We work together. And play together. Everything is separate. I get it."

"It's just—"

"Aidan. I *get* it. Could we please not make me feel more mortified than I already do?"

He looked at her in surprise. He'd thought *he* was the one who should be feeling mortified—not her. Lying about his true feelings…? He was most definitely not onto a winner with *that* tack.

"You shouldn't feel badly. I'm the one who stuck my foot in it," Aidan persisted, not entirely sure why he had to get the record straight when in fact that was the last thing he was doing. "I just want to make sure we're good." He reached over and started to trace a finger along her arm in tickly little leaps and hops.

She started laughing and swatted at him. "I thought we weren't going to talk about this anymore?"

"Talk about what?" Shoving everything under the proverbial bed seemed to be working for them. Why change now?

"Precisely." She gave him a mischievous smirk.

Something in the air between them shifted. The awkwardness was replaced with that crackling electricity they shared so well.

"What do you want to do instead?"

Aidan moved his hand up into her hair, tucking little strands back into place. Perfect. He drew his fingers along the thick swatch of hair that trailed down to her collarbone and traced that, too. He'd yet to complete the freckle-count on her décolletage.

"Weeell…" Ali drew out the word as she moved the pizza box to the low table they'd been using as a footrest. "I could think of a couple of things. But I *am* terribly busy, as you can see."

Aidan pulled her onto his lap, no longer interested in the distance between them, however paltry. "C'mere, you."

He drew her to him for a deep kiss, savoring the taste of her salty lips. He could kiss these lips when they were sweet, salty—whatever. His focus narrowed. He traced his finger along her lower lip as her tongue darted out, ultimately capturing his finger between her teeth and drawing it into her mouth. He sucked in a sharp breath.

Two more weeks. That was all they had. He knew they hadn't really cleared the air between them, but their bodies seemed to have a language of their own, and that would do for now. Ali was on his lap now, her thighs opening wide as she pressed her body to his, her hands holding on to the back of the sofa, her mouth teasing, urging him to commit to something deeper, something more intimate.

He rucked up her shirt and ran his fingertips along her bare back as she dropped kisses and wicked little licks along his neck. Her skin was like silk. He pressed her tightly into him in the vain hope that her scent would be seared into his memory banks. The thought of losing her—not having her with him—threatened his composure. This wasn't enough. Two weeks... Six weeks... It would never be enough. But it was all he had and he was going to be damn sure to make the most of it.

"C'mon." He helped her to her feet and took her hand in his. "I think it's bedtime."

Ali slipped her arm along his waist and gave him a light squeeze.

"I couldn't have put it better myself."

"Doc, we've really got to stop meeting like this."

"Afraid your teammates might start whispering, Mack?" Ali popped a second blood-soaked swab into the medical waste bin. "You're beginning to look a bit like Scarface!"

"That's all part of the plan! The girls love it." Mack gave her a wink.

"Oh, yeah. We just *love* a good ol' roughed up face. The more scars the better!" Ali laughed along with the rookie player. Mack was an up-and-coming star for the North Stars, and was definitely living up to his "Mack

Attack" tagline. There wasn't a scrum he didn't want to be a part of.

"Is that why you've gone off Dr. Tate?"

Ali could barely stop her eyes from boinging out of her head at the question, and quickly busied herself with preparing the suture kit. How could she tell him that she and Aidan had shared just about every night together since "That Night" at hot yoga nearly three months ago?

She might as well call their nocturnal liaisons Kama Sutra Class for all the new tiers of lovemaking she was discovering. Last night had been particularly illuminating. And intense. It was as if their bodies knew there wasn't much time left and saturated every move with greater intensity. Microblasts of heat started detonating inside her as her body relived Aidan's rhythmic movements as she—*ahem*!

She waited to speak until her voice wouldn't sound like a choirboy's. "What makes you say that?"

"Oh, we thought you and Tatey had a thing going on a few weeks back—but obviously even the powerful Harty-attack couldn't tear down the fortress of The Monk's heart."

Well... That's partly true.

"Okay—here's the part that's going to hurt." Ali picked up the needle and was just about to take the first stitch when Mack quickly turned away.

"What? You're not afraid of my needlework, are you?" Ali asked, but she too turned to see what had caught her patient's eye.

"Harty!" Jonesy staggered in, his huge hand covering his face, blood pouring everywhere, "Just got a hands-off." He plopped onto the second examination table in the room and tilted his head back.

"Holy crow, man. Who did *that*?" Mack looked enthralled.

Little boys. The lot of 'em.

"Looks more like a hands-*on* to me."

Ali tried her best not to recoil. Ballet stars very rarely had bloody noses, but these guys collected them like badges of honor—and once their noses started spurting they were like unstoppable geysers. At the very least she was developing an incredibly strong stomach.

"Hey, Jonesy. Harty and Tate have broken up."

Ali tutted and tried her best to look nonchalant. Since when had her social life become a discussion point for the team?

"What? No way! I thought you two were cute together. Are we supposed to be like your girlfriends and ask you what happened? Or can we skip that part and let everyone know you're back on the market?" Jonesy sent her a sympathetic yet hopeful look through his bloodied fingers.

"No way! You've both got the wrong idea. There's never been anything going on between us. *Ever*. Never."

Ali lied through her teeth with a slice of genuine horror thrown in. And a splash of admiration for the fact that their "sleeping together" plan had made the atmosphere between them at work seem visibly cooler. Even if it had done the total opposite to her heart. She was still wrestling with that one—big-time.

And as for the couple part? *Hmm...* Aidan had insisted upon regular reminders on that front. A big, fat no-go zone.

Not that she'd protested. They were having fun, weren't they? Just two adults enjoying each other's company. In various stages of undress, mind, but there was no doubting they were enjoying one another. For now.

Besides, this sort of explosive attraction never worked out long-term. Short-term suited them, Ali insisted to herself: *a limited edition couple.*

"But when did you break up?" Mack persisted. Since when was he a stickler for details?

"There was never anything to break up *from*! We were never a couple. You boys have clearly suffered too many head injuries."

"What?" Both men protested in unison. Concussions were taken seriously. "Any doubt and you're out" was the coach's motto.

"Enough! The both of you." She wagged a stern finger in each of their directions. Then scowled.

Rugby players needed tough love. It was a world away from the ballet, where cosseting and cajoling worked a treat. She grabbed an ice pack from the well-stocked mini freezer.

"Jonesy, put this on your face. Mack, sit still like a good boy and let me finish these stitches—otherwise you really will look like Scarface. I'm going for a Southern Cross effect. Will that suit?"

"Yes, miss." Mack responded meekly.

"These boys giving you guff?"

"We're all good!" Ali forced herself to reply evenly to the sound of Aidan's voice.

She refused to turn around, focusing fastidiously on the stitches she'd begun. If she was going to continue this highly successful charade, going weak-kneed when their eyes met would be a bit of a giveaway.

"Grand. Lockhart—my office when you're done."

"Yup! Just give me a few minutes with these lugheads and I'll be there."

"Ooh. Harty's in *trouble*!"

Ali couldn't stop herself from swatting at Mack's

arm with a bonus glare. It was a bit like wafting tissue paper at a steel beam, but a girl had to try.

"Methinks the lady doth protest too much," Jonesy blurted from beneath his ice cubes.

"Since when do you quote Shakespeare?" Mack guffawed.

"Since I got my degree in English Literature, with a special emphasis on the Elizabethan era. We're not all noodleheads like you, Mack."

"I knew it was Shakespeare," the player retorted.

"Hoo! Color me impressed!" Ali meant it. "Do you have plans to do anything with it, Jonesy? Your degree?"

"I thought I'd go back and get my Masters in teaching once we show the South who dominates the world of rugby. It's not like this gig is going to last forever, and I don't think I'd be any good at coaching. The sidelines aren't my gig."

"Impressive. Not everyone plans for the future. There you go, Mack. All done." Ali tied off the stitches and pressed on a bit of tape. "That should hold your brains in for a while."

She gave him a grin and a "scoot" gesture. Time to sort out Jonesy's nose.

She was really impressed, and strangely proud of this player. It wasn't as if she'd known the man for long, but in the short time she had they had developed a really solid working relationship—heavy with ribbing. She was seriously pleased for him. He was smart to plan for the future. It was something *she'd* have to do, since this little secret liaison thing with Aidan was obviously not going to carry her off into the sunset. Not that she'd ever banked on *that* scenario coming to pass.

Medicine was the only thing she could rely on. But

it would be a shame to go all ostrich on herself again—sticking her head back into the medical sandpit of no return. She'd enjoyed setting up the clinic. A lot. And it had eaten up her entire life. That would definitely help keep her mind off Aidan. Maybe she should set up a new one. But where?

Jonesey plonked himself down in front of her, unveiling a blood-slathered face.

America, maybe?

Aidan stared at the whiteboard as if it would help give him some answers.

The only sound in the locker room was the ticking of the clock. He'd never realized how much time elapsed between each second.

He rubbed his eyes, then gave it another inspection.

Nope. No good. That day's skinfold results just weren't going to help him find a way to tell Ali their late-night trysts had to end.

He kicked one of the towels lying on the ground straight up and into the basket on the other side of the room. If only it would be that easy to deal with his father. The man really had unbelievable timing. They had a perfectly amicable long-distance relationship, and now he wanted to come home and show off a new bride…

He let himself sink onto one of the benches, holding his head in his hands. Unbelievable. Two tiny weeks left with the love of his life and now he had houseguests.

Tick. Tick.

Hold on a minute.

Love of his life?

No dice. He wouldn't be going down *that* street again. He couldn't. Not after everything life had thrown at him. Five years of holding vigil for a woman—a life—that would never happen. Had it been worth it? Was it worth changing the rulebook now? For this woman who'd whirled into his life, knocked everything sideways and seemed intent on whirling straight back out again?

"Hey!" Ali leaned through the locker room door, giving it a quick knock as she poked her head into the room. "Couldn't find you in your office. Is everything all right?"

"No."

"Oh? It's not Rory, is it? He hasn't been sneaking into the weight room again? I've told him—"

"No."

Ali walked into the room, the door swinging back with into place with a hushed *thwffft*.

Tick. Tick.

"Aidan?"

Ali stood in front of him, her brow working on the beginnings of a furrow. *Just look at her.* The most wonderful creature he'd ever known.

Just two more weeks! All he'd wanted was to make the most of these two past weeks with her—this amazing woman he was finally beginning to realize he loved. Was that *so* much to ask? Did *everything* he planned have to be swept away before he had a chance to see it through?

Hadn't he paid enough penance for Mary's death?

Couldn't he just have two more weeks before he had to say goodbye?

"I'm presuming this isn't a guessing game and that you are eventually going to tell me what's going on?" Ali nudged his foot with her toe.

"Yes—sorry." He pushed his hands onto his thighs

and stood up. He might as well look her in the eye when he did this. He owed her that at least.

"I'm afraid our nocturnal trysts are going to have to end sooner than I thought."

From the look on her face, the news had hit her hard.

"And you thought the locker room was a good place to let me know?"

"Ali, I—I didn't want to draw things out. Now seemed just as bad a time as later."

"Right. Okay."

She gave him a thin smile and looked away. He could hardly blame her.

"That's your fake *I'm cool with it* voice, isn't it?"

"Well, it *is* a bit out of the blue, Aidan. I thought we were—" She broke off to look around the room and ensure they were on their own. "I thought we were enjoying ourselves."

"We were! *Are!*" He raked a hand through his hair. "It's my dad. He's coming to stay."

"Oh!" Her face brightened. "Well, that's not so bad, is it? You can sneak over to mine."

"He's coming with his *new wife*." Aidan tried to weight the words with the depth of meaning they held for him.

"Why are you looking so gloomy? That's great news! Isn't it?"

She peered at him for answers he just didn't have the heart to give. When none were forthcoming, she, too, stared at the skinfold analysis, as if it would offer some code of understanding as to what was going on here.

"You could still come over to mine, couldn't you? It's not like you're sixteen and need your father's permission for a sleepover. Besides..." A bright smile lit up her face. "It would give the newlyweds their own space while they stay with you."

"It's more complicated than that, Ali." Aidan tugged a hand through his hair, fighting an urge to howl at the moon… He looked up at the ceiling. Well…just *howl*. "You and I were meant to be short-term anyway—with my dad here, there would just be too many secrets to worry about keeping. We'd be best just to nip it in the bud now."

A sharp, searing look of pain passed across her eyes as she slowly turned to leave the room. If he could've pulled her into his arms and told her everything was going to be all right he would've. The churning in his gut told him he owed her more than he was giving her—and the best but most painful way to do that was to let her go.

"Ali, I—"

"Please don't, Aidan. Really. I get it. If you don't mind, I think I'll just get back to work in lieu of you rubbing some more salt into my wounds."

"This was hardly what I wanted, Ali. I just received my father's email. I'm still reeling myself."

"From *what*, exactly, Aidan? A visit from your *dad*?" She threw her hands up in bewilderment. "That sounds like a *nice* thing to me. The money I wouldn't give to have my mum back for a just a few hours, let alone a proper visit… You're lucky to have him."

"It's not—*aaarghhh*! It's not the same."

"Right."

Ali squared herself up to him, arms crossed firmly over her chest. He had to give it to her: she wasn't one to give up ground lightly.

"What's so different about your dad that makes having him alive and wanting to visit his son with his new wife so awful?"

"Long story."

She glanced at her watch. "I've got until the next groin injury or bleeding beak comes stumbling in that door. Could be minutes. Could be hours." She pointed at the bench. "Sit. Speak. If you're going to rob me of my final days of the best booty calls I've ever had, I deserve an explanation."

Aidan couldn't help himself. He had to laugh. This woman had mettle. It was going to eat him alive that their final few days together would be relegated to pitch-side.

"Spill it, Tate." She sat down on the bench beside him, giving him a poke in the arm for good measure.

And he did. He told her about his mother leaving when he was a teen. How his father had been absolutely destroyed by her departure. He told her how he'd had to take over making meals, cleaning the house, making sure his father—a successful sportswriter—got to work, went to games, took showers, turned in his stories on time so he would get paid. How his teenaged girlfriend had become his helpmeet. Had risen to the occasion. How she'd been there for him and his father—particularly his father—when they had needed it, and—

"And…?" Ali asked quietly.

"And when I went to med school, she took over for me. You know—checking in on him, making sure he didn't get scurvy or anything. She just looked after him up until he moved to the West Indies for work."

Ali shot him a questioning look.

"He needed to move on. And he did. Successfully. I thought it was time for me to take the next step with my girlfriend, so we went away to the Pacific Islands—"

Ali's breath froze in her chest. *The tropical storm. The charity work.* Everything fell into place with a riotous clash in her heart. Aidan was caught. Caught in the thick nets of the past. And he couldn't see his way to break free.

She tipped her head so she could see what was happening in Aidan's eyes. They normally sparked with life. She'd never seen him this down.

Her stomach sank. Aidan's words were really beginning to sink in now. It was over. His father was too close a link to the past he had never recovered from. No wonder he compartmentalized everything so much. It made his life bearable.

Aidan stared straight ahead and continued to speak. "I was busy being pragmatic. Sensible. Life with my dad had taught me to hold every card I had tight to my chest. He'd already had a series of girlfriends by that point, and I'd learned better than to expect to see any of them for more than a few weeks or months before a new one would turn up."

The words began pouring out of him. Ali pressed her fingers to her lips, eyes widening as he spoke. She knew what was coming.

"I thought it would be prudent to wait a few days into our holiday before I proposed. You know—make sure we could relax together as well as we worked together."

"And did you?"

Ali knew she shouldn't be jealous, but a teensy bit of her was envious of the woman who had known a younger Aidan. An Aidan who would've looked at the world through less jaded eyes. The more time she spent with him, the more she wanted. And now he was spelling it out in triplicate why it was all over between them.

She scuffed at the locker room floor with the toe of

her shoe. Aidan wasn't the only one who thought life was harsh.

"We were one of those steady couples. It had always been…" His eyes wandered around the locker room as if hunting for the best word "*Easy*. It had always just been easy with her. I liked her. She liked me. No wild fireworks like—" He tipped his head in her direction with a wry smile playing along his lips.

His face was wreathed in such unbearable sadness it nearly broke Ali's heart. She wanted to touch him. Hold him. She knew how awful it was to lose someone. And she also knew there was nothing she could say to make it better. She wished for her mother to be back every day of her life, and only just managed to fill the void with medicine. It seemed as though Aidan had done the same thing for different reasons.

She watched as his dark eyes locked on the wall across from him. His voice took on a wrenchingly hollow tone.

"The tropical storm hit in the morning. I was up on the balcony of our room, reading, and she'd gone out snorkeling with a couple we had met the night before. I had this paper I wanted to write and some reading to finish up—I thought I'd save the proposal for the evening. You know—the romance of moonlight and all that claptrap."

Ali clapped her fingers to her mouth. *How awful*. Her heart ached for him.

"Did you ever see her again?"

Ali didn't know why, but if she'd been in the same situation she would have wanted to see the body, to say goodbye properly. She'd been able to say farewell to her mother before she'd passed. The painful heartbreak of those moments haunted her to this day, but at least she had had them. She had no doubt of the love her mother had for her—and she knew her mother had died with the knowledge that her daughter would honor her forever.

"No. I stayed on for a few months, helping with the volunteer medical corps, but after a while it was obvious it was a futile search. They'd been snorkeling out on a boat beyond the cluster of islands where we'd been staying. The whole thing was a nightmare. An absolute living nightmare."

She couldn't even begin to imagine. And for the first time in a long time felt at an utter loss for words. What did you say to someone who had experienced something like that? How did you pick the words that could even begin to explain how deeply you felt for their loss? You tried your best...

"And yet you still watch zombie films?"

Aidan turned to her as her face snapped into a horrified *oops* expression.

"Sorry—that was about the least sensitive thing I could've said."

"No." He patted her leg as he rose from the bench with a sad smile. "The one thing I can always count on when I spend time with you is to be cheered up." He added, "Truly," when she raised a dubious eyebrow. "Thanks, Ali. I mean it. Having you around makes the world a nicer place."

Ali felt cemented to the bench as she watched Aidan push through the swinging doors of the locker room toward the corridor where his office lay.

The world hadn't really given him much of a break, had it? No wonder he preferred to keep her at arm's length. A heartbroken father? A young love that never had a chance to see itself through? It couldn't have been that long ago... Maybe five...six years? If time had done to him what it had done to her after her mum died, he would hardly have noticed it flashing by.

She pressed herself up from the bench, wondering what had broken his heart more—the loss of his girlfriend or never knowing what would have happened if he had proposed. Maybe the two were so interwoven it was impossible to tell.

She pushed out of the locker room and headed toward her own office. She could always count on work to be there for her. But this time she should learn from the past—make progress, as Aidan had said his father eventually had. She would work hard—but be realistic. Not push life to the wayside as she had before.

Losing her booty calls with Aidan was definitely going to be a tough ask, but she knew in her heart she would do anything to see that bright spark of life in his eyes again—even if it meant backing off. For good.

CHAPTER EIGHT

"CAN YOU SEE who it is?" Ali went onto her tiptoes, as if that would help her see through the thick wall of uniforms surrounding a player on the ground.

The referee looked to their side of the pitch and made a signal.

"One of ours. Head injury. I'll take it," Aidan replied grimly as he grabbed his bag and began to jog toward the huddle of players.

Grim was the only tone he'd been using lately, and work was the only thing that was helping him get through the day. Not that he wished his players ill—but focusing on them was a damn sight easier than thinking about his father's impending arrival. It had churned up just about every bit of history he'd worked so hard to tamp down into the past.

And being away from Ali hadn't brought the balm of Alone Time he'd thought it would. The only thing he'd achieved was a first-class foul mood.

A couple of nights on his own had seemed sensible—pragmatic. Time to rebuild the protective barrier around his heart. If his father fell to pieces again he wasn't so sure how strong a support system he would be. Not now. No one to lean on. No one to just—*be there*.

The emptiness of the past forty-eight hours had only

drilled into him how much a part of his life Ali had become. Instead of feeling empowered by the absence of their entanglement all he felt was an overwhelming desire to tell Ali more. Hash out his past and untangle the weave of his history to create something new. Something that made him feel ridiculously alive—as he had ever since he'd met her. This whole "nipping it in the bud" idea was beginning to look like a contender for Stupidest Idea Ever.

"Doc, it's Chris." One of the players opened a gap in the huddle around the North Stars player to let him in.

"That's a nice egg you're growing on your pate, Chris."

"Thanks, Doc. Anything for some sympathy." He remained flat on the ground despite his stab at humor.

"That'd be about right. Do you know what half we're in?"

"Don't be ridiculous. We're not playing in a match. This is a practice."

"Can you take your hands away from your head for a minute? I need you to focus on my finger." He held his index finger up and began a slow arc across Chris's eyeline.

"Don't take the mick, Doc. You've got two fingers up there. I know a trick question when I see one. I mean two…"

"Right!" Aidan pushed himself up decisively. "Nice and easy, boys. Can you help Chris up?"

"I'm perfectly fine to— *Whoooooahhh*!" Chris lurched up and then clonked back down to the ground. "I. Want. To. Play." He spoke progressively more and more slowly.

"Lads?" Aidan signaled to two of the players to lift him up.

It was definitely a concussion. How severe it was

remained to be seen. For now he just needed to get
Chris off of the field and into the stadium's clinic. The
stretcher team was right behind him if he needed more
help, and there was an ambulance standing by if he was
concerned about internal bleeding.

He tucked his shoulder underneath one of Chris's
lumberjack-sized arms and began a slow walk off the
field, to the supportive cheers of the fans.

"Easy, there, Chris. I've gotcha."

"Do you need a hand bringing him down the tunnel?" Ali rushed to help as they reached the edge of
the field.

"No. You need to stay here!" Aidan snapped.

"No need to bite Harty's head off, Doc. It's obvious
the woman just wanted a chance to put her arms around
me," Chris joked through his very obvious pain.

"Dr. Tate's right." Ali gave the player's arm a pat.
"You just look after yourself and do as you're told."

"Yes, miss." Chris threw her a grin as a stony-faced
Aidan led him down the tunnel toward the medical
room.

Ali didn't think Aidan had smiled once since he'd
told her the news of his father's arrival, and her heart
ached for him. She was trying her best to give him room
to breathe, but being at this away game had meant an
enforced coach ride together because the coach had
wanted to talk through some of their players' injuries,
and the hotel had put their rooms adjacent to the others. She had actually laughed out loud when she'd gone
to her room to drop her tote and had seen it had one of
those connecting doors that would've allowed her to
slip into his room unnoticed. If it weren't locked tight.

Ha-bloody-ha! Wasn't life sweet?

She went back to the bench as play recommenced

and joined Rory, who insisted on watching all of the games from the sidelines in full uniform despite still being on the mend.

"You don't leave your teammates in the lurch just because you're hurtin', Harty," he'd quipped.

She'd nearly burst into tears at the words. It was physically painful not to be there for Aidan when he was so obviously hurting. But she knew well enough when someone needed to go through something on their own. She'd gone through her own dark tunnel and… Was she out of it? At the very least she knew she could see the light.

She pressed her fingernails into her palms and threw a forlorn look in the direction of the medical room. No sign of Aidan. Probably just as well. What had seemed a short two weeks when they had been "together" had suddenly turned into an endless stretch of seconds, minutes and hours that would never end. They were down to eight days now. One hundred and ninety-two more hours. Fewer if she could escape to the train station right after the final match. She thought steering clear of airports would be a wise move.

"So, Harty. You think I'll be ready for the final?" Rory gave her a good-natured elbow in the ribs.

"Let's see what Mr. X-ray Machine has to say when we get back tomorrow, okay? How much training have you been doing?"

"Same as the other lads, minus any weights. Well, *heavy* weights. I've even been back to that hot yoga you made us all do a few weeks back. It's good, that."

Ali smiled at the memory and just as quickly felt it fade. That had been the night she and Aidan had been honest with one another and set the world alight.

Well, *her* world, anyway. So much for honesty being the best policy...

"Sounds good, Rory. As long as you're listening to your body and playing it safe I don't see any reason why we won't see you out there."

"Ace. Thanks, Doc."

"Don't take that as a sure thing!" she warned, knowing she was the one who needed to be taking her own advice.

If only her heart—not to mention her body—would stop telling her how much she wanted Aidan, life would be a whole lot easier.

"Hey, Harty!"

One of the players called her from the entrance to the hotel bar—the only quiet spot she'd been able to find where the internet worked.

"You joining us for dinner? We've found a ripper of a steakhouse—coach approves!"

"Ooh, you risk-takers! Skinfold tests tomorrow! Beware the banoffee pie!" she teased, then waved away his invitation. "I'm going to have a quiet one, I think. See you in the morning."

"You bet."

He disappeared around the corner and she stared at her laptop, willing it to offer her some guidance. Who could she email for some advice? The cursor blinked at her, as if daring her to type in someone's name. She really needed a friend, and the one she really needed—wanted—right now was a closed book.

That telltale stinging began in her nose and it took real effort to swallow down the threat of tears. She wasn't much of a crier, but the past few days had seen her teetering on the brink of weeping more than once.

It didn't take a brain surgeon—or in this case a highly trained doctor—to figure out what the problem was. One six-foot-something, black-haired, chestnut-eyed problem was her problem. She was in love with Aidan, and he couldn't be making it clearer that a future together was about as likely as Ali getting up in her toe shoes again.

She closed down the email program. She'd dealt with that part of her life. Not dancing again. She loved medicine and, whilst dancing with the best would've been amazing, she wouldn't change her life one bit.

Or would she? Would she reel back the past few months? The hours of scorching passion she'd spent with Aidan? The days of working with him, growing and learning together?

The part of her that could look at the situation with clinical accuracy was beyond reach. Then again, the truth boiled down to something very simple: she wanted Aidan in her life and that wasn't an option—so she was just going to have to get a grip.

"For the lady." The bartender appeared in front of her with a cocktail.

A Cosmopolitan.

Her heart rate instantly accelerated and she looked to the other end of the bar. There he was, as gorgeous as the first day she'd laid eyes on him—Aidan Tate.

"May I join you?"

"Aren't you eating with the team?"

"Doesn't look like it, does it?" He walked over minus an invitation.

"No need to raise your hackles—it was only a question."

Ali pressed her lips together tightly. Maybe she should

just call Cole at En Pointe and say she needed her old life back. The cold-blooded one. Immediately.

Eight days suddenly seemed like an eternity.

"I wasn't—" Aidan began sharply, then stopped himself with an equally abrupt change of demeanor. "When I saw you in here it just reminded me..." He didn't bother finishing.

"I know," Ali replied softly, not trusting herself to touch him despite the fact that his hand was resting just within temptation's reach. Three days ago she would have. But now wasn't then. "It reminded me, too."

She let her finger trace up the slender stem of the cocktail glass, already beading with condensation. She'd never believed it was possible to actually feel your heart breaking until this very moment.

"Well, aren't *we* the happy couple?" Aidan lifted his glass with a sad smile. "Cheers."

Ali raised her cocktail and clinked glasses with him. As she brought the glass to her lips the scent of the alcohol in the drink went straight to her gut. It was all she could do to keep her tummy in check as intense waves of nausea began to build within her.

"I'm sorry, Aidan. Will you excuse me?"

"No time for a drink with a colleague?"

It was unbearable to see the disappointment in his face. She felt it too. But she had to get out of there—and fast.

"It's not that. Sorry... I'm just not feeling very well."

"Anything I can do?" He reached toward her and she pulled away, tucking her laptop in front of her chest as if it would protect her heart from any more pain.

Oh, blimey. She really wasn't feeling well at all.

"No, no. I'll be all right. Sorry about the drink."

She winced as she said the words, but knew time

wasn't on her side. If she didn't get to her room... *Too late*. Ali grabbed hold of the doorframe to the bar and, despite her best efforts, returned her lunch to the world.

Talk about mortifying!

"Ali! Are you all right?"

"What do you think?" She didn't have the where-withal to pull her elbow away from Aidan's support-ive hold.

"Don't worry, madam. We'll get it cleaned up for you." The bartender had arrived with several cloths and handed her a dampened serviette. "Would you like me to call a doctor?"

"I *am* a doctor."

"*I* am a doctor." Aidan's voice was stronger than hers.

She glared at him, as if that would help take away the relief she felt that he was there by her side. But having him as her support system wasn't her destiny.

"I'd just like to go to my room, if that's all right."

"I'll walk you there."

"No." She gritted her teeth together, then forced her-self to offer Aidan a polite smile. They were in public, after all. "Thank you."

"Don't be ridiculous. My room is next to yours any-way, so it's not like it's out of my way."

"Would you like your drinks sent to your room? Rooms...?" the bartender asked, obviously unsure how to wrap up a situation of this nature.

"No!" They each answered definitively.

"Right you are, then. I'll just call Housekeeping." He turned away on his heel, obviously annoyed at their collective terseness.

Aidan started to giggle first. Ali couldn't help but join him. By the time they hit the elevator and its doors had firmly shut they were in the throes of a full-on belly laugh.

It felt nice. To be laughing with Aidan. She chanced a glance up at him and saw he felt the same thing. It would've been so easy to step right back into his arms, feel the warmth of his chest. Nestle into that perfect little spot that made it so easy for him to rest his cheek on her head while she listened to his heartbeat.

The elevator lurched to a halt, instantly reminding Ali of why they were headed to their rooms in the first place. Another wave of nausea was threatening to defeat her ability to retain control over her stomach. What on earth was going on? She hadn't eaten anything suspect for lunch. It couldn't be food poisoning.

"Are you all right? You look awfully pale."

"I'll be fine. I think a good lie-down is all I need."

Ali slipped her key into the door and pushed it open before turning to face Aidan. *C'mon, girl, be nice. He's trying to help.*

"Maybe this is the other team's attempt to take us all out with food poisoning!"

"Great hypothesis—except you're the only one being sick."

"It's a working theory. I'm willing to explore more options."

Aidan looked down at her with an expression that was anything but amused. "I'm right next door if you need anything."

"I'll be fine."

She tucked herself behind the door, making it clear she was going solo. He was too close. And, no matter how much she could do with an Aidan-shaped pillow in bed, right now she needed him elsewhere. *Now.*

"Honestly." She gave him what she hoped looked like a nonchalant smile. "I'll be fine."

Two hours later, "fine" was the last thing Ali felt. She'd forced herself to lie in bed after Aidan had left and had gone through a medical checklist as to what could have caused her to be sick so suddenly.

One panicked trip to a nearby chemists later and feeling "fine" was something she knew would be unbelievably hard to come by.

Excited, confused, terrified...

Those she could do.

She stared at the plastic stick in her hand again as if it might have been lying to her. Then she stared at the other one.

Nope. Two stripes on each, and she hadn't got a concussion.

She was pregnant.

And the only man who could be the father was one very thin wall away.

CHAPTER NINE

AIDAN STOOD IN the airport Arrivals hall, a stream of speeches already going through his head. None of them were particularly fair. His father hadn't been the bad guy in his first marriage, and if he'd found happiness at long last the only thing Aidan should be feeling was happiness.

His dad was an amazing guy. Social, laser-smart, professionally still at the fore of his game. He was a great catch. And yet he couldn't help but think, *Why him and not me?*

It wasn't jealousy. It was pure frustration that his dad had managed to move beyond his unhappy past and *he* hadn't. He just hadn't reconciled a way to move forward after Mary had died.

Ah! There he was. Richard Tate. Definitely a contender for the "silver-haired fox" category. He'd recognize that head of hair anywhere and—

Oh, my word.
Is that...?
Did he...?

Aidan didn't know whether to be happy or mystified at the strangeness of humankind. It appeared, from the beaming faces of the happy couple, that his father had gone and married his divorce lawyer. How on earth...?

"Hello, son!"

"Hey, Dad. And it's Marianne, isn't it?"

"Well, I'm not going to start making you call me 'Mother,' if that's what you're worried about."

Marianne gave him a warm smile and much to his amazement he felt himself returning it. He was *genuinely* happy for his father. After the tightness in his heart these past few days it was a relief to let the clamps loosen—if only just a bit.

"I take it you approve?" His father gave him a knowing look.

"Father! What on earth do you mean?" Aidan took charge of their luggage trolley and began guiding them toward the car park, a big grin playing on his lips. "I approve of *all* your wise decisions."

"Oh, don't be coy with me, son." He made an unsuccessful attempt to commandeer the luggage trolley and then opted to swing an arm over his wife's shoulders instead. "I think you'll be happy to know I have finally—after some rather extensive and heavily faulty experimentation—found 'The One.'"

Aidan had to work hard not to give him a dubious look.

Marianne gave a happy laugh at her new husband's declaration of love and smiled knowingly at Aidan. "At least you can be sure if it doesn't work out I know how to *really* put the screws in when it comes to the divorce."

The couple began to absolutely crease themselves with laughter, as if she'd just said the funniest thing in the entire world. Divorce didn't seem on the immediate horizon from the looks of things.

Aidan shook his head and smiled. You could've knocked him over with a feather right now. What was it they said? There was nowt so queer as folk...

Too bad life hadn't been as generous to him and Ali. His lips settled into a straight line. They'd hardly exchanged a word since they'd left that away game, and he could hardly blame her.

What was he doing, anyway? Keeping her at arm's length for exactly *what* benefit? Closing down what had been a perfect fit? She was smart, sexy as hell and she had no quarrel with standing up to him—there was definitely a bit of "like father, like son" in *that* department. Was he carving his own history into something he had predetermined it to be? An unhappy one?

Aidan began to unload their luggage into the trunk of his car as Marianne and his father play-bickered over who would get the front seat. They looked happy. Genuinely happy. Which was exactly how he felt when he was with Ali. Excepting these past torturous seventy-two hours, when he'd most likely ruined any chance of getting back into her good books.

He hoped she was all right. Leaving her on her own after she had been unwell at the hotel hadn't sat right—but he was trying to respect her wishes. It was the least he could do after unceremoniously dumping her. Because that was what he'd done. Just like he'd done to every other woman he'd dated. Only this time it had been different. This time he hadn't meant a single word. Seeing his father so happy, so content, was a glaring confirmation that he'd done the wrong thing when it came to Ali.

And the chances of fixing it? Making things right with her?

An image of her closing the door in his face flickered through his mind's eye.

Nil.

She'd accepted the terms of their deal. And he didn't

blame her. She would think herself a fool to fly back into the arms of a man who played hot and cold. Unless he were to tell her that he loved her.

The thought unsettled him. He didn't do love. He did casual.

This was all just sentiment, right? He was letting surprise at his father's choice of bride soften his resolve. Sure, they were happy *now*—but that was how relationships were in the beginning. All giggly and fun in the first few months.

Even as the words flowed through his mind they felt wrong. He'd known about Ali from the moment he'd laid eyes on her. Getting to know her had only cemented in stone what he hadn't been brave enough to put into words then: he loved her. Heart and soul.

He raked a hand through his hair and slammed the lid of the trunk down with a satisfying clang. He'd blown it with Ali and it was just as well. He'd just have to find a way to live with the consequences.

"Son! You've got human beings in the car here!" His father stuck his head out the window. "What gives?"

"Sorry, Dad... Marianne. Forgot about your old jangling bones!" he joked, not feeling the remotest bit cheery. "Just a bit distracted by work." He slipped into the car and started the engine.

"Anything we can do to help?" Marianne asked from the back seat.

Apart from winning back the heart of the woman I love and proving true love can last? No. Not really.

"How about you magically heal our flanker's clavicle and pray for no more groin injuries?"

Marianne made a *youch* face in the rearview mirror.

"What about we take you out to dinner tonight after

work, son? Then you won't have to worry about cooking or anything.

"Sounds good, Dad."

And for the first time in a very, very long time a night with his father and his new wife sounded like something he would genuinely look forward to.

Ali looked up from her desk at the sound of Aidan's knock on her office doorframe. Her tummy did a flip as their eyes caught. Was it the baby or her who was reacting to seeing him? Surely the baby was too small? And it wasn't as if she was unaware of the effect Aidan had on her.

As if to press the point, her fingers began to tingle. So she sat on them. "How'd it go at the airport?"

"Good! They're sleeping off their jetlag and we're meeting up for dinner later. But it went well! She's really nice."

"You look surprised."

"It seems my father has gone and done something wise."

Aidan leaned against the doorframe, all lean-sexy-man-style. Oh, she *really* wished he wouldn't do that. This was what he would do in the mornings when he brought her coffee. Stand in the doorframe and watch her for a moment, before coming into the room and giving her a long, slow kiss.

Her hand snuck out from under her leg and began to trace her lips. She couldn't help it. They were missing his touch. *All of her* was missing his touch.

Didn't he have work to do? As long as he was out of sight she'd have more time to think up the right combination of words to tell him he was going to be a father. He had a right to know. Then she'd tell him he didn't have to worry. That she and the baby would be all right on their own.

She blinked up at Aidan and realized he was looking at her expectantly. Was she meant to have said something?

"Sorry—what was that?"

"My father..."

Aidan peered at her curiously. She guessed she hadn't hidden the thoughts racing round her mind all that well.

"He's married quite a wonderful woman."

"That's great!" Ali enthused, using every bit of strength she had to maintain a bright smile.

Now what? Should she say, *Give them my best, and while you're at it you may as well let them know they're going to be grandparents in about seven months' time!*

"Yeah. You should meet her. You'd like her."

"Sure. Absolutely! That'd be great!"

Lordy. She sounded like a wind-up fairy on a sugar high.

"Um..." She pointed at the paperwork on her desk. "I've just got to go through these stats. Shall we catch up later?"

"No problem."

Aidan gave her a sideways glance. One that told her in an instant that he knew something was up but wasn't going to push it. For which she was grateful. She still needed time. Time to formulate a Big Picture plan before dropping her bombshell.

Her little, tiny, baby-shaped bombshell.

Ali had to face facts. There were only so many cotton buds a person could fit into the plastic container she was twirling round and round, trying to divine a small spot for just one more teeny-tiny bud. Was that so much to ask? A bit more room to make things fit? Ditto cotton swabs, knee braces, ankle braces, crepe bandages, sock tape, grip enhancers and zinc oxide tapes. Her run bag was officially full to bursting.

She sat back in her chair with a huff.

She had to face facts. No amount of tidying was going to change the reality that she still hadn't told Aidan she was pregnant with his baby. And that instead of feeling absolutely horrified she felt abuzz with a myriad of sensations.

The sensation she felt most of all was *happy*. Really, truly, fire-burning-in-her-belly happy. Not a literal fire, of course, because that would hurt the baby, and already—just one attack of nausea and a few early nights in—she felt a fierce need to protect the microscopic little creature.

By her estimation the baby would be eight weeks, one day and—she glanced up at the wall clock—thirteen or so hours old. Not that she'd been racking her brains trying to figure out the moment of conception or anything. There had been that "incident" with a condom on the first night they'd shared, so it looked as if she was living proof that nothing was foolproof.

It wasn't too strange that she'd missed the signs. She'd had a period after "The Great Airport Liaison," so hadn't thought twice about the protection malfunction.

Ali stared at the tip of the cotton bud. Was this how big it was? The baby? A little four-and-a-half-millimeter being, busy developing a circulatory system, buds for arms and legs, all of its teeny-tiny internal organs taking shape.

If she was eight weeks along it would already be forming itsy-bitsy ears, eyes, and a little-bitty upper

lip. One that, when it was fully developed and she was
holding their—*her*—baby in her arms, she would trace
with her finger as if it was the most amazing thing in
the world. Which it was, considering she was using all
sorts of gooey baby talk in her head.

She was a *scientist*, for heaven's sake. Someone who
always retained her cool.

A memory of raking her nails down Aidan's back as
he teased first his fingers and then his—*stop*!

Almost always retained her cool.

When she hadn't had her period last month she'd
just written it off to a combination of adrenaline, a new
level of fitness because she'd been working out so much
and…well…honestly…? Who wanted a monthly visitor when you were having such a great time mattress-
testing? Besides, her periods had never been regular.

She'd been too busy sliding down rainbows and
twirling round pots of gold, thinking how happy she
was with her life up here. A dreamy little life, way up
here on Cloud Nine. Until Aidan had yanked away the
fluffy cloud and abruptly plonked her back down to
planet earth.

Jerk.

Perfectly perfect jerk.

How on earth was she going to tell him? It ate at her
heart that he couldn't see beyond his past, but that was
the way their cookie crumbled. She'd certainly let her
lack of a future in dance maul her soul for a while. She
understood how disappointment could eat away at you.

Apart from which, if the baby *had* been conceived
on that night at the airport there really would have been
every chance she'd never have seen him again. Two people put together by a heavy snowfall to make a baby.
Her baby. If she thought of it that way—took away the

Aidan she had fallen in love with—it was easier to bear. By a smidge.

So... She drew in a deep breath. This was how it would be: Ali and her very own little baby, creating a brand-new family. The Lockhart Duo! Just like she and her mother had been. She'd never dreamed of being anything but on her own after her mother died—so this was good. Just different than what she'd planned.

Ali leaned back in her chair, using her toes to push herself back and forth. She'd known for about five days and seventeen hours and she wasn't sure the news had sunk in with her—let alone given her enough time to calmly tell Aidan he was going to be a father. Each time she'd opened her mouth to say something there had either been an interruption or she'd lost the courage.

She had to tell him. At the very least it was his right to know. Especially since she was going to see this through. She was going to have the baby.

As the thought paraded through her brain a whole new set of nerves sent a fresh course of adrenaline through her. She'd have to go to yoga tonight after work—not hot yoga...that wouldn't be good for the baby. But yoga—the calming sort—was a must if she was ever going to rein in her composure enough to tell Aidan. Which she would. When she found the right time. *If* she found the right time.

Oh, golly, gosh—and a Moses basket to boot!

She was simply going to *have* to find a time.

She tried to picture what his face would look like after she told him—said the words *We're having a baby.* Or *I'm having a baby.* Maybe that would be better. No. Then it might sound like someone else could've been in the picture. *As if.*

There is a baby.

No. Too scientific. And vague.

Remember at the airport, when we were pretending we didn't care it was Valentine's Day, decided to skip dinner and went straight to the great sex part? We ate ice cream after. Choc chip mint. With fudge sauce. Which I licked off your—

No. Inappropriate for a baby-reveal.

Then again… Maybe it hadn't been that night after all. It could have been that night they'd each got rug burns. Or…

Aaaaaargh! No, no, no, no, no, noooooooooo!

She plonked her head down on her desk with a clonk. Her speech needed work.

"Lockhart?" Coach Stone gave the doorframe of her office a quick knock before entering. "You all right to do the skinfolds this morning? Tate's off doing X-rays with Rory."

"Absolutely." She smiled and grabbed her caliper. "Be there in a mo."

Work. The perfect distraction. It had helped her get through tough times before. But this time it was going to be much harder to put the blinkers on and block out the obvious. She was in love with Aidan Tate and she was going to have his baby—and those weren't things Aidan wanted in his life: a relationship, a baby. A family. The sooner she got that through her thick skull, the better.

She pushed into the locker room and as the fug of sweaty man scent, dirty towels, smelly rugby cleats and fifteen different varieties of deodorant hit her she found herself trying to knock back another powerful wave of nausea.

"You all right, Harty?" one of the players asked as she barely stopped herself from swooning at the sensation. "You're looking a bit green around the gills."

"Did you guys run out of shower gel or something?" She cracked a smile but had to hold on to the doorframe to help her collect herself before entering the locker room. It had never seemed this rank before. What had these guys been *doing* all morning?

"You didn't go and get yourself pregnant at one of our away games, did you, Harty?"

Her stomach turned again. "Ha-ha. Very funny." She forced herself to let go of the doorframe.

Must remember to mouth-breathe. That should just about get her through the next half hour in here.

"Come on, Mack. You're up first, fatty!" She opened the calipers in an evil scientist clamping motion and left the doorway. She could do this.

As she tried to stride into the center of the room a huge waft of tropical heat hit her when one of the players came out of the steam room. Unsteadiness began to work its way through her, as if she were a huge bobble woman. The players and the lockers began to spin around her. She could see but not hear Mack as he approached her, arms outstretched, and then—darkness.

Aidan gave the coach an incredulous look. Ali? *His* Ali had fainted?

"I don't know what happened, Aidan. She just came into the locker room to do the caliper tests, and next thing you know was out like a light in Mack's arms. One of the boys found some salts and she was back up at work as if nothing had happened a few minutes later, but it was strange."

"What? She fainted because Mack was holding her?" That didn't sound like Ali—and he didn't like the idea of her being in another man's arms.

"No, no. She fainted and he caught her because he

was on his way to her to get his skinfold test." Coach Stone gave him a sideways glance. "What does it matter, anyway? Point is, Lockhart fainted for no apparent reason, and you need her on top form tomorrow for the final or you need to get someone new in here. *Stat.* Are we clear?"

"Absolutely, Coach. I'll go speak with her."

"You do that. We need absolutely no diversions tomorrow."

The coach was serious. The team had done incredibly well this season, and he had all but cleared a prime spot in the display cabinets of the North Stars' trophy room. They were all in the same place—on the same mission. Fainting doctors weren't really a goer at this point.

Strange, though. When he'd last seen Ali she'd been perfectly... No, she hadn't. She'd been distracted. *Very* distracted. Maybe she had some sort of bug. There was always something going around this time of year as the seasons shifted. If that was the case he didn't want her anywhere near the team. It wasn't how he'd been hoping to see out the last day he had with her—but if he had to ban her from the game, he would. He'd chosen work and he needed to stay true to that.

Aidan pushed out of the locker room's double doors and headed for her office. They'd barely spoken since his father had arrived. Everything between them was the opposite of how he'd imagined their final days together would be. If he had been a wall-puncher his apartment would have been riddled with holes.

This was just the sort of scenario he should've pictured before he'd let himself get carried away with—with *what*, exactly? Falling in love with Ali Lockhart? That was about the size of it. He just didn't know how to picture it, though. Never had. Marriage to the girl of his dreams and living happily ever...? Didn't he give himself an annual reminder as to why that was *never* going to happen?

He stuck his head round Ali's office door. She was wholly engrossed in finishing up some paperwork and he stole the few moments to soak her in. Ebony hair falling down her back and over her shoulder in thick waves. Long fingers playing at her lips while she chose what to write on the forms. He narrowed his focus to the pads of her fingers, tip-tapping along her lips—lips he knew he could never tire of kissing.

He straightened and abruptly cleared his throat. This sort of mooning wasn't going to get him anywhere.

"Hey, there." Ali turned round in her chair, eyebrows slightly raised in expectation.

"Mind if I come in?"

"Please." Ali indicated a chair—not the one closest to her desk, he noticed. Fair enough. It wasn't as if he'd been unleashing a welcoming parade of late.

"Coach wanted me to check on how you were feeling."

She tilted her head to the side, as if she were considering what to say, then gave a dry laugh. "I'm fine." She looked him in the eye. "Anything else?"

"Are you sure? You don't think you've got a bug or something? I heard about the fainting."

Ali pressed her lips together. Hard. Then let them scrape past her teeth before allowing herself to answer. She'd left it too long to tell Aidan now. The day before the final. Destroying his focus when he needed it most Was not really the plan of action she'd been going for. She would tell him directly after the final. And then she'd leave.

"I'm fine, Aidan. Just putting together the team's final set of health stats before the big day."

He nodded, rubbed his hands along his thighs and gave his hands a clap, as if he was gearing up to saying something big. "Good, good. Anything interesting?"

Uh... I'm pregnant with your baby.

Out loud, voice—please! Otherwise Aidan's going to keep hovering, and the longer he stands here the more you're going to want to slip into his arms and be held for one lovely, long, Aidan-scented last time before you have to say goodbye.

"Mack seems to have the most consistently low resting heart rate of the lot," she mustered, in her bright-as-a-bluebird voice. "And..." She ran her finger along the chart she was currently working on. "Looks like Jonesey wins on the skinfold test—although they're all really in peak condition. I would say there's not much more than a hair's breadth between them."

"Great. As well they should be. Coach has been working them hard." Aidan moved to the doorway but didn't seem to be making much of an effort to actually leave the room, which would've been the ideal outcome.

"That he has!" Ali smiled at him, hoping her expression said *We're done now.* Her veneer of cheer was about to crack, so his departure would be good.

"You wouldn't...?" Aidan's voice trailed off.

For the sweet love of an ending! Spit it out, man! There are not so many hours left in this day, and that means there are fewer than twenty-four more before you hear you're going to be a father.

"Wouldn't *what*, Aidan?" Ali was finding it hard to mask her exasperation.

"You wouldn't like to come out to dinner with me tonight? To meet my dad and his wife," he added hastily.

Unexpected.

He gave her one of those pretty-please smiles of his that she found virtually impossible to resist.

"There's a lot to do before tomorrow..." she stalled.

"C'mon Ali. You've got to eat."

Aidan sat down in the chair next to her desk and took her hand in his. Her nerve endings shot to attention and it was all she could do not to climb into his lap, wrap her arms around his neck and tell him everything.

"Help me out here."

"What? By having dinner with your dad and your new *stepmum*?"

She knew the word would rankle. Which was precisely why she'd said it. He pulled his hand away from hers—just as she'd predicted.

"She's not that bad, actually." He rested his hand on his chin and began to draw rugby-ball-shaped doodles on a notepad. "I know it's not what we'd planned for tonight."

Ali sat back in her chair. This was interesting. They had, over the past weeks, made a very distinct point of not having *any* plans. Ever. They'd "just happened" to end up in one or the other's kitchens, or sofas, and just about always beds every single night since "That Night" a few months ago.

"And what exactly *was* it we had planned for tonight?"

"Hanging out with my dad didn't really top the list."

Aidan's face lit up with one of those irascible smiles of his, and despite her best intentions Ali's tummy went all effervescent in a way that had nothing to do with her pregnancy.

"I really need to pack tonight, Aidan."

She tried to look aggrieved at the choice she had to

make, but dining out as a family when she knew there was a whole lot more "family" on the cards than anyone else knew was not a chart-topper for her.

"C'mon, Ali. We both know you only have enough things to put in a run bag." His eyes met hers. "I know it's weird, but I'd like you to come. You know me. I'm hardly the king of lively conversation and I promise to be really irritating. It'll make your forget-about-Aidan campaign much easier."

"I don't think anything will make that easier."

Ali wished she could swallow the words back down her throat. She would never, *ever* forget Aidan Tate. Not in a million years.

"Hey... C'mon..." Aidan's fingers crept across the desk toward hers. "It hasn't been all bad, has it?"

"You know it has been the total *opposite* of that, you barmstick."

"Easy on the language, Lockhart. You'll get yourself kicked off the field tomorrow if you don't watch it."

Ali didn't reply. She just gave him a sad smile. She could feel the choke of tears begin in her throat. This was going to be so tough. Harder than anything. Why did he have to carry on being so *nice*? If he could go back to being the irascible, arrogant, know-it-all she'd first met this would be a whole lot easier. But if he really had been that haughty guy she knew she wouldn't have fallen in love with him as deeply as she had.

"Look. I'm not going to take no for an answer. We'll eat early. They're still jet-lagged, and you and I both need an early night." Aidan put his hands up in the air as if he was showing her his final card. His ace. "Besides, you'll need your energy for tomorrow and it's not like you're going to eat well at home." He pulled a face. "I've tasted your cooking."

"What are you saying, exactly? I make delicious bowls of cereal!" Ali was laughing now. He had that way with her. Always teasing away the protective layers and unveiling one of her unabashed smiles when she least expected to give it.

She felt her smile fade and had to look away from those dark eyes of his.

She'd wanted change when she came up here to Tealside, and she had received the super-deluxe treatment.

"So, I'll pick you up around six-thirty?"

Aidan rose from his chair as if it were a done deal. Then he smiled again, the little crinkles by his eyes doing their cute little dimple thing.

It was only dinner. And she was a grown-up. Might as well meet the future grandparents of her child!

"Great. See you then."

CHAPTER TEN

"AIDAN TELLS US you work with dancers?"

Richard Tate was definitely a man who liked to keep the flow of conversation moving. Not that he had much work on his hands tonight. He and his wife were great fun, and Ali would've been hard pressed to recall a single awkward moment. Even Aidan, whom she'd thought might easily revert into "annoyed son mode," seemed on good form.

"Most of the work I do—*did*—was with dancers. But En Pointe does a lot of work with gymnasts, as well. They have similar injuries. It's mostly women, so working up here has been quite a change."

Understatement of the universe!

"Ali's made some great alterations to the team's training."

Aidan jumped in with details of all the changes they'd made since her arrival. In fact all night he'd been on some sort of mission to put all her plus-points on display. It was flattering, sure. But not what she was used to. Particularly after having worked with shut-down, grim-faced Aidan for the past few days.

It felt as though she'd grabbed on to an enormous emotion-laden pendulum and was holding on for dear life. He was acting like a young man showing off his new girlfriend to his parents—not someone who'd brought her along just to keep the chitchat lively. Talk about a sea change.

"I'd like to make sure Ali's work here stays in play." He gave her a wink before taking a bite of his steak.

He liked it medium rare: super-seared on the outside with a dark seam of rare in the center. With chips. And a mountain of salad. Not that she had been getting to know everything he liked over the past three months or anything. *Nothing like that at all.*

"In fact," he continued after a moment, "we might start calling the exercises 'Lockharts.'"

Everyone at the table laughed apart from Ali, who just managed not to choke on her wild mushroom gratin. *Classy.*

Lockharts? *Really?* All that was going to remain of her time here were some ankle-strengthening exercises? Or was all of this just Aidan's way of trying to sugarcoat the truth? He was looking forward to her departure. He liked being in charge. That much had been clear when she'd arrived.

Her hand slipped onto her belly for a protective rub. All she had to do was make it through this dinner and the game tomorrow, and then she would be done. Oh! And tell Aidan he was going to be a father before she hopped on the train. Other than that—she had just about wrapped everything up.

"Are your plans to return to London straight away?" Marianne asked.

"That's the idea," Ali quipped, grabbing her water and fastidiously avoiding eye contact with Aidan.

Her mouth had gone dry about a thousand times already that night and this moment was no different.

Until she told Aidan about their baby, and that he was off the hook in the responsibility department, everything was going to be off-kilter. Time to steer the conversation off of her.

"How did you and Richard meet?"

If Ali could've opened her mouth and stuffed her foot directly into it she would have. Aidan stared at her in disbelief until Marianne and Richard broke the silence with near-hysterical giggles.

"I thought Aidan would've told you!"

"Well..." Ali desperately started backpedaling. "He did mention something about—about your profession."

"Don't worry, dear." Marianne reached across the table and patted her arm comfortingly. "I like to look at our introduction as a sort of primer into The Full Richard Tate Package." She gave her new husband a warm smile. "I knew what I was getting into when I agreed to marry this man—and I also knew exactly what sort of woman he didn't want."

"What's ridiculous," Richard jumped in, "is how long it took me to figure it out. They do say women are smarter than men. I can assure you, Ali, that is definitely the case in this scenario. Truth be told, I'm grateful for my past. If I hadn't made so many mistakes, hit rock-bottom, I never would've ended up at this one's doorstep. I'm just annoyed it took me so long to realize Cupid was pointing his big neon arrow right over her cute little head."

He gave Marianne's hand a squeeze and lifted his glass of wine.

"A toast."

Ali raised the glass of wine she'd been fastidiously avoiding all night.

"A toast," Richard repeated, making eye contact with each of them. "To finding 'The One.'"

As Ali raised her glass to the chorus of "Hear! Hear!" her stomach dropped, then catapulted up to her throat.

There had been a ridiculously untethered moment in time when she'd thought Aidan might have been The One—but he had been very clear that family life was not for him. She watched as Richard gave Marianne a moon-eyed gaze, followed by a kiss... If his goal in bringing her here to meet his dad had been to illustrate just how messed up his father was, it wasn't working.

"You're not drinking to the toast?"

Aidan's hand slipped onto her knee under the table. She wished he wouldn't do that. It was all too easy to imagine him touching her elsewhere, and they weren't doing that anymore. She jogged her knee away from his hand.

"I took a sip," she lied. "Just trying to keep my wits about me for the match tomorrow. We're lucky it's a home game, aren't we?"

Excellent topic-changer, Ali! You're getting good at this.

"Good point, love." Richard took a final swig of his wine whilst signaling to the waiter that they wanted the check. "We could do with slipping off to bed and letting you both get your rest." He gave a wink to Aidan. "I don't want to shoulder the blame for any poorly set noses tomorrow."

"Dad." Aidan sent his father a dry look. "I think I can handle a broken nose in my sleep, thank you very much."

"I know, son." He gave Aidan a pointed look. "There isn't much you *can't* do once you set your mind to something."

* * *

"You really didn't have to walk me to my car. I'm a big girl, you know."

Ali fumbled amidst her handbag debris for her key. Was being discombobulated part of being pregnant? Or was being next to Aidan the reason her well-honed cool demeanor had deteriorated into a jumble of jitters?

"Of course I did. You were incredibly indulgent in accompanying me here. 'Meeting the parents.'" He flicked his fingers in the quotes symbol then put his hands on her shoulders and turned her toward him.

The jangle factor of her nerve endings shot up another notch. He slid his hands along the collar of her coat and tucked it up close round her neck.

Oh...why do you always have to smell so nice? And be so nice. I don't want to say goodbye.

The thought lay like lead in her heart. "Right. So, I'll see you at the stadium tomorrow, bright and early?"

"Yeah, of course—the big game!" Aidan let his hands dawdle on her coat collar, his index fingers tracing along the stitched edging of the woolen fabric, thumbs circling in a slow swirl. He'd done it before. That swirl. Her skin remembered it well—her tummy, her breasts... It took all her power not to arch into him, press herself tight against his chest.

But she couldn't do anything to give away what she was really feeling. Not now that she knew his heart would never belong to her.

They each stared at his fingers—lost, she presumed, in different lines of thought. His mind was on the game... Hers was on—what else?—the new life she carried.

Ali wondered if he could sense the changes she had already noticed. She wasn't showing, but she felt more like a woman than she ever had. She was used to feeling lanky—all legs and arms and a long torso to stick it all together—but here, so close to Aidan, with their child in her belly, she felt about as soft and feminine as they came.

"Ali? It meant a lot to me."

"What? Having dinner? You already said that, silly." She looked up into his eyes. She'd miss exploring their deep brown depths, trying to figure out if they were espresso, mahogany, teak or any other deliciously brown color.

"No, I mean—" He broke off and shot a look in his father's direction. He and his wife were standing beside his car. "You being here. All of it." He ducked his head lower, trying his best to give her a meaningful look.

Ali shrugged herself out of his hold on the premise of needing to rub her hands together. She didn't need this. Couldn't bear it. Trite goodbyes for an affair that had enveloped her body and soul were too painful.

She forced herself to look up at him. He wasn't the man he thought he was. Dispassionate. All business. He was kind. Caring. And *so* off-limits. It tore at her heart that his heart was tethered to the past. If only he could see the future for what it was—an amazing gift.

"Well, all good things must come to an end, right?" If they were going to go with trite she might as well embrace the truisms with a fresh smile.

"You're right." he acquiesced. "What's the point in making rules if you don't stick to them?"

Ali pressed her lips together and gave him what she hoped looked like a nod. She didn't agree. Not now. This was definitely a time when rules were meant to be broken. Meant to be reformed, reshaped. Why not the whole shebang? This was a time when they needed an entirely new rulebook—one that bent and flowed with the wind. One that would allow them to be together. One that allowed them to have a baby.

"Son, we're freezing to death out here. Mind if you toss us the keys?"

"I'm coming, Dad."

Aidan turned to go, then swiftly turned back and bent his head to kiss her on the cheek. It was one of those instants she wished she could have frozen in time. His scent. His touch. His breath slipping along her cheek down to the bit of neck not snuggled in the depths of her woolly scarf. She'd never know those sensations again.

Choking back a sob, Ali nodded again and gave him a wave goodbye. She plunged back into her handbag and came up trumps on the first forage. Car keys. Thank God. She needed to get away. Clear her head. Write the script—the farewell script—and make sure the North Stars won their final match before she set about figuring out what she and her baby would do with the rest of their lives.

Nothing to it. Nothing at all.

"Are you going to tell me why you won't admit to dating that young woman?"

Aidan's father dunked an herbal teabag in and out of his mug as he waited for Aidan to answer. Since when did Mr. Meat and Potatoes drink *herbal tea*?

"Not sure what you're talking about, Dad."

"Ali. The young woman we just dined with."

His father spoke slowly, as if Aidan had suddenly become hard of hearing.

"We work together. That's all."

"Yes, son, and I'm the Emperor of China." His father laughed, squeezed the teabag on the side of the mug with a spoon and took it out. "You're in love with that woman—it's plain as the hand at the end of my arm."

Aidan all but choked on his own tea. Traditional English tea, with milk in. *He* hadn't changed. Unlike his father, who kept throwing new components of himself out into the universe to be seen by one and all. Wasn't this the man who'd taught him that there was no sure thing in life? That love was as fleeting as the seasons? *It comes and goes—it comes and goes—and you can never rely on it.*

"Sorry, Dad." Aidan gave him a rueful look. "Just colleagues."

His father walked round the kitchen island and pulled out one of the stools. "Against company rules, is it?"

Aidan's stomach clenched. "Something like that." He nodded, hoping his father would let the subject drop, and took another sip of tea. Against Aidan's rules was more like it, but he didn't need to tell his father that.

"No. I don't buy it, son. What happened? You two have a fight or something?"

Aidan looked at his father in surprise. What was this? An inquisition? "What would make you say something like that?"

"I don't know. There definitely seemed to be something going on between the two of you—but Ali seemed..." He sought the perfect word just as Marianne came into the kitchen, made a beeline for her husband's mug and took a sip. "Sugar, what was that thing you said about Aidan and Ali?"

Aidan's eyebrows just about popped off his forehead. *What*? They'd been *discussing* him and Ali? They'd only been home from supper for five minutes!

Marianne gave him a guilty smile. "Don't worry,

love. It's one of the side effects of my trade. I just can't help analyzing every couple I come across."

"We're *not* a couple! How many times do I have to tell you?"

"Well, if you're not you should be," Marianne rejoined. "I have seen thousands of couples come in and out of my offices. Most of them end up divorced. But the ones with a connection like you two have...? Those ones always end up leaving hand in hand."

"Like you and me, eh?" Aidan's father grabbed her round the waist and gave her a cuddle.

"Most of my suitors didn't show up with their wives. Or wait twenty more years to propose, for that matter."

"I wanted to be original!"

"You definitely are that, love. You definitely are that." She gave Richard a peck on the cheek and stole his mug again for another sip.

"We're not a couple," Aidan muttered into his mug, acutely aware that no one was remotely listening to his side of the conversation.

He should just go to bed. Watching these two canoodle was getting him nowhere. The whole reason he'd put a halt to things between Ali and himself was because you couldn't change the past. It was part of you—no matter what.

"Besides, son..." Aidan's father re-engaged him, with Marianne's shoulder safely tucked under his arm. "It's like your mother said the other day—"

"Wait a minute." Aidan could hardly believe his ears. "You still *talk* to Mum?"

"'Course I do, son. We may not have been a love match—and I can assure you we don't talk much—but we've got an eternal bond."

Aidan opened his hands in a *what bond?* gesture.

"*You*, son. We'll always be proud of having done that together. If I hadn't met your mother I wouldn't have you, and there is not a chance in high heaven that I would've gone through my life without knowing the absolute pleasure of fatherhood."

This was a bit of a blindsider.

They'd never really had a traditional father-son relationship. It wasn't as though Aidan had ever felt unloved, he just hadn't felt a part of his father's life, except on an administrative level. Particularly since Mary had died, It was hardly as if his dad had been seeking Father of the Year points.

"That's right, Aidan." Marianne nodded. "In fact your father was quite reluctant about our tying the knot without you being there. He was really hoping you'd join us, but with the season running the way it does he thought you'd be wrapped up in work."

Aidan's face must've been screaming *Seriously?* because both of them burst out laughing.

"It's true, son." His father nodded earnestly. "I was hoping you would be our ring bearer. You would've looked a treat in that 'Little Boy Blue' getup they wear."

Aidan had to join in their laughter. The picture of himself in a little pastel suit with a satin cushion, carrying the rings down the aisle for his father's golden years wedding, was too funny a picture not to laugh at.

"Thanks, Dad. I would've liked to have been there."

"You're always welcome to join us, son. Now that I've found myself a proper wife, who seems intent on keeping me chipper, you are welcome. Anytime."

And from the look on his father's face Aidan could see he meant it. Maybe things really *had* changed for his father. He'd never really invited Aidan along to things before—and he'd always just presumed it was because he didn't want him around.

"Well, son. We're going to pop off to bed. I imagine you'll be up and out of here early. Shall we meet you after the game?"

"That'd be great," Aidan replied with a smile. He meant it, too. "You two have a good night. There will be tickets for you at the gate."

Half an hour later Aidan could still hear them giggling through the walls of the guest bedroom. They really were the picture of a happy couple. Which was a lot more than he could say for Ali and himself. Not that they *were* a couple. They'd been fastidious in that respect—keeping the boundaries clear. Boundaries that had melted away in the bedroom.

Beyond that...? Aidan sank into his sofa, barely seeing the twinkling lights of the city beyond.

He and Ali worked well together. Played well together. They did just about *everything* well together. But was that because they'd made their time limit? Set the boundaries? Was that the only way he functioned? By being able to shut and lock the door on his feelings? It was the way he'd always worked after he'd lost his girlfriend, and it had worked perfectly well. Until now.

Aidan shook his head and pushed up from the sofa. He'd better get some sleep before the match. The last day he'd work with Ali. The last time they would be together. He would never hold her in his arms again.

He hastened to remind himself that it was all for one very pragmatic and practiced reason: he didn't do affairs of the heart. There would be no honoring of what he'd had—or could have had—with Mary if he did. They would have been married now—maybe even had children...

The thought sent a sour taste down his throat. He'd always wanted a family. A big one to make up for his pretty lonely excuse of a childhood. He just had to face facts now. Once Ali was gone he could get back to structure, routine, to his well-practiced comfort zone.

He pulled the duvet up around his head as if it would help block out the truth. This time it had been different. He'd stepped outside the outline of their agreement. This time he'd fallen in love.

Ali felt as though she was having a flashback to the first day she'd met Aidan. Well...not *that* day. Their first day at work. She was kneeling on the ground next to Rory and could see Aidan's size eleven shoes in her eyeline. Only this time he was letting her get on with things. At least they'd made progress in the professional respect department.

"How's it feeling, Rory?"

"Just a turf burn, Doc. It's that new artificial turf. Doesn't suit my baby-soft skin." He tried to wink away her concerns.

"Rory! You were writhing around clutching your shoulder."

"It's not my shoulder. Honest. Just giving the crowd a bit of bonus drama." He popped up from the field with a grin, despite the expanse of raw skin on his arm. "C'mon!" he pleaded. "We've got to get this show on the road! We're three up!"

Ali turned to consult Aidan—who, she could now see, was already jogging back to the benches. *Terrific.* So much for a conference with her colleague. She guessed it was going to be a day of his and hers injuries.

He had hardly said *boo* to her all day. "Exasperating" didn't begin to explain how frustrating the situation was. Where had the "Chatty Kathy" from the night before gone? They were back to the days of Dr. Jekyll and Aidan Hyde. Hide 'n' seek was more like it. The man had been avoiding her from the moment they'd arrived at the stadium.

Or maybe she was just being super-sensitive. They were all hopped up today. The boys were definitely running on high-caliber adrenaline.

The team as a whole had only clocked up a couple of minor injuries, and if they carried on as they had been they'd charge through the rest of the game like bulls. They were super-charged. Everyone was. This was the biggest match of the year, and it felt as if the whole of England had jammed itself into the stands. The roar of the crowd was deafening.

If only it could stifle all the thoughts lurching round her head like out-of-control billiard balls —clanking against each other before careening off in an entirely different direction.

Some focus might be in order.

After a quick examination to make sure his collarbone was still in one piece Ali nodded a reluctant assent. Play could recommence. She jogged off the pitch and headed toward a different bench than the one Aidan had chosen. The number of times she'd almost blurted out her news in the past hour alone was running into double digits.

She glanced up at the game clock. Thirty-seven more minutes. That was it. Thirty-seven minutes and the game would be over, the trophy would—Lord willing—be in the hands of the North Stars, and she could let Aidan know she was pregnant then jump on the train and go back to her old life.

It was what she had decided in the witching hours

of the previous night. She had enjoyed setting up En Pointe, and now that she had a baby on the way maybe being around people she knew wouldn't be such a bad thing. Not that that wasn't the case here.

She took a mental panoramic shot of the stadium in its full glory. Leaving the team behind—the work she'd begun with them, her apartment, the bicycle rides, all of it—was going to be much harder than she'd thought. And as for leaving Aidan...

Pure, unadulterated denial was the only way she was going to get through that goodbye.

Would she prefer to stay with him and watch their baby grow up together? There wasn't a *yes* big enough to encapsulate how much she wanted that to be the case. But there was no getting away from the fact that it was absolutely *not* what Aidan wanted. And she couldn't blame him. He hadn't exactly been handed the smoothest ride in life. No doubt the pain of moving forward—moving on and away from what had never been... Well... He'd made it clear that was never going to happen.

She pressed her hands together between her knees and forced herself to focus on the game. The two sides were going into formation for a new play. What had originally been a massive huddle of muscles and numbered shirts now pinged into individual components for her. She saw repaired ligaments, strengthened ankle joints, improved flexibility, increased speed, heightened stamina. These were some of the fittest people on earth and she had played a role in keeping them that way. Making them more than what they'd thought they could be. It was truly satisfying work.

The huddle of men broke apart as play recommenced, with players running long to catch the rugby ball spinning toward them in a meters-high arc. Mack, unsurprisingly, was at the center of the action, arms reaching up high, cleats giving him the traction to push harder, further than the other players. But as he leapt into the air his arms suddenly snapped to his chest, his feet giving way to the bend of his knees as he crumpled to the ground.

It took the rest of the players a moment to realize anything had happened, but Ali had already taken off from her bench at full speed, calling for a defibrillator to be brought immediately. Everything she knew about him reeled through her mind. The consistently low heart-rate, the intense training, his young age, the occasional bouts of dizziness during training he had always put down to getting overheated.

Hypertrophic cardiomyopathy.

She should have seen it earlier. All the signs would've come together if they had scanned all of the players like the Italians were required to. *Mack was having a heart attack.* Sudden cardiac death in young athletes had been hitting the headlines too often lately, and it looked like this match would now hit the front page for all the wrong reasons.

As each microsecond passed his life would be in increasing danger. Her lungs tightened as she ran faster. Aidan passed her with an AED kit before she'd even become aware of him. He had obviously put the pieces of the puzzle together, as well. The crowd went collectively silent as Ali reached the group of players around Mack.

One of the opposing team players was already doing compressions on Mack's chest.

"Did you check the airway?" Aidan knelt down opposite the player.

"Yes, Doc. No heartbeat."

The player continued his compressions until Aidan indicated that they should switch roles. "Ali! Grab the AED."

She took the player's place, checking the switches on the automated external defibrillator. They glowed green. Aidan must've flicked it on while running. These portable devices were a godsend in this sort of scenario. The only truly effective way to shock the heart back into action.

If Mack's heart was strong enough...

Without seeing a scan it was impossible to say, but Ali would have bet any amount of money it would reveal a thickened wall of heart muscle around the septum, where the left and right sides of the heart were separated. When the muscle between the lower heart chambers thickened blood flow could be blocked—particularly when the body was undergoing intense physical strain.

"Pulse?" Aidan looked to her for an answer.

Ali placed her fingers on both Mack's wrist and his carotid artery. *Nothing.* She shook her head.

"Are you charged?"

"Yes."

Ali rucked up Mack's shirt, stopping only for Aidan to finish a series of compressions. He lifted his hands so she could place the electrode pads on his bare chest. She gave each cable a quick tug to ensure they were firmly in place.

"Clear!"

Aidan raised his hands. She pressed the shock button and watched as the voltage bucked through Mack's chest. Aidan began chest compressions again. Thirty chest compressions and then two breaths of air. It would be up to two minutes before the AED could read Mack's obs and let them know if it had worked—if they'd tricked his body into working again.

She held her breath along with the rest of the crowd, her eyes trained on Aidan's woven fingers as he pressed the ball of his hand into Mack's chest again and again.

She tried to picture everything happening inside of the young player's body. With his heart in a state of ventricular fibrillation nerve impulses would still be shooting from the brain, but so irregularly the heart would not be receiving a strong enough message to continue expelling blood into the circulatory system.

The AED should have shocked his heart into a regular heartbeat...

"Again."

She didn't need to be asked twice. It hadn't worked. She'd already prepped the charging pads with gel.

"Clear!"

Aidan began compressions again. At least two minutes had passed. Two incredibly precious minutes. The microscopic child inside her would have found it impossible to battle those odds. Mack was a fit twenty-two-year-old man. She prayed he had better chances.

After four to six minutes the brain would begin to suffer from oxygen deprivation and cells would begin to die. Each second ticking away as Aidan's hands systematically pulsed out an artificial heartbeat were buying time for the shock they'd just sent through Mack's body to stop the heart's spasm. If it worked this time his nerve impulses would resume their normal pattern and his heart would resume its normal pacing. If it was strong enough.

"Twenty-nine. Thirty."

They both leaned back on their heels and looked at the AED for a reading.

It was slight. But it was there.

Relief washed through Ali. It was near impossible to hold back the tears. Mack had made it. He wasn't out of the woods, but he was with them. She looked up, surprised to realize that an ambulance had arrived on the pitch and the players had formed an orderly row, heads all bowed as each man made a silent prayer for his fellow player.

"Load him up!" Aidan called to the medics. "You'll be all right?"

Aidan rubbed a hand along her arm as he indicated that he would be going along with the paramedics to the hospital. It was impossible to tell if his eyes were asking her something more—something deeper.

She *would* be all right. One day.

As Ali watched the ambulance doors closing Aidan out of her sight, she felt all of her senses come back into play, as if she'd flicked them off one by one in order to focus on Mack. Sight, sound, touch—everything returned to her with an added appreciation that she was there at all. She was aware of the scent of the grass, the somber applause from the crowd as the ambulance left the arena, the bright, bright blue sky above them on the crisp March day. The gratitude she felt for the gift of life growing within her.

Ali's hands slipped to her belly as she strode off the playing field. It was growing within her. Life. *Precious, precious life.* And she would do everything in her power to make sure her baby had the best shot at happiness she could offer.

The ride to the hospital had been tense, to say the least. Mack's heart had failed again. And one more time as they'd entered the A&E courtyard. Aidan had ridden atop the gurney, pressing an endless flow of syncopated pulses into Mack's body, willing his young heart to hold on.

A half hour later the player was still in Critical Care, but had been stabilized for the time being. Aidan stood outside his room, barely hearing the beeps and whirrs of all the equipment the young man was connected to. Hypertrophic cardiomyopathy. It would change Mack's life forever.

He should stick around to tell him the news. It wasn't the sort of thing he should hear from a stranger. His family—parents and two sisters, who had been watching the game—had been told. They were surrounding him now, his mother holding on to her son's hand as if it would give him the extra strength he needed. Perhaps it would. He wouldn't know about that sort of thing. His mother hadn't stuck around long enough to see him through much of anything.

Aidan turned away from the room and shrugged off the thought. He'd passed being bitter about that part of his life long ago. It was just one of the compartments he'd shut and closed before he'd moved on to the next compartment and the next.

His phone bleeped as a message appeared on the screen. It was Coach Stone.

We won. Tell the boy.

He looked back at Mack's room with a smile. At least he would have some good news when he woke up.

CHAPTER ELEVEN

ALI KNEW HIDING out in the ICU wasn't the most secret of locations, but her fingers were crossed that Aidan wanted to enjoy the celebrations with the team. She'd seen neither hide nor hair of him when she'd arrived in the department, and had just assumed he'd stayed with the team after he'd returned to update them about Mack.

Visiting hours were over, so Mack's family had had to leave. Ali had pushed her train journey to London back a few hours so she could sit with him a bit. If he woke up over the course of the evening it'd be nice for him to have someone there he knew.

She pulled a chair over from the corner of the room and parked it next to Mack, who was sleeping like a baby. A big, muscly baby, who had scared the living daylights out of everyone on and off the pitch today. He'd have some big decisions to make about his future. He was an amazing player, and rugby was his very raison d'être. But was it worth it if the sport could take his life? Maybe he would take a page out of Jonesey's book and go back to uni.

Ali looked upward to the invisible heavens, grateful that her decisions weren't life or death. She propped an elbow on the side of Mack's bed and cupped her chin in her hand. Her decisions were very much about life. Her life. Her baby's. Aidan's…

"Oh, Mack…" she whispered. "How am I going to tell him?"

"Tell him what?"

Ali froze at the sound of Aidan's voice. She barely trusted herself to turn around, let alone start speaking. There was a pretty big list she could spool out. She could tell him she was carrying his child—their child. Tell him she wanted to keep it more than anything in the world, which had completely taken her by surprise. Falling pregnant had already made her feel more alive than she could possibly have imagined. More accurately, falling pregnant by the man she was absolutely bonkers, head-over-heels in love with had brought out a side of her she'd never known existed. A life-charged, high-beamed wonder that just being alive could be so good—and so heartbreakingly difficult.

She could tell him all those things. But she wanted to make it easier for him. Make the transition back into his old life fluid. Simple. She wanted him to be happy.

"Is it Mack? Any updates?"

Ali swiped at the tears threatening to spill onto her cheeks. "Yes. No. I mean, he's stable. Not totally out of the woods yet—but he'll make it. Indications are he has a strong enough heart to beat this."

If only hers was as strong.

"Excellent work out there on the field today."

The compliment felt like one she might get from one of the players. One usually accompanied by a punch on the arm or a playful elbow-jab. Was that ultimately how he saw her? As one of the lads? A ladette with benefits?

She let her head fall back into her hands as her mouth formed into a silent scream.

Nooooooooooooooooooo!

She'd told herself again and again that that was the reality, but there had been a part of her that had believed otherwise. Had hoped he might love her.

How could she have let herself be so foolish? She cracked an eye open, sizing up Aidan through her fingers. He was still there. He was looking deeply uncomfortable, but he was still there. Each gorgeous little centimeter of him, his brow rising in—bewilderment? Concern?

A deep-seated sense of resolve began to steady her, to clear her thoughts, so that only a single truth remained. She was having a baby and would do anything in the world to protect it. Aidan had a right to know. Then she and her baby could get on with their lives.

"Is there somewhere we can talk?"

Aidan put down the paper cups of tea on the table and closed the door to the conference room they'd slipped into. Ali had been worryingly silent as they'd first gone to the cafeteria, then wandered through the hospital trying to find a quiet corner.

What on earth could she need to tell him behind closed doors?

As the door clicked into place, so too did the bits of information whirling around his head. Each little piece dropped into perfect place. The nausea. The dizziness. Those looks weighted with so much more than the feelings of a woman building up to a bittersweet farewell.

"You're pregnant."

Everything went into a strange slow motion. A feeling akin to seeing the towering waves arch and curve toward him all those years ago. He could hear the roar of the ocean in his ears as he watched Ali nod a confirmation, her teeth pressing into her lower lip, her eyes trained on him.

"How far along?"

"About eight weeks or more. I haven't had a scan yet."

He skimmed a mental calendar. On or around Valentine's Day. The first day he'd laid eyes on Miss Cosmopolitan and wanted, more than anything, to make her his.

"And you want to…?"

The words coming out of his mouth bore no relation to the thoughts pitching between his heart and his mind. *A child?* A baby to care for and raise and assure that the world was a safe, secure place to live in?

"I am going to keep it."

Ali's eyes sparked with a determination he'd not seen in her before—and that was saying something.

She raised a hand before he could interject. "Don't worry. I'm not expecting anything."

"Are you sure?"

The question came out before he could stem it. It wasn't that he wanted there *not* to be a baby—extraordinarily, that wasn't it at all. But this was a life-changing piece of information to take in. And she had already decided his role for him—or rather the absence of a role.

How well she knew him. She saw through his shoddy veneer of calm and bored straight to the heart of the matter. She already knew he wasn't someone who could give Ali or the baby—*his child*—the stability and commitment they deserved. Sure, he did steady as they came within the confines of work—but outside the stadium… They had agreed on a one-time, one-place deal—and she was holding up her end of the bargain.

The white noise in his head grew even louder. Was

it actually possible to hear the cogs whirling between one's ears? He rubbed at his temples, the roar making it impossible to train his focus on exactly what he wanted—needed—to do.

Ali was watching him with cool reserve. She was unreadable. As the words had come out of his mouth he'd known they were off-center, but the future Ali had placed before him was one he had never let himself consider and she knew it. He'd been more than clear on that matter. Aidan Tate didn't do long-term.

He looked into her eyes, searching for an answer—the right answer. Was she telling him what she really wanted? To be a single mother? From what he knew of Ali, she felt as let down by love as he did. Striking out on her own would be the safest way to go.

She arched an eyebrow as if daring him to question her decision. She was telling him what she wanted loud and clear. *Get out of my life.*

"I'm happy to contribute."

Pathetic! C'mon, man. You're better than this!

"Don't worry. I'm fine in that department."

"Of course. But you will let me know if—?"

She gave him a sad smile with a shake of her head and pushed up from the table. "I will."

He couldn't help letting his eyes linger on her waistline as she rose. His fingertips twitched at the thought of the smooth expanse of skin beneath the loose swing of her jumper. His hands knew every contour of her body. The dip from her rib cage along her belly—a belly that would soon grow round and pronounced. A belly he could rest his hand on and wait, eyes locked with hers, for a hiccough or a kick.

"Ali—" He rose with her and reached out.

If he could just hold her in his arms for a minute—

rest his cheek on that silky black hair of hers and have a chance to digest everything—maybe he could fix this.

That her gut reaction was to pull back with a flinch told him all he needed to know. She was ready to move on and he needed to respect that. Aidan was no longer part of her life. What happened to her was now her business and hers only.

Silence was the best thing he could muster as she picked up her bag and spun her woolen scarf around her neck. If he told her he loved her he would only make things worse, more painful. As she did up the buttons of her coat it was all he could do to stop himself from asking her to stay, to see what would happen if they gave "being real" a chance. Being human—open to the aches and pains and joys of loving someone.

"Goodbye, Aidan."

She laid her hand on his shoulder for just a moment. And then she was gone.

Where are you????? Ali sent the message and took another scan of the bar. Trust Cole to ask a pregnant woman to meet him at a *bar*. He was going to be the most inappropriate godfather going, but he was her best friend and—like it or not—he was all she had right now when it came to family.

As soon as the tease of tears began to sting at the back of her throat she took another gulp of water. *Swallow it down. It's just the hormones. Everything's good. Exactly as you want it.*

No Aidan. No broken heart.

She took another gulp of water. One day she'd believe her new mantra. *Really.* She would. It had already been over a week since she'd left and she was virtually swinging from the rafters with all the freedom she was feeling. Seriously. She *was*.

She caught a glimpse of herself in the bar mirror. Frowning. Big-time.

Okay. Maybe she'd have to work on the footloose and fancy-free thing a bit—but she'd get there.

"For the lady."

Ali looked up at the bartender in surprise. He was placing a Cosmopolitan onto a bar mat in front of her. Er...this was going to be awkward.

"The gentleman wanted me to say it's alcohol-free." The bartender gave her a look, as if to say he knew it was weird, too, but whatever, he was just doing his job.

Ali's heart lurched, before taking off at an accelerated rate. She hardly trusted herself to turn around. It would have been a bit of a no-brainer for Aidan to find her at the clinic if he'd wanted to, but over a week had gone by and she hadn't heard a peep.

She stared at the icy rim of the cocktail glass as if it would turn into an oracle and give her some answers. Only one man knew that was her drink. A mug of tea was slid onto the bar alongside her cocktail. She arched an eyebrow at it. Not quite what she had been expecting.

"I thought I'd lay off the wine to keep you company."

Aidan's voice swept along Ali's spine, unleashing an all-over spray of body shivers. For goodness' sake! A few goosebumps along her arms was not good enough? *Hormones, definitely.* Had to be hormones. Not the fact that the love of her life had just appeared beside her.

"Mind if I sit down?"

Ali's hand automatically moved to her belly as she turned to face him. It was almost impossible to believe how happy she felt at the sight of him. Suppressing the smile she knew she wanted to give him was a mammoth task, but she did it. Aidan didn't have a right to be here. Not while she was patching up her heart.

"I'd rather you didn't."

"Even if I am prepared to announce to everyone in this bar—or the whole of London, for that matter—the fact that I've been a complete and utter idiot?"

Ali felt her lips twitch, teasing at her composure. She leaned back and gave him an appraising look. "Depends upon just how big an idiot you think you've been."

"Oh, I can assure you…" Aidan drummed his fingers along the bar-top as if his body was humming with as much excess energy as hers was. "I have been a *colossal* idiot. Epic-style. So much so I've been nominated Chief Idiot of Idiotsville and I expect to win."

A full smile lit up her face. She couldn't help it. Aidan had a way of bringing out Fun Ali with just one of those knowing winks of his. She really was going to have to toughen up if keeping this man out of her life was her goal. It *was* her goal. Wasn't it?

"I suppose my mate at En Pointe is behind all of this?" She pushed the stool next to hers out from under the bar so that he could join her.

"I didn't really think I stood much chance if I tried to get in touch with you."

"Mmm… Well…" She felt her smile fade away. "I think you were more than clear about where you stood when we last spoke."

"That's just it, Ali. I wasn't clear at all." Aidan reached out for her hand.

She balled it up like a fist inside his fingers. *No! You don't get access to me. Not now. Not now that I have a baby to protect.*

Aidan kept his hand on hers, his thumb rubbing along the surface of her fist. Back and forth. Back and forth. Soothing her. Like he would a child. She couldn't do this. Ali pulled her hand away and crossed her arms protectively across her chest.

"Ali," Aidan persisted. "I was wrong. About everything."

"When you say everything—what exactly are you talking about? 'Everything' covers a pretty big—"

"I mean about the baby, about you, about me and how we all fit in together."

Ali sucked her lower lip into her mouth, pushing it back and forth along the edge of her teeth as if it would add clarity to what he was saying.

"And what conclusion did you reach?"

"That I needed to grow up, move on."

"What do you mean? Move on from—?"

"From the island and what happened there."

"So...have you found a way to do that?"

"I think I have. First—and it took my dad, of all people, to come up with this one—I would like to set up a scholarship fund, so more people there can train in medicine. I mean, it won't be huge—but it would be a help."

Ali nodded along. That sounded good. Really good. Healing...

"And secondly..."

He paused and cleared his throat—first once, then a second time—then twisted a swizzle stick into a knot.

"Are you keeping that one a secret or have you just come down here to torture me?" Ali teased, her heart careening round her rib cage.

He looked up at her and pulled her hands into his, eyes bright with emotion.

"I'm trying, Alexis Lockhart—defender of the people—in a really bad, terribly awkward way, to ask you to marry me."

Ali's eyes popped wide open. She felt the word *yes*
form in her mouth but couldn't get her lips and tongue
to join in on the action. She loved Aidan, heart and soul.
Loved him as she had never loved another—particularly
now that she had this little teensy, tiny baby of his tucked
up safe and sound in her belly. But he'd never expressed
any desire for a wife, a family…

"Don't answer yet." Aidan put a finger to her lips.
"None of this is how I wanted it to be."

"I thought you never wanted *any* of this to be?" Ali
indicated the two of them and then her belly.

"A few short months ago you would've been absolutely right."

"And then what happened?"

"You."

"Aidan—don't." Ali fixed him with her steeliest gaze.
She had to. There weren't many more trips through the
emotional wringer she could survive. "We had a one-
night stand at an airport."

"Alexis Lockhart, what we had was most certainly
more than a one-night stand. I began to fall in love
with you that night, and fate gave me a chance to put
things right."

"How? By making it clear that the last thing you
wanted was a relationship?"

"Making me face the truth is more like it. I messed
things up. I know I did. It's just—I thought you deserved
more. So much more than I believed I was capable of
giving. But the day you left it became ridiculously clear
I was making the hugest mistake of my life. Even my
dad could see things more clearly than I could. But now
I can. I wouldn't be honoring what was good about my
past by keeping my heart clamped shut for the rest of
my life. And you—my sweet, amazing, irascible, sexy

tigress of a wonder woman—you made my heart come to life again, and I want nothing more than to create a family with you."

He took her hand in his and pressed his lips to it.

"Ali, you are the woman I love—heart and soul. I would be the happiest man alive if you agreed to marry me."

It was all Ali could do to stop herself from nodding like a lunatic. If she hadn't known better she would've sworn her heart was soaring round inside her rib cage— held aloft by little tweeting birds. She loved Aidan with all of her heart, but she wasn't just making a decision for one now. She had to be sure he meant what he said.

"You know there are going to be changes in your life if I say yes? Lots of them?"

"The day I met you my life changed—for the better. You've taught me what my dad has known all along— that love is worth taking a risk for. Worth changing for."

"Well…" Ali toyed with a cocktail swizzler. "When you put it that way…"

"Ali." Aidan placed his hands on either side of her face. "I love you. Please say you'll marry me."

"Do we have to tell our baby about the airport?"

Aidan's laugh lines crinkled as his lips formed a broad smile. "Is this a yes?"

"Only if you promise to keep that little nugget of information our very own secret." Ali rested her forehead on his, closing her eyes as she took a deep breath of him. It was as if breathing him in made her whole again.

"I promise." Aidan gave her a soft peck on the lips. "And I promise never to tell the next baby we have, or the next one." He kissed and teased at her lips as he continued, "Or the next one…"

"How many babies are we going to have?" Ali laughed, slipping her arms over his shoulders.

"Oh, I was thinking a dozen or so." He pulled back, eyes twinkling.

"Oh, *reeeeally?* That was what you were thinking?" She tipped her head to the side as Aidan traced a finger along her jawline.

"I thought we could have our own little rugby squad."

Ali was giggling like a lunatic now. "Is that what you thought?"

"Oh, I could think of quite a few things for us to do over the years. But I know what we could do right now..." He pulled out the key to a hotel room and flashed it between his fingers like a magician.

"What do you say to a one-million-night stand?"

"One million?"

Ali gave him a kiss, then pulled back to study his face. That perfectly gorgeous face she would love until the end of time.

"I don't think that will be nearly long enough, but I'm happy to give it a go."

* * * * *

MILLS & BOON®

MEDICAL ROMANCE™

THE ULTIMATE IN ROMANTIC MEDICAL DRAMA

A sneak peek at next month's titles...

In stores from 28th January 2016:

- **His Shock Valentine's Proposal** *and*
  Craving Her Ex-Army Doc – Amy Ruttan

- **The Man She Could Never Forget** – Meredith Webber
  and **The Nurse Who Stole His Heart** – Alison Roberts

- **Her Holiday Miracle** – Joanna Neil
- **Discovering Dr Riley** – Annie Claydon

Available at WHSmith, Tesco, Asda, Eason, Amazon and Apple

Just can't wait?
Buy our books online a month before they hit the shops!
visit www.millsandboon.co.uk

These books are also available in eBook format!

MILLS & BOON®

The Billionaires Collection!

This fabulous 6 book collection features stories from some of our talented writers. Feel the temperature rise with our ultra-sexy and powerful billionaires. Don't miss this great offer – buy the collection today to get two books free!

2 FREE BOOKS!

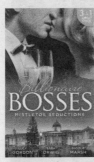

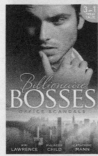

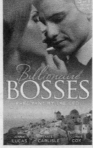

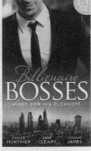

Order yours at
**www.millsandboon.co.uk
/billionaires**

MILLS & BOON®

Man of the Year

Our winning cover star will be revealed next month!

**Don't miss out on your copy
– order from millsandboon.co.uk**

Read more about Man of the Year 2016 at

www.millsandboon.co.uk/moty2016

**Have you been following our
Man of the Year 2016 campaign?
#MOTY2016**

MILLS & BOON®

Want to get more from Mills & Boon?

Here's what's available to you if you join the exclusive **Mills & Boon eBook Club** today:

- ✦ *Convenience – choose your books each month*
- ✦ *Exclusive – receive your books a month before anywhere else*
- ✦ *Flexibility – change your subscription at any time*
- ✦ *Variety – gain access to eBook-only series*
- ✦ *Value – subscriptions from just £3.99 a month*

So visit **www.millsandboon.co.uk/esubs** today to be a part of this exclusive eBook Club!